Actors

Actors

KEVIN O'BRIEN

St. Martin's Press
New York

Design by Amy R. Bernstein

Library of Congress Cataloging in Publication Data

O'Brien, Kevin.
  Actors.

  I. Title.
PS3565.B714A65   1986   813'.54   86–13902
ISBN 0–312–00393–5

First Edition
10 9 8 7 6 5 4 3 2 1

This book is for my parents, with love from the Boy

I am indebted to my editor at St. Martin's Press, Victoria Skurnick, who gambled on an unknown commodity, and to her assistant, Robin Desser; to my terrific agents, Sherry Robb and Bart Andrews; to Mary Ryan, whose editing skills and input improved this book immeasurably; to my creative writing teacher, Zola Helen Ross, who first encouraged me to write this novel; and to all my fellow writers in Zola's class, whose feedback and support were a great help, especially Bonny Becker, Bob Welshons, Scott Wyatt, and Brenda Wilbee; to Patrick Sheldon for his legal advice and kindness; to my friends, George Stydahar and Shannon Sheldon, who weathered early drafts of this book and came back with suggestions for improvement; to my family for their love and support; and to my dear friend who perhaps helped me most with her encouragement, honesty, intelligence, and patience, Cate Goethals.

Actors

PROLOGUE

New York City—October 1978

The owner of the Shell station sat behind a beat-up metal desk. His chair was tilted back so that it rested against the Coke machine. One of the overhead lights gave a flicker, but the man ignored it. He wasn't about to fix it now; those fluorescent jobs were a pain in the ass, and he was tired. He had just finished up the last of the theater crowd. Nice cars, though—Cadillacs, Continentals, a few Mercedeses. He'd let Tony on the graveyard shift mess with the light.

Bob Pierce stared up at it. Then he turned away and studied his reflection in the darkened window. It was an actor's habit, one he'd never broken—studying his own expressions. He smiled. This one would be called "Contempt for a Lightbulb."

He'd held onto these habits. Still practicing and preparing, clinging to the dream he'd officially pronounced dead. He'd even found this station in the theater district. He still needed the atmosphere, just as he needed the habits. Like a mother who kept setting a place at the table for the child who'd run away, Bob Pierce refused to give up hope.

In some ways, he was still acting. He wore a grease-stained workshirt a few sizes too big that said "Art," sewn in red script. Tonight he was Art. It gave Bob an uneasy feeling, because Art had been dead for three years now, shot in a hold-up during the night shift.

He stared at his reflection. At forty-seven, he was still an attractive man. Age hadn't added many pounds to his athletic body. But the wavy black hair was starting to thin and give way to gray. The blue eyes were becoming more languid. He threw his image a sardonic smile. "Give up, asshole," he whispered. "Give up already."

A handsome young man in his early twenties stepped into the station. Bob turned from the window and directed his smile at the boy. "In the crapper again, aye, Rusty? You're going to wear out that mirror, kid."

"Sorry." He shrugged. "I got some grease on my face and I had to wash it off. Last thing I need right now is zits."

Bob put his feet up on the desk and clasped his hands behind his head. "You know, Rusty, Tony says he'd like to bust that mirror in the men's room. Tell me the truth. Why did you take this job? Were you hoping some big-shot Broadway producer was going to pull in for gas and make you the next Robert Redford?"

Rusty squirmed. "Come on, Mr. Pierce. Give me a break, will ya?"

"Okay. But see if you can't save your trips to the toilet for when you've got to piss. You have plenty of chances to look at yourself cleaning the customers' windshields."

The boy pushed back his blond hair. It framed a face so beautiful it might belong to a girl, except for a once-broken nose. He leaned against the Coke machine and shoved his hands in his pockets. "Sorry, Mr. Pierce."

"Tell me. Are you doing anything besides trying to look ravishing for the day Joseph Papp drives in here for gas?"

Rusty looked flustered. "I've been working! I cleaned up the garage, and I took those boxes of air filters—"

"No, no," Bob said, more gently. "I meant, what have you done to get yourself some acting jobs?"

"How did you know I wanted to be an actor?"

Bob pulled his feet off the desk. "Well, let's see. When Tony's on lunch, he reads the sports page or an old copy of *Swank* he keeps hidden in the desk. You read *Variety*. And every time one of us tells you we had a celebrity come through here, you look like you just missed the last bus home."

"Pretty obvious, huh?"

Bob nodded. "You'd better be doing more than just hoping you'll get discovered in this dump, kiddo, because it doesn't happen that way. I was no different at your age. Only I was parking cars at Metro Broadcasting downtown."

"You're kidding!" Rusty sat on the edge of the desk. "You mean you wanted to be an actor too?"

"I *was* an actor." He was surprised how easily he'd said it. Rusty's face was full of interest now. He knew what he could tell the kid. How he'd tried out for the Actors Studio, when the Method was being taught to Marilyn Monroe, Brando, Dean, Newman. How he'd fought for—and gotten—roles in movies, plays, and live shows at the peak of television's Golden Age.

And he could tell Rusty about Lisa Weller. Because he'd known her better than anyone. He'd lived with her. He was there when she got started. The same Lisa Weller who was now packing them in over at the Helen Hayes.

Bob looked at Rusty's pretty face with its expectant smile. Suddenly, he felt ridiculous. He got to his feet and walked over to the cash register.

"Damn overhead's got to be changed," he said. "Guess I'll leave it for Tony." He opened the register drawer and began sorting out the receipts. "He should be here soon. You better cut out. I don't feel like playing referee tonight."

A curious look passed over Rusty's face. He edged off the desk and ambled to the door. Then he paused.

Without turning around, Bob said, "See ya later, kiddo."

Rusty gave a slight shrug. "Well, g'night, Mr. Pierce," he said and closed the door.

Bob put down the receipts. He'd come close to telling Rusty the whole story. But after twenty-five years of chasing the dream, he was no different from the kid. Whenever a limousine pulled in, he too hoped there'd be someone important in the back, some producer, some agent. When no one was around, he'd even dig out Rusty's discarded *Variety* and flip through the pages to check the casting calls.

He looked up. A car had driven into the station. Bob glanced out the window. A limousine. He chuckled. "Okay, asshole, here's your big chance. Joe Papp needs his oil checked. Look sharp."

He suddenly felt as if he were onstage. The old actor's question, what to do with your hands, rattled him. He stuck them in his back pockets and sauntered toward the pumps.

The driver had gotten out and was leaning against the open door of the limousine. He was a slight, uniformed man with curly, silver hair. When he saw Bob, the man ducked his head into the car and spoke to the passenger in back.

"Sorry, ma'am. This will only take a few minutes. Should have filled her up before I left the barn."

The woman in the back seat smiled. Bob's heart froze in his chest. She hadn't changed much over the years. The honey-colored hair was the same, and the somber gray eyes didn't look much older, only more reflective. She still had that nose, slightly crooked near the bridge. Twenty years before, it had prevented her from getting modeling jobs and bit parts. Bob had talked her out of a nose job. And he was right. The starlets and the models were forgotten, but the girl with the unusual face became famous.

Standing ten feet away, he wondered if she would recognize him. Her looks hadn't changed, but maybe she had. She was no longer the shy twenty-two-year-old he'd loved. Part of Bob wanted to rush up to her; part of him recoiled from the thought. A few breathless questions, some brief reminiscing, and then the inevitable strained silence. And after that, he'd still have to fill her gas tank. God, it was too funny, too pathetic.

"Fill her up with unleaded, okay, buddy?" the driver called.

"Okeydoke." Grabbing the hose and switching on the pump, he stole a glance at her. She looked drained, but the fatigue didn't diminish her beauty. The chinchilla stole she was clutching reminded Bob that she'd always been cold. The apartment they'd shared was poorly heated. During the winter months, she had

4

worn sweaters to bed. Late at night, she'd read audition scripts curled on the floor with a hair-dryer blowing warmth onto her stocking feet. Remembering, his heart ached.

She rolled down the window and gave him a brief, patient smile, a smile reserved for strangers. Uncertainly, Bob returned the smile. The gas tank was on her side of the car, and he pulled the hose over to the limousine and unscrewed the cap.

"Recognize her?" It was the driver. "I'm carrying precious cargo tonight. That's Lisa Weller, the actress."

"For God's sakes, Buzz," she said in a good-natured voice. She turned and gave Bob a curt, embarrassed smile.

He stepped out of the shadows and walked over to her window. "Well, I'll be! Whaddaya know. It *is* Lisa Weller." He spoke with an affected Brooklyn accent.

"See?" the driver said. "You made his night, Miss Weller."

Lisa turned and shot back a reply.

Bob leaned against the hood of the car. "I seen all yer movies. I seen that one, *Fate Is My Destiny*, five times . . ."

She looked back and blinked. "You sat through that turkey five times?"

"Yeah. I thought you was great in it."

"Well, thank you. That's very sweet. Thanks very much."

Bob's smile faded. She hadn't recognized him at all. "I'm your biggest fan," he went on.

"Thank you," she said again, her smile growing strained.

He eased his arm off the hood and got out the squeegee and paper towel. As he worked on the windshield, he studied her, huddled under the chinchilla in the back seat. But her face was turned away.

"Well, you're sure as hell getting it clean." The driver chuckled and nodded toward her. "She's something, huh? You know, she's not one of those stuck-up types, either. She'll give you an autograph, I bet. All you gotta do is ask." He called into the car, "Isn't that right, Miss Weller? You'll give our friend here your Jane Hancock."

"Buzz, please." She looked embarrassed. "Just pay the man. I'm sure he gets a lot of show business people in here."

Bob put the squeegee away. The pump shut itself off, and he briskly went over to retrieve the hose. Just get her out of here, he thought. Why in God's name had he wanted her to recognize him? What could she say? "Well, Bobby, I see you've really hit the skids"?

He replaced the gas cap and took the hose back to the pump. "That's $15.20," he told the driver.

"Now, Buzz," she said, "give him a good tip. He's been very patient with us."

The man met Bob in front of the car and grudgingly handed him a twenty. "Keep the change."

"Thanks."

The driver started back toward the car. Bob turned and looked at her. She was staring at him. Nervously, he took a few steps toward the window. He noticed she was looking a little nervous too. Maybe she had butterflies, he thought. He felt them—the curtain lifting—no doubt about that. He wished he had a script so he could check whose line it was. Maybe he should leave it to her. She'd always been good at improv.

But she remained silent, her eyes fixed on him. Bob looked down at his feet. Finally, he said, "You know, I really would like your autograph, Miss Weller. I mean, if it's no trouble . . ."

A sad smile crossed her face. She pulled an envelope out of her purse. Taking out a pen, she glanced up at him. "Your name?" she asked, the pen poised above the envelope.

Bob closed his eyes. He stepped away from the car and looked at the grease-stained pavement. "Art," he said, fingering the name on his shirt. "Make it out to Art."

"Art." She scribbled on the envelope and absently spoke to her chauffeur. "Buzz, be a dear and reach in that glove compartment. There're some passes in there—give a couple to Art here."

"Sure thing, Miss Weller." He reached out and handed Bob a pair of theater tickets. Bob thanked him. "See, I told you, buddy. Isn't she nice?"

"Yes, I'm a saint," she said, still writing. Bob returned to the window. She was putting the pen away. "Bring your wife or sweetheart to see the show," she said. "It isn't bad, even with me in it. Feel free to come backstage afterward." She gave him the envelope. "There you go. It was nice meeting you, Art."

"Thanks a lot, Miss Weller," he said, trying to keep the vacant smile fixed on his face.

Slowly, she rolled up the window. "Okay, Buzz," she said and gave Bob a quick wave.

He nodded grimly, allowing himself one moment out of character before the curtain fell. The driver started the engine. Bob saw her sit back. He took one step toward the car.

"Lisa? Lisa, wait a minute—"

But she hadn't heard. He put his hand out to her window as the car began to move. Then it picked up speed and pulled out of the station, and he had to restrain himself to keep from running after it. He watched as the sleek black limousine disappeared around the corner.

Taking a deep breath, he counted to ten. Another trick. It was supposed to clear the head, bring calm and control. He finished counting. It hadn't worked.

He looked down at the tickets in his hand. Then he looked at the envelope. *To Art*, it said. *Best wishes, Lisa Weller.*

He started to crumple the envelope in his fist. As he did, the flap opened, and he stared down at what was written there:

You're still a great actor, Bobby, she'd written. *Love, Lisa.*

ONE

Seattle, Washington—1947

Bobby Pierce screamed.

Then he watched as the five judges in the front row sat up with attention. He congratulated himself on having dreamt up the screaming business. His audition piece was Othello's suicide speech. He wore his father's red robe open in front (those two weeks of push-ups weren't for nothing) and a single, gold-painted earring from the five-and-dime. The scream had definitely awakened the judges, who had been nodding off after Melissa Chaffy's boring Lady MacBeth. She'd sounded as if she were reading the directions off a prescription bottle: "Out-damn-spot."

His voice choked with emotion, Bobby ranted and raved at the dead Desdemona. He just had to win the Garfield High School Drama Prize. He was the only junior who had entered the contest.

After three years, he still hadn't made a name for himself in school. He was an "outtie," striving to be an "innie." To most, he was just the kid who worked and lived at the country club with his oddball father. He wasn't special at anything. He couldn't participate in sports, because he'd had a bad knee since childhood. An apathy for studies had excluded him from the Honor Roll Society.

But on stage, no one could ignore him, and that was where Bobby was determined to make his mark—not only in high school, but beyond. He'd be famous. Gary Cooper the Second.

Another Errol Flynn or Clark Gable. Fans would clamor for his autograph. All the kids who snubbed him would talk about how they used to know him. As a movie star, he would attend his high school reunion and be very kind to all the former bobby-soxers and lettermen. He'd have their love and admiration. He'd be a very important man.

Someday.

For now, he was trying to make the most of his small roles in school plays. His co-stars accused him of scene-stealing and up-staging them. "You're no actor," one girl told him. "You're just a ham."

If that were true, he thought, then why did the audience laugh at his cross-eyed policeman in *You Can't Take It With You?* How come he'd scared the bejesus out of them as The Ghost of Christmas Yet to Come in *A Christmas Carol?* And if he was just a ham, why were the contest judges gaping at him in awe? He knew they were impressed.

> *—Set you down this;*
>
> *And say, besides, that in Aleppo once,*
>
> *Where a malignant and turban'd Turk*
>
> *Beat a Venetian and traduc'd the state,*
>
> *I took by the throat, this circumsised dog,*
>
> *And smote him—thus.*

He loved it. The speech last two minutes. He stood alone on stage, the spotlight focused on him, all eyes focused on him, Bobby Pierce, as he pulled a knife from the pocket of his robe—a real knife too, not some phony rubber job. Drawing up the knife, he felt a rush of excitement and power. He held it in the air for a moment, letting the blade catch the spotlight's glare. Then he plunged it between his ribs and forearm, and let out a blood-curdling cry. Dropping the knife, he staggered toward the footlights and gasped his last two lines. Then he fell to the floor, one arm dangling over the edge of the stage.

He listened to the applause, basking in the knowledge that he *had* them. There was no way he could lose.

Gail Gilmore won. She accepted the award still dressed in her Southern belle rags in which she'd recited Scarlett O'Hara's "I'll never go hungry again" speech.

But Bobby snared one small moment of glory. After the presentation, Gail came over to him. "Gosh," said the beautiful senior. "I was so scared you'd win. You were really good!"

"Aw, you were better," Bobby said. When she smiled, he figured he deserved some kind of acting award for that line alone. Still, one of the most popular girls in school had paid him a compliment, and she actually smiled at him.

Bobby lugged a grocery bag up the backstairs of the country club's employee residence. He and his father shared a tiny, two-bedroom apartment on the second floor. Ricardo, the cart-master, lived next door on their right, and Jose, the groundskeeper, had the apartment on their left. The club refused to hire Negroes or Orientals, so the employee residence was like Spanish Harlem with a golf-course view.

He stepped inside the apartment and found his father sitting naked at the kitchen table. Cameron Pierce was fifty-two years old, but a decade of heavy drinking had taken its toll on the once-handsome face. The bloated, sad-eyed creature staring down at a glass of rye bore little resemblance to the strapping, dark-haired young man Bobby had seen in old photos.

"Hi, Poppy," he said, setting the bag on the counter.

"Goddamn weatherman said it's gonna rain tomorrow," Cameron announced in his husky monotone. "You know what that means, boy?"

Bobby nodded. "Dirty golf shoes. Well, cheer up, Poppy. Maybe the rain will discourage the old farts from playing."

His father was the club's locker room attendant. He cleaned golf shoes, and scrubbed the toilets and showers. Bobby helped him on weekends, and, during the summer, he worked there full-time.

"Here," Bobby said, pulling his father's robe from the grocery bag. "Were you looking for this? Put it on."

Cameron got to his feet. As Bobby held up the robe, he spied his father's hairy, dilapidated body, and he silently swore he'd never let himself go like that no matter how old he got.

"There's a rip in the sleeve," Cameron said, climbing into the robe.

Othello had torn it with the knife. "I'll sew it up for you," Bobby offered. "Leave it on the bedpost tonight. You eat dinner yet?"

Cameron sat down again and sipped his drink. "We had Chef's Stew."

"God, how can you eat that crap, Poppy? It's just leftovers and all the crud that wasn't good enough for the club members. So they unload it on us . . ."

"Delicious," said Cameron, smacking his lips.

Bobby took a can of corned beef hash from the bag and turned on the hotplate. "Sorry I'm late tonight," he said, busily preparing his dinner. "I had something after school."

"Football game?"

"Naw. C'mon, Poppy, you know I can't play with my knee. Besides, it's baseball season. This thing I did was for the drama department—"

"What was the score, Danny?"

Bobby glanced over his shoulder at the old man. "Danny's dead, Pop," he said quietly. "You remember . . ."

Cameron frowned. "Oh. Well, I don't have a clean uniform for tomorrow, boy."

"I'm doing the laundry tonight. Pile up your stuff and I'll take it down after dinner." He set a bag of cookies in front of his father. "Here, I bought you Fig Newtons."

Cameron ripped open the bag, grabbed a handful of cookies, and stood up. Bobby turned to watch him hobble toward the bedroom. Beneath the hem of his robe was one white, hairy leg, and a prosthesis—a wooden leg, not a hollow one. Cameron had a hard time walking after a few drinks. Bobby always kept an eye on his father, afraid the old man might fall or hurt himself.

Stuffing a cookie in his mouth, Cameron opened his closet door and started to gather up the dirty clothes. When Bobby saw that his father was all right, he turned and went back to fixing his dinner.

The clothes still had fifteen minutes in the spin cycle. Bobby sat on the front porch railing outside their apartment. He lit up a cigarette and stared out at the darkened golf course. It was drizzling. The sound of rain on the roof blended with the Spanish music coming from Ricardo's apartment next door.

Bobby puffed on his cigarette. Through the thin drapes, he saw his father asleep on the couch. Eight-thirty, and the old man was passed out. He used to be a social drinker, back when he had a social life and a "normal" job. Cameron had been a switchman for the Union Pacific Railroad.

His wife had always fretted about him. She'd heard so many horror stories about accidents in the switchyards, men getting killed or losing limbs. But it hadn't happened to Cameron that way.

It had been Christmas night when the family drove back from dinner at Uncle Cliff and Aunt Dorothy's house in Olympia. Bobby had been sitting in the back seat with his brother, Danny. Bobby was seven and Danny was ten. Already, it was clear that Danny, the tough, little athlete, was his father's favorite. But Bobby had won his mother's heart, and if his father sometimes seemed cold and unloving, the little boy knew that *she* loved him.

The boys were shoving each other. Their mother shot a look back at them. "Danny, stop picking on your brother. And for heaven's sake, sit down. Come on, now. Let's all behave and sing along with Poppy. 'We Three Kings . . .' "

Cameron Pierce, the social drinker, was known to burst into song after a few snorts. He was singing in the car that night, very loud, when he ran a stop sign.

Bobby had little recollection of the accident that killed his mother and brother, and crippled his father. He only remembered lying on the floor of the back seat, pinned under something heavy and hard. Half-conscious, he had barely been able to breathe from the pain in his right leg. He couldn't see anything, but heard his father's anguished cries. Bobby had wanted to call back to him, tell him he was alive, but there wasn't any air in his lungs. He wondered how he'd answer if his father cried out for him. Yet he had never heard his father utter his name, only Danny's—over and over again.

Bobby tossed away the cigarette, then rubbed his knee. It was bothering him tonight, probably the rain. The door of Ricardo's apartment opened. The short, muscular man ambled out, one hand grabbing at his crotch. He smirked at Bobby. "Hey, little shit," he said. "I'm goin' to Karla's room. You come and she'll fuck you, too."

Karla was a slightly retarded thirty-year-old who was in charge of the laundry. Bobby shook his head at Ricardo. "No, thanks." He smiled.

"You still a virgin?" Ricardo said. His black eyes narrowed as he grinned.

"I'm saving myself for Ava Gardner."

"I think you're a homo."

"Fuck off, Ricardo."

The cart-master chuckled and strolled away. Bobby threw a sneer at his back. He wasn't sure who he hated more, the rich, tightwad club-members or the repulsive employees. He wanted to rise above all of them. Just being rich wasn't enough. He was going to be a famous actor, an important man, loved by millions.

Bobby imagined himself on magazine covers, receiving awards, at movie premieres with fans swarming around him. They would call out his name—over and over again.

That summer, Bobby became very aware of his looks. The club was closed on Mondays, and he'd spend his free time at the beach, swimming and working on his tan. Despite an occasional pimple, he liked what he saw in the mirror. The constant running around at work had kept his five-foot, eleven-inch frame lean and wiry. He pilfered bathroom supplies from the club, tamed his wavy, black hair with Wildroot, sustained a smooth tan with coconut oil, and kept his blue eyes forever clear with Eye-giene. Sometimes at the beach, he noticed women gazing at him. And he liked it.

Unfortunately, he never got a glance from girls his own age. To them, he was the invisible man. He'd sit alone on his blanket, eyeing the inaccessible high school girls in their swimsuits. He knew all of them, and they knew him. But they never said hello. Snobs. He'd asked a few of them out during the school year. Two girls were "grounded." One had an aunt who had died. Another had to study—on a Saturday night. Still another just said, "God, no way."

Bobby was sure that his senior year would go by like the previous three—without a girlfriend or even a date. He was starting to think, however, that he was in love.

When there was a lull in the locker room, he was supposed to go out front and haul golf clubs from the cars to the caddy-master. He also held open doors for the members and their wives. Mrs. Helmore, the pert, blond wife of one of the club's youngest members, always smiled at him. She wore bright red lipstick and said, "Thank you, Robert," when he held open the clubhouse door for her. He'd sneak a glance at her retreating figure—the Ann Sheridan hairdo, the hem of her summer dress floating around the backs of her knees.

She played golf with Mrs. Swift, the wife of the club's president. Mrs. Swift was a small woman in her early forties. She had short, copper-colored hair and a deep, year-round tan that had aged her face prematurely. Sometimes, Mrs. Swift stopped to talk to Bobby at the front door. He didn't mind, because it gave him more time to study her golf partner.

"I'm going to tell my husband what a splendid job you're doing," Mrs. Swift trilled one morning.

"Thank you, ma'am. Have a nice golf game." He ushered them into the clubhouse.

"Mmmm," he heard Mrs. Swift giggle. "I wouldn't mind handling *his* six iron!"

"Oh, Marsha!" Mrs. Helmore laughed. "You're terrible!"

"I'd kill to have his eyelashes . . ."

Bobby began to feel uncomfortable when Mrs. Swift came to the club. But she was there almost every day. He felt she was flirting with him, but he told himself that she was an older, married lady. Why the hell would she be interested in him?

One Sunday in late July, she stopped and smiled at him. "Tomorrow's your day off, isn't it? If you're not busy, would you be interested in making ten dollars?"

"Sure," he shrugged. "I mean, yes, ma'am."

"Good. The deck and cabin of our yacht need to be cleaned. I think you're just the man for the job. I'll pick you up at nine-thirty tomorrow morning. All right?"

"Yes. Thank you, Mrs. Swift."

Actually, he would have *paid* ten dollars just to spend his day off at the beach—alone. Mr. Swift was ga-ga about his yacht. Bobby knew he'd have to work his butt off to please the club president.

"I should have told you to bring your trunks," Mrs. Swift said, as they stepped onto the twenty-eight-footer that bore the name *The Marsha*. She took him below and showed him where the cleaning supplies were kept.

As he started working on the windows, he saw her slip off her sundress. He eyed her nervously. She was wearing a two-piece swimsuit with light blue polka dots. She looked like that pin-up girl, Chili Williams. Her body was tanned and firm, like that of a much younger woman. He stared at Mrs. Swift and became aware of how the polka dots accentuated her less-than-ample bust. Bobby began to sweat.

She hung the dress on a hook and picked up a towel. "Don't forget the head," she called to Bobby. "I'll be up on deck if you need anything." Then she climbed up the steps.

In two hours, the cabin was immaculate. Bobby's sports shirt was dripping wet. Panting, he brought the mop and pail topside.

She was lying on the towel face down. Her bronzed body was covered with oil; the top of her suit was unhooked and she'd slipped her arms out of the straps. She squinted at Bobby as he climbed onto the deck, then reached for her sunglasses. As she put them on, he could see her breasts, white against her tan, the rose-brown nipples grazing the towel.

"I'm dying of thirst," she called out, fumbling with the top of her bathing suit. "There's a cooler of lemonade in the galley. Run and get it before I simply perish."

When Bobby returned with the cooler, she was in the cabin. There were two empty tumblers on the table. Her sunglasses were pushed back in her hair and her bathing suit top was refastened. "Pour yourself a glass, too," she said, smiling.

Bobby filled the glasses and they both drank thirstily. Mrs. Swift held the cool glass against Bobby's forehead. "Looks nice down here," she said, glancing around. "You've done a splendid job."

"Thank you."

She began to run the wet tumbler over her neck and down to the cleavage between her breasts. Bobby pretended not to notice the droplets trickling down the top of the polka-dotted suit. Finally, she stood up.

"I hope I won't be in your way on deck. I'm sure you can work around me. But take your break. You've earned it." Holding her drink, she started back up to the deck.

When he finished his lemonade, he followed her up and began to mop the deck. She reclined on one elbow and watched him work. "You must be sweltering in that shirt," she said, after a moment or two. "You can take it off if you want."

Bobby nodded sheepishly and pulled the damp shirt over his head. Then he tucked the shirt into the waist of his pants and picked up the mop.

"Careful you don't get sunburned," Mrs. Swift said. She unscrewed her bottle of suntan lotion. "Better put some of this on."

"That's okay," he said.

"Come on. I won't have you scalded while you work on my yacht."

Reluctantly, he laid down the mop and went over to her blanket. "Sit down," she said. "Let me do your back."

He sat down Indian-style in front of her and gripped his knees with nervous hands. The oil felt warm on his shoulders. She slowly moved down to the center of his back, her supple fingers kneading each bump of his vertebrae.

"You have a nice body," she remarked.

He tried to sit up straighter. "Thank you, ma'am," he said.

She was working on his lower back now. He smelled the coconut oil mixing with his sweat. Her hands glided around him and she rubbed his stomach, touching the top of his pants. Her fingers began to trace the line of hair that grew below his navel. Bobby held his breath. He could feel her breasts nudging against his back. Then her hand moved up his chest and she gently pinched each of his nipples.

He stared straight ahead at the blue-gray waters of the lake. He tried to think of everything except what she was doing to him. Nothing worked—dead dogs, mutilated squirrels, car crashes. Nothing. He wished his jeans weren't so tight. She'd see, and then he'd die of embarrassment.

She was tracing oily circles on his shoulders. Then she stopped. Her hand was out, holding the bottle of lotion. "Your turn," she said. "Do me now. There's this tricky place on my back I can never reach."

Slowly, he took the bottle. She had moved around so that her back faced him. He tried to discreetly adjust the bulge in his crotch. When he looked up at her again, Mrs. Swift was unhooking the top of her suit. She lowered the straps and held the top to cover her breasts. Bobby stared at her naked back, with delicate freckles turning sepia under the deep golden tan.

"Well?" she said, turning her head to smile at him.

He shook out some oil and quickly rubbed it into her back.

"So what kind of classes do you take in school?"

"Th-the usual stuff. Math, English, stuff like that."

"Sounds fascinating," she said. "More oil, darling, and don't be in such a hurry. Any favorite classes?"

"I like drama."

"Oh, so you want to be an actor? Well, I must say, you certainly have the looks for it . . . A little lower, dear."

He spread some oil at the base of her spine. Her skin felt smooth and warm.

"You know, Bob, a very dear friend of mine is a sponsor for the Seattle Players. Maybe I could talk to him about you. He might find a job for you there. Would you be interested?"

"Uh, yes ma'am. I—I really would. That'd be great."

"Fine. Then I'll talk to my friend. A favor—for a favor, wouldn't you say, Bob?"

A favor for a favor. He didn't say anything.

"We're losing our sun," she sighed, glancing up at the clouds. An offshore breeze swept over the boat, and he felt her skin come up goosebumps against his slick fingers. "That's enough, darling. I think I'll take a swim. You finish your work."

As he washed the deck, he watched Mrs. Swift untie the mooring lines from the dock cleats. The boat began to drift offshore. Bobby's stomach was tight with nerves. Mrs. Swift scared the shit out of him. But the Seattle Players!

He tried to look as if he were hard at work while she stretched out on the blanket and watched him over the frames of her sunglasses.

When he'd finally finished, she slowly got up and strolled over to the mast, moving like a lazy cat. "Put the cleaning things below," she said. "Then we'll take a swim."

He started to remind her that he hadn't brought his trunks, but then figured he could swim in his blue jeans. While he was below, he heard her drop the sail. When he returned topside, he saw that the boat lay ahull not far from a deserted beach. Mrs. Swift stood near the rails. She smirked at him. "You can't go swimming like that. You'll sink straight to the bottom."

He sat down and pulled off his shoes, trying not to look at her. As he stared at his feet, the top of her polka dot bathing suit suddenly drifted down to the deck.

"You really shouldn't swim half-dressed," she said. The polka dot panties landed on his knee. He looked up. She was standing before him naked.

He glanced away, but not before he'd seen the white patches

of her body against the tan. She stretched and yawned. Then she dove into the lake. "What are you waiting for?" she called, giggling like a little girl. "Come on in! The water's marvelous!"

Bobby went over to the side of the boat and prepared to dive.

"No clothes allowed! Come on, no one can see. Take them off!"

Hesitantly, he looked around. The lake was empty.

"I won't look," she said, and covered her eyes.

Clumsily, he pulled off his pants and, after a moment, took off his shorts as well. For a second, he stood in the wind, aware of his own nakedness, the sun and air touching his exposed flesh. Finally, he jumped in the water. The lake was cool but refreshing.

When he came to the surface, Mrs. Swift was there. She splashed him and laughed. "I lied," she said. "I peeked!"

It didn't feel so different from skinny-dipping at night in the country club's pool. But he felt the urge to look at her body, and every time he did, she giggled and splashed him. Teasingly, she rubbed against him, touching his heavy penis, pinching his buttocks. All he managed in response was a feeble laugh.

Suddenly, she let out a cry of surprised pain. She threw her arm around his neck, and gasped, "Oh damn! A cramp . . . I've got a cramp." Her arm tightened. "Oh God, I can't breathe—help me—"

Frantically, he struggled to keep their heads above water as he pulled her back to the boat. Mrs. Swift was clawing at him, pulling him down. Dear God, he thought, don't let her drown. Please, don't let her drown.

Finally, they reached the boat and he dragged her aboard. She was doubled up in pain. Bobby wanted to ask if she was all right, then put his clothes on and leave. But she was still clinging to him, and he was getting a hard-on. He couldn't believe it. The woman was dying on him, and he was getting a hard-on. She didn't seem to notice.

"Help me below," she said with a wince of pain. "Please—I've got to lie down. My side—"

He carried her below and set her down on the cushioned

19

bench. Mrs. Swift sighed. Then she suddenly pressed her slim body against his and pulled him on top of her. Her slippery arms went around him and she squeezed his buttocks.

"Come on," she said. "Fuck me. I want you to . . ." Trembling, he looked at her. She was moaning in anticipation. "Do it," she whispered. "I want you to. Come on, put it in me . . ."

Bobby was terrified.

And obedient.

And so it went for the rest of the summer. Every Monday, he would come to the docks where he'd clean the boat, and then receive his "reward" below in the cabin. Sometimes she called Bobby her "sun-god," other times it was "slave." Occasionally, she would forget to pay him. He'd be too embarrassed to ask for the ten dollars, or, for that matter, about the acting job with the Seattle Players. She never mentioned it again.

Bobby worried about himself, because he didn't like her, didn't even like having sex with her. Something had to be wrong with him. He looked forward to school so he could stop working aboard The Marsha every Monday. One day during the last week of vacation, they were below in the cabin. Mrs. Swift lay naked on the cushioned bench. She was smoking a cigarette. An ashtray was balanced on her flat stomach, and her feet were nestled in Bobby's lap. From time to time, she would curl her toes and pinch the hair on his thighs.

"I start school next week," Bobby said. "So I guess this will be our last time for a while." Forever, he hoped.

She picked a piece of tobacco off her tongue. "Yes, well, hand me my swimsuit, will you?"

He got up, pulled on his shorts, and handed her the suit. Mrs. Swift stubbed out her cigarette and gave him the ashtray. "Here," she said. "Clean this out."

Bobby went to empty it in the head. He could hear her voice from the cabin. "So," she called, "you're quitting on me, huh?" She laughed. "Well, no matter. My husband and I are going east. By the time we get back, the sailing season will be over anyway.

So everything works out fine. I was worried you'd figured we'd continue like this . . . but I can see you're a smart kid."

He came out of the bathroom. She was pulling the straps of her suit over her shoulders. "Good-looking, too," she said. "You'll do all right for yourself."

In the car, they drew closer to the country club. She still hadn't said anything about the theater job. Mrs. Swift looked cool and formidable behind her sunglasses. Bobby cleared his throat.

"Uh, I was kind of wondering about that friend of yours. The one with the Seattle Players?"

"Oh, that," she said, watching the road. "His name's Perry. Perry Martino. Just trot down to the theater and introduce yourself. I'll give Perry a call."

Bobby stared at her. She didn't look at him. A favor for a favor. But all he said was, "Thank you, Mrs. Swift."

A woman sat in the lobby of the Seattle Playhouse addressing envelopes. Bobby estimated she was in her late thirties. Glasses rested in her reddish hair.

Hesitantly, he approached and told her a friend of Mr. Martino's had suggested that he come by. "She said he's one of your sponsors," he added.

She looked up wearily. "We have lots of sponsors." She put down her pen, took off her glasses, and rubbed the bridge of her nose. "What kind of work are you looking for? Right now, all we've got is volunteer stuff."

"I want to act," Bobby said.

"Well, at the moment, *Desire Under the Elms* is on, but it's already cast. Check back in a month or so. We'll be auditioning for another production."

"A month or two?" he said, crestfallen.

The woman shrugged and put her glasses on. "Well, we're always looking for volunteers. If you hang around long enough, you might get first crack at an audition."

She looked at him until Bobby finally nodded.

Every night, Bobby would pedal his bike the six blocks to the playhouse. There he'd assemble extra rows of folding chairs in the auditorium. After the show, he'd fold them up again, store them in the closet, and sweep up. He did this for free. If Mrs. Swift had made him feel like a chump, she had nothing on the folks who ran the Seattle Players Theater.

On those nights, he'd return home and find his father passed out on the couch. He'd wake up the old man, help him into bed, then fall onto his own bed, exhausted.

Desire Under the Elms finished its run in late October of his senior year. Bobby got a part in the next production, *The Man Who Came to Dinner.* The reading was an anticlimax: no one else bothered to try out for the part.

His role was Richard Stanley, the unhappy son who ran away in the second act and then was dragged home in the third. It wasn't very big, but Bobby got a few juicy scenes, which he played to the hilt.

Sometimes there were only a dozen people in the audience. The show went on anyway. At the curtain, Bobby would listen to the dull smattering of applause, and he'd have to force himself to smile and bow.

The reason Bobby didn't drop out of the play was because of Roxanne Blout, who played his mother. She was a big woman with lustrous black hair and a great stage presence. She lived near the club and began giving Bobby a lift to and from the theater. Sometimes after the show, they'd stop at a coffeehouse called The Nook and share a banana split.

"Richard, honey, you can't give up." She always called him by the name of his character. "I know it gets depressing, especially when the audience is a couple of nuns, a few bums, and the director's second cousin." She smiled. "But you've got to stick with it. I think you're really going to be something someday. It just takes patience, lover."

"But don't you ever get fed up?" he asked. "You're a fabulous actress. Don't you hate being stuck in a third-rate community playhouse?"

"Sure I do," Roxanne said. "But when you're thirty-one, with no husband, no boyfriend, no one to make you feel special, and you hate your daytime job, you'd better find something that gives you a feeling of importance."

She smiled again and pushed the ice cream to his side of the table. "You finish," she said. "I'm too fat already."

"No, you're not," Bobby said.

"Yes," she said, "I am. But I'm a damn fine actress."

The Man Who Came to Dinner folded the week after Thanksgiving. Bobby was surprised by how sad it made him. The cast had become like a second family. It was hard saying good-bye to them, especially Roxanne.

"No," she said at the set-striking party. "None of that good-bye crap, Richard. *Our Town* goes up in February. You'd be perfect for George. That's the lead, lover. If you haven't run off to Hollywood, come back and audition. Everyone here loves you." She pinched his cheek. "I'll probably play your mother again, you know. I'll have to start calling you George."

It wasn't yet December, but Bobby was already counting the days until auditions opened.

"Aw, the sweater looks good on you, Poppy, if I do say so myself." Bobby smiled at his father, who did look handsome— like a regular father, his face clean-shaven and hair combed. He was wearing a tie with the navy blue cardigan, Bobby's Christmas present to him.

"You like what I got you, boy?" he asked.

"Oh, yeah, Poppy. The football's swell." Bobby knew for whom his father had really bought it. "Maybe we can toss it around tomorrow, you and me."

"Well, you'll have to go easy on me, Danny. Mind my leg—"

Bobby sighed. "Danny's dead, Pop." He straightened his own tie and grabbed his sportscoat. "Don't slip and call me Danny in front of Uncle Cliff and Aunt Dorothy, 'cause it embarrasses the shit out of them. Okay, Poppy?" He turned and gathered up the presents he'd gotten for his aunt and uncle. "We'd better scram.

The cab should be here soon, and we don't want to miss our train. Next one isn't till—"

Bobby stared at his father, who stood by the door. Slowly, he put down the packages as the dark stain bloomed at the crotch of Cameron's gray trousers. Bobby took a deep breath. "C'mon, Poppy, let's clean you up and change your pants," he said patiently. "Real quick now."

Christmas dinner at Cliff and Dorothy's house in Olympia had become an annual ordeal. It wasn't just the painful memories evoked by the yuletide visits. Bobby's aunt and uncle were boring. Bobby knew the visits from him and Cameron put a strain on them too, and it made going there even worse. Still, Cliff and Dorothy kept inviting them back every year.

The one bright spot to the Olympia ordeal was the train ride back. There was no booze at Cliff Pierce's house, so Cameron was conscious and coherent for the journey home. Bobby would sit with his father in the nearly deserted smoker car as Cameron went into a comical tirade about his brother, Cliff, the stuffed shirt. Then they'd sing Christmas carols, and sometimes a few lonely strangers would join in.

But not this trip. Elderberry wine was served at dinner, and Cameron had passed out by dessert. Then, Bobby's uncle announced that, instead of driving them to the station, he would take them all the way back to Seattle.

Bobby sat up front with his uncle, a stocky, gray-haired, sixty-year-old with glasses. Cameron was asleep in the back seat. As Cliff turned the Hudson out of the driveway, Bobby dreaded the next hour of boring small talk and long, silent lapses.

"I guess we shouldn't have had that wine with dinner," Cliff said, glancing in the rearview mirror at his brother. "Well, at least this gives us a chance to talk, Bob."

Bobby detected a stiffness in his uncle's voice. He sounded too forced, like an actor unsure of his delivery. Bobby wondered if the elderberry wine had really been a mistake, if this ride home weren't somehow prearranged. He kept silent and stared at the dark road ahead.

"Have you given any thought to your future, Bob?"

He shrugged. "Sure, I guess."

"What do you want to do?"

"I'm going to be an actor."

"Well, now," said Cliff patronizingly. "That's a fine ambition. Do people go to college to study that?"

"Sometimes, I guess. But I'm not going to college. Who'd take care of Cameron?"

"Exactly. That's my point," said Cliff.

"What point? I don't understand . . ."

"Maybe you don't notice it, being with him every day. But your aunt and I—every time we see him, he's worse and worse. Bob, something has to be done about it."

Bobby glared at him, but Cliff's eyes were fixed on the road. "By 'it,' do you mean my father?"

"I think it's time we—put him somewhere, Bob. Now, when your grandfather died four years ago, he left some money for just such a purpose. He knew even then that your father—"

"Listen, Uncle Cliff," Bobby cut in, "I know you're trying to help and all that, but I can take care of Cameron myself. We're doing fine . . ."

"Maybe for now. But your grandfather also left money for your first year of college. It was his wish—"

"But I'm not going to college. I'm staying with my father."

"So you're going to work at that country club forever?" Cliff asked. "Bob, your father will only get worse. We've got to put him—some place where they can look after him, keep him away from the booze . . ."

"I'll get him to lighten up on the drinking," Bobby said hotly. "Okay?"

"It's not just his drinking, Bob."

Bobby glanced around the car. He felt like he was suffocating. *So you're going to work at that country club forever?* Cliff's question kept ringing in his ears. More than anything, he wanted to get out of the car and forget this entire conversation. "Listen, Uncle Cliff. Maybe you should turn back and drop us off at the station. There's still time to catch our train."

"I'm not saying all this to be mean, Bob," Cliff whispered. "I'm only thinking about your future. You can't expect to pursue a career in—acting or whatever you eventually decide on—when you're looking after a sick old man."

"I've *already decided* to be an *actor*, Uncle Cliff," Bobby hissed. "I'm in a Seattle theater group now, and getting paid for it. And I've managed to take care of Poppy in the meantime. So thanks anyway, but I don't need your help or advice." Yet even as he spoke, Bobby knew his uncle was right. During the run of the play, he'd felt guilty about neglecting his father, and he'd seen how the old man had deteriorated.

After a long silence, Cliff finally spoke. "I won't say any more about it, Bob. Just give the matter some thought. I'm sure there are a lot of good theater schools around the country—if that's what you want—and you're throwing away a good opportunity. You have the money for a year of college. And your father is better off some place where professionals can look after him. That's all I'm going to say."

Biting his lip, Bobby turned and glanced at his father in the back seat. Shadows from streetlights moved across Cameron's face. His head was thrown back and he was snoring.

Bobby felt a pang of homesickness. He wished they were on that smoker car, singing Christmas carols with the other lonely strangers.

"I'm sorry to have to call you up here about this, Bob." Mr. Kirkabee, the country club manager, took off his glasses, then ran a hand over his nearly bald head. He sat behind his desk. The usually jolly fat man looked very grim that March afternoon. "Sit down, son," he said. "I've had a very long and very disconcerting talk with Mr. Swift."

Bobby gripped the arms of his chair. Somehow, he'd always known that the summer before would come back to haunt him. He wondered what had taken so long, and how Mr. Swift had found out about those Mondays aboard the yacht.

"Mr. Swift said some of the other club members have come to him about your father."

Bobby opened his mouth, but no words came out. He just shook his head.

"Now, it hasn't been so bad these past winter months," Mr. Kirkabee continued. "With your father's custodian job during this period, he hasn't had any contact with the club members. But he's back in the locker room, and I'm afraid he's slipping. He can't keep up with the work, and the golf season isn't even in full swing yet. That locker room is a shambles, dirty towels all over the place . . ."

"I—I'll talk to him, Mr. Kirkabee."

"Well, it's not only that, Bob. Mr. Swift says some of the club members . . . Well, your father's been rude to them, testy. I understand he's been drinking on the job, too."

"I'll talk to him about the drinking, sir. I can get him to stop." Now, won't *you* please stop? he thought, squirming in the chair.

"And his appearance, Bob. He's unshaven and his hair is never combed." Mr. Kirkabee closed his eyes in a pained way. "I'm told this last Monday he—he was wandering around the locker room in full view of all the members and it was obvious that he'd—wet himself . . ."

Bobby nodded quickly. "Yes, well, he's been having trouble w-with his bladder. We're going to see a doctor about it. I promise it won't happen again, sir."

"Well, I'm afraid if things don't get better, I'll have no choice but to let him go. Naturally, you could stay on, work fulltime in his place. You'd still have room and board here. We have no complaints about you. Nothing but praise . . ."

"Thank you, sir. I'll talk to my father. He'll do a good job from now on, I promise."

But he'd already had that talk with the old man, a dozen such talks. He'd already heard from club members and other employees that Cameron was *slipping*. Bobby knew why, too. He was never around to keep an eye on him. Between school and the play (*Our Town*—Bobby had the lead), there was no time to look

27

after the old man. He would come home after the show each night and have to clean the mess his father had left behind in the locker room. Nearly every morning, he'd give his father pep-talks that were more like lectures: "Now, promise me, Poppy, you won't have a drink until *after* work and *try* to be nice to those old farts and remember to check the showers once in a while to make sure the stalls are clean . . ." Nag, nag, nag. He knew his father was beginning to hate him, because the old man didn't call him Danny anymore.

"So it boils down to two choices," said Roxanne. She and Bobby sat in their usual booth at The Nook, spooning up ice cream. A Jo Stafford record was playing on the jukebox.

"You can pack Dad off to the funny farm, then go to college and pursue your acting career. Or you can stay put, look after him, and be the best darn locker room attendant in Seattle—if not for the rest of your life, at least for the rest of *his* life. Those are your options, Georgie, put bluntly and insensitively. And I think you already know what you're going to do."

Bobby gave her a troubled, confused look, then glanced down at the tabletop.

"Do you want me to tell you what to do?" she asked quietly. "I'm your mother only in this play, honey. Don't expect me to make the decision for you. Don't expect me to take on all the guilt and responsibility, either. Same goes for mean old Uncle Cliff."

"But the asshole keeps calling me every week about this thing!" Bobby exploded. "The only time I used to hear from him—"

"It's your decision, honey," Roxanne interrupted, her voice firm, yet gentle. "And you've already made it."

His throat tightened and he stared at her. "Why do you keep saying that?"

She smiled sadly. "You said something a couple of weeks ago about taking your college entrance exams. You said you did pretty well. Why'd you take them?"

He shrugged. "Everybody took them. I just—" He let out a strangled sigh and lowered his head.

Roxanne shoved the banana split to his side of the table. "Here, eat," she said. "Best thing for depression. I should know. Where do you want to go to college?"

"UCLA," he mumbled. Bobby wiped his eyes, then fiddled with the dessert spoon. "It's got a good drama department, and maybe I could check out some of the movie studios while I'm down there. Oh, God, I don't know . . ."

She handed him her napkin. "Blow your nose, toots. And don't look so miserable."

The tears were streaming down his face, but he managed a weak laugh. "I'm gonna remember how this feels. I can put it to use later on stage. I'm gonna remember this."

It wasn't really a funny farm. It was a *rest home.* No bars on the windows or padded cells, just a lot of senile people wandering the long, stark corridors in their bathrobes. Bobby had seen the place two weeks before when he and Cliff had brought Cameron there.

Bobby stayed at his uncle and aunt's house—a miserable fourteen days full of boredom and guilt. He so looked forward to Los Angeles, yet he knew the guilt would follow him there. The Sunday before he left, Bobby went to say goodbye to his father.

They were in the game room, a large, uncarpeted place filled with rickety card tables, painting easels, and couches. Syrupy music churned over a radio. A few of the old folks—in pajamas, robes, or clothes that looked slept in—milled around, playing cards or checkers, or painting. Bobby sat with his father at one of the tables. Cameron wore a blue cardigan over a dirty undershirt and his pajama bottoms. He was unshaven, but his hair was combed, obviously a last minute touch-up job by one of the nurses. He was playing solitaire, not paying any attention to his son.

"Anyway, I'll be back at Christmas," Bobby was saying. "We'll spend it at Cliff and Dorothy's. That should be about as much fun as a case of typhoid, huh, Poppy?"

Cameron kept turning over the cards.

"Maybe you'd like to spend a few days away from this place

at Christmas time. I can arrange it. And—and we won't have to stay with Cliff and Dorothy, not if you don't want to. How does that sound, Poppy?"

Cameron didn't raise his head. He drew more cards from the pile.

"How's the food here? Can't be any worse than at the club."

Again no response.

"Listen, Poppy. If you don't like it here, tell me."

The old man stared down at his solitaire game. Bobby reached over and grabbed his hands. The cards fell to the table. Cameron finally looked up, his eyes listless.

"Poppy, I put you in this place," Bobby said. "You just say the word and I'll get you out. I don't have to go to school. I can get a job—some kind of job—and we can stay together, look after each other. Please, just tell me what to do."

"Do what you need to do, boy," Cameron said simply. "I don't care."

"But I care," Bobby said, still clutching his father's hands. "If you want out, I'll get you out. You don't have to stay in this place if you don't like it."

Cameron gently pulled back and dropped his hands in his lap. "It's all right," he said, staring at his son. "I'll just wait here until Danny comes and takes me away."

Bobby rubbed his forehead. "Danny's dead, Pop."

"I know that, son," Cameron whispered. "I know that."

November 7, 1949

Dear Roxanne,

I'm in History class right now & I'm bored. The teacher is yapping away about the Spanish Inquisition (sp?). How's knowing about this crap going to fry my toast? My classes stink & I'm way behind in everything (more on that later).

I miss you. Sorry I've been so bad about writing. I'll probably phone you before you get this letter, but better a letter and a phone call than only a phone call, right? Well, as usual, I'm not making sense. But if I did, you'd think something was wrong. Right?

Actually, something is. My father died two weeks ago. He had a heart attack and keeled over in that place which was supposed to take such good care of him. I came up to Seattle for the funeral (sorry I didn't call or anything, but I was so messed up I couldn't see anybody). I'll spare you all the depressing details. Suffice it to say I feel like a shit for deserting him in the first place. Anyway, I missed a week of school & all my mid-terms. So I'm way behind.

—Hello again. Now I'm in English class. We're discussing "Romeo & Juliet" (wherefore art thou, Roxanne?).

It's hard to give a shit about school (or anything) since coming back last week. But my tuition is paid up through May, and room & board is good through December. So I'm sticking it out till then.

The Performing Arts classes here at U.C.L.A. are O.K., but most of the people in P.A. are stuck-up. The only one I hang around with at all is a Junior named Brad Dalton. I think he might be queer, but he's a nice guy & he's actually done a few movies, bit parts. He says he might be able to scare up some work for me too.

The real exciting news (& lately, the only thing keeping me going) is that they're doing <u>Our Town</u> here in January. Yes, <u>Our Town</u>! I'm going to audition for George & they've got to give me the part, otherwise <u>there is no God</u>!

Well, nothing else to report. No steadies yet (still an L.A. virgin). Hope your love life's better than mine. Sorry this letter was so boring and depressing. Let me know how the new play is doing. Write when you get the chance. I miss your sexy body!

> *Love,*
> *Richard/George/*
> *Bobby*

There was no God.

He'd attended every acting class, hung around the prominent students and ass-kissed the drama teachers, coyly mentioning to them now and again that he had played George Gibbs in a Seattle theater production of *Our Town*. He'd rehearsed with Brad Dalton for two weeks before the auditions. Still he didn't get the part.

Bobby decided he hated the school and everyone in it. Brad won the role of The Narrator. Out of pity, he invited Bobby to stay at his apartment the night after the outcome was announced. "We can bend a few elbows. Stay up late. What do you say?" Brad had asked.

Bobby looked at Brad, with his soft green eyes, sandy hair, and movie star smile. Even if he was queer, he told himself, Brad was a nice person—and his only friend. He felt ashamed for his long silence. "Sure, Brad, thanks," he said. "Thanks a lot."

Brad's studio loft had bad plumbing, a good view, and a Murphy bed. There was also a couch on which Bobby slept, undisturbed. He stopped feeling guarded around his friend. He no longer questioned Brad's kindness or his masculinity—at least, he didn't question it vocally.

That December, Bobby moved out of the dorm and into Brad's apartment. Together, they looked for work, Brad between classes, and Bobby during them. Losing the part in *Our Town* had soured him on school.

He was hired to fill out crowd scenes in several major productions. At MGM, he was a face in the congregation while Elizabeth Taylor got married in *Father of the Bride*. At the same studio, he applauded Ava Gardner's lip-synching in *Showboat*, and did the same for Mario Lanza in *The Great Caruso*. But he never got to see any of the stars up close.

His luck was better at Warner Brothers, where as an anonymous deckhand, he stood behind Gregory Peck in a scene from *Captain Horatio Hornblower*. Another day, dressed as a cadet, he got to shake Doris Day's hand between takes in *West Point Story*. But so many people were talking to her at the same time that he felt lost in the crowd. Extra work was like high school: he was still on the outside striving for recognition.

He decided he needed an agent. Brad had one, but he wasn't

taking on new clients. So Bobby began to shop around.

"I'm here to see Mr. Hanley," he told the receptionist at the first talent agency. She looked up. She was very blond, and very bored.

"Do you have an appointment?"

"No, but I thought if he had a minute—"

"I'm sorry. He's very busy."

"Could I make an appointment?"

She sighed. "What did you want to see him about?"

"I'd like him to represent me."

"Oh," she said. "An actor."

"Well . . . I want to be—yes, I'm an actor."

"Any experience?"

"A few movies, crowd scenes mostly. But I—"

"Mr. Hanley doesn't represent beginners. You'd just be wasting his time and yours. Now, I'm busy."

Bobby nodded politely. "Well, fuck you very much, ma'am."

"You're welcome," she said, without looking up.

"If I could just make an appointment," Bobby told the receptionist at the Kendall Agency.

"I'm sorry. Mr. Kendall is booked up through the week. If you'll just—"

"I can wait till he's free."

A dapper, middle-aged man with a dark mustache and an expensive suit emerged from the office. "Rita, hold my calls," he told the receptionist. "I'm going to be at Twentieth for the next few hours."

"Yes, Mr. Kendall."

Bobby hurried after the man, who was pressing the button for the elevator. "Mr. Kendall? Mr. Kendall, my name's Robert Pierce—"

Kendall looked at him, annoyed. "Sorry, son. I'm afraid I'm in a hurry right now."

"Couldn't I just ride down in the elevator with you? See, I'm an actor and I hear you're one of the best agents around—"

"Why don't you leave your name and résumé with my secretary and we'll—"

The elevator arrived and Kendall stepped inside. Bobby got in behind him. Kendall frowned. "We'll get back to you, Mr. Peters, I promise you. If you'll just—"

"Pierce," Bobby hissed. "Robert Pierce. And no, you won't. I've been to eleven different agencies and they all say they'll get back to me, but they never do." Another man was already on the elevator, but Bobby ignored him. "You don't give a damn, none of you guys! Ya-got-any-experience-ya-got-any-experience? That's all you ever want to know. Well, how the hell am I supposed to get any without an agent? Unless one of you big shots gives me a break? All I'm doing are stupid crowd scenes and I can't even get work there anymore."

Kendall's mouth tightened.

"Look, I'm sorry, Mr. Kendall," Bobby said. "I don't mean to be rude. But, please, I know I'm a good actor. I've done plays in high school and shows in Seattle. If you'll just give me a chance—"

The doors opened on the ground floor and Kendall hurried out. "Yes, well, that's wonderful. We'll get back to you, Mr. Pierce. Now good day."

"Thank you, Mr. Kendall," Bobby called. He watched the agent hasten across the lobby and out to a waiting car.

"Pretty discouraging, huh?"

He turned and saw the young man who had been in the elevator during his tirade. He was in his mid-twenties, well-dressed and handsome, with wavy brown hair and a familiar smile.

"You ain't just flapping your gums, bub," Bobby said.

"Not much work since Liz Taylor's wedding, huh?"

Bobby squinted at him.

"You don't recognize me, I guess," he smiled. "*Father of the Bride?* I sat in the pew in front of you during the wedding scene."

Bobby nodded. "Oh, sure, I remember now," he lied. "That

was a few months ago. You still doing extra work? I'm having a tough time finding any myself."

"So I heard," he replied, with a superior grin. "I quit doing extra work. I'm getting speaking parts now. In fact, I'm going for a screen test tomorrow. Things are really starting to happen for me."

"Huh, well, congratulations," Bobby said, trying not to look envious. "Who'd you have to kill?"

"All it takes is talent and perseverance." A smirk came to his face and he nudged Bobby with his elbow. "Plus giving the casting director a blow job helps."

Bobby laughed, until he noticed the man was serious. "You're kidding . . . aren't you?"

"Hey, listen, that's how I got my first speaking part. Five lines and a close-up in this western. Just a couple of fag tricks, that's all. I haven't had to do any crowd scenes since. Anyway, like I said, things are starting to happen for me."

Bobby stared at him. His lip involuntarily curled.

The young man shook his head and chuckled in a condescending way. "I guess you haven't learned how to play their game yet," he said. Then he started for the door. "Good luck finding extra work, kid."

Alone in the lobby, he watched the former extra walk away, a bounce in his step. Bobby didn't wonder how anyone could be so desperate, because he felt that desperation now. He knew what it was like to want something so badly. He didn't question the young man's morality, or his motives, or even his manhood. Bobby just wondered if it really could "start to happen" that easily.

An independent studio was making a low-budget World War II melodrama that required soldiers. Bobby stood in line with the other extras, filling out applications. He eyed the men seated at the desk at the head of the line. They jotted down names and collected the cards. They were low men on the totem pole, who didn't have much influence, but standing behind them was some-one who looked important.

Bobby tried to guess his age. He had a boyish face, but his short, neatly groomed hair was white. Like Brad, the man was almost too handsome. His casual attire looked expensive: a tweed sports-coat over an Ivy League, crewnecked sweater, and no tie. His dark, black-browed eyes met Bobby's.

Bobby looked away and took a step up in line. He'd caught men staring at him before, but he'd never considered encouraging them. He peeked up. The man was still watching him. Bobby didn't look away this time. He gathered up his courage and smiled. He almost wished the man wouldn't respond, but a smile was returned.

Then Bobby was at the front of the line. "Name?" asked the man seated behind the desk.

"Pierce, Robert."

He scribbled on a card. "Pierce Roberts."

"No, um, Pierce is the last name," Bobby stammered. "Robert Pierce."

"Sounds sexier the other way around," the white-haired man said. His voice was effeminate; Brad sounded like a truck driver compared to him.

Bobby looked up and smiled. He knew the remark was a con-versational lead-in, but he couldn't think of anything to say.

"Have you ever considered changing it?"

Bobby still had the stupid smile frozen on his face. "I'd change it if I got a speaking part," he said.

Folding his arms, Mr. Ivy League looked Bobby up and down. "Do you have any experience?"

"Oh, yessir! Professional theater in Seattle, and I've been an extra in about a dozen movies."

The man smiled. "Put him down for a bit part, Frank."

"We'll call you, Mr. Pierce," said the other man, setting Bobby's card on a separate, smaller pile.

Bobby felt elation rise above his nervousness. "Thank you," he said, smiling at his white-haired redeemer. "Thanks very much!"

Victory achieved, he quickly retreated toward the door. The cool spring air and the street noise brought reassurance. His heart was still racing, but the tightness in his gut began to fade. He'd made it. He'd gotten what he wanted with just a bit of flirting. A speaking part in a movie! Bobby took a deep breath and a real smile came to his face.

"You look hungry."

He gulped. Bobby turned and saw the white-haired man standing beside him. His first impulse was to run like hell. But he thought about how easily his application card could get lost.

"I was just about to grab a cheeseburger," the man said. "Care to join me?"

His name was Don Lockridge. He was thirty-six years old and *Guns in the Pacific* was his first film as an associate producer. "And it'll be your first movie with a speaking part," he told Bobby. "I think we should drink to that."

They clinked beer steins at a chic little restaurant where a lot of well-dressed men seemed to know Don. They also gave Bobby some long, appraising stares. He was too nervous to eat, and took only a few bites of his BLT.

"The food here is just like the drinks at The Basement Door," said Don. "Mediocre. You ever go to The Basement Door?"

"Um, no. What's that, a bar?"

Don looked disappointed for a second, then he smiled tightly and nodded.

The entire conversation was like that. Don kept mentioning bars and clubs Bobby had never heard of. It was as if Don were speaking in some sort of code. Bobby began to feel stupid, having lived in Los Angeles for a year and not known any of these popular places. Finally, he lied and said, yes, he'd been at Woody's Cavern—a couple of times, in fact.

Don looked very pleased at this news. "Well, of course, Woody's has its own breed of clientele," he said. "Mostly a lot of pretty California boys standing around, posing. Ask one of them to dance and they snub you. A bunch of teases. Good scenery, but that's about it. *Finis.*"

Bobby suddenly realized all the places Don had mentioned were homosexual nightspots. His mouth dropped open and he quickly shook his head. "I lied about that Woody's place," he said. "I've never been there. In fact, I've never even heard of it. I'm not—" He fell silent.

Don stared at him for a moment, then he leaned forward. "You mean, you're not gay?" he whispered.

"Oh, yes, sir. I'm really happy—and grateful to you for giving me the bit part in your movie."

Don closed his eyes and chuckled. "No, Bob. 'Gay' is another word for homosexual. It's a new term."

"Oh."

"Oh," Don echoed him, smiling shrewdly. "Bob, what were all those cute, coy looks about while you were in line? From where I stood, it seemed like you were flirting with me."

Bobby glanced down at his half-eaten sandwich.

Don took a deep breath. "Well, I'd say this lunch is comparable to a night at Woody's. You should hang out there, Bob. It's your kind of crowd." He slapped down some money for the check and got to his feet.

Bobby looked up. "I'm sorry, Mr. Lockridge."

"That makes it unanimous," said the man. He turned and started for the door.

Bobby sprang up from his chair and started after him. He caught up with Don on the sidewalk. "Listen," he said. "Does this mean I won't get the speaking part in your movie?"

Don stopped and gave him a deadpan stare. "Make an educated guess." He started to walk away again.

"I'll do whatever you want," Bobby heard himself say in a loud voice.

Don stopped once more. He turned and smiled. "You're that desperate for the part, huh?"

"Yes."

"Well, *I'm* not that desperate," said Don, moving closer to him. "In case you haven't noticed, dear boy—all modesty aside —I'm not exactly hard on the eyes. I don't have to resort to sexual

38

deals with little hustlers—even if one of them happens to look like Montgomery Clift, though I'm tempted." He paused, assessing Bobby with his eyes. Don's expression softened. "Tell you what," he said. "Your address is on that application card, isn't it?"

Wide-eyed, Bobby nodded.

"I'll drive by your place at seven-thirty tonight. If you still want that part, be outside waiting for me." He turned and walked away.

"Sorry I'm late," Don said, as Bobby climbed into the front seat of the Ferrari. "I was detained at the studio. *Unbelievable* confusion. I love your shirt. Pretty shade of blue. Matches your eyes."

"Thanks," Bobby said, trying to breathe normally. His stomach had been in knots all afternoon, and now the knots were tightening. But the sickly dread was nothing compared to how he'd felt ten minutes before. He had been so worried Don had found another more enterprising young actor to take home.

One hand on the steering wheel, Don pulled a shriveled, hand-rolled cigarette from his breast pocket. With a gold lighter, he lit up and inhaled deeply. Staring at the road ahead, he handed the cigarette to Bobby. "Here. This will relax you. You look like you're driving to your own execution."

That's just how I feel, Bobby wanted to say. But he was silent and took a drag off the cigarette. Immediately, he went into a coughing fit and his eyes watered up. "God, this is strong!" he gasped.

Don glanced at him. "Haven't you ever smoked reefer before?"

"Is *that* what this is?"

Shaking his head in disbelief, Don returned his attention to the road. "Your first marijuana cigarette and your first time with a man. Save me a seat in hell. I'm corrupting you. This *is* your first time with a man, isn't it?"

"I guess it will be," Bobby said nervously.

"What about women? *Please* tell me I'm not leading a virgin down the path of sin and corruption."

"No, I've had plenty of girlfriends." A lie. Mrs. Swift was the only one. Funny, he'd felt kind of trapped into sleeping with her, too. But this time, he knew he would get something out of it: a speaking part in a movie, a better chance at landing an agent, and bigger roles in other movies.

Don slowed down as he approached the corner of Hollywood and Vine, where some boys stood. They were about Bobby's age or older—an odd assortment, some dressed in biker's leather, others dressed like rich college boys. "Well, the nighthawks are out early tonight," said Don, stealing a peek at the young men. "Do you know who they are?"

"Hustlers?" Bobby said. He'd seen them before.

"Well, I'm glad you're not totally naive. You know who used to be a regular out there about two years ago? Earl Eastman. You know, the star of that silly picture—"

"*Free All the Sinners?*" Bobby asked. "*That* Earl Eastman?"

Don nodded. "I used to drive by and see him *posing* out there practically every night. He had a wicked reputation. Would do just about anything—or so I heard."

"You mean, Earl Eastman is a—"

"Homo?" Don interjected lightly. "Not necessarily. Most of those street vendors are like you—in it for the money or the off-chance that the next trick will give them a part in a movie."

Bobby glanced back out the rear window, noting the street corner where Earl Eastman had gotten his start. He turned around again. "I'm not in it for the money," he said.

"That's only half an answer." Don smiled. "Independently wealthy, hmmm?"

"No. In fact, I owe my roommate two months' back rent. But it's not money I'm after."

"Then it must be your career. Or perhaps you're just a teensy bit curious to see how the other half lives?"

"I want a speaking part in your movie."

Don's mouth tightened. "It means that much to you?" he asked coolly.

"Means everything to me," Bobby said. "I'm going to be a famous actor, even bigger than Earl Eastman."

"So you're taking his route to stardom." Don laughed, "*He stoops to conquer!*"

Bobby sighed and stared at the road ahead. "Don't make fun of me, okay?" he asked quietly.

"All right. But don't insult *me*. I've just given you every opportunity to tell me that you like me or you're attracted to me or at least curious. And all I get is a lecture on show business Machiavellianism. You could at least *try* to convince me that tonight isn't purely a business venture for you. Insults to my intelligence I can take. Blatant insults to my pride are another story."

"I'm sorry," Bobby muttered. "I'm just nervous."

"Finish that cigarette. You need it."

Bobby took another puff of the awful-tasting thing. He remembered what that other actor had said to him: *I guess you haven't learned how to play their game yet.* Well, he was sure learning a lot today. About the boys on the street corner, smoking reefer, and how to pretend an act of desperation was an act of desire. He glanced over at Don. "Well, you're—a handsome guy, Mr. Lockridge," he stammered. "I'm not just saying that, either. I mean it."

Don glanced at himself in the rearview mirror. "Really? What do you think is my best feature?"

"You've got nice hair, real distinguished-looking."

"It was gray in high school. I used to get drinks in bars without being carded. Turned completely white about five years ago. You know, I grew a mustache once and it came out black. The hair on my chest is black too—as you'll soon see."

Bobby forced himself to take another hit off the cigarette. The ride he'd hoped would last at least another hour was coming to an end. Don turned into the underground garage of a swank, high-rise apartment. A large door automatically opened to swallow them up. He parked the car and turned off the ignition. In the darkness, he glanced at Bobby and sighed. "You look positively catatonic."

"Is that a compliment?" Bobby asked sheepishly.

Don laughed. "Oh, God. You're actually sweet." He reached over and took Bobby's hand in his. "Don't be afraid, okay?"

"I'm sorry. I can't help it. My stomach is all turned around and I'm shaking inside."

"Me too," Don whispered. "It's sexual tension, part of the fun."

Bobby never considered the feeling that he was about to throw up fun.

Don squeezed his hand. "Since this is your first time, we'll go easy, okay? Just tell me whenever I'm doing something that makes you uncomfortable. Now, this is the point of no return. I can give you cabfare home or you can come upstairs with me."

Bobby thought about the speaking part in the movie. Then he said in a determined voice, "Let's go."

He had one line: "Hey, Doc! The Poet's hurt bad!" The camera lingered on him for a two-second close-up, but his face was obscured by dirt and an oversized army helmet. *Guns in the Pacific* was quickly edited and distributed without fanfare. When the film got second billing at a nearby theater, Bobby dragged Brad to see it. The movie was awful, but they both applauded when Bobby's big moment came. He sat through the film three times. Unfortunately, not many people sat through it even once. No offers came, and the agents weren't pounding on his door. Even extra work was hard to find.

Meanwhile, Brad was starring in campus productions and he'd nabbed a featured role in a CBS radio soap opera. He'd also paid Bobby's share of the last two months' rent. Bobby felt obliged to listen to Brad's frequent lectures.

"You should go to a few of your acting classes. God, Bob, you're supposed to be a student here. You know, they're starting to draft guys, what with this business in Korea. You better hold on to your student deferment."

"I've got a bad knee. They won't take me."

"You've got a bad attitude, too. Sleeping all day. Out all night. Where do you go till all hours, anyway?"

"I'm practicing to become a vampire," Bobby sighed. "Listen,

Brad, I appreciate your concern. But I can take care of myself. And I'll take care of the rent I owe, too, I promise. Now, let's just drop it, okay?"

He didn't want Brad to know about some of his shortcuts to fame.

That summer of 1950, with nothing to his credit but a few extra bit parts, Bobby didn't feel much like the actor he was trying to be. Then something happened. He wandered into a movie theater on Wilshire Boulevard. It was showing a film he'd never heard of, starring an actor he'd never heard of, either. The movie was *The Men*, starring a guy with a weird-sounding name—Marlon Brando.

The minute the movie let out, Bobby rushed to the library to find out more about this Brando guy. He read the reviews of *The Men* and *A Streetcar Named Desire*, the interviews describing Brando's nonconformist attitude and the famous mumbling he'd learned at a place called The Actors Studio in New York.

New York.

Bobby made a decision.

Dressed in an undershirt and jeans, Bobby leaned against the side of the building, lit up a cigarette, and watched the traffic go by. It was a hot, suffocating night in early September. Most of the drivers assessed him and his "co-workers" from open windows, but those weren't the ones Bobby would let pick him up. Tonight, the car had to be air-conditioned, and the driver had to be rich.

"Hey, Bob. Haven't seen ya here in a while." The twenty-year-old wore only a pair of jeans and sneakers. His shirt was tied around his waist. He had a good build and a tan that complemented his blond-dyed hair. "I thought you were giving this up," he said.

"I need dough," Bobby mumbled, puffing on his cigarette. "Going to New York as soon as I get enough scraped together. What's the action tonight, Rick?"

"Slow. A lot of cops on the prowl, creeps in unmarked cars.

Watch out who you get a ride with. Christ, it's hot. Got another cig?"

Bobby handed him one, then went back to his standard hustler's pose: hands in pockets, cigarette dangling from his mouth, a surly gaze at the cars cruising by. Very Brando. He was tired of being told he had such a "sensitive" face, even if it was the kind of face they liked. He didn't want to come off like a wimp; he wanted to be tough, like Brando.

A beat-up, white LaSalle slowed down near the corner. He ignored it. A dumpy car meant its driver didn't have a lot of money or show business connections. Much to Bobby's irritation, the car stopped, blocking the way for other potential customers. He glanced toward it with his best "get lost" sneer. But the expression fell off his face as he saw the young man gaping back at him from the passenger's window. Bobby's heart stopped. Instinctively, he stepped back and bumped into the wall. He almost put a hand in front of his face, but that would have been too obvious, and too late. The young man anxiously nudged his friend behind the wheel to get moving, and the LaSalle sped down the street. It was only a brief moment, yet Bobby knew Brad had seen him.

Trembling, he dropped his cigarette and hurried away. He wasn't sure where he was going, but he didn't want to be on that street corner if Brad came back. Any ambition to make a buck that night had been knocked out of him. Bobby just wandered for two hours, afraid to go home.

When he finally decided to return to the apartment, he stopped and glanced up at the building to make sure the lights were off in the window. Brad would be asleep, and maybe (please, God!) he wouldn't say anything the next morning.

Bobby crept inside the apartment and quietly closed the door. In the darkness, he spied Brad beneath the covers of the Murphy bed. He tiptoed to the couch and pulled his shirt off. He spread the bedsheet over the sofa, then unzipped his jeans.

The light went on.

"Home kind of early tonight," said Brad, sitting up in bed. He was wearing undershorts, but Bobby knew he'd waited up for him. He usually put some acne cream on his face before going to bed, and tonight he wasn't wearing it.

Bobby glanced over his shoulder. "Yeah, I'm bushed," he said, shucking off his jeans and climbing on the couch. He pulled the sheet over himself. "Kill the light, will ya?"

"Bobby—"

"Hope I didn't wake ya," Bobby said, turning away so he didn't have to face him.

"Bobby, there's a job opening at CBS. I think you should take it."

He swiveled around and sat up. "Really? What? The radio soap? Is it a big part?"

"No." Brad grimly shook his head. "It's in the commissary. Doing dishes. Dollar-sixty an hour."

Bobby sank back. "Give me a break, will ya?"

"It's work, Bobby. And *obviously* you need the money."

"No, thanks." He sighed. "Now, will ya kill the light, please?"

"I saw you out there tonight, Bobby. I saw you with all the other hustlers. What the hell were you doing there?"

"Hey, y'know, I could ask you the same thing," he shot back. "What were *you* doing cruising around there?"

With an indignant look, Brad shook his head. "Steve D'Angelo and I drove by to laugh at all the street urchins. Thank God, Steve didn't recognize you!"

"Well, I hope you guys had a jolly time."

Moving to the foot of the bed, Brad reached over and rested a hand on Bobby's shoulder. "I'm trying to understand," he said. "I don't know what's happened to you these past few months, but you're nothing like the nice guy I met a year ago. I mean, your appearance, the hours you keep, even the way you talk. Mumbling all the time. What is it with you? Do you think by butchering the English language you sound more masculine or something?"

"Oh, yeah," Bobby sneered. "You're a great one to give lessons on masculinity."

Brad took his hand away and glared at him. "You goddamn crumb," he hissed. "Don't point a finger at me because you can't face yourself. I'm not the one working the street corner."

"No, you never had to," Bobby said. He threw off the bedsheet and sat up. "So where the hell did you get your big break, huh? Were you 'nice' to some bigshot at CBS? Is that how you got that part in the soap?"

"What are you talking about?" Brad shot back. "I auditioned with thirty-nine other applicants. That's how I got the part."

"So you mean you never had to put out for anyone?"

"No, for God's sakes—"

"Then you're damn lucky."

"Yeah. I'm lucky." Brad gazed at him in a pained and wondering way. "Bobby, is that what happened to you?"

Bobby grabbed his pants off the floor and fished a cigarette out of the pocket. "Remember *Guns in the Pacific?* I was 'nice' to the associate producer, and got a speaking part out of it." He lit his cigarette and frowned. "That was the first time. He was a nice guy, so my—initiation was pretty painless. And he kept his promise, not like all the others."

"Others?" Brad asked numbly.

"Yeah, others. On the streetcorner. All the people who picked me up, who said they were in show business—producers, old actors and actresses I'd never heard of, ad executives, all types. If I had a nickle for every empty promise, there'd be enough to pay you all the back rent I owe. I didn't make much money at it, *obviously.*"

Brad rubbed his forearms as if he felt a chill, but the room was sweltering. He uncrossed his legs and his foot brushed against Bobby's. Brad flinched. "What did you—have to do for them exactly?"

Bobby ran his thumb under the elastic band of his shorts. He was sweaty and tired, and didn't feel like explaining things. He sighed. "Most of the time I just had to stand there naked. Didn't have to touch them. They did it all themselves." Tiredly, he made a jerking motion with his hand. Then he brushed a stray ash from

46

his chest. "Sometimes, they blew me or jerked me off. I was too scared to let them do anything else. I got to call the shots. Ain't that a kick in the teeth? These guys and these old ladies pawed at me, worshipped me practically. And all I wanted from them was a line or two in some movie, a part in a show . . . just something to get me started."

Brad's eyes avoided him. Only when Bobby glanced away could he feel his roommate looking at him. "All for a part in a movie?" Brad asked quietly. "You must really want it bad."

Bobby nodded and squashed out his cigarette. "Y'know, if I'm not a famous actor in ten years, I think I'll bump myself off. Really. I won't want to go on living."

Brad climbed off the bed and sat down beside him. "You can't mean that."

"Why not?" Bobby laughed weakly, then patted Brad's knee. "Anyway, you don't have to worry about it for ten years."

Brad said nothing. He gave Bobby a long look.

Suddenly, Bobby felt the same tightening in his gut as when Don Lockridge had first noticed him standing in line. He discreetly edged away from Brad and pulled the rumpled bedsheet over his lap.

"I've seen you without your clothes on, Bobby."

Bobby let out a skittish laugh. "What do you mean?"

"You sit here telling me all about these disgusting things. Then you look at me as if I—" Brad drew in a sharp breath. He got to his feet and climbed into the Murphy bed.

"I'm sorry, Brad. I just—"

"You're just suspicious of me. What did you think I was going to do? Molest you or something? Shit." He snapped off the light and yanked the bedsheet over himself. "You'd better stop working the street corner. It's turning you into a real creep. And you're stupid if you think you'll get any career breaks from it."

"I caught on to that," Bobby murmured, sitting in the darkness. "The only reason I went there tonight was money. I need bus fare to New York."

"That dishwashing job pays a dollar-sixty an hour. Take it,

Bobby." Then Brad's voice became softer. "Please, take it, okay?"

After a moment, Bobby nodded. "Okay," he said. "Thanks, Brad. I—I'm sorry about earlier."

"Forget it."

"Were you—" Bobby hesitated. "Were you going to do anything?"

Brad turned his back to him. He took a deep breath. "Nothing. Maybe I wanted to hold you, I don't know. I felt bad for you."

"Do you still want to?" Bobby asked. "I'm sorry to act like such a shit. If that's all you wanted to do—"

"Go to sleep, Bobby. It's late. You have to go apply for that job in the morning."

"I'm really sorry, Brad."

"Shut up and go to sleep, Bobby."

For two months, Bobby scrubbed pots in the network's kitchen. Eight sweating hours a day, five days a week. But his meals were free, and he saved money. He paid Brad the back rent he owed.

There were no more lectures from his roommate. In fact, they barely spoke to each other.

One day in late November, Bobby got up from the kitchen table. He looked around the apartment, and then with a final glance, opened the door and walked out.

The note he'd left read:

Dear Brad,

For a year you've put up with my crap. You helped me when you didn't have to and I'll never forget that. Anyway, you're the best friend I ever had. I hate long goodbyes. Sentimental crap. So here's my share of the rent for next month. I'm headed for New York. I'll miss you.

Your friend,
Bobby

TWO

Evanston, Illinois—1951

The sign was posted above the soda fountain counter. "Ask our waitress about the Dimwit Delight!"

The handsome, dark-haired man sat down on the stool and smiled at the waitress. "So, what's your Dimwit Delight?"

Lisa Weller was sponging off the counter. Tiredly, she looked up. "Six flavors of ice cream, eight toppings—bananas, strawberries, Melba peach, nuts, cherries, tutti fruitti, pineapple, and whipped cream. The management assumes no responsibility for the state of the customer's stomach. Anyone who can finish a Dimwit Delight is eligible for membership in the Brotherhood of Dimwits. And it only costs a dollar."

"I'll have a Pepsi," the man said.

"Someday I'm going to tear down that stupid sign," Lisa sighed. She loaded a glass with ice and took it over to the soda fountain. There was nothing playing on the jukebox, so she sang, "Pepsi Cola hits the spot/ Twelve full ounces, that's a lot/ Twice as much for a nickel, too/ Pepsi Cola is the drink for you!"

The man smiled as she set down the drink and handed him a straw. She could see he wasn't one of the local college students. He was older, smoother, and had a Florida tan, not one of those phony-looking sunlamp jobs.

"That was pretty good," the man said. "You're a talented singer."

Lisa grinned. "I don't think Teresa Brewer is staying awake

nights. Can I get you anything else?"

"No thanks." He glanced at her. "Say, weren't you on television a couple of days ago?"

She laughed. "Who me?"

"They had a fashion show on Dave Garroway's program. You look just like one of the models. Do you model?"

"No, I'm just a student here at Northwestern."

The man shook his head. "You ought to be a model. If I were an agent, I'd sign you up right here and now."

"Thanks," Lisa said. "I'm awfully flattered." Shyly, she backed away and went over to clear the tables. As she scooped up the dirty glasses, she thought about the man who had come into Hermy's the week before. He'd said the same thing.

She certainly didn't feel very glamorous at the moment. The hamburger grill left her face and hair greasy, and the faded blue waitress uniform wasn't exactly becoming. Still, when her hair was clean, it was blond and wavy. Madeup, her skin was clear and translucent, almost an apricot color. The bump on her nose was noticeable only from certain angles. When she felt confident, even Lisa had to admit she was kind of pretty.

People at Northwestern University apparently agreed. One of the fraternities had even voted her as its Dream Girl, quite an accomplishment for a day-hopping freshman. The next year she won the title of Campus Sweater Queen. When she brought home the trophy, her younger brother, Buddy, snorted, "Hey, must be a bad year for boobs."

She was embarrassed by all the attention and hid the awards in the back of her closet. At the same time, being recognized as beautiful gave her a secret thrill. It was vanity, and she hated herself for it, the same way she hated the unexplainable excitement certain boys gave her. Bad boys, not hoods or J.D.'s, but the smooth operators, the notorious cads who thought they were God's gift to women. They terrified her. Yet she found herself attracted to the danger. They were the only ones cocky enough to ask out the Campus Sweater Queen, and the dates always ended up the same—parked somewhere off Lake Shore

Drive, her stomach in knots as Mr. Smooth made the slow attack. She'd start out with weak protests, and as her excitement grew, so would her terror. She'd commence screaming until she was driven home. There, Lisa would start to breathe normally again.

The boys who dated Lisa Weller considered her a stuck-up tease.

She didn't think she was *stuck-up*, but the *tease* part bothered her. She was a flirt. She liked the attention. Wasn't that normal, for God's sake? Apparently not. No, not when she was terrified about what might happen if she let a boy have his way.

It had happened to Lisa's mother twenty years before, as a high school senior "in trouble." Lisa still hadn't fully forgiven her mother for it. She wasn't going to make the same mistake.

Her studies were a good excuse to avoid dating altogether. When she saw a "Help Wanted" sign in Hermy's Soda Shop, she applied for the job. Something to keep her busy, a good excuse. The shop was a favorite haunt for students, and the job was just three nights a week. She liked the customers. It gave her a chance to be friendly, unavailable, and prove to them that she wasn't *stuck-up* after all.

The man had finished his Pepsi when she got back to the counter. "Say, doing anything Saturday night?"

She looked up and met his smile. Definitely a smooth operator. Robert Mitchum eyes.

"Afraid I'll be working," she said, trying to look busy as she wrote out the check.

"What about Friday? Seen *The African Queen* yet?"

"No, I-I haven't, no."

"How about seeing it with me?"

"Sorry, I don't date customers."

He looked at her for a moment. Then he slapped down a dollar to cover the ten-cent check. "There. I'm no longer a customer. Keep the change."

She glanced surreptitiously at his left hand. No wedding ring, but a telltale white strip around his finger. Lisa hid the smile of relief. She could turn away this attractive cad and feel like a "good girl" instead of a coward. "I don't date married men, either," she said.

He laughed loudly. "What makes you think I'm married?"

"You have a nice tan. Just get back from vacation?"

"Yeah, as a matter of fact, I did. Cuba. It was absolutely beautiful." Smiling, he leaned over the counter. "Just like you."

Boy, what an operator! "Did your wife enjoy Cuba?" she asked. "She must have been there, because I see you wore your wedding ring to the beach."

The man glanced down. "Observant girl," he said. "And bright. You know, I'm in the ad game. Advertising. I'm not an agent, but I know a few. I can get you a better job than this—a female soda jerk."

"I like to think of myself as a soda jerkette," Lisa said lightly.

"You could make good money modeling. What do you say we discuss it over dinner sometime?"

She smiled. "I'm sorry to disappoint you, but my father happens to be creative director at J. Winston Evans. The ad game—you know, advertising? If I wanted a modeling job that badly, all I'd have to do is ask him." Lisa tucked the dollar bill in her pocket. "Thanks for the generous tip and the compliments."

The man slid off the stool and started for the door. Then he turned and shrugged. "Can't blame a guy for trying," he said.

"Unless he's married," Lisa replied.

Two weeks later, Cathy DeRoca sat on the same stool, listening to Lisa. She was a short, energetic girl with curly black hair. She had come from Des Moines, Iowa to attend Northwestern. Cathy was majoring in performing arts, but the real degree she wanted was the M.R.S.

"Don't be ridic," Lisa was saying.

"You're just chicken, Lisa."

"Why should I be scared? I won't get the dumb part—I'm no actress. So, how's your cheeseburger?"

"It's fine and don't change the subject. The play only runs two weeks, Lisa. Right when Hermy closes up to go to Florida. You have no excuse not to audition."

"How about midterms? Anyway, I'm studying to be a teacher, not an actress. You're the drama major. Why don't you try out?"

"I am," Cathy said, "for a supporting role. For the lead, they need someone like you."

"They need someone who'll stink? Listen, Cath, I wouldn't stand a chance at the audition. I'd faint dead away before I said one word. And I could never memorize all those lines. So forget it. I've got to go bus some tables."

"Bet you five dollars you get the part—if you audition."

Lisa paused. Cathy held up the money and smiled.

Lisa lost the bet. The play was an original melodrama written by a graduate student in the English Department. It was called *Farewell to Yesterday*. Lisa played the part of Eve Thornton, a woman forced from her small town because of her bad reputation, only to find notoriety and riches in New York. The play dealt with Eve's return to the town and her plan to avenge those who had banished her. In the end, she fell in love with the mayor's son.

Throughout rehearsals, everyone in the show praised Lisa's acting. By opening night, she felt confident. She knew her lines and her cues, and before the curtain went up, she'd only thrown up twice.

Everything went well in the first act. However, two fraternity boys had plotted their own vengeance—a day of reckoning for the campus "Strike Out Queen." They'd gotten hold of a script and knew about the beginning of Act Two:

Scene One

Later that day in Eve's hotel suite. Eve wears a long satin robe. She sits at her vanity, brushing her hair. The telephone rings. Eve goes to answer it:

EVE: Hello? Yes? Mr. David Grant is on his way up? Mayor Grant's son is here to visit me? Thank you. Get me room service, please. Hello, room

53

service? This is Miss Thornton in three-oh-eight.
Send up a bottle of your finest champagne. Yes,
right away!

EVE hangs up and goes behind the changing screen, where she throws off the robe and dons a beautiful evening gown. There is a KNOCK ON THE DOOR.

EVE: Just a minute!

She emerges from behind the screen, goes to the door, and opens it.

Enter David. He is tall, good-looking, and a bit cautious.

DAVID: My father said you were beautiful, but he didn't
say just how beautiful.

EVE: What else did your father say?

DAVID: He said you were wicked, evil, no good . . .

EVE: Do you believe everything your Daddy tells you?

So began the second act.

The boys sneaked backstage during intermission and locked "David" in his dressing room.

The curtain went up for Act Two. Lisa, as Eve, tried to ignore the commotion off stage in the wings as she did her business at the vanity table and said her lines on the telephone. She strolled behind the screen and shed her robe. Underneath, she wore a strapless peach swimsuit.

At first, she paid no attention to the stagehand who stood in the wing. Just there for a peek, she thought. But out of the corner of her eye, she noticed him signaling to her. He drew his hands apart. "Stretch it out!" he silently mouthed.

Dumbfounded, Lisa stared at him for a moment. Then she remembered six hundred people were watching her alone on the stage, and they were waiting for her to do something.

Take your time getting dressed, she told herself. They were bored. Maybe she could tease them. (That was supposed to be her specialty, wasn't it?) She showed a leg at the side of the screen, then a bare arm. The audience was still bored. She could feel them shifting in their seats. What was she supposed to do? Where was that guy?

She glanced over at the stagehand. He looked panic-stricken and continued to give her the stretch signal.

Lisa wiggled into the evening gown. She rolled her shoulders and let out a wicked laugh. "Get ready, David Grant, because Eve is going to get you!"

God, what a stupid thing to say!

She stepped out from behind the screen and ran her hands up and down the form-fitting evening dress. There were murmurs from the audience. At least they weren't bored. Lisa twirled and glided to the vanity and admired her reflection. She threw her head back and laughed. These people probably thought her character was a lunatic; this was the second time she'd laughed for no reason. Where the hell was that stupid actor?

"Oh, David," she cooed. "David, David . . ." *Say something else for God's sakes.* "Oh, David, why do you take so long?" Yes, why? I'm dying out here, Lisa thought. She floated toward the door and opened it. "David?" she chirped. "Are you hiding out in the hall?"

The stagehand was there, away from the audience's view. "He's locked in his dressing room. We're trying to get him out. Stall!"

Omygod.

She returned to center stage, where the six hundred people watched her, waiting. They had to know something was wrong. Her mouth open, Lisa stepped up to the footlights and stared out at the ominous darkness. "He isn't coming," she said in a tiny voice. "He . . . he . . ."

Helplessly shaking her head, she turned away. Then she saw the prop telephone by the sofa. Her salvation. "That stupid desk clerk!" she bellowed. "I'm going to give him a piece of my mind!"

She faced the audience, picked up the receiver, and dialed.

"Hello? Front desk? This is Miss Thornton. You phoned me and said Mr. David Grant was on his way up. Was that supposed to be a joke? He isn't here . . ." She paused. "He's stuck in the elevator? Oh, that's marvelous, simply marvelous, just marvelous . . ."

Okay, they got the point. It's marvelous already.

Forcing herself to relax, Lisa reclined seductively on the sofa. "Well, you know, you have a nice voice. Are you the tall, blond man behind the desk? I thought so. You're very handsome." She lifted her dress above her knee and smoothed out one of her stockings. "Will you forgive me for being mad at you? Oh, thank you. I can never stay mad at a handsome man for too long."

For the next three minutes, the audience sat spellbound as they watched Eve on the telephone, enticing the imaginary desk clerk. She told him she'd like to be trapped in an elevator with him. Curling the phone cord around her finger, she described the hot, cramped elevator and the two of them together, alone.

"I'll bet it would be dark in there," Lisa said in her sultriest Lauren Bacall voice. "You know, I'm afraid of the dark. You'd have to wrap your strong arms around me—hold me. Kiss me until I feel better. I can almost feel your lips right now . . . soft. You kiss my neck, and I'm kissing you back. I can feel you pressing against me. You're strong. Oh, tell me how strong you are! Right now, I want to—"

There was a knock from the sound-effects man backstage, and a few disappointed groans from the audience. Lisa glanced over to the wing. The stagehand whispered, "David," and he pointed to the set door.

"They must have fixed the elevator," she said into the phone. "Um, listen, maybe we can ride it together sometime when it breaks down again." She kissed the mouthpiece and hung up.

She hurried to the door and opened it. The young man playing David was frazzled and out of breath. Lisa spoke quickly, jumping his line: "I know. You were stuck in the elevator. The desk clerk told me. So don't you tell me. I don't want to hear about it."

56

He looked at her, momentarily confused. Then he vaguely delivered his line: "My father said you were beautiful, but he didn't say just how beautiful."

"What else did your father say?"

The next day, it was the *Chicago Sun-Times* that had something to say:

> . . . The play treads along rather sluggishly until the beginning of the second act. Then, Lisa Weller sizzles as the vengeful seductress, with her bold proposition to an unseen desk clerk over the telephone. Her enticing tone and alluring movements are startlingly effective. The all-too-brief scene was the best moment in the play. This young actress breathes life into an otherwise tepid, talky production. We're sure we'll be hearing more from Lisa Weller.

"Beautiful bone structure. And high cheekbones—that's a definite plus." The silver-haired woman studied Lisa's face as if it were a piece of china. Lisa studied her, too. She was about fifty, very carefully made up, and well preserved. Her name was Rita Fabor and she wore a stylish black dress, a leopard skin beret, and waved a cigarette holder like a scepter before her.

Dressed in a gray skirt and a gray cardigan, with pearls, Lisa felt like a country bumpkin. She evaded the woman's cool, appraising eyes by staring out the office window at the traffic below on Michigan Avenue. "Pretty hair," said Miss Fabor.

"Thank you," Lisa said.

"Let me see your teeth, dear," the woman said, leaning closer. Lisa gave her a wide, nervous smile. "I know you must feel like a melon in the supermarket, but teeth are very important. Yes, very nice. You've got a healthy, well-scrubbed look. Nice figure too."

"Thank you."

"And just how did you find us, dear?"

"My father—" Lisa hesitated. "He knows some people in advertising and they said your talent agency was the best in the city."

"You want to be an actress, as well? What kind of experience do you have?"

"Well, I was in a few plays at Northwestern."

"You're still in school?"

Lisa nodded. "Until next June. I'd like to work part-time up until graduation, and then full-time."

Her voice trailed off. It had been too presumptuous to say that, she realized. She glanced up nervously at Rita Fabor.

Miss Fabor was nodding. "You'd make a wonderful girl-next-door type," she mused. "I'd like you to come back next week with some photographs. Out of the family album, whatever. Then my partner can look you over and we'll see how you photograph."

Valentina D'Ambroise, Rita's partner, was one of those gaunt French women who looked as if they'd lived forever and still had another eternity left. She seemed more impressed with Lisa's pictures than with Lisa herself. "Have you considered to fix the nose?" Valentina asked, in a thick accent.

Lisa was startled. "I hadn't thought about it," she said.

"You should. The bump—is no good."

Miss Fabor stood over her partner, studying the photographs. "Actually, it doesn't show up in these."

Valentina got up and stalked around the table. "Let me see your hands." Lisa held them out. She was also asked to show off her bustline and pile her hair on top of her head. Valentina barked out commands like a drill sergeant.

But at last, she seemed satisfied. Lisa was given the name of a photographer, who for forty dollars would make up a composite sheet. The photographs were duly taken, and Lisa wasn't crazy about them, though Rita seemed pleased.

"Now we print these along with your measurements, sizes, etcetera. Then we'll send these around and see what we get."

But it wasn't until March that Rita finally called. She said she had gotten Lisa a part in a TV commercial. Her first professional

58

job was spooning mayonnaise onto a salad. There weren't any lines, but Lisa prepared for the part at home by practicing spooning mayo and giving herself a manicure.

For the next ad, she headed a conga line advertising footwear. "Shoes to dance in, prance in, romance in!" went the slogan. For another part paying twenty-three dollars, she woke up to start a beautiful day, thanks to Milk of Magnesia for prompt relief. All the talking was done with a voice-over narration as Lisa yawned, smiled, climbed out of bed, smiled, went to the window, opened the drapes, and smiled.

"Can I have a line or two in the next commercial?" she asked Rita, after five more non-speaking assignments. "I'm supposed to be an actress, not a prop!"

Rita got her parts with lines. "Gosh, Diana," complained Lisa, in her next role, "Bill won't come near me!" "It could be your breath, Madge," was the reply. Lisa received seventeen dollars for having halitosis; $29.50 for almost poisoning her new husband with bad coffee; $32.50 because her deodorant didn't prevent underarm wetness ("Gee, Ann, why can't *I* get a date?"); and $37.00 for that dull, gray film on her kitchen floor.

Lisa was a good loser, until finally she was cast as a glamour princess in a Hudnuts Egg Cream Shampoo commercial. The producer of a Chicago children's program spotted Lisa sitting at her dressing table wearing a tiara and gown, and signed her for his show. He needed a replacement for Pretty Princess Pamela, who was suspected to be a fellow traveler. "Pretty Pinko Pamela," the director had called her.

Lisa felt a little uneasy taking over the part. The show itself was called "Uncle Bob's Kiddie Good-Time Hour." Uncle Bob was a kindly family man with a mouth that would make a sailor blush. The program featured four cartoons, a clown named Chucklehead, an onstage studio audience of giggling kids, and several commercial breaks, which were introduced by Pretty Princess Pamela: "And now, a word from our sponsors!"

The highlight of the show was the Big Prize Contest. Pretty

Pamela would stroll among the children and tap her wand on preselected heads. She had been told their seat numbers before the show.

Lisa didn't like that part of the job. The losing children were always full of despair; they didn't understand that the whole thing was a prearranged set-up. Sometimes they grabbed at her gown or burst into tears.

"Don't mind the little bastards," Uncle Bob advised her. "Great kids, but sometimes they can sure be a pain in the ass."

But the show was steady work and didn't interfere with school or her commercial spots. By January graduation, Lisa had saved over eight hundred dollars. It was enough, she figured, to go to New York and become an actress. A real one.

"New York?" Dee Weller set down her coffee cup. She shot her husband a distressed look, then turned to Lisa. "You want to move to New York?"

"Yes, Mother." Lisa glanced down at the dinner table. "I'd like to leave in a few weeks."

"Isn't this a little—sudden?"

"I've told you several times that I've been planning this. New York's got the best theaters and drama schools. If I'm going to be an actress, that's the place to be."

"And how, may I ask, do you intend to support yourself?"

"Doing what I am now. Commercials. TV."

Dee frowned. At forty, she was an elegant, blond, suburban matron, her battles with poverty and self-image long behind. Sometimes it was hard for Lisa to envision her twenty-two years before: a scared high-school girl "in trouble."

Matthew Weller, tall and lean, with gray hair and dashing looks, rivaled Robert Young as the perfect father. Lisa loved him so much that she often wished to go back and rewrite the circumstances of her own birth.

Matt smiled at her. "Lisa, honey, where do you plan to live in New York?"

"Greenwich Village."

"Oh Lord," Dee groaned. "There's nothing but beatniks there!"

"Why Greenwich Village, sweetheart?" Matt asked her.

"Well, I know this girl who graduated last year, Patty Bushman. She's a dancer and she's got an apartment there. I heard through her family that she was looking for a roommate."

"Patty Bushman?" Dee studied Lisa. "How come we've never heard of this girl until today?"

Patty Bushman was one of the most obnoxious dips in the forty-eight states, but Lisa wasn't about to tell her parents. She figured she could stand Patty for a few months until she found a place of her own. Lisa sighed. "I'm sure I've mentioned her, Mother. And she's very nice. So please, don't worry. I have enough money for at least three or four months. And I promise to set aside enough for a return ticket on the Twentieth Century Limited. Anyway, I wasn't planning to leave 'til next month."

Dee Weller sipped her coffee and sighed.

On Soundstage Five, the players took their marks minutes before the live broadcast began. In Lisa's first national telecast, her role was the unseen secretary, Miss Gray. Over an intercom, she would announce to her employer, "Miss Baker is here to see you, sir, and I've got your wife on line three."

Lisa was terrified. Her sixteen words would be heard by millions of people across the country. If she screwed up, there would be no one to blame but herself. They'd stuck her offstage—away from the other actors—in a glass booth that seemed like a gas chamber. She'd had to go to the bathroom ever since they'd locked her in there twenty minutes before. Lisa had been told to speak in a low voice, precisely two inches from a special filter mike.

She sat in the booth and waited for her cue. What if she missed it? What if she sneezed? What if she spoke too loudly—or so softly no one would hear her? Good God, maybe she wouldn't be able to speak at all.

That would be it. Good-bye, New York; hello, Chicago. For

three months, she had made rounds from Radio City to Madison Avenue. Every day, she put in an appearance wherever a job could be found.

Since her arrival in New York, Lisa had worn out four pairs of shoes from walking her rounds. Her savings had dwindled to sixty-three dollars and thirty-five cents. Most of it had gone to pay for singing lessons and drama classes, plus fifty dollars a month for her rent.

She made some money taking modeling jobs. The agencies played up her supposed resemblance to Grace Kelly—another "ladylike blonde," they claimed. But some sponsors didn't like her height, or found her face too narrow or her figure too flat. One casting director told her, "You're no Suzy Parker, that's for sure."

"Would it help if I dyed my hair red?" Lisa had asked sweetly.

"A nose job would be more useful. Anyone ever tell you it's crooked at the top?"

"Gosh, no," Lisa said. "Thanks for the tip."

At least they couldn't criticize her looks as the invisible secretary. All she had to do was speak. Good God, had she missed her cue? No, they were still talking.

What was her line? "Your mother is here to see—" *No, damn it.* "Your *wife* is on line four—" *Three. Calm down.* "Miss Gray is here to see you—" *No, you're Miss Gray, stupid.*

"What is it, Miss Gray?"

Lisa started. Drawing a deep breath, she leaned close to the mike and murmured, "Miss Baker is here to see you, sir, and I've got your wife on line three."

Lisa Weller was now a professional television actress. The year was 1954.

THREE

It was five-thirty in the morning. Bobby strolled down West Fifty-seventh Street, looking for a place to sleep. He concealed a wire coat-hanger inside the front of his parking attendant's jacket. Everyone in this city locked their goddamn cars.

He felt awful from lack of sleep, much older than his twenty-three years. Prowling the bars all night, he looked so seedy that no one wanted to get near him.

The streetlamps were being turned off, and the news-vendor piled the morning papers in his shack. Bobby stopped for a moment to eye the girlie magazines on the top shelf. It reminded him of when he was a kid, so often alone in the apartment while his father was working.

He used to search his father's bedroom for dirty magazines or playing cards with naked ladies on them. Some of his friends' fathers kept such treasures hidden in their underwear drawers. But Cameron's underwear drawer contained just underwear; he kept nothing beneath the bed.

In his father's closet, Bobby had discovered a brown envelope. Inside were Danny's athletic certificates, drawings, and report cards. There was only one report card of Bobby's. He had torn through the closet, hoping to find an envelope of his things. He found his father's medical reports, old bills, his parents' marriage license, his mother's and Danny's death certificates.

Then he had found his own birth certificate, and stared at it with a strange sense of relief. At least it seemed to prove his existence, prove that, in some small way, he mattered. But as Bobby had shut the closet door, he didn't feel very important to anyone. Even himself.

Shit. Why the hell did he have to think about that now? He was depressed enough already.

Bobby crossed the street and headed for the Metro Broadcasting parking lot. Only a few cars were there at this hour. He decided on the chrome green Mercedes. If he was going to get arrested for breaking into someone's car, he might as well go in style.

After ten minutes of manipulating the hanger through the crack in the car window, he unlocked the door. Climbing inside, he shut the door and curled up on the front seat.

Someday, he thought, he'd own a car like this, instead of just sleeping in it. Someday, he'd be an important man.

The owner of the green Mercedes was Raymond J. Bartlett, a very important man at Metro Broadcasting.

The cab driver had a cold. When Ruth Bartlett counted the tenth sneeze in fifteen minutes, she checked the cabbie's license for his name and leaned forward. "Excuse me, it says here your name's George."

"Well, it ain't No Smoking." He coughed.

"George," she said, "forgive me, but should you be out driving a cab when you're so sick? That sounds like a terrible cold. Is it an allergy?"

"Yeah, I got an allergy, lady," he said. "I'm allergic to poverty. That's why I been driving ten hours straight, half-dead with a cold."

"Ten hours! But it's eight in the morning! You ought to be home in bed."

The driver grunted.

Ruth sat back against the cracked leather seat and stared out the window. She felt foolish. Old and foolish. In two days, she'd be fifty. She had never thought growing older would be so disagreeable. If she had been thirty, the cab driver would have thought she was just being kind, even flirtatious. At fifty, she was just nagging.

"I'm sorry," she said, trying to smile into the mirror. "Maybe you're allergic to snoopy old women."

He coughed and spat out the window.

"I have this awful habit of sticking my nose into other people's business," Ruth went on. "It drives my husband crazy. I'm particularly insufferable when I'm in a good mood. Unfortunately, you caught me in a good mood this morning."

The cabbie said nothing. Ruth began to regret she hadn't just stuck with "God bless you." It was stuffy in the cab, which smelled of stale smoke and Vicks Vaporub. Ruth rolled down her window. The driver sneezed and she mumbled, "God bless you," for the eleventh time.

"Thanks, lady." The man sniffled. "I don't mean to be a stinker. It's this cold. I guess I should be glad somebody's in a good mood, at any rate."

Ruth smiled. "Oh, I am. My husband's been away on business and—"

"Yeah, right. Good to have him out of your hair. I know what you mean, lady."

"Good heavens, no!" Ruth laughed. "I've missed him. He got into La Guardia last night and stayed over at his club. I'm meeting him for breakfast. Then we're going shopping for my daughter and her husband. It's their anniversary."

The driver shifted his rheumy eyes to the mirror. The lady in back was rich. No question. He'd picked her up at one of those Old Money estates in Glen Cove. His initial glimpse had recorded her classy clothes and figure, a little thin. He liked them fleshy. Now he studied her more carefully. She was a blonde, with a kind face. The only real sign of age was traced in her vulnerable eyes.

"You don't look old enough to have a married daughter," he said, trying to be polite.

"Really?" She beamed. "Well, George, your tip just went up a few dollars."

When he dropped her off at the entrance to Metro Broadcasting's midtown studios, Ruth paid and tipped him, and made him promise he'd go straight home to nurse his cold.

She walked into the building and took the elevator up to the executive offices. She paused outside the plush suite occupied by the Vice President of Programming. Raymond's office.

She was disappointed to see a new girl at the reception desk. Raymond's regular secretary, Jane Benchley, was a very sweet girl. She always chatted with Ruth and brought her coffee. The sad part was that she usually enjoyed seeing Jane more than her husband.

But Ruth refused to think of that now. Whenever Raymond returned from a long trip, she saw it as a fresh start—another chance for things to improve.

The new receptionist was pretty. Tan, brunette, with an Italian haircut and bright red lipstick. She wore glasses and a low-cut blouse. She wasn't exactly to Ruth's taste. Still, she decided to be gracious and welcome the new girl. She walked over to the desk with a smile.

"Hello, how are you today?"

The girl looked up from the letters she was opening. "May I help you?"

"Yes, I'm Mrs. Bartlett. Raymond didn't tell me he'd hired someone new."

The secretary smiled coldly. "I'm not new. I work down the hall. I'm filling in for Jane."

"Oh? Is she sick?"

"I believe she has a cold," the girl said, letting her smile fade.

"Something must be going around. My cab driver had the same thing."

The receptionist didn't look up. "If you're here to see Mr. Bartlett, you missed him. He left for London an hour ago."

"*London?* There must be some mistake. I talked to him last night. We arranged to have breakfast."

The receptionist merely opened a drawer in her desk and took out a set of keys. "Mr. Bartlett was called to London early this morning. He'll be gone for about ten days. He left word he'd get in touch with you." She handed the keys to Ruth. "He'd like you to take his car home."

"But he just got in from Los Angeles last night!"

The girl picked up her letter opener. "Mr. Bartlett didn't trust the club's valet. He said there were some extra miles on the Mercedes. The car's parked in the lot out back."

"He didn't leave a message?"

"Just the car," the girl said.

Ruth stared down at the keys. "Thank you," she said, in a low voice. "I'm sorry, I didn't catch your name."

"Miss Wallace."

"Thank you, Miss Wallace. Nice meeting you."

Miss Wallace nodded curtly and returned to her mail.

As the elevator hurtled down to the lobby, Ruth stood and stared at the panel of lighted numbers above the door. Ten days. He would miss her birthday. She would spend it at home, sitting in the huge dining room at the long, empty table, listening to the servants' hushed voices in the kitchen. They would bring her a glorious cake and sing "Happy Birthday" and she would act pleased.

The elevator doors opened. Ruth walked down the hall to the rear exit. There would be a call from her daughter, and one from her son at college.

Raymond would forget. He'd be busy in London with Valerie Bounty, his latest discovery. Ruth had seen her picture. A vulgar-looking girl—a bottle blonde who wore tight, low-cut gowns. Falsies, probably. What did Raymond see in this one? Now Christina Slade, the Los Angeles starlet—at least she had some talent.

Raymond wasn't even discreet about it. If only he would show some trace of shame or remorse, some sign that he cared what Ruth thought. But he seemed to enjoy flaunting his infidelities, like a hunter displaying his trophies. He never admitted his indiscretions to Ruth, and she never acknowledged them. But everyone knew. The public humiliation was real—the talk behind her back, the innuendos dropped at parties. Sometimes Ruth thought she should have been paid as an actress herself. She always played the role of the happy idiot.

She stepped into the chilly, gray morning and looked over the vast parking lot. Moving down the steps, she stumbled on the last one and gripped the railing, glaring at the keys in her hand. Tears stung her eyes.

"Goddamn him!" she cried and threw the keys onto the pavement. No self-pity, Ruth, she told herself, closing her eyes. Stop it. He does care about you. This thing with these other women. It's just a phase. He's a vain man, and he's getting older. He has to save his ego. Those girls don't mean any more to him than a sport car. He cares. Now *stop* it.

She bent down, picked up the keys, and walked across the lot to her husband's car. Raymond and his damn Mercedes. Another of his trophies. Sometimes she wished she had married someone unattractive. Instead, Raymond was a man's man. Six-foot-two, black hair streaked with silver, forever tan. She recalled the party where Raymond had stripped down to his trousers and done chin-ups by the pool. All the guests had gathered, whistling, cheering him on, counting in unison while the number of chin-ups grew. Ruth had watched, too, smiling patiently, secretly hoping he'd have a coronary in front of his adoring fans.

She approached the Mercedes and was about to unlock it when she glanced inside. Her heart almost stopped. Dropping the keys, she staggered away, stuffing her hand in her mouth. "My God!"

A young man lay inside the car, curled up on the front seat. His stocking feet were jammed under the steering wheel, his ribs pressed against the gear shift. A parking attendant's jacket was thrown over his body.

Nervously, Ruth peered through the window and was thankful to see he was still breathing. The exposed half of his face revealed fine features, a fair complexion, and wavy black hair. Asleep, he looked young and innocent, a drop of saliva trickling from his parted lips onto Raymond's expensive upholstery.

She glanced around the parking lot. No one was in sight. Don't be a coward, she told herself, and tapped on the window. The boy stirred, moving his left foot so it lodged against the steering column. Finally, Ruth unlocked the front door and opened it.

"Excuse me, it's time to get up," she said. The young man didn't budge. Ruth shook him. "Excuse me, I hate to be a spoilsport, but you'll have to wake up. I don't want you to get in trouble—"

Agitated, he kicked her hand away and mumbled an obscenity, but that was all. Flustered, Ruth reached into the car and pressed the horn.

Bobby jerked upright, hitting his head on the dome light. "Jesus! What do you think you're doing? Trying to scare the shit out of me? Jesus, lady!"

Ruth drew back. "This happens to be my car," she said. "Rather, my husband's."

Bobby rubbed his head. He gave her a contrite look. "Okay, okay. Sorry, lady." He squirmed into his jacket and reached for his shoes. "Don't worry. I didn't mess it up. I'm leaving."

"The car doesn't matter," she heard herself say. She held out the keys to him. "Here. Drive it off a cliff for me."

Shoes in hand, he was edging across the seat. "Look, it's okay, lady. I'm leaving."

Gently, she pushed him back down. "Put your shoes on. You'll catch cold. Something's going around."

Bobby glanced at her warily.

"I'm not crazy, if that's what you're thinking," she said, with a faint smile.

"I didn't say anything."

"They'd fire you if they knew you slept in customers' cars, you know."

He got to his feet. "That's already been taken care of."

"Oh, I'm sorry to hear that," she said.

"Don't lose any sleep over it. I haven't."

"Why did they fire you?"

Bobby gave her a jaded smile. "Why do you give a rat's ass?" he said.

She flushed. "Shouldn't people care about other people?"

"You're a real yo-yo, you know that, lady?" He rested an elbow on the hood of the car. "Well, if you're really panting to hear the story—some clown drove in here last night late. Gave me crap about being careful with his precious DeSoto. Kept poking me with his umbrella. So I very politely told him if he didn't stop with the umbrella, I'd jam it up his tailpipe. He went bananas. Told me he could get me fired and bla bla bla. I kept my cool, though. Just stood there and took it."

"That's what I would have done," Ruth said quietly.

"But I guess he was testing me, because then he gave me another jab with the umbrella. So I decked him."

"You decked him," she repeated.

"That's right. But the joke was on me, because this clown turns out to be some big shot. I got the royal ax a few minutes later."

She stood staring at this crude young man with some amusement. Even with the bags under his eyes, he was very good-looking. But there was something else about him, a boyishness, a vulnerability that his tough façade couldn't hide. "Why were you sleeping in my husband's car?" she asked. "I mean, if they fired you, why didn't you just go home?"

"Couldn't. Got evicted from my apartment last week. Landlady locked me out. She's holding my stuff till I can cough up the last few months' rent."

"You poor man!"

"I get by," he said, with a hint of pride in his voice. "I keep a change of clothes in a locker at Port Authority."

"But where do you sleep?"

"That's never been a problem," he said slyly. "Until last night, I guess. I was a little strapped. So I came back here looking for a place to catch a few winks. Anyway, your old man left the window open a crack, and I was able to get in. Hope ya don't mind. I mean, I didn't hurt anything." He started to walk away and threw her a lazy wave. "Well, lady, it's been a slice. Real swell talking with ya."

"But where will you go?"

"I don't know. Here, there—around." Turning, he walked off, stretching out his arms and rolling the crimp out of his neck.

"What are you going to do?" Ruth called after him.

Pausing, Bobby turned and grinned at her. Ruth fidgeted with the car keys. Finally she smiled back. "Why don't you have some breakfast with me?" she heard herself say.

He nodded agreeably. "I could go for that." Peeling off the attendant's jacket, he slung it over his shoulder and strolled back to Ruth. "I know a great place around the corner. Real cheap. Just don't order the sausage."

Ruth felt strange as she left the parking lot with this handsome young man. He was muscular, but so thin. His eyes were a guileless blue with long, thick lashes. When he caught her studying him, she stared at the pavement.

"I'm an actor," he told Ruth. "Pierce Roberts."

"Ruth Bartlett," she said. "Are you really an actor?"

"Yep. I'm gonna be the best. Better than Brando, better than Clift. Better than anybody."

She glanced up at him. "You don't mind yourself one bit, do you?"

"You gotta think that way if you wanna get anywhere."

"And have you gotten anywhere?"

"All the way to nowheresville." He shrugged. "I've been in movies, done some TV, but it's all just been background crap." Bobby looked up at the tall buildings that stabbed the gray sky. He scowled. "That's what I've been doing the past three years. Extra work. Hustling. I thought I might get a break parking cars at Metro, but that's history now. You gotta have some connections in this business. Know some bigshot. That's the whole game. Who ya know. But how the hell do you meet the right person?"

Ruth stared straight ahead. She smiled faintly. "I think you just met her."

Ruth felt conspicuous as she and Bobby entered the greasy spoon. No one in a Bergdorf suit had stepped inside in years, she was sure. It was a nameless café, hidden in the lobby of a building on West Fifty-second. Business was slow. Three booths were empty. At the counter sat two truck drivers and a bag lady mumbling to herself about Queen Elizabeth's coronation. A cook in stained whites leaned on the counter with his nose in a Mickey Spillane paperback. There was no sign of a waitress.

Every head lifted as Ruth entered the diner. Blushing, she followed Bobby to a booth. The tabletop was wet and smeared, the red plastic seat torn and its stuffing spilling onto the dingy floor.

The cook returned to the Spillane book; the woman resumed her bitter monologue; the truck drivers went back to ignoring each other. "Well, the coffee smells good, at any rate," Ruth said, with forced cheerfulness.

"Yo, Bobby!" a voice cried. They looked back at the kitchen and saw a waitress, a homely girl in her thirties. Her grin revealed a missing front tooth. A pencil was stuck in her brown hair, which she'd pulled back in a greasy ponytail. Her stained yellow uniform stretched across an enormous belly. Pad in hand, she hurried over to their booth.

"Charlene!" Bobby grinned. "Why, you gorgeous piece of womanhood. How the hell are you?"

"Shmo. Where you been? I haven't seen ya all week."

"Busy, sexpot, busy. Give me a smooch. C'mon."

Ruth's smile froze as the waitress planted a kiss on his cheek. He wiped it off with one hand and then nibbled at his fingers.

"Cornball," the waitress laughed. She glanced at Ruth, then took the pencil out of her hair and poised it above the pad. "What'll you have? Special today—eggs, toast, skinless frank, and all the rot-gut coffee you can drink. Seventy cents." She flashed her gap-toothed grin at Ruth. "Personally, honey, I don't recommend it. The franks here could gag a maggot."

"Thanks for the tip," Ruth said.

"How about a couple of menus?" Bobby said.

Charlene gasped in mock wonder. "Well, *menus*. I'm impressed. Comin' right up."

"And two coffees while you're at it, babe. I love ya!" he called after her.

Ruth waited until the waitress had gone. "Is that your girl?"

"Christ, no. She's married. We just fool around."

Ruth shifted in her seat. "Do you—fool around a lot with married women?"

"God, no. Well, only sometimes." Smiling at her, he took out a pack of Chesterfields and lit one. "Anyway, you've got it all wrong about me and Charlene. I flirt with her, okay? The bum she's married to roughs her up. Check it out—she's got marks all over her. A few months ago, he knocked out her front tooth." He took a thoughtful drag. "With us, it's all in fun. She knows that —Charlene's swell. But her old man . . . " His voice trailed off in disgust.

"Do you know the husband?"

He blew out a stream of smoke. "I know the type. And you want to hear the punch line? She loves him. You figure it. He treats her like dirt, and still she loves him. Can you believe that?"

"Yes, I can," Ruth answered quietly.

The waitress returned balancing cups, saucers, and menus. She placed the coffee in front of them and then handed a menu to Ruth with an elaborate curtsy. "One for madame?"

"Thank you," Ruth said, trying not to look at the welts on Charlene's arm.

Charlene gave Bobby a menu. "And one for Brando, Jr. I'll be back in a couple of minutes, okay, Bob?"

"Thanks, doll."

Charlene grinned and left.

"Did you see those arms?" he asked Ruth, grinding out his Chesterfield.

"That poor girl."

"Oh, she'll be okay," he said.

"She called you Bob."

"Yeah, that's my name. Bobby Pierce."

"But you told me it was Pierce Roberts."

"That's what it's gonna be, when I'm legit. When I'm a star.

Aw, Equity's probably already stuffed with Bobs and Robert Pierces. So I turned it around. Sounds sexier, don't you think?"

"I think it sounds awful," Ruth said. She looked back at her menu. When she looked up, he was glaring at her, wounded. Impulsively, she touched his arm.

"I'm sorry. I just think your name is fine the way it is. It suits you. Pierce Roberts sounds, well, like you ought to be wearing black leotards and reciting poetry. I didn't mean to offend you, Bobby—that's just the impression I got."

"Well," he said, reaching over to stroke the palm of her hand with his thumb. "Maybe I'll wait and see how Robert Pierce goes over first."

"I think he'll go a lot farther than Pierce Roberts," Ruth said with a smile. Withdrawing her hand, she returned to the menu.

Staring at the items, she wondered why he had done that. Her hand tingled. He couldn't be interested in her. She was old enough to—well, her daughter Laura was certainly older than he. And when Ruth had been pregnant with Brendon, this boy was probably in kindergarten.

He was so good-looking. Not like Raymond, whose handsomeness was the result of careful grooming and tailored clothes. This boy had the kind of looks she pretended not to notice on shirtless street workers, careless young men in beat-up cars. A smooth, defined bone structure, and a strong jaw. His hair needed cutting, but its disarray somehow added to his looks. He could have all the pretty, young girls he wanted. So why was he playing up to her?

She had hinted she might be able to help him, but so far, he hadn't pounced on that, at least not yet. Maybe he hadn't realized whose car he'd chosen to sleep in. Or maybe, he had. And if so . . .

She peered over the menu. He was looking at her with those blue eyes. And that smile. "I think I'll have bacon and eggs," she said. "How about you, Bobby? See anything you like?"

His grin widened.

She sat back in the booth. "Listen, I'll pay. For the breakfast, I mean."

"It's okay, Mrs. Bartlett." Bobby nodded coolly. "I know what you mean."

After they left the diner, Bobby said his day was "free." They went to Gimbel's, where Ruth shopped for her daughter's anniversary. She'd planned on getting Laura and Frank a lamp, a notion Bobby dismissed as "squaresville." He suggested a his-and-hers set of bongo drums. Ruth lied and said her daughter was tone-deaf. Finally. they agreed on an expensive camera. She paid for it and had it sent to her daughter in Boston.

In Ladies' Apparel, he coaxed her into trying on some clothes. Reluctantly, she agreed, emerging from the dressing room as Bobby made her laugh with wolf-whistles and applause. She didn't buy any of the clothes, but insisted on getting Bobby a tie, an idea he wasn't crazy about but endured stoically.

They lunched at the Plaza, where the newly purchased tie proved a requirement. Bobby checked his parking jacket at the coat room. The head waiter gave him a suitcoat to wear that was a couple of sizes too big. At the table, Ruth noticed his manners were borderline as he lit one cigarette off another, elbows planted on the table, and gobbled up food. But he made up for them with self-conscious pleases and thank-yous, and an appealing timidity over which fork to use. There was something touching about the way the borrowed jacket came down to his knuckles. Beyond the tough façade, Ruth sensed that he was nervous and lost.

By the time they finished, it was three-thirty and starting to drizzle. Walking back to Metro, they were caught in a downpour and paused to huddle in a doorway. Ruth's arms were crossed in front of her. She found herself fighting the impulse to cling to him for warmth. They watched passersby struggling with umbrellas, vainly trying to hail taxis. Finally, Bobby put his attendant's coat around her shoulders.

"Thank you." She smiled. She tried not to notice how his white shirt had become transparent with rain and clung to his broad young chest.

"What do you say we make a run for the car?" His eyes danced in his wet, chiseled face. "It's only a few blocks away. Okay?"

Ruth nodded. He grabbed her hand and they dashed down the avenue together. After they reached the Mercedes, they stood by it panting. Then Ruth heard herself asking Bobby to drive her home.

"I hate driving Raymond's car, especially in the rain," she said. He'd catch his death walking around in this downpour, she told herself, as Bobby nodded. She'd make him a nice warm dinner, call a cab, and pay for his ride back.

He drove over the speed limit most of the way. An hour later, he pulled down the long, tree-lined drive leading to the house. The lights inside were few, and the big, brick house looked lonely and cold.

Bobby kept up a steady series of exclamations as Ruth led him through the large, oval foyer to the richly paneled study. One wall had floor-to-ceiling bookshelves filled with books, vases, and expensively framed photographs. Bobby picked up one of the pictures—it showed a beautiful blond girl with a sweet smile and sad, vulnerable eyes.

"Was this you?" he asked.

"It still is," Ruth said. "I've only changed on the outside."

"You still look pretty good," he said.

She went over to the bar and poured him a brandy. "You'll be warmer over here," she said, nodding to a fire crackling in the hearth. "Owen must have laid the fire before he left."

"Who's Owen? I thought your husband's name was Ray."

"Raymond's in London at the moment. Owen is our butler. He and the maid have the evening off." She handed Bobby the brandy. "Well, I'd better get out of these wet clothes. There's plenty to read in here. I shouldn't be long."

Bobby nodded and wandered back to the bookcase, where he stood studying the photograph. Ruth was watching him from the doorway. "Is it so hard to believe it's me?"

"No. It's just a beautiful picture."

"You know what's really hard to believe?" she asked, with just a trace of sadness. "When I look in the mirror now, I don't see that girl anymore."

* * *

Pulling on a fresh slip, Ruth went into her bathroom and began to towel-dry her hair. She wondered what Bobby was doing. How could she explain tonight, of all nights, she had given the servants the evening off? She should have explained that the cozy evening had been arranged for her and Raymond. She'd bought Raymond's favorite foods and had planned on cooking an intimate meal. A quiet, romantic homecoming. It must look like a set-up. It was, but it was for Raymond, not this boy!

Working the comb through her tangled hair, she tried to ignore the reflection in the full-length mirror. She'd stopped counting the lines on her slender neck. Scarves and high-collared blouses would have to be added to her wardrobe. Just as well, she thought. She never had gone for low necklines anyway, probably because she didn't have much to show. She allowed herself a glance at her legs, which were still good. But not against those of a Valerie Bounty or Christina Slade.

In the bedroom, she opened the closet and pulled out a blouse and skirt, then tossed them on the bed. She took a new pair of stockings from the bureau and sat on the bed to put them on. Yes, she still had good legs. She paused to admire her slender thighs. As she clasped the garter to the second stocking, she looked up. Bobby was standing in the bedroom door.

Quickly, she pulled her slip down and snatched up the blouse to cover herself. "Bobby, I'm getting dressed!"

He didn't seem to hear. He strolled into the bedroom and began to unbutton his shirt. It came off to reveal his white muscular torso, the patch of black hair in the center of his chest.

Still clutching the blouse to her breast, Ruth got up. She began to back away. "Listen, Bobby. If you need to change your . . . your wet things, my son's room is right across the hall."

The shirt fell to the floor as he kicked off his shoes. He began walking toward her.

"Just down the hall," she repeated, backing against the open closet. "You can borrow something of his. You seem about Brendon's size. Take anything . . . it's just down the hall, you can't miss it—"

Stopping at the bed, he grabbed the bedpost for balance and peeled off his socks.

"Or if you want a shower, there's a bathroom in there. You could take a shower while I run downstairs and fix us some dinner. Just as soon as I finish dressing."

"That sounds like a good idea," Bobby said, unfastening his belt. "I'll wait to take my shower later, though."

Ruth closed her eyes. She heard his pants unzip. "Bobby," she whispered. "Please leave." She looked up and saw he had his hands on his trousers, which were open, revealing a glimpse of black pubic hair against his flat, white pelvis.

"Get out."

He smiled hesitantly. "I don't get it."

"Get out!" she shouted. "Out of my house!"

Frowning, he zipped up his pants. He started to move toward her and Ruth recoiled. "Come on, now, Ruth . . . "

"I mean it, Bobby. I want you out." Turning toward the closet, she buried her face in the racks of clothes. "Please just go."

"But you said you'd help me. I just thought . . . " Shaking his head, he buckled his belt. "Let's see. We got breakfast, lunch, and dinner. And 'drive me home.' All the help's off for the night. The old man's outta town. And now—this? I thought—"

"Get out! How many times do I have to tell you?"

He gathered his things off the floor. "It's okay. Don't worry. I'm leaving."

Pressing her forehead against the side of the closet, Ruth tried not to cry. Biting her lip, she listened to his angry footsteps clattering down the stairs. Good, she thought. In a moment, he'd be gone. But when she heard the door slam, she only felt worse.

Bobby walked through the rain, cursing under his breath. Water oozed through his cheap shoes with every step he took. His coat was soaked through. Don't start bawling, ya jerk! he told himself. No, he was cool. All he needed was a ride back to civilization. Where the hell was he, anyway? Nowheresville. At least an hour's drive back to the city. They'd be ice-skating in hell before he'd catch a ride out of this cake-eaters' ghetto.

He wished the damn rain would let up. There wasn't a bar or even a phone booth in sight. Just mansions, with acres and acres of empty grounds. Some had No Trespassing signs posted on the gates; others didn't need any signs. It was understood in this neck of the woods. Keep Out.

The rain was dredging up unwelcome thoughts of how he'd pissed away the last three years in New York getting nowhere. Some actor. His stage was the street corner, the bars. Private auditions in hotel rooms with producers' wives, agents, and casting directors. But the only talent that had interested them was between his thighs.

That first year, he'd been lucky. A thirty-six-year-old ad executive named Alfred Weeks had become infatuated with him. Alfred had gotten Bobby some bits on television, but never a speaking part. He told Bobby he wasn't ready for larger roles, that he needed more training. "The grooming, Robert," he'd said. "You're still in your apprenticeship. We mustn't rush. You have to learn, develop yourself, before you can take on bigger roles and handle the exposure. I can teach you, be your mentor."

So Bobby had moved into Alfred's Park Avenue apartment. They'd kept separate beds; Weeks insisted on maintaining decorum. But the extra bed was there for show, and show was what Alfred Weeks was all about. Alfred was an immaculately groomed, well-tailored, civilized man. He was handsome because he worked at it, and intelligent and charming for the same reason. He gave Bobby books to read, had him fitted with expensive clothes, and taught him how to enter a room and charm the pants off a block of ice.

Weeks had loved to give parties. His guests were writers, poets, critics, artists, show-biz types. Weeks said he wanted Bobby to meet only "the right people." Bobby had thought they were a bunch of snobs. Phonies, every single one. The women were cold, stuck-up vampires. The men were effeminate and snide, trying to outdo each other for the current favorite's attention. But worst of all were the ones like himself, the "pretty" boys who confided that they were only living off some "old fairy" for the money or a shot at a part in a show. Bobby had hated them most of all, because he saw himself in them. He was the phoniest of the phonies—a queen, all prettied up to Alfred's specs. A veal cutlet for his mentor's pals to drool over. "He looks scrumptious," they would say. "What a delicious boy."

Eventually, Weeks had lost his appetite. He had accused Bobby of sleeping around. That much was true. In the year they'd lived together, Bobby had slept with dozens of nameless girls. He'd had to, he told Weeks, or he'd have gone crazy.

Weeks, as usual, was civilized about it, insisting Bobby keep all the clothes he had bought him. Three days after Bobby had moved out, he'd found a room at the Iroquois Hotel. Weeks had found a new protégé, an eighteen-year-old blond who didn't wear Bobby's shirt size.

For the next few years, Bobby had lived in many places and had had many mentors, an endless line of matrons and patrons of the arts. He'd forgotten their names and faces as quickly as they'd forgotten their promises. Like Weeks, none of them really wanted him to accomplish anything, because that would have meant his independence. And independence wasn't the name of this particular game.

One rich divorcée had had enough connections to get him an agent, who didn't give a shit about Bobby. After a week, neither had the divorcée. The agent was always out and, when he was in, he was too busy to see Bobby. Still, he'd gotten Bobby a handful of bit parts in plays and commercials. He'd also starred in a fifteen-minute Army training film called *A Moment's Pleasure, A Lifetime of Anguish.* Then the agent had dropped him without explanation.

Bobby washed dishes and bussed tables in slop joints in which he wouldn't have eaten five years before. But too often, he'd skip work to answer open auditions—cattle calls with hundreds of actors vying for a small part in a new show. He had never gotten a part and had never held a job for long, either.

Now the rain beat down. He didn't have a job or even a place to live, and he didn't know where the hell he was anymore. Here he was, busting his butt to get back to the city and the only thing waiting for him was a park bench or an unlocked car. He could forget any hopes of getting picked up, because he looked like hell. He hadn't slept in a regular bed, alone and undisturbed, in two weeks.

Bobby wiped the rain from his face; it felt warm. Jesus, he was crying. So what? There was no one to notice.

He wanted to give up, call it quits, and hightail it home. But he had nothing to give up, and nowhere to go. What was he supposed to do? Go back to Seattle and see if they had an opening at the goddamn country club? Even that looked good now. At least he had liked himself back then.

"I'm sorry!" a voice called out.

Bobby looked back, startled.

"Please, Bobby," Ruth said. "Get in the car."

She was standing in the rain next to the open door of the Mercedes. The headlights shone on the slick road and he could see the worried expression on Ruth's face. "Please," she said again. "Let me take you back. You'll catch your death out here."

Bobby didn't move. He was afraid if he stepped toward her, she'd see he'd been crying. "Back where?" he said. "I got no place to go."

She sighed. "You can spend the night at the house. There's plenty of room."

"You wouldn't toss me out again?"

"Good Lord, Bobby. Just get in the car, will you, please?"

He cleared his throat and got into the Mercedes. The heater was on and he shivered gratefully at the change in temperature. But the sudden warmth also thawed his stoic front. He turned his head away so she wouldn't see the tears in his eyes. "Thanks," he managed to say, but it was almost a whisper.

Hands on the steering wheel, Ruth gazed past the hypnotic beat of the wipers. "I think I overreacted back there at the house," she said. "It was, well, a misunderstanding."

"It was dumb," Bobby said through the tightening in his throat. "I'm sorry, Ruth—"

"Bobby?" She looked at him. "Are you alright?"

"I'm so screwed up," he said tearfully. "I've made a mess out of my whole life. Please, don't—don't look at me—"

"It's alright." She reached over and smoothed back his wet hair.

"I'm sorry . . ."

Ruth took his face in her hands. "Bobby, listen to me. Never mind about that. It's okay."

Shaking, he put his damp arms around her as she comforted him. His sighs and the constant patter of rain were the only sounds in the quiet car. "It's alright," she whispered, kissing his cheek. "It's alright." Her lips skimmed his moist skin and met his slightly open mouth. They pressed against each other, suddenly jolted by the warm shock of each other's bodies.

Then Ruth broke away, gasping, "I'm sorry!" She grabbed the steering wheel. "I don't know why I did that."

"It's okay," Bobby murmured. "Happens to me all the time."

"Well, it's never happened to me," Ruth said, still shaken. "I'm a married woman with two grown children. I'm going to be fifty in a few days—"

"Happy birthday," Bobby said softly.

She wrestled with the gear shift and began to turn the car. The Mercedes went over a curb as it made its circle, and Ruth grimaced. "See? I really needed someone to drive for me. I hate this awful car!" She tightened her grip on the steering wheel as they started down the road. "I realize, Bobby, that what you did in my —room, you only did because you thought I expected it from you, that I lured you to my house for one thing. Isn't that right?"

He wiped his eyes. "Something like that."

"I'd like to think that kindness was my only motive. But I'm not sure. Maybe I really did want just what you thought I was after." She sighed. "Lord, I'm a horrible person."

"If you really felt that way," Bobby said, "you wouldn't have tossed me out when I made that stupid pass."

"I knew you just wanted me to help your career," she said quietly. "I knew you weren't attracted to me. A young man like you wouldn't be interested in me."

82

"But I like you, Ruth," he said. "That should count for something."

Gazing at the road, she smiled briefly. "Well, I like you too, Bobby. And I want to help you. I do. But I won't make you jump through any hoops for me."

She took a deep breath. "You won't have to do anything you don't want to do. No strings attached. Tonight you'll sleep in my son's room. And tomorrow morning, I'll call Amelia Foster. She's a friend of mine, and one of the best agents in town. I'll ask if she'll see you. Amelia's very good at getting young people started in this business. I think she'll be good for you."

Bobby sat up. The stranglehold on his throat was gone. He could swallow again. But why was he still so empty inside? He should be excited about this new chance. So why, he wondered, didn't it feel right?

FOUR

The minute Bobby saw the building, his nervousness vanished. Smiling a little, he pulled off the tie Ruth had bought him and shoved it in his pocket.

He'd expected to find Amelia Foster in some swank high-rise on Madison Avenue. Instead, he stood facing a modest, five-story slate dump on West Fifty-seventh.

Even the elevator didn't work. Her damned office had to be on the fourth floor, but the climb drained his nerves of any jitters about the interview.

The doors along the corridor were old-fashioned, with windows of bubbled glass. Bobby strolled down the hall reading the printed names: KAISER TRAVEL SERVICES; M.K. FEINBERG, D.D.S.; A. FOSTER, TALENT REPRESENTATIVE.

Then he heard someone typing on the other side of the door. He opened it. A pretty blonde sat at a large, antique desk, ripping a piece of paper out of the old-fashioned Underwood. She crumpled the paper, tossed it on the floor, and slammed her hand down on the desk in frustration. Then she saw him and looked down, embarrassed.

"Hi," he said, stepping inside the office.

"Hello," the girl replied. She rolled another sheet of paper into the carriage, put her fingers to the keys, then hesitated.

Bobby glanced around the room. He'd expected to see glossies of movie stars on the walls. Well, there were pictures all right, but he recognized no one. The furniture was old and mismatched.

Piles of paper covered the aging file cabinets behind the desk where the girl sat typing. It looked like a fly-by-night bookie joint.

She was the nicest thing in the place. She wore a striped shirt with the sleeves rolled up and a gray skirt. From what he could see of her figure, she was slim, even willowy, and her skin was a pale gold. Her nose was a little crooked, but it gave her face character, setting her apart from most blondes Bobby knew, who were blandly pretty.

He wandered over to the desk. "Watcha doing?"

The girl stopped and frowned. "I'm swimming! Jeesh . . . " She went back to typing.

Bobby laughed. "You do a nice breaststroke," he said. "Have you considered the freestyle?"

She dropped her hands into her lap. "Look," she said, "I'm sorry. If you want to see Miss Foster, just knock." She nodded to a closed door behind her desk.

"I'd rather watch her secretary," Bobby said.

"Miss Foster's secretary is about sixty years old and right now she's on her lunch break. But I'll leave her the message," the girl said dryly.

He leaned on the desk. "So who are you?"

She sighed and returned to her typing.

"When do you go to lunch? Maybe we could have it together?"

The girl ripped the paper out of the machine. "Look, ace. I'm really in a sore mood right now. So could you do me a huge favor and get lost?"

"Okay," Bobby said, "I love you, too." He backed away.

They glared at each other. Bobby could tell she felt badly about being bitchy, but decided it was to his advantage to leave her feeling that way for a while. He knocked on the office door. A deep female voice answered. "Come in already!"

The office was even smaller than the anteroom. A cluttered desk occupied most of the room, allowing barely enough space for two cushioned armchairs, a philodendron plant, and Amelia Foster.

She was on the telephone, but motioned for him to enter and

sit down. She had a dark, dissipated beauty and smoky eyes to match the wry, gravelly voice. She was the same age as Ruth, but looked years older, the lines more apparent on her face. But she had a brassy vigor that was evident to Bobby all the way across the room.

She sat twirling a pair of glasses in her free hand. "Nicky, darling, go to Italy and do the rotten movie if you want. I just think you're gonna have a helluva time learning Italian. Don't forget how long it took you to change that Southern accent, honey. We're talking a whole new language here, Nickita. Just a sec, darling." She covered the mouthpiece and looked at Bobby. "Can you close the door? I'll be off in a second. Don't leave!"

As Bobby closed the door, he heard the typing start up again. He sat down and studied Amelia Foster.

"Well, Nicky," she was saying. "That's my advice. Anything more, and I'll have to charge ten percent. I don't have time for ex-clients, darling. Besides, a young man just walked into my office and he's every bit as gorgeous as you are. So I have to give you the heave-ho now . . . Love you, too, Nickies. Ciao." She hung up and sighed. "Sorry about the wait. Also for the 'gorgeous' crack. Hope you didn't mind."

Bobby grinned. "Depends who I'm being compared to."

"Nick Hunter."

"Nick *Hunter?*"

She nodded, pulling out a cigarette and lighting it. "He still calls for advice. I stopped being his agent two years ago. Gave me the ax the same day he won the *Photoscreen* Award for Best Newcomer."

"That's a little heartless," Bobby said.

"Heartless?" Amelia smiled. "I expect it, dear heart. If I'm still someone's agent after three years, I've failed them. Out in the waiting room are dozens of pictures—faces you probably wouldn't know from Adam. Come back in a year, and seventy percent of them will be hot potatoes. But their pictures won't be on my wall anymore. That's my job. To help people get started in this business. I'm just a midwife, easing the birth pains, so that by the time people give their acceptance speeches on Oscar night, they can thank all the other mothers." Amelia got up and perched on the edge of the desk. "It hasn't made me rich, but there's a . . . satisfaction in guessing right. So," she said, "you're the kid Ruth called about."

He straightened. "Yes, ma'am. Bob Pierce."

She glanced at her watch. "Eleven-fifteen. Well, you're punctual, at least. Good. The best actors are always on time." She looked at him and then frowned. "But you're not wearing a tie. Not so good. If I represent you, you'll wear a tie to your appointments. When you're Brando, then you can look like a slob. Okay?"

Bobby reached in his pocket and pulled out the necktie. "I'll put it back on if you want."

She ground her cigarette and grinned. "Too late. For now, go ahead and show off your sexy throat."

He shoved the tie back into his pocket. "Next time I'll wear it. I promise."

Amelia folded her arms and studied him as if he were a painting hanging in the Louvre. "The last time Ruth recommended anyone was three years ago. She told me about a young man she'd seen in New Orleans, in some community playhouse production. She talked him into coming to New York. That turned out to be His Nibs, Nick Hunter. You're in good company, Bob. That's why I agreed to see you on such short notice. Ruthie can spot them."

"Ruth never told me about Nick Hunter."

"Well, she was pretty vague about you, too. Where did she dig you up? Some off-Broadway showcase?"

"Her husband's car."

"Is that something playing down in the Village?"

"No. I was asleep in her husband's car, yesterday morning. She found me in the Metro parking lot."

"Let me get this straight. Ruth didn't see you in a play? She discovered you sleeping in Raymond's car?"

"That's about it."

"Are you sleeping in his bed, too?"

Bobby reddened. He didn't answer, but sat listening to the typing outside the door. "Is that really any of your concern, ma'am?" he said finally.

She regarded him with her sharp eyes. Then Amelia got off the desk and sat back down behind it. "All right," she said. "I withdraw the question. But let me tell you one thing, honey. Whatever your relationship is with Ruth, you sure as hell better treat her right. She's already got one heartless bastard on her hands. She doesn't need another one."

Bobby stared back levelly. "Yes, ma'am."

"Okay." She smiled. "Down to business. What have you done? What's your experience read like?"

He told her about the plays in Seattle, the extra work in Los Angeles, the TV bit parts in New York. She put on her glasses and took notes.

"Singing? Dancing?" She looked like a nurse filling out a medical report.

"No. I'm no Donald O'Connor."

"All actors should be capable of both," she said without looking up from her notes. "Passably, at least. I'll sign you up for lessons. Do you have a résumé? Eight by ten's? Cards?"

"No."

Amelia tore off her glasses. "Look, sonny, just what have you been doing in this town for the last three years? Riding the subways?"

Bobby squirmed.

"All right. Never mind." She sighed and rummaged through a drawer. "I want you to write up all your credits for me. For the extra work, say you were *featured* in the following, dot dot dot. Up your age a few years in terms of those Seattle shows. Jazz it up." She slapped a folder on the desk. "Here's a good example of a résumé. It'll give you some idea of the correct format. And here's the name of a reliable photographer. Give him a call and set up an appointment. Tell him I sent you. He'll know what to do."

Bobby reached across the desk and took the résumé and the card. The typewriter in the next room had stopped clicking.

"The photographer's going to set you back about fifty bucks," Amelia said. "Come and see me when you get the proofs. I'll see that you earn back the fifty in a week. Then we'll get you started." She consulted her watch again. "I'm ten minutes late for a meeting at the Plaza. *Ciao, bello.*" She wagged her fingers at him until he got to his feet.

"Um, well, thank you, Miss Foster."

"Amelia." She smiled. "Now get to work on those photos. You know, I think Ruth was right about you, honey. You've got potential. Now get a haircut."

Nodding, he turned and opened the door. The blond typist was standing before it, ready to knock. She held a few pages in her hand.

"Oh, excuse me," she said.

"My pleasure," Bobby said.

Amelia was slipping into her coat. "Lisa Weller." She nodded. "Bob Pierce."

"How do you do," Lisa said quickly. She called past him, "I'm finished, Amelia. Thanks for letting me use the typewriter."

Amelia picked up her briefcase and bag. "Let me see it tomorrow, Lisa. Do me a favor and make sure everything's locked. Beatrice has her key. Bye y'all." She dashed out the door.

Bobby stared after her. Then he turned to Lisa. "You in a hurry, too? Or do you have time for a cup of coffee?"

Lisa was closing the door to Amelia's office. She came back to the desk, where her coat lay over the back of the chair. "I'm sorry, I—"

"Still in a bad mood, huh?"

She slipped her typed pages into her coat and draped it over her arm. She stared at Bobby. Her face seemed to undergo a small change and she said, "I was rude earlier. I'm sorry."

"That's okay," he replied, a bit more eagerly than he'd planned. "And the coffee?"

"I don't think so. I have an audition."

"After the audition?"

She picked up her purse and walked to the door. "I'm afraid not. I go to work at five. Thanks anyway."

They walked out to the hallway together. "You know," he said, "I really thought you were Amelia's secretary. Guess I was wrong."

"Amelia's my agent," Lisa said. "She lets me write while Beatrice is at lunch. I'm trying to throw together an original scene to use for an audition."

"Can I walk you over to the theater?" he asked, as they started down the stairs.

Lisa smiled a bit stiffly. "It's not for another hour," she said, "so you needn't bother—"

"Then you *do* have time for some coffee," Bobby said. He was smiling broadly.

They paused on the third-floor landing. Lisa looked at him and sighed. "Sure. Coffee would be fine. We'll go Dutch though, okay?"

Bobby shrugged, but it seemed further proof of her suspicion toward him. Then he remembered he'd arranged to meet Ruth at the Plaza for lunch. He'd just have to tell her the interview took longer than he'd expected.

They stepped outside. The day was chilly, with most of the sky the same slate color as the buildings. Bobby helped Lisa on with her polo coat, and they started down Fifty-seventh Street.

"I have time for just one cup," she said.

"Fine," he said. "What do you do at five? Job?"

"That's right. Waitressing."

"I see. So what's the audition for?"

"The one today is for a TV pilot. A stupid comedy series they're planning about doctor-crazy nurses. They need a Kookie Blonde." She sighed and smiled.

It felt great, walking beside her. He wanted the whole city to see them together on Fifty-seventh. Bobby shoved his hands deep in his pockets. "So—you're trying to be an actress?"

"Actually, I'm trying to be a waitress. I'm just taking these

90

acting jobs till I can make a name for myself in the restaurant business." They laughed together. "Are you an actor?"

"Kind of. Well, sort of. I'm trying to be, if you know what I mean." Something about her made him feel stupid, but still eager to please. Maybe it was her smile, or the way her blond hair caught the fleeting sun in one small moment.

"I'm sorry I didn't catch your name when Amelia introduced us," she said.

"Bob. Bob Pierce."

"Mine's Lisa."

The automat was crowded, but they managed to squeeze into line and get their coffee, then find a wobbly table by the window.

"I love sitting here," she said. "You get to watch all the people on the street, all the interesting faces."

"All the weirdos, too."

"I suppose," she allowed, looking at him. She took a sip of the hot, bitter coffee. "So you're an actor," she tried again.

He nodded.

"You know what drives me crazy?" Lisa said. "When someone asks me what I do and I tell them I'm an actress. And they always ask, 'Have I seen you in anything?' Just like that, as if I'm supposed to know what they watch. Doesn't that drive you crazy?"

"Huh, yeah." He tried to think of something charming to say.

"Then I rattle off all the commercials and shows, and I feel like I'm bragging or being a bore. It's like a job interview. You have to tell them how great you are and what you've accomplished. I hate that, feeling like I have to prove something over and over."

"Yeah."

She idly fingered the sugar dispenser. Then she laughed. "So —have I seen you in anything?"

Bobby shrugged. "I doubt it. Background crap. Extra stuff. I haven't exactly made my mark yet." He didn't want to talk, or watch the people outside. He just wanted to look at her and play it cool. He lit a cigarette and hoped she wouldn't notice how his hands were trembling slightly.

"Listen, Bob, I hope you're not mad about the way I acted back there. Really, I hope not."

"It's okay."

"That's good." She sat back. "So where are you from?"

"Seattle."

"Oh? How long have you been in New York?"

"Three years."

Then there was silence. He sat back, smoked his cigarette, and smiled at her. She pointed out a man standing on the corner. "That man in the trenchcoat looks like a spy. See how he clutches his briefcase? Like it's full of top-secret documents?"

He threw a quick glance at the window. "Yeah."

She looked impatient. "Well, tell me. How long has Amelia been representing you?"

"About an hour now."

"How did the interview go? What did you think of Amelia?"

Bobby stubbed out his cigarette. "It went okay. She comes on like a bulldozer, if you know what I mean."

"Well, she's a little abrasive at first, but I think that's good. An agent is supposed to be tough."

"I guess," he said. "It sort of unnerved me, though."

"Oh, but she's a good agent. You'll see. Until I signed with Amelia, I was going nowhere. I've only been with her three months, and I've landed some parts on TV and even gotten close to a couple of Broadway plays." She grinned. "Huh, it must sound like I'm bragging. But it's really Amelia's work."

"Yeah, well, how about that voice of hers?"

"I love her voice," Lisa said. "That low, sultry baritone. Like Lauren Bacall or Tallulah Bankhead. I wish I had a voice like that."

"Like a truckdriver?" He chuckled. "Small wonder she's not married."

"What's that supposed to mean?"

He sat back in his chair. "Come on, you know what those pushy old broads really are. I know a dyke when I see one."

"A what?" she asked, incredulous.

"Look, don't get me wrong. I got nothing against them, but I do resent the way they like to push guys around."

"You know something?" Lisa said, grabbing her purse. "You're a real jerk!" She got to her feet and walked out of the automat.

For an hour, Ruth had been sitting at a table in The Oak Room. She had sipped her tea and pretended to read *A Man Called Peter*. It was a good book, but she just didn't need any religious inspiration at the moment. She kept glancing over the pages at the door. The hundredth time she did so, she saw Amelia Foster standing at the table.

"Amelia . . .?"

Amelia tossed down her purse and sank into a chair. "I can't believe I've been suffering through this tedious wheeling and dealing, and I didn't even notice you over here. Are you meeting Raymond?"

Ruth closed the book. "No, he's in London. I—"

"I thought he just got back from Los Angeles. What's he doing in London?"

Ruth shrugged. "Working?"

"On Valerie Bounty, perhaps," Amelia said and drew out a cigarette.

"Don't start, Amelia. All right?"

"Sure, Ruthie, but on one condition. You must tell me all about that divine boy you sent over today. I want all the dirt."

Ruth smiled warily. "There's no dirt, Amelia. He's just an out-of-work actor who—"

"Happens to be gorgeous, darling, in case you hadn't noticed, and I daresay you had. Now what's going on?"

"There's nothing to tell. I'm just trying to help him. How did the interview go?"

"Fine. I scared the hell out of him."

Ruth sipped her cold tea. "How long ago did Bobby—I mean, Bob—how long ago did he leave your office?"

"Maybe forty-five minutes. We call him *Bobby*, do we?" Her

sharp eyes strayed over the face of her friend. "Not even a whiff of romance in all this?"

"Don't be silly."

"You know," she said, "I wish just once you would be 'silly,' Ruth. I mean Nick Hunter. He practically threw himself at you, and you never touched him. And you wanted to."

"Now, really—"

"Don't be ashamed. I still have a soft spot for Nick myself."

"I happen to be married."

"Well, I'll throw rice at your divorce," Amelia said. "It's about time you picked up a few of Raymond's hobbies yourself and stopped trying to volunteer for canonization. Our Lady of the Martyred Wives. For God's sake, Ruth. You have a gorgeous young man here who'd do anything for you. Why fight it? Raymond certainly doesn't."

"Two wrongs don't make a marriage, Amelia."

"Neither does one," Amelia said curtly. She stood up and gathered her coat. "Have a happy thirty-ninth tomorrow."

"Thanks, Amelia. Take care."

Ten minutes later, Bobby arrived. The captain stopped him at the door. As Ruth watched, Bobby pulled out his necktie and put it on. He was still tying the knot as he walked over to Ruth's table.

"God, sorry I'm so late," he said, taking a seat.

Ruth smiled faintly. "I was worried something might have happened to you," she said with rehearsed concern.

"No, I—" He glanced up at the waiter. Ruth ordered the brook trout. Bobby asked for a cheeseburger and Coke.

"Where was I?" he asked, after the waiter left.

"I was wondering the same thing myself," she sighed. "I've been sitting here for over an hour, Bobby."

He shook his head. "Gee, Ruth, I'm really sorry. The interview took longer than I'd expected."

"Oh?"

Her reply hung in the air for a moment. Bobby frowned at the tablecloth. "No," he said. "The stupid interview ended almost an hour ago. I forgot about our date, and I asked some girl out for coffee. It wasn't until after we got to the coffee shop that I remembered—" He shook his head. "I'm honestly very sorry."

"I'll settle for the 'honest,' " she murmured. She tried to smile. "Oh, well, no harm done."

He glanced up at her. "Ruth, would you say I was a jerk?"

"A what?"

"A jerk. You know, a creep . . . "

"Not exactly a jerk," she said. "I'd say you were capable of being pretty thoughtless." She paused. "I don't think a real jerk would ever ask that question. He wouldn't care enough. He'd never worry about what others thought of him. And he wouldn't mind who got hurt. A real jerk wouldn't care."

As she spoke, Ruth realized that, at that moment, she was thinking of her husband.

After lunch, she drove Bobby to his building on Fifty-fourth and Sixth. On the way, he told her about the interview—that he thought his foot was in the door of Amelia's agency. He didn't think he'd get as far with his landlady, however.

His landlady was a heavy woman who usually came to the door wearing a flowered bathrobe and a cheaply made blond wig. She always seemed annoyed with her tenants, and spent most of the time stuffing the tufts of her own hair back under her wig.

She looked perturbed to see Ruth and Bobby waiting in the corridor. "You owe me one hundred and forty dollars!" she said immediately. "And I don't want to see you around here until you pay me that two months' rent."

Ruth pulled two hundred-dollar bills and a ten from her purse. "This should cover it," she said quietly. "Here's this month's rent in advance. Now will you please unlock his door?"

The landlady peered at her suspiciously, but stuffed the bills into her bathrobe. She lumbered to Bobby's door and took off the padlock. "I'm keeping this," she hissed, shaking the lock in his face. "Just remember that the next time!" She turned and strutted down the hall, her bathrobe billowing.

"Oh, blow it out your ass," Bobby said under his breath. He

shrugged an apology to Ruth, then opened the door.

The apartment was a dark, airless studio, with a kitchenette the size of a phone booth. The room was built around a lone window that offered a view of a brick wall. There was a bookcase cluttered with dusty books and record albums, and a desk and chair in reach of the unmade bed. Clothes were scattered on the floor.

Ruth picked up a blue sweater from the chair.

"I'm not much of a housekeeper," Bobby said.

But Ruth was glancing inside the sweater. "Why, Bobby, this is cashmere—" She went to the closet and gazed at the rack of expensive suits and Italian sportshirts. "Why, just look at these clothes!"

"They're all mine," he said defensively.

"I didn't say they weren't. I'm just surprised, that's all." She fingered the lapel of a sportscoat. "My goodness, this is camel's hair."

"I didn't steal it, Ruth!" he said hotly. "An . . . acquaintance of mine bought those clothes for me."

"A very generous friend," she remarked. She folded the cashmere sweater and placed it on the closet shelf.

"I earned every damn thread."

"All right. I'm sure you did. No need to get all worked up."

"I don't care about clothes," he said. "But sometimes it pays to look slick, you know? And I'll pay you back, too, Ruth, I promise," he said in a rush, "if I have to hock every suit in there."

"Don't worry about it, Bobby."

"No, I mean it. You've just been forking out the dough—by the pitchfork. I want to repay you."

"Don't be silly. It's Raymond's money. And you don't owe him a thing."

But Bobby had gotten up and gone over to the desk. He pulled open the file drawer and took out a small set of bongo drums. He buffed the wooden cylinders with the bottom of the bedspread and then handed the drums to Ruth.

She laughed. "What on earth is this?"

"My bongo drums. They're not much, but I bought them myself. My first major purchase in the Big Apple. They mean a lot to me. I want you to have them. A down-payment . . . " He looked like an anxious little boy.

Ruth swallowed. "I don't feel right taking these, Bobby."

"Naw, it's okay," he mumbled. "Neighbors raise hell whenever I play 'em. Anyway, uh, happy birthday."

"Thank you," she said gently.

"Gonna throw a bash?"

"No. My husband's gone on business and the children live in other cities. I'll just have a quiet evening to myself."

Bobby edged away from the bed. "Could I give you a birthday kiss?"

Ruth nodded. He put his arms around her. Her body went tense. As he was about to kiss her, Ruth turned her head aside so that his lips brushed her cheek. After a moment, she pulled away and patted Bobby on the shoulder. Her eyes avoided his. "Goodbye, Bobby."

She picked up the drums. Bobby sat down on the chair, hooked his arms over the back of it, and rested his chin on his fist. With a little smile, she turned and walked out the door.

Bobby stared after her. After a moment, he lightly tapped on the top of the desk, as if he were playing a drum.

It had been a lousy day. Lisa hated what she'd written for the Actors Studio audition. Corny and dull, she thought, riding home from work on the crosstown bus. Amelia had told her that the Studio discouraged original material. The audition instruction sheet warned against "testing one's writing ability when auditioning as an actor." Contemporary scenes were recommended. But Lisa had felt intimidated using Odets, Williams, or Miller. So she was trying to write her own five-minute scene about a girl telling her boyfriend she was pregnant. She knew it hit close to home, since it had happened to her mother, but that was the point of training at the Studio, wasn't it?

She still hadn't found a partner for the scene. No monologues were allowed for the auditions. But the type of man she needed was the type she always tried to avoid—the kind she kept at a distance, the kind she found attractive.

When she'd met that arrogant Bob at Amelia's office, she'd thought he might make a good audition partner. But he'd turned out to be a real heel. Just because he was attractive, she was supposed to roll over and play dead. No thanks, Lisa thought.

The audition that afternoon had been a disaster. She was to read for a part in "Girls In White," the comedy show about nurses. But before she'd had a chance to read, the casting director had told her bluntly she wasn't buxom or daffy-looking enough, and the script had been taken out of her hands.

The restaurant was a madhouse. One couple had bolted without paying their bill, two tables had stiffed her, and at another table five college boys with fake I.D.s had taken turns propositioning her.

She just wanted to go home, take a bath, and crawl into bed. Or rather, go home and find Frank Sinatra or Nick Hunter waiting with a snifter of brandy, ready to massage her feet by a roaring fire. But the apartment didn't have a fireplace, and Lisa didn't drink. It would have to be a movie magazine and hot chocolate by the radiator.

But when she got in, she found her roommate, Patty, sprawled on the couch, eating from a container of chocolate ice cream. Her brown hair was up in curlers and she was wearing a pink kimono. An Eddie Fisher album blared from the phonograph.

Lisa hung up her coat and turned down the volume. "The neighbors have already complained this week," she told Patty, trying not to sound severe.

Patty shrugged and giggled. "It's not my fault if they don't dig 'Oh My Papa'."

Lisa sighed. Patty was in one of her aren't-I-kookie moods. She retreated to the bedroom and slipped out of her waitress uniform. She gazed around the room. Patty's half was strewn with discarded underwear and leotards. The whole place smelled of

Patty's gardenia and musk perfume. It was starting to make Lisa sick.

Lisa pulled on her robe and shook her hair out of its ponytail. Patty appeared in the door, still holding her ice cream. "Guess what?" she said. "You'll never guess."

"No, I won't," Lisa said. She began to brush her hair emphatically. "Ike is divorcing Mamie to marry you?"

"Guess again."

Lisa glanced tiredly around the room. "*House Beautiful* is coming to photograph the apartment?"

"Nope."

"Patty, I'm just exhausted—"

"I'm pregnant!"

"Well," Lisa said. "That explains the ice cream."

"Really and truly. I am!"

Lisa slowly set down the brush. "My God, Patty. You're serious. What on earth are you going to do?"

Patty licked her spoon. "Guess."

"Have you told Todd? It *is* Todd, isn't it?"

"Of course," Patty said, a little huffily.

"Well, what are you going to do? Have you told him?"

"Uh-huh," Patty said. "And guess what?"

"Patty, for God's sake—"

"We're gonna get married!" she squealed. "Next week. We're eloping. Isn't that just the most romantic thing you've ever heard?"

"Yes, that's very sweet," Lisa said. She managed a smile. "I'm happy for you, Patty."

"He's kicking his brother out of the apartment. And he's gonna move the barbells to the living room, so there'll be room for a bassinet in the bedroom. It'll be so cute. We're gonna start moving my junk out of here tomorrow. I can't wait to see how my wicker rocking chair looks at Todd's place."

"Patty," Lisa said. "The rocking chair is—er—mine."

Patty put down her spoon. "Are you sure?"

Lisa nodded. "It's one of the only things here that does belong to me. Remember? I bought it at that second-hand store a few weeks after I moved in?" Lisa sighed. "Look, forget it. Consider it a wedding present."

Patty was still squinting. "I could have sworn that chair was mine."

Later, when Lisa was in bed, she slid her hand under the pillow and wondered why she resented Patty so much. And she wondered what it was like to have a boyfriend. Of course, she didn't have time—there was her career to think of. Deep down, she was aware it was all fear—fear of getting involved, fear of what they might do to her. The only men she let herself fall in love with were movie stars: unattainable and safe.

Then she suddenly realized there were more practical things to consider. She'd be minus a roommate soon. She couldn't afford the flat on her own, or even refurnishing it. Maybe she should look around for a cheap studio. She could keep an eye out for a nice rocking chair while she was at it.

Yes, it had been one hell of a long day.

The dining room was dark, except for the flickering light that came from the kitchen. Ruth sat alone at the head of the table and sipped her wine. It was her second glass of the evening. Another glass would get her sufficiently stewed, and she was determined to drink it.

Owen and his wife marched in from the kitchen, singing a rather somber rendition of "Happy Birthday to You." Selma carried a cake covered with cream frosting roses and ten candles. Ruth felt a frozen smile cling to her face as she blew out the candles. She almost wanted to ask Owen and Selma to sit down and have some cake with her, but she knew it would strike them as inappropriate. So she told them to help themselves and take the rest of the night off.

She refilled her glass and nibbled at a thin slice of cake. Her daughter and son had already telephoned. She'd tried to sound cheerful for them. Of course, Raymond hadn't called. The least the jerk could do was call. She was really starting to feel that third glass of wine.

"Excuse me, Mrs. Bartlett."

Selma stood in the doorway holding a hatbox. "A young man just delivered this."

"What?"

Selma put the box on the table. Ruth opened it. Inside was a lopsided cake. Globs of frosting clung to the side of the box. The writing was clumsy and childlike. *Happy Birthday, Ru.* The *th* had come off on the side of the box.

"Where is he?" Ruth asked softly.

"The young man? He's out back. He didn't want to come in."

"Show him in," Ruth said. "Oh, wait—" She handed Selma her plate. "Take this. And wrap up the other cake, all right?"

"Yes, ma'am."

"By the way, Selma, it was delicious."

"Thank you, Mrs. Bartlett."

The maid withdrew, and Ruth sat smiling at the dilapidated cake as if it were a sleeping infant.

"I hitched." Bobby sat at the table, wearing the same blue cashmere sweater Ruth had noticed the day before. He had a glass of wine and a slice of cake in front of him. He pointed to the cake with his fork. "You know, this tastes like—well, it sure doesn't taste good."

Ruth ate some. "Nonsense," she said. "Did you make it from scratch?"

"Betty Cockett."

"Crocker."

"Yeah. I—I used to be a much better cook. Guess I've lost my touch."

Ruth took a large swallow of wine. "No, it's just wonderful, Bobby. And a very sweet gesture. Why didn't you want to come in when you delivered it?"

"I thought you might have guests."

"No. Just me, myself, and I." She smiled. "Would you like more wine?"

"No, thanks."

"Well, I'll just have a touch more." She refilled her glass.

"So what's up with old Ray? He still in London?" Bobby asked, sounding casual.

"Yes. His job takes him all over. He's the Vice President of Programming at Metro. He's planning to start his own studio eventually. Why not? He's got the money. His parents were very wealthy. And Raymond has a flair for uncovering new talent." She laughed. "He wouldn't help you, though. Raymond's more interested in budding young actresses. His latest discovery is in London. Her name's Valerie Bounty. That says it all."

Bobby could tell she was plastered. Still, there was dignity in her drunkenness. Every blond hair was in place and not a wrinkle appeared in her beige angora dress. She sat straight in her chair, staring down into her wineglass.

"No, Raymond only helps the little actresses," she said. Her eyes closed, but she raised her brows in pain. "I, however, have helped a number of actors. But not precisely in the same way."

"Amelia told me about Nick Hunter," Bobby said.

Ruth smiled dreamily. "I'll always have a soft spot in my heart for Nicky. I'm so glad he's become a success. I still run into him every once in a while, and he's always so sweet. And he sends me a potted poinsettia every Christmas."

She drank some more wine. "You know, sometimes I just want to bang my head against the wall. I've been married for twenty-seven years and in all that time, I've never cheated on that jerk."

"But not Raymond, huh?"

Ruth snorted. "No, not Raymond," she said. "I first found out about five years ago. It was going on before then, but I refused to—recognize it. I had to read about it in the newspaper. They didn't name names, but it was obvious. They referred to Raymond by his initials. 'A very dashing—'let me get this right—'a very dashing, very married television executive.' The girl was called, 'the scarlet starlet.' Or was it harlot? I can't remember now. Anyway, that one blew over fast, and no one got hurt."

"Except you," Bobby said.

Ruth let out a weak laugh. "Nice to read about your husband in the newspaper."

"What did you do?"

"I cried a lot at first. Then I put down the newspaper, walked into the billiards room, and broke Raymond's favorite cue stick."

"That's showing him!"

"Oh, a lot of good it did," Ruth said. "The day before he came back, I ran out and bought him another, just like it. Took me forever to find."

"So you never let him have it, huh?"

"No. I never even let on that I knew."

Bobby stared at her. "Why do you let him get away with it, Ruth?"

"Because I'm not a fighter," she murmured.

"And you never considered—evening the score?"

There was a silence while Ruth raised her eyes and regarded him. "Not until I met you," she said finally. "Have I shocked you? I bet you thought I was the Mary Worth of Glen Cove, right?"

"No," Bobby said quickly. "No, I think you're a real nice lady."

"Oh, yes. Nice and sweet. And old. I used to be nice and sweet and young." She looked at Bobby with a sad, drunken grimace. "For God's sake, why did you have to come here tonight?"

He stared back. "I don't know what you mean."

"I thought yesterday was the end of it. I'd gotten you an agent and gotten your apartment back. You didn't need me anymore. I was so relieved, driving home, that I hadn't let anything happen. Relieved and sorry, too. Why did you have to come here and make everything so difficult again?"

Bobby cleared his throat. "I'm just grateful, that's all."

Her eyes narrowed. "And how do you plan to show your gratitude? How far do you intend to go, Bobby?"

"As far as you want me to go, Ruth," he answered quietly.

"My," she said. "You are a young man of principle, aren't you? All debts accounted for. You certainly do earn everything you get. Like that expensive sweater you're wearing. You can't just let the nice lady help you out a little. You have to show your gratitude, even if she's old and wrinkled and—"

"Stop it!" he hissed. "Just stop it, okay?"

Ruth got unsteadily to her feet and made her way around the table. She rested a hand on Bobby's shoulder. "I'm sorry. I'm drunk. It's the prize excuse. You showed your gratitude by bringing me the cake tonight. It was very nice. Tell you what, you can send me a potted poinsettia at Christmas if you still feel—beholden to me."

Then she called for a cab and handed him taxi fare. Ten minutes after Bobby had left, there was a call from London. It was Raymond. The connection was terrible.

"What?" She said into the crackling receiver.

"I said, 'Did you get the Mercedes back to the house?' " he shouted.

"Yes, Raymond. The car's fine."

"No problem driving?"

"I paid a young man to drive it for me."

"What did the mileage gauge happen to say?"

"I didn't look."

"I bet that kid at the club has been taking it out again. I'll bet anything."

"That's a shame."

"What? I can't hear you."

"I said, 'Let's hope not'!" she said loudly. "What time is it there?"

"Two in the morning. I just got in from a dinner party. Business—"

"What day is it?"

"It's Saturday. Why do you ask?"

She was silent.

"Hey, wait a minute," he said. "Today's your birthday, isn't it?" He sounded uncertain.

"It's yesterday here," Ruth said slowly. "You missed my birthday, Raymond."

"No, I didn't. It's still Friday there. Happy birthday, darling."

"Drop dead," she said.

"What's that?"

"I said, 'Thank you, dear.' "

"Sounded like you said you were in bed."

"No, I should have gone to bed an hour ago. I was silly not to. Raymond, this connection is awful. I better hang up now."

"Yes. Well, I'll bring you something from London. Be home on Thursday."

"I can't wait," she said. "Good-bye, dear."

"Happy birthday, Ruth."

FIVE

"Please don't shoot me," Lisa whimpered. "Please, don't shoot. I've got a baby at home."

"Just give me the money in the cashbox, sister, and quit yer yappin!" The man in the leather jacket poked his revolver through the bars at the teller's window. His partner stood nearby, holding the bank manager and three customers at gunpoint.

With trembling hands, Lisa gathered up the stacks of bills and put them in a bag.

"Hurry up!" the man growled.

"I'm trying—" A tear began to slide down her cheek.

The director hadn't specified crying, but Lisa figured it wouldn't hurt. Now that the tears had come, she hoped he'd kill her in one take, because she had a toothpaste commercial at eleven o'clock. Not that a lousy ad was more important than a spot on "G.E. Theater," but she needed the money. Patty was leaving in two days, and she still hadn't found a replacement. A hundred a month for that roach trap! She might as well move to the Bowery.

"Come on, sister. Hand me that cash!"

"Here!" She thrust the bag at him. "Now get out!"

"I don't take no lip from no dame," he snarled.

Lisa backed away, cringing. "I'm sorry, please—"

The gun fired twice. The blanks were loud, and Lisa started, before clutching her stomach and falling sideways. She conven-

106

iently bumped against the alarm, and as the bell rang out, Lisa slumped to the floor and died.

"Let's cheese it!" the hold-up man yelled to his partner, and they hurried out the door.

"Cut!" the director called. "That was a beaut. Let's set up for the next scene."

Lisa opened her eyes. She got to her feet and brushed off her dress. The alarm was cut, and she went over to the director. "Do you need me for anything else?"

"Not today, doll. But those tears were great. What's your name again, honey?"

"Lisa Weller."

"Well, you were a knockout, Lisa. Hope we'll be working together again soon."

"Thanks," she smiled. She said a quick good-bye to the crew and cast, and then hurried off.

She was five minutes early to the commercial shoot. In the dressing room, she applied an extra layer of mascara and Scarlet Passion lipstick. With a half-dozen bobby pins, she neatly piled her hair on top of her head, then changed into her costume: a crinoline petticoat and a strapless, blue princess party dress. She checked her teeth, which were white enough, and in preparation for the goodnight kiss (the highlight of the ad), she gargled with a small bottle of Listerine she'd brought along in her purse.

Then she hurried to the soundstage and found the director, a lean, gray-haired man who was correcting some lights.

"There you are," he said, when he saw her. "We were just setting up the smooch scene. Your leading man is still getting ready." He led her to the set, a brightly lit mock-up of a doorway surrounded by a fake front porch and picket fence. "He'll kiss you here, by the door," the director said. "First, we want some coy chitchat—anything, just mouth it. The sequence will be voiced-over anyway. I'll yell when I want the kiss. Look encouraging, but let Lover Boy make the move."

"Yes," Lisa said. "I've got my mark."

"Good." The director glanced off into the darkness beyond the set. "Come on," he called. "Let's go, kiddo." He turned back to Lisa. "Here's the lucky man. Lisa Weller, meet Bob—what's your name, kid?"

"Pierce," he said, walking into the pool of light that spilled around the set.

Lisa sighed. "We've met," she said. He was dressed in an expensive suit, his black hair neatly combed. Still, at the sight of him, a wave of irritation swept through her. She glared at him and tugged up the bosom of her party dress.

The director slapped Bobby on the back. "Okay, kid. Take your mark. You know what to do."

"Yes, sir."

"Let's try a run-through. Keep it long on the conversation until I say kiss." He clapped his hands together and walked into the shadows. His voice rang out from the darkness. "I want to see how you look together. Hold her a little closer, Bob."

Lisa and Bobby exchanged awkward smiles. His hands slid around her back. Lisa's hands limply rested on his shoulders. It appeared to be very romantic.

"Well, hello again," Bobby whispered. "Isn't this a nice coincidence?"

"Well, it's a coincidence, anyway." She smiled angelically.

"You don't like me much, do you?"

"It's not a question of like or dislike," she whispered. "I just find you boring."

"Okay," the director called. "That's terrif. Let's go with the kiss."

Bobby parted his lips and slowly brought his mouth to Lisa's. His tongue poked past her lips and tasted her clean breath. Then her teeth clenched, and she very discreetly ground her heel into his foot.

"That's good, kids," the director said. "That'll do fine."

Pushing Bobby away, Lisa hissed, "You keep your forked tongue to yourself, buster."

He rubbed his foot. "God, I think you've crippled me."

A makeup lady appeared to powder Lisa's face. She held up a mirror for Lisa to fix her lipstick. "What was the big idea, anyway?" Lisa muttered.

"I just got carried away." Bobby shrugged helplessly. "This is my first part in five months. I'm just over anxious, I guess. Sorry."

She scowled at him. The makeup lady tissued off Bobby's smudged face and then vanished. They could hear the director muttering to his assistant. Then he called out, "Bob? How tall are you?"

Bobby straightened his tie and squinted into the lights. "About five-eleven. Why?"

"He still looks too short," the assistant said. "We can get someone else in here. It shouldn't take long."

Lisa glanced at Bobby. The blood had drained from his face. She bit her lip and stared out at the darkness. Finally, she called out, "Couldn't he just stand on a box or something?"

The director stepped forward, shaking his head. "We'll be tracking in from a long shot. Can't use a box. I'm afraid we can't use you, Bob. Sorry. You kids looked good together, except for the height thing."

Lisa quickly pulled the pins from her tall hairdo, and the blond curls fell to her shoulder. "Look," she said. "How's this? That's a good two inches right there." She kicked off her high heels. "And I can carry these for the kiss. It could look sort of cute and romantic. Then you can keep the long shot." She slipped the hairpins in Bobby's coat pocket, then rested her hands on his shoulders. "Stand up straight," she whispered. He obeyed and gave a wary, sidelong glance toward the darkness.

"How does this look?" she called. "He's taller now, isn't he?"

The makeup woman came over to straighten Lisa's hair. "Looks good," Lisa heard someone say. "I like the hair down, and the shoe thing's a nice touch. Corny as hell, but the sponsor won't mind."

Finally, the director nodded. "Okay then. Let's try it for the camera this time. Ready?"

"Thanks," Bobby whispered, wrapping his arms around Lisa.

109

"You saved my skin. Maybe you like me after all, huh?"

Lisa smiled. "I just didn't want to hold up shooting while they looked for another actor. By the way, your breath is no treat."

"I smoke," he said.

"Well, it's already stunted your growth. Too bad it couldn't have done the same for your ego."

"I wish you'd like me," he said softly. "Just a little bit."

"Hey, Bob," the director called. "Keep smiling. You're supposed to look happy for chrissakes!"

"That's right, Bobby," Lisa whispered. "Be happy."

"It's nice to hear you say my name."

"Hmmm, that's a line if I ever heard one."

"Good, kids. Now try the kiss again."

"That tongue comes near me, I'll bite it off," Lisa cooed, as she tilted her head.

Bobby eased into the kiss, pressing against the small of her back with his fingertips. He closed his eyes and took a deep breath. He could smell the fragrance of her hair. For a moment, he really was on that front porch, and they were alone after a late evening stroll. She would open the door, take him by the hand, and lead him inside and up the stairs—

"Cut! Okay, terrif, kids."

Lisa pulled away and caught her breath. Her shoe dropped to the floor, and Bobby picked it up.

"Was that better?" he asked.

"Just fine," Lisa said. She took the shoe out of his hands. "Very —nice, just fine."

The director announced a break while some lights were readjusted. Bobby and Lisa milled around the set. Bobby stuck his hands in his pockets. "I guess I was kind of out of line the other day with what I said about Amelia."

"You were wrong about her, you know."

"Yeah," he said. "My photos aren't even ready yet, and she already got me this job."

"First impressions aren't always the whole story," Lisa said gently.

"Does that go for me, too? I mean, can you always tell a jerk when you see one?"

She blushed. "How's your foot?" she asked.

He studied her, the pale gold skin against her light blue costume. "It's fine. I can almost feel my toes again," he smiled.

On the third run-through, Bobby whispered, "Doing anything Saturday night?"

"I have to work. Keep smiling."

"What about Friday? I think we should rehearse this scene again, make sure we got our motivations right today."

She raised her eyebrows. "I work Friday, too," she said.

"How do you expect me to look happy when you keep turning me down?" he asked.

"I don't," she said. "You haven't asked me anything except my schedule."

"Okay. Lisa, will you go out with me Saturday afternoon?"

"I'll be—"

"Okay kids—let's have the smooch."

"Will you?"

Lisa smiled. "Shut up and kiss me."

By the time the filming was over, he had her address and phone number. Their "date," they agreed, would be an apartment-hunting expedition.

Changing his clothes before he left the studio, he pulled out the scrap of paper on which she'd scribbled her address. He found something else in the coat pocket—her hairpins. He looked down at them and smiled. He'd hold onto them for her.

Bobby kept his hands in his pockets as he limped off the bus at his stop. Camouflage. He'd had a hard-on for the last five blocks of the ride home.

He'd never thought he'd get horny filming a toothpaste commercial. Lisa was so beautiful; he kept remembering her skin and her hair, the way she'd kissed him. She actually seemed to like him now. That made him feel guilty, because he was anxious to get back to the apartment and relieve himself in the most expedient way possible.

But when he opened the door to his room, he found Ruth sitting on the bed. Next to her lay her purse and the bongo drums.

"Your landlady let me in," she said. "I hope you don't mind."

He stood in the door, staring at her. "No, it's okay." He kept his hands in his pockets.

"I had to come into the city and thought I'd stop by and return these." She placed the drums on his desk. "It was a lovely gesture, Bobby, but I don't think I should keep them. They're yours. I also wanted to apologize for my condition the other night."

He closed the door. "Don't mention it." He shrugged.

"I recall saying some awful things. I'm sorry. I can't imagine anything more annoying than a drunk, self-pitying, old woman."

Bobby walked over to the desk and sat down. He gave her a narrow glance. "You know something, Ruth? You've got a real beef about age."

She swallowed. "Maybe so." She took off her black, flowery hat and set it on the bed. "Lord, this is a silly-looking thing, isn't it?" She idly picked at the black fabric petals and sighed. "I guess I might not mind this 'landmark birthday' if I hadn't been feeling so alone lately. I haven't seen my children in months, and my husband's been away. He was supposed to return from London today. So I made myself an appointment at Elizabeth Arden. Wouldn't you know, he called this morning? Said he won't be back for another week. I went to the salon anyway. That's why I came into the city—to have my hair done. Kind of a waste, considering." She shook her head and tried to chuckle. "Maybe I should set this to music."

"So you were in the city for a 'do job,' huh?" Bobby said. "That's good. The way you're dressed, I thought you'd been to a funeral or something."

Chagrined, Ruth glanced down at her black outfit. "It's supposed to look chic."

"Oh, well, it does—"

"I should be going—"

"Don't be insulted. I mean, what do I know about chic? I just know you look nice, Ruth." He smiled. "Listen, I got paid for this commercial today. Let me take you to dinner. After all, if it weren't for you, I wouldn't have gotten the part in the first place."

Ruth stood up. "That's not necessary, Bobby."

He hopped out of the chair and started to unbutton his shirt. "No, I want to. I just need to take a quick shower and I'll be ready." He headed for the bathroom.

As he pulled off his shirt, Ruth turned away. "No, really," she said nervously.

"Just sit there, okay?" He tossed his shirt on the floor and kicked off his shoes. "If we don't go out, your new hairdo really will be wasted. I'll just be a few seconds in here."

"Bobby, wait. You don't have to take me to dinner."

Bobby stood in the bathroom doorway. "I want to do this for you," he said. "Just a little dinner to show I'm grateful for all you've done."

Trying not to look at him, Ruth nodded a few more times than was necessary, then sank down on the bed.

"Good." He smiled again and then ducked into the bathroom.

Ruth watched the door move, but Bobby didn't close it completely. From where she sat, she could see part of the tub and the clear plastic shower curtain. His pants dropped to the floor; the belt buckle clinked against the tiles. She heard the shower curtain swish open, and she quickly glanced over at the window.

The water started up with a roar. Ruth allowed herself a peek toward the bathroom and caught the flesh-colored blur behind the curtain. Steam rose and escaped out the door. He was washing his face, she could tell. He turned slightly, and his hands made circular motions down his chest. Through the fog and the curtain, she could see only the dark triangle at the top of his legs. His hands continued down to the shadowy area.

As she listened to the constant rush of water, Ruth wished he hadn't left the door half-open. She wanted to close it—and go beyond it—at the same time. Perspiration formed on her forehead. Watching him turn under the spray, Ruth held a hand to her throat. Slowly, she stood up, then froze. Could he see her through the curtain?

Ruth stepped back and bumped into the bookcase.

The water was turned off with a surrendering squeak. Ruth grabbed a book and hurried back to the bed. Brushing the dust off the cover, she opened to page eleven. She heard the shower curtain move.

"You still out there?" he called.

"Yes, I'm reading . . . a book here." She peeked up toward the bathroom. His pants still lay on the floor, but she couldn't see Bobby.

"Any place in particular you'd like to go eat? Remember, it's my treat."

Ruth tried to sound preoccupied. "Let me, all right? I don't want you spending your paycheck on my dinner."

Bobby stepped out of the bathroom, holding a white towel around his waist. She nervously peered up from the book. His hair was in wet tangles. The hair on his chest and legs was matted down, dark against his pale skin. Water glistened on the muscles of his shoulders and chest. He gave her a sheepish smile. "After all you've done for me, can't I do something for you?"

She tried to appear interested in the book, but her eyes kept coming back to him. "Of course, Bobby," she said. "Dinner will be fine."

"I'm not just talking about that, Ruth. I'm not talking about a lousy dinner I can't afford, or a set of drums you've got no use for. Or a birthday cake that tasted like hell. I think you know what I mean."

Ruth's stomach tightened. She wished he'd go back into the bathroom and get dressed. "If you're talking about what I think you are," she said steadily, "it wouldn't be right. Yes, I find you attractive. But there's no love. So it wouldn't be right."

"And Raymond loves you? That's the way someone treats a woman he loves? I probably care a hell of a lot more about making you happy than he does. I don't mean to sound like I'm bragging, or I'm stud of the year or something like that. But I haven't got anything else to give you that might make you happy. It's that simple."

She looked up. Suddenly, she couldn't think of any reason why she shouldn't go to bed with him. The thought terrified her. Her lips moved, but no words came.

He was holding the towel in front of him now. She could see the angle of his hip, the curved ivory line of his abdomen, the top of his thigh.

"Tell me what to do," she said. "I-I've never done this with anyone besides my husband. I'm at a loss—I don't know . . . "

"Why don't you take off your dress?" His smile was reassuring.

"All right." Unsteadily, she got to her feet and reached in back for the zipper.

"Let me," he said, stepping behind her. The towel dropped near her feet. Ruth's throat tightened and closed as the zipper slowly descended. She felt his head lower and his warm kisses on the back of her neck, his damp cheek against her skin.

"Thank you," she whispered. She climbed out of the dress, feeling clumsy and awkward. She placed the dress over the chair and stood before him in her black slip.

"You look very sexy," he whispered. She stole a glance at him. He seemed unabashed about his nakedness and his erection. Ruth leaned forward to unhook her stocking. His hand closed over hers. "Let me do that," he said.

She managed to nod. He reached under her slip and unclasped the stockings. He rubbed against her as he peeled the stocking to the ground. Then he lifted her other foot to the chair. Hesitant, she traced her hand down his curved backbone as he carefully unrolled the other stocking. When they finally lay in a pool of silk at her feet, she faced him.

"I still have to—take off my girdle," she faltered. "I better do this part myself."

"Whatever you say." Bobby smiled and kissed her. Then he

walked over to the bed. She watched him, staring at his tight young buttocks as he got into bed and propped himself up on one elbow.

She felt embarrassed, but reached under the slip and struggled out of her bra and girdle. When they were off, she walked, still in her slip, over to the bed.

It wasn't until some time later that Ruth began to cross the border from self-consciousness to pleasure. The creaking bedsprings sounded loud at first in the tiny room, but then began to fade. Bobby's face was still with concentration. He buried his face in her breasts, breathed in the hollow of her neck, and she shivered with satisfaction. Her hands explored his smooth young skin. She lifted his head and kissed him deeply.

Then he was entering her, and she was young and lovely again. He arched his body rhythmically and she could see the muscles in his back and buttocks tighten and relax. When he climaxed, his face spread into a boyish grimace and he let out a soundless cry. Ruth drank in the look on his face and smiled.

He had finished too soon. It wasn't good enough, he thought. She deserved better. He'd have to make up for it the next time, and the time after that, and all the times until she grew tired of him.

He lay on top of her. The sweat from his body spread over her, making the silk slip moist and sticky like flesh. Her eyes were closed. He touched his lips to her blond hair. He kissed her neck, and then the pale gold hair that was almost the color of Lisa's.

SIX

Sitting at Walgreen's counter, Lisa sipped her soda. She looked across at Bobby and sighed. "D'you ever want a Coke so bad, the first gulp makes your eyes water?"

He had already drained his glass, and he rattled the ice cubes so the soda jerk would bring him another. He looked back at Lisa. "That last place was a real dump," he said. "How many did that make? Eight? Nine?"

"Seven-and-a-half. Not counting the place where we just looked at the lobby and left." She managed a smile. "I can't imagine this is much fun for you. But I appreciate it, Bobby—"

"Well, I appreciate being able to sit down for a moment. I feel like Admiral Perry discovering Greenwich Village."

"I'm sorry," she said. "Why didn't you say something sooner? I guess I'm just used to walking."

She told him of her daily job-hunting rounds in between Amelia's assignments. Then she admitted she had nabbed the part of a visiting troublemaker on one of the daytime soaps.

"I start on Monday," she said. "I wish it wasn't live. Anyway, that's what comes of sticking to rounds. Don't you ever try them?"

"I have my own system," he said.

"Oh? What's that?"

He shrugged and glanced down at the counter. "I hang out in the right places. Make the right connections. It all depends on where you hang out and how you play their game." He shifted uneasily. "I mean, it always boils down to what you've got to do for them before they do something for you."

"Like an audition," she said, nodding.

He bit his lip and nodded back.

The counter boy brought them two more Cokes. Bobby didn't even look up. Lisa studied him for a moment. Then she nudged him. "What's bothering you, Bobby?" she said softly.

"Nothing. I was just thinking about auditions. They can be pretty degrading at times."

Lisa nodded. She stirred her Coke and swiveled absently on her stool. "You know, Bobby, I've been writing this scene to use for the Actors Studio auditions. It's still pretty rough, so I haven't applied yet. The thing is—" She paused. "I need a partner to audition. A man in his early twenties." She smiled briefly. "Dark hair, blue eyes, maybe five-foot-eleven or so. It's okay if he smokes. Know anybody who'd be available?"

He stirred. "Hmm?"

"Come on. Would you like to be my partner? I mean, are you at all interested in the Studio?"

"The place where Brando studied?"

She began to gush about Strasberg and Kazan, all the movie stars who had studied there. "It's not only good artistically," she finished, "but it's a real chance for success, Bobby."

"So who do you have to know to get in?" He sounded skeptical.

"You just apply!" She looked astonished. "Anyone over eighteen can audition. So what about it?"

"What if I blow it for you?"

"Well, I'll just have to shoot you." She grinned. "Anyway, there's always next year. I wouldn't blame you if we didn't make it on the first try. Lots of people don't."

He stared at her for a minute. Then his face lit up and he pounded on the counter. "Well, hell! What are we waiting for? Let's see this script you've written."

Lisa laughed. "Can you wait till next week? You could come over Monday and we could go over it then."

"Next week? But Lisa—"

"I need time to polish the script. I've waited this long. I'd like to wait a little longer."

He sank his chin into his hand and frowned at her.

When they left the drugstore, he walked her home. She ran lightly up the steps. "Thanks again," she said. "You made house hunting today a lot of fun."

Bobby followed her. He leaned against the door frame as she unlocked the door.

"Well, bye, Bobby." With a determined little smile, she kissed his cheek and stepped inside.

"What was that?" Ruth asked. She held the bongo drums in her lap. Wearing only a slip, she sat cross-legged on Bobby's bed. He was perched beside her in his undershorts.

"My neighbor, Mrs. Dreyfuss. I sneeze too loud and the old witch is pounding on the wall. Don't mind her. Keep playing. You're starting to get the hang of it."

She gave him back the drums. "I don't want to get you evicted."

He leaned across her to put away the drums, and she reached up and stroked his back. "This is so nice," she whispered. He turned and put his arm around her. "I mean, with Raymond—after he's finished, he's finished. He just goes to sleep."

"Sounds like a hell of a guy."

Ruth traced her fingers down his chest. She sighed. "He comes back tomorrow. I never thought I'd dread saying that. I guess it's a cliché, but I don't want this to end—you and me."

Bobby was silent. This was the kiss-off. He'd heard it a hundred times before, usually from someone who had grown tired of him, welshing on promises for help. Sometimes a few dollars accompanied the farewell speech, but he'd still feel cheated and used. He'd always held his mentors in contempt, but not Ruth.

For the first time, he felt like the user, and his contempt was aimed at himself. Ruth had already helped him—more so than anyone else before. He was relieved it would be over, and his debts paid up. Ruth would go away happy. No repercussions from his agent for dumping her best friend. Bobby was glad that the nice lady was dumping him. He shrugged and gazed up at the ceiling. "I'll miss you, Ruth," he said. In a way, he meant it too.

She kissed his shoulder. "It'll be hard enough keeping myself from calling you while he's here," she said. "I hate to think what it'll be like when Raymond goes out of town again. He's away so frequently."

Her words hung heavily in the air, waiting for some kind of reply. Bobby swallowed. "Well, um, next time he blows town, give me a call."

"Oh, you don't have to say that, Bobby. After all, this is a break for you—Raymond coming back. You're a young man and you don't want to get tied down with the likes of me."

Why did she have to be so smart, so sensitive? His eyes avoided her. "No, really. I'd like to keep on seeing you," he lied.

She sat up and leaned over him. "Bobby, I'm giving you a chance to bow out gracefully. If this is it for us, I understand."

But she'd never understand, he thought. If she didn't end it herself, then he'd be the heel, the user. "What's to understand?" he heard himself say. "When he blows town again, give me a call."

"It's really that simple?"

"Sure, if that's what you want."

"I—think so."

He worked up a smile and kissed her. "So okay then."

She searched his face. "I've never met anyone quite like you," she said. "So anxious to please, to be loved. You'd do anything to make people care about you, wouldn't you, Bobby? Is that why you want to be a movie star? So people will love you?"

He drew away. "What's wrong with that?"

She kissed him. "Nothing." She smiled. "But someday, maybe

120

you'll find one person who'll make you feel that important. I hope you do, Bobby." He was still staring at her, puzzled. Ruth patted his knee. "Well, let's get dressed. I'll take you to dinner. And no place dark this time. We'll go someplace expensive and crowded. Tonight, I don't care who sees us together."

The arrival of Brenda Dare on "Live for Today" had been eventful. Already she had seduced a happily married doctor, told his wife all about it over coffee, been responsible for little Kitty Bradshaw's miscarriage, and made life hell for her sister and brother-in-law.

Lisa loved playing a vamp. Audiences loved hating her, too. The ratings had gone up one-half point with the addition of the new character, and the producers were considering signing Lisa on as a permanent member of the cast. They had some pictures taken of Lisa wearing a long cocktail dress, brandishing a cigarette holder. Underneath, the caption read: "Lisa Weller sizzles as Brenda Dare on 'Live For Today'!"

In Lisa's second week with the show, thirty-one letters were waiting for her when she got to the studio. "What's all this?" she asked the actress who played the unfortunate Kitty.

"Fan mail," the girl said. "Read it. Ought to be good for a few laughs."

When they finished the show, Lisa put the mail in a paper bag and caught the bus to Amelia's office. Beatrice, the secretary, had already gone for the day, and Amelia was at her desk reading a script.

"Mind if I use the typewriter?" Lisa called.

Amelia glanced up. "Still working on that Actors Studio piece?"

Lisa held up her bag of letters. "Answering fan mail! How about that?"

Amelia looked delighted. She put down her script. "That's terrific. The show's taking off for you, Lisa. Listen, dear, I'm glad you stopped by. I need to talk to you for a minute. Powwow time."

Lisa sat down and watched Amelia light up a cigarette.

"I understand you might become a regular on the show. Have they said anything definite?"

"Not really. I guess they're still mulling it over."

"Well, if the offer comes through, don't grab at it. They've gotten you cheap for two weeks, but they'll have to pay a hell of a lot more for your name on a yearly contract."

"They didn't get me cheap!" Lisa exclaimed. "I've been able to keep my apartment. I'm lucky. Most actresses wait years for a break like this."

"Yes, you are lucky. Most actresses wait even longer to do a Hollywood screen test."

Lisa stared at her. "A screen test—for me?"

"Yes, honey." Amelia smiled. "For you, little Lisa Weller. Paramount seems to think it might want you for a bit in the next Martin and Lewis comedy. You'd have a five-minute scene on a train with Jerry. The part's a lot like Brenda Dare—another siren. I said I'd have your answer by tomorrow afternoon." She paused. "Naturally, there's a hitch. If you agree to do the film, assuming the test is good, you'd have to sign an exclusive three-year contract with Paramount. The key word here's *exclusive*. But it's steady employment with a great studio. Pay is a hundred a week. Not bad for an ingenue," Amelia finished.

Lisa chewed her lip. "But I have to sign the contract to do the film, right?"

Amelia nodded. "You wouldn't get to choose scripts. You'd be shoved in with all the other starlets. They'd arrange all your acting jobs. You'd take what they gave you, no matter how lousy the part was. You'd be lucky to get half-a-dozen walk-ons over the three years." She stubbed out her cigarette and sat back. "My advice is to give them a firm no. There'll be other offers, Lisa. Better ones. You won't have long to wait, honey. Then you'll be able to write your own ticket."

Lisa sighed. "It sounded so wonderful. But maybe you're right."

"My advice is to sleep on it, if you're not sure."

"No, I'm sure. After all, the Actors Studio is here, not in Hollywood. But you know, Amelia, it hurts like hell."

"I know, sweetheart. Smart decisions are hard to make. It's the dumb ones that seem easy. But in the long run, I think you'll be doing the right thing." She smiled. "By the way, how is that Studio audition piece coming along?"

Lisa shrugged. "I'm still working on it. But I think I finally have a partner for the scene. In fact, we're going over it tonight. He's one of your clients—Bob Pierce."

Amelia raised her eyebrows. "Bobby Pierce? Frankly, dear, I'm a little surprised. I didn't think he was quite your style. But if you think he's right for the part—"

"Is something wrong?" Lisa asked. She'd expected Amelia to be pleased. "I mean, if you don't think so—"

"No, I suppose he'll be fine." Amelia sounded ambivalent.

"Then it's okay?"

"Of course, honey. Anyway, it's your decision, not mine." Amelia stood up and smiled. "Now go write thank-you notes to your fans."

Bobby was waiting on the front steps when Lisa reached her building. He stood up when he saw her. "Guess I'm a little early."

"That's okay." They stepped into the lobby. Lisa stopped at her mailbox. It was empty. Then she laughed and held up her bag of fan mail. "Oh well, guess I have enough to read tonight. It's fan mail!"

Bobby's eyes widened.

"Actually, most of it is hate mail. Brenda Dare's a pretty bad apple. But mail's mail."

They went down to Lisa's basement flat. "Wish I could see your show," Bobby said. "But I'm never near a TV set. It's going well, huh?"

"Oh, terrific." She grinned. "Tomorrow I get to make a pass at my sister's husband. I ought to get a few letters about that!" She unlocked the door, stepped inside, and switched on the light. "It's not much, but I call it a rat-hole."

Since Patty's desertion, the apartment had become pretty sparse. The main room was furnished with a couch and coffee table bought from the Salvation Army. There were a few feminine touches, though—lace curtains on the high, barred windows, plants arranged along the bookcase shelves, prints of Paris street scenes taped to the walls.

He followed her into the kitchen. Quaint but cute, he thought. A wall rack held pans, utensils, and rooster-shaped potholders. There was an old-fashioned breadbox on the counter, and round tea and coffee canisters. The rickety table was coverd with a checkered tablecloth and held a wicker Chianti bottle complete with a dripping candle.

He liked it. Girls were amazing, he thought. They could move into a dump, stick a flower pot in the corner, and the place was suddenly a home. "Nice place," he remarked.

"Pretty corny, though," she said. "A living cliché. Struggling young actress comes to New York, gets a basement in Greenwich Village. I'm still waiting to meet a millionaire on the subway." She went to the cabinet and took out a package of macaroni and cheese. "Featured tonight is our 'Eat Cheap' special. Can I induce you to join me?"

"Sure," he said. "Sounds great."

She poured them each a Coke while he told her about his day working on a razorblade commercial. She smiled and nodded, while he warmed to his story. He suddenly flashed on a hokey image of marriage—the husband coming home to a cozy apartment and telling the pretty wife about his day while she fixed dinner.

The bag of letters lay on the table, and they began to poke through them. Lisa glanced at the postmark as she opened the first envelope. "Okay. This is from a faithful fan in St. Petersburg, Florida."

"Let's hear it for St. Petersburg!" Bobby called.

Lisa unfolded the letter. "Dear Brenda—'" She looked at Bobby. "That's my character on the soap. This should be a dilly

. . . 'Dear Brenda. I don't know what you're really like in person, but if you're anything like the Brenda Dare on the show, you ought to be shot.' "

Bobby laughed. "Ah, another adoring fan."

"They love me. What can I say? There's more: 'How can you sleep nights knowing you've practically killed Kitty, to say nothing of the baby? You should be ashamed of yourself! Do you get to keep the clothes you wear on the show? I really need to know.' "

Lisa had to stop reading for a moment, because Bobby's laughter was contagious. " 'Please reply quick. Send me an autographed photo. And it wouldn't hurt if you visited Kitty in the hospital since you put her there in the first place.' Oh, God, it's signed, 'Regards, Mrs. Emma Hilsendorfer!' "

Bobby beat his hands on the tabletop. "Emma Hilsendorfer! The name is poetry!" He wiped a tear from his eye and handed her another envelope. "God, these are great. Here, read the next one."

Lisa glanced at the postmark. "This one's from beautiful East St. Louis, Illinois."

"Let's hear it for East St. Louis!"

"Hooray!" she said, pulling out the letter. "It says: 'Dear Lisa . . . ' Well, they used my real name. 'Dear Lisa. I seen you on TV.' " She grinned at Bobby. "Another fan who wasn't an English major: 'I seen.' " She went back to the letter. " 'You were really something on that show. I seen it on TV at the bar I go to, and I tell all the guys that it's my daughter up there—' "

She choked. Her smile died as she looked at the letter. Bobby saw her pale gold complexion turn a sickly white.

"Jesus, what's wrong?"

She crumbled the letter in her grasp, then dropped it to the table. Her eyes squeezed shut, Lisa whispered, "Oh, damn. Damn him . . . "

"What's wrong?" he asked. "I—thought you liked your father."

"He's not my father!" She nervously rubbed her forehead and sighed. "It's—it's a crank, just a stupid crank letter. I'm sorry to overreact. I'm not used to them."

"Let's see." He reached for the crumpled page, but Lisa quickly snatched it away and shoved the letter in the bag. She got to her feet and tossed the bag on the counter.

"If it's a crank, why don't you just throw it out?" he asked innocently. "If it bothers you so much—"

"Can we just forget about it, please?" Her voice had a hostile edge to it. Lisa glanced at the stove. The pot of noodles was boiling over; the water hissed as it spilled onto the red coils. She grabbed the hot steel handle, then let out a sharp cry. She didn't rub her hand, but made a fist and hit the countertop. "Dammit! Dammit!"

Bobby jumped up from his chair and went to her. "Jesus. Put it under some cold water." He took her wrist and led her to the sink. But Lisa wrenched away.

"I'm okay. Just—just leave it, all right?" She turned on the water, and spoke with her back to him. "Could you turn off the stove, please?"

When the stove was off, he walked up behind her. He wished he could do something. He felt so useless and clumsy. "You okay now?" he asked.

"Yes." She kept her head down. "I'm sorry if I snapped at you."

Bobby ached to hold her, comfort her. He reached out and touched Lisa's hair.

With alarm, she swiveled around. "What are you doing?"

"Nothing. I—"

"Listen. I'm not very good company right now," she said, turning off the sink. "Maybe you'd better go."

"What did I do?"

After a moment, she took a deep breath and smiled tightly. "Nothing, Bobby," she said. "I'm sorry to act like such a pill. Please, stay."

He tried to give her a reassuring smile. "Listen, if that letter

126

really was from your old man, and you're embarrassed or something, don't be—"

"It wasn't from my father. I already told you that."

"Well, even if it was," he said, sitting down at the table, "it doesn't mean anything. Believe me, Lisa, I had a weird father myself. I know what it's like—"

"But my father isn't weird," she said. "I happen to love my father, corny as that sounds."

"I loved mine, too," Bobby said. "Only that didn't change the fact that he was nuts and sometimes I felt embarrassed being his son."

She took the pot off the stove. "Oh, everybody goes through that with their parents. I used to think my mother was crazy."

Bobby drew a deep breath. "Well, my father was actually a bit funny in the head, Lisa." He let out a weak laugh. "I guess there's no nice way to say it."

Numbly she gazed at him. "You mean, he was eccentric?"

"I mean he was nuts."

"In what way?"

"In the way that I had to put him in a rest home when he was only fifty-three years old. He couldn't look after himself."

Lisa came over to the table and sat down. "I'm sorry," she whispered. "If—you don't want to talk about it . . ."

"But I do," he said. "You're the first person I ever wanted to talk about it with. God, I know that sounds like a line, but it's true. Did you ever have some secret that made you ashamed and you didn't want anyone to know?"

Lisa put a hand to her throat. She stole a glance at the bag of mail, then looked back at him.

"That's how I felt about my father after I put him in this place," Bobby continued. "Only now, I want to tell you. I don't know why, but I do. Somehow, I feel I won't be so ashamed telling you, Lisa. That is, if you want to listen."

"Of course I want to listen, Bobby." She reached over and touched his face. He closed his eyes an she felt his warm breath on her fingertips. The warmth seemed to go right through her.

127

When he looked up, his blue eyes were clear and free from pain.

Then, in a rush he was telling her about Cameron and Danny and his mother. They talked through dinner, and then after dinner. Curled up on the sofa, Lisa hugged a throw-pillow and listened as Bobby told her about the country club, the Seattle Theater group, and UCLA. He made no mention of Mrs. Swift or her successors. Someday he would tell her, but not tonight. Finally, he yawned and announced that maybe it was time to think about the audition piece.

She climbed off the sofa. "Yes, we'd better. It's got to be eleven, at least." Lisa went into the kitchen and called to him, "I only have one copy of the script. It's in my bag here. Oh, my God! This stove clock can't be right. It's a quarter to two!"

Lisa stepped back into the living room. "I can't believe this," she groaned. "In five hours, I have to persuade Dr. Morton to leave his wife for me."

Bobby got to his feet and stretched. "Well, I guess we'd better call it a night."

She sighed. "I hate to say this, but I think the last bus left ten minutes ago." She glanced at the barred window. "And it's starting to rain." Lisa hesitated. "I could fix up the couch for you."

"The couch?" He studied her.

She folded her arms. "Or you can stand out in the rain and try to find a cab."

"I'll take the couch. Thanks."

She dug out a blanket and sheets. Bobby smiled when she appeared in a plaid bathrobe, oversized, with the sleeves rolled up. She explained that it used to belong to her father. She looked so damn sweet padding around the place, he thought, her hair pulled back and her face shiny clean.

By the time he came out of the bathroom, hopeful and shirtless, she was already in her bedroom. "Goodnight," he called. "And thanks."

"See you in the morning," came the voice from the other side of the door.

He stripped down to his undershorts, cut the light, and lay down on the couch. It was a little too short for him, but comfortable. The sofa pillow was hard and small, but he could smell her hair on it. Bobby fell asleep clutching Lisa's pillow to his bare chest.

In her room, Lisa dug out the letter. She forced herself to read it several times. But it was so pathetic, she felt almost disappointed.

> Dear Lisa,
>
> *I seen you on TV. You were really something on that show. I seen it on the TV at the bar I go to, and I tell all the guys that's my daughter up there on the screen. But of course no one believes me. Dummies.*
>
> *You grew up real pretty, just like your mother. But I still see some of me in the way you look. It makes me glad. You must be doing all right for yourself, and making a lot of money.*
>
> *Maybe I'll come to New York one of these days, and you and your old man can get together. I'd like that.*
>
> *Take care. You're my girl.*
>
> Your Dad,
> Johnny

She hadn't seen John Rogan or heard from him in ten years. Lisa put down the letter and reached over to her nightstand. From the drawer, she pulled out a man's chain necklace. Holding the thin string of silver beads in her hand, she thought back to when her father had sent it to her.

She had been in love with him, of course. And Lisa had been devastated when Matthew Weller received his draft notice shortly after her twelfth birthday. The day he left, she locked herself in the bathroom and cried. She found one of his dirty undershirts in the laundry hamper and decided to wear it to bed —every night until he got back. Her mother wanted to wash it, but Lisa refused. "No. You'll wash Daddy off!"

She wrote to him nearly every day while he was at boot camp.

Whenever she got a letter back, she'd hurry into the bathroom, lock the door, sit on the side of the tub, and read. She hid the letters under her mattress and then took them out at night to pore over.

One of the letters had rattled as she went to open the envelope. A necklace had fallen out. She had scooped it off the bathroom floor and seen that it was a St. Christopher medal, dangling from an Army-issue chain. Eagerly, she turned to the letter that accompanied it.

Atlanta, Georgia
Nov. 12, 1944

Dear Lisa,

I've been wearing this chain around my neck for a month. It held my dog tags and the medal. Yesterday, the chain broke during a hand-to-hand combat exercise (lots of fun). They gave me another chain for my tags, but I had this one repaired and am sending it to you.

Now it's yours, along with the medal which I've had since high school. Be a sweetheart and wear them for me. And would you do your Mom a big favor and give her that dirty undershirt so she could throw it out? Thanks.

They're shipping me out to London next week, as I'm sure Mom's told you. Don't worry, honey. It's pretty safe there. I'll send you a postcard of Big Ben. Congrats on that A in History. I'm very proud. Pay no attention to Marcie Cawell. You aren't stupid at all. Sounds to me like she's just jealous.

Well, the mail will be picked up soon, so I'd better finish this up. My love to Mom and Buddy. I miss you, angel.

Love,
Dad

Lisa slipped the chain around her neck. She was determined to wear it forever—or at least until she saw her father again.

Her mother had taken a job in shipping and receiving at a

meatpacking plant on Ashland Avenue. Lisa helped with the housework. She liked to cook and shop, even within the limitations of wartime rationing.

Work began to take up her mother's nights, as well as days. Sometimes Dee came home at six o'clock to change her dress and fix her blond hair into a Veronica Lake peekaboo-bang style. "Dinner with a client," she'd explain. Then she'd go off, telling Lisa and Buddy not to wait up or answer the door for anyone unless they knew who it was.

Lisa would wait up anyway. She'd lie awake in bed until she heard the front door click and her mother peek in to check on her. Sometimes she would hear muffled sounds coming from her mother's room late at night. It sounded like crying.

On Buddy's eleventh birthday, Dee came home early, carrying a bakery box and presents. A little later, a delivery man from Sears-Roebuck arrived, carrying a large package. It was addressed to Buddy. Inside were forty pounds of barbells that Matt had ordered. Buddy was ecstatic.

After dinner, Dee was about to light the candles on the cake when they heard a knock on the front door. All day, Lisa had been secretly hoping her father would show up to surprise them. The war in Europe was supposed to end soon. All the papers said so. Maybe, she thought, they didn't need him in London anymore.

"I'll get it," she called, and almost tripped over her chair with excitement. She raced to the door and threw it open.

A strange man stood there, smiling at her. He carried a suitcase. Lisa's face fell. She had been so sure it would be her father.

Dee looked frightened as she rose from the dinner table. Going to the door, she gently pulled Lisa away. "Johnny," she said in a funny voice. "Well, this is a surprise. What are you doing here?"

"Aren't you going to ask me in?" he said. Lisa saw him glance at the table, where Buddy was gawking from his chair.

"Yes, of course," Dee said, backing away. The man stepped inside and set down his suitcase. He smiled down at Lisa. "You must be Lisa. Your mommy has told me all about you."

She didn't like the way he spoke to her as if she were a dumb little kid. Still, he was handsome. He looked like he needed a shave, but the shadowed jaw was square and strong. He had pretty, dark eyes and a nose with a bump near the bridge. Lisa felt uneasy. Her mother looked very nervous.

"Lisa," she said, "this is a friend of mine from years ago. Mr. Rogan. He's a friend of Daddy's too. They went to high school together."

"You can call me Uncle Johnny." He smiled.

"How do you do?" Lisa said politely.

"Why, aren't you the little lady?" He grinned. "How do you do yourself?"

"I'm fine." And not so little, she wanted to say.

"Did you really go to school with my dad?" Buddy asked.

"You bet, kid."

"This is Buddy," Dee told him. "Buddy, have you forgotten your manners?" She turned back to the man. "It's his birthday today. He's eleven."

"And I'm twelve-and-a-half," Lisa piped up.

Buddy got up from the table. "Hi," he said, suddenly shy. He shook hands with the dark-haired man. "Were you on the basket-ball team with Dad?"

"No, I was too short. I bet you're a good ball-player, though. Only eleven and almost as tall as I am. Just like your old man, so tall. You've got more to you, though. Matt was always kind of puny."

Lisa saw her mother shoot a look at the man.

"I mean skinny!" He chuckled. "Tall, but skinny."

"What'd you say your name was again?" Buddy asked.

"Rogan. John Rogan. Happy birthday, kid. Sorry I didn't bring a present."

"That's okay," Buddy said. He stared at the man for a moment and then walked down the hall toward his parents' room.

"I'll clear the table," Lisa said. She went back to the dining room, but glanced at the door while she was stacking the dishes.

"Are you planning a trip, Johnny?" Dee asked, looking down at the suitcase.

"Not exactly. I got evicted. Couldn't make the rent."

Dee sighed. "I told you last week that was going to happen. What about the money you had?"

Lisa lowered her head and took the plates into the kitchen. She heard the man mentioning "a sure thing at the track," and her mother angrily whispering a reply.

When she came back for the glasses, Dee looked over at her. "Lisa, dear, Mr. Rogan and I are going to step out in the hallway for a minute. I'll be right back."

Lisa nodded. She watched them go and noticed the man had left his suitcase in the living room. Then she crept over to the door and pressed her ear to the wood.

She heard her mother's muffled voice. "You promised me! We had an agreement. I might have known—I should never have started seeing you again, Johnny."

"What did you want me to do, babe? I was strapped. No place to go. I'm down to my last nickel."

"Well, I don't have any money. I spent it all on Buddy's birthday presents. Please, Johnny. Leave us alone."

"I just told you, I got no place to go. At least let me stay the night."

She heard her mother laugh. "Are you kidding? It's funny how things have a way of turning around, Johnny. I seem to recall back in high school, coming to you for help when I was in trouble. And you turned me down."

"Yeah, but you came back to me, babe. I've been plenty 'helpful' keeping you company these last few weeks. Now, c'mon. Let me stay the night. Tomorrow, you can lend me twenty and I'll be on my way."

"I don't have twenty," Dee said. "Everything's tied up in war bonds. I won't have anything until payday."

"Then just the night."

"Oh, sure! And what am I supposed to tell the neighbors? Or my children? What are they supposed to think?"

"I don't mind using the couch. Not for one night. Don't worry, Dee. Come on, babe."

"Stop it, Johnny," Dee said weakly.

The man chuckled. "You love it."

Then Buddy came into the living room with a book in his hand. It was their father's yearbook. "Where'd that Rogan guy go?" He asked.

Lisa held a finger to her lips and tiptoed back from the door. She pulled Buddy into the dining room. "He's out in the hall. He and Mom are talking."

"What about?"

"How he doesn't have any money," Lisa said. "He wants to sleep here tonight."

Buddy scowled. He opened the dusty yearbook. "Look at this. That guy's not in here. He didn't go to school with Dad. Mom was lying."

Lisa stared at Buddy. "Mom would never lie."

"Well then, who is he?" Buddy demanded, closing the book.

Lisa picked up the empty glasses from the table and went into the kitchen. Buddy followed her. "Well?"

She set down the glasses. "I guess he's a friend of Mom's from work." She turned back and went to collect the silverware. Buddy was waiting for her.

"I don't like that guy," he said.

"Well, don't worry. Mom told him he couldn't stay here."

"Do you think he and mom are doing it?"

"*Buddy!*" Lisa dropped the silverware into the sink. "What kind of thing is that to say? You're really disgusting." She moved over to the counter. "Listen, get lost, okay? I'm going to take out your cake."

"So what?"

"So—you shouldn't see."

They heard the front door open and turned to watch their mother and Mr. Rogan step back inside. Dee came into the kitchen. She shooed Buddy away and began hunting for the matches. Lisa helped her light the candles on the cake. She noticed her mother's hand was trembling.

"Mr. Rogan wasn't in Dad's yearbook. Buddy and I looked."

Dee burned her finger and nervously waved out the match. "No, honey," she said, lighting another. "Mr. Rogan didn't finish school. Now, he's a very nice man, and he needs a place to sleep tonight. I want you and Buddy to be nice to him. It's just one night. Okay?"

Lisa sighed. "Okay, Mom."

Dee picked up the cake. "Here we come!" she called gaily into the darkened dining room.

They sang "Happy Birthday" as Dee set down the cake. By the flickering candlelight, Lisa could see that her brother wasn't smiling, but the man who wanted to be called "Uncle Johnny" was. He sang loudly and grinned at her. Lisa tried to smile back, but she could feel the effort showing on her face.

"Make a wish," Dee suggested, when they finished singing.

Buddy paused, took a deep breath, and blew out the candles. Everyone applauded. Then Dee switched on the lights. "What did you wish for, Buddy?"

"It won't come true if he tells," Lisa said.

Buddy glanced across the table at John Rogan. Then he said, "I wished that Dad would come home."

John Rogan took Lisa's room, and she slept with her mother. After three nights, Lisa began to resent being deprived of her bed. But she remained polite to Uncle Johnny, as he insisted on calling himself. He was always friendly toward her, but he wasn't quite so friendly to Buddy. Buddy, for the most part, did his best to ignore him.

The third night Rogan had been staying with them, Buddy was silent and withdrawn as they sat at the dinner table. But he sat up when "Uncle Johnny" said, "Lisa honey, I think it's time you got your bed back. Tonight I'll use the couch."

"That's okay," she said politely.

Buddy smirked. Then he said, loud enough for the others to hear, "Better change the sheets, Lisa."

Dee looked scandalized. "Buddy!"

John Rogan reached over and cuffed Buddy on the side of his head. Lisa could see that her brother was surprised, trying to cover the hurt and humiliation. "Nobody likes a smart-ass, kid," Rogan said.

"Buddy, apologize to Mr. Rogan at once," said Dee.

Lisa turned to her mother. "*What?*"

Buddy stood up, threw down his napkin, and went to his room. Rogan chuckled. "Don't mind him. He's just being a sourpuss."

Lisa glared at Rogan. "You big—"

"That's enough out of you, young lady," Dee warned. "Or would you like to go to your room?"

"Yes, Mother, I would. I have to change the sheets on my bed." She didn't look at them as she left the room.

As she replaced the linen, Lisa came across her father's letters stuck under the mattress. She pulled them out and reread them several times. It occurred to her to write her father and tell him about Uncle Johnny. How could her Dad be friends with such a jerk?

She was still at her desk, staring at the letters, when Rogan came into the room. She quickly stashed them in her desk drawer. Rogan placed a crumpled paper bag on the bed.

"What's that?" Lisa said, frowning.

"Take a look-see," he said. He sat down on the bed. Lisa remained at her desk. Finally, he reached inside the bag and pulled out a stuffed animal, a yellow giraffe with green spots. It looked old and dirty. "Surprise!" He smiled, and handed it to her.

Lisa looked at the stuffed animal. It smelled creepy. "Thank you," she mumbled.

"How's about giving your Uncle Johnny a thank-you kiss?"

She wondered what spot on his face would be the least painful to kiss. She leaned over and gave him a quick peck on the forehead. He pulled her down into his lap. She tried to sandwich the moldy stuffed animal between them.

"You're my girl," he said. "You know that?"

"Thanks," she managed to say, as she crawled out of his embrace.

Rogan got up from the bed, took his suitcase, and opened the door. "Goodnight, honey."

"Night."

"Night, Uncle Johnny," he corrected.

Lisa nodded. "Uncle . . . Johnny . . ."

He gave her a wink and left the room. Lisa went over and shut the door. She started to put the giraffe back in the bag. Then she noticed a receipt in the bottom of the sack and picked it up. It was from the Salvation Army store.

She suddenly felt sorry for Mr. Rogan, but not so sorry that she'd sleep with his smelly giraffe. She put it on her bookshelf, changed into her nightgown, then crawled into bed. The last thing she heard before falling asleep was the murmur of voices from her mother's room across the hall.

"Where's Mr. Rogan?" Lisa asked at breakfast.

"Eat your eggs before they get cold," Dee told Buddy. She set a glass of juice in front of Lisa. "He left early this morning."

"Let's hope for good," Buddy said.

"That's enough out of you, young man." Dee sat down and picked up her fork.

"He shouldn't have hit Buddy," Lisa said. "Besides, he was only supposed to stay here that one night."

Dee put down her fork and stared at Lisa. "Why, I'm surprised at you. Mr. Rogan gave you back your room. He could have slept in a bed, but he took the lumpy sofa—all for you. And he told me he gave you a lovely present."

Buddy looked at Lisa as if she'd betrayed him.

Lisa tossed her head. "Well, it was gross and smelly and he got it from the Salvation Army," she said, mostly to appease Buddy. "It was an awful present."

"That's the most ungrateful thing I've ever heard," Dee said. Buddy suddenly got to his feet, muttering something about baseball, and ran out of the room. Dee stared after him with exasperation. Lisa looked at her mother and nibbled a piece of toast.

After a moment, Dee cleared her throat. "Lisa, I miss your father very much. Maybe you don't think I do, but I miss him terribly. I want him back just as much as you do."

Lisa said nothing.

"Maybe I was wrong about Mr. Rogan hitting Buddy. But Buddy wasn't very nice to Mr. Rogan, honey—"

"Dad's never hit us."

"I know that. But Mr. Rogan isn't your . . . he's not like Daddy." Dee paused. "I got paid yesterday. I'll give him some money. Then he can go and stay somewhere else. I'll talk to him tonight, and he'll leave tomorrow."

Lisa stood up. "Okay," she said, feeling awkward. It was as if her mother was trying to convince her of something and not succeeding. She started to leave the room.

Dee raised her voice. "Oh, and Lisa? After Mr. Rogan's gone, you can get rid of that giraffe."

Rogan returned shortly before dinner. As usual, Lisa and Buddy retreated to their rooms the minute they heard his voice. Lisa fervently hoped her mother would keep her promise, that she should make "Uncle Johnny" leave.

Sprawled on her bed, she flipped through a movie magazine. She was halfway through an article called "The Day Van Johnson Broke Judy's Heart," when there was a knock on the door. Rogan walked into the room. "Hi, honey," he said.

She sat up. "Hi."

He came over and sat down on the bed. "This is my last night here. Will you be sorry to see your Uncle Johnny go?"

She was a terrible liar. "I guess . . ."

He glanced down at the picture of Betty Grable on the cover of *Screen Stories*. "You know, you're a whole lot prettier than she is."

Lisa laughed feebly. "I don't think so."

"Pretty girls should have pretty things." He fingered the chain around her neck, with Matt's St. Christopher medal dangling from it. Rogan made a sour face. "Where'd you get this thing? You wear it all the time."

Lisa squirmed away. "My father gave this to me. I love it."

"Looks cheap. You ought to have nice things to wear. Here," he said, "I got something a whole lot better than that piece of junk." He reached into his pocket and pulled out a gold chain on which hung an ornate locket. It was beautiful—no Salvation Army store bargain.

"That must've cost a lot," she murmured.

"Yeah, I guess it did. Here, try it on. First take off that ugly chain."

"Well," Lisa hesitated. She clutched her father's medal. "Thank you anyway—Uncle Johnny, but I can't."

His face was darkening. "You'd rather wear some piece of junk than something I got you?"

"It's my father's. I promised I'd wear it until he came back—"

"C'mon, it's ugly," he said, reaching toward her neck.

She recoiled. "Please, don't—"

"Whaddaya pulling away from me for? That's just a piece of garbage. Take it off!"

"But it means something to me."

"It doesn't mean shit!"

Lisa glared at him. "My father gave this to me!"

"He's not your father. I am! I'm your daddy!" He grabbed at the chain Matt had given her. She ducked and screamed as Rogan pulled at it. The chain dug into the back of her neck until it broke. Lisa clawed at him, trying to get it back.

The door opened, and Dee came into the room. "My God, what happened?"

"Ask her!" Rogan said, pointing at Dee. He stared down at Lisa. "Ask her who your real father is!" He threw down the chain. Lisa fell to the floor to retrieve it.

Dee's face was ashen. "No, Johnny," she whispered. "No, please, don't. Not like this—"

"Tell her, Dee. Go on! She should know her real father!"

"Get out of here," Dee said, shaking. "Please, just get out of here."

Sobbing, Lisa crawled to the foot of the bed. She wondered why her mother wouldn't call him a liar. She clutched the broken chain. "Make him go away, Mom," she cried.

But Rogan grabbed Dee's arm. "She's my kid. Tell her, goddamn it!" He struck her across the face. Dee fell to the floor, covering her mouth and nose. Dark blood oozed between her fingers.

"You're nothing but a goddamn—" Rogan stood over her, his face full of fury and contempt. He had his back to the door. He didn't see Buddy or the baseball bat Buddy was holding until it slammed down on his shoulder.

Rogan roared with pain.

"Get out!" Buddy said.

Rogan jerked around. He started toward Buddy, but the boy didn't move. With a quick motion, he jabbed the thick end of the bat into Rogan's gut. Letting out a strangled gasp, the man fell to his knees. He coughed, his mouth twisting to one side. He blinked and shook his head like a wounded dog.

Buddy stood over him, the bat poised. "Mom," he said, not taking his eyes off Rogan, "are you okay? I think you better get his stuff together so he can go."

Dee got to her feet. Her mouth and chin were smeared crimson. "Buddy, I don't want to leave you alone in here."

"I'm okay, Mom. Just hurry."

After casting a cautious glance at Rogan, she ran out of the room.

Lisa remained on the floor, curled up at the foot of the bed. Buddy was standing over Rogan's crumpled form. "Lisa," he said, "go call the police."

She got up and walked gingerly around Rogan, as if he were a snake that might coil and strike.

"Hurry up," Buddy said. "Call the cops."

Lisa backed out the door. She found her mother in the living room, throwing Rogan's clothes into his suitcase. She glanced up at Lisa. "Hand me my purse, honey. Quickly now."

"I've got to call the police. Buddy told me to," Lisa said.

"No!" Dee darted across the room and stood in front of the phone. "No. Please. You can't."

She stared at her mother. The blood was caked around her nose; her hair was wildly mussed. Lisa studied the pleading eyes, red and moist with tears.

"Don't you see, honey? If he's arrested, they'll ask questions. We've got to think about Daddy. We can't—please, Lisa, don't call."

Lisa gazed steadily back. "He was . . . lying. Wasn't he? It wasn't true, Mom. It was a lie."

"Forgive me, Lisa. Please—"

Dee broke away. Running over to her purse, she rummaged through her wallet until she pulled out three twenty-dollar bills. Clutching them, she hurried back to Lisa's room.

As if in a trance, Lisa started for the front door. She could hear her mother's voice: "Hurry, Johnny. Take this money. The police will be coming. You've got to get out of here."

The moon cast an eerie light on the monkeybars in the playground. To Lisa, the bars seemed to glow; the jungle gym and swingset looked like shells of burnt-out houses.

It was dark now and chilly. The vacant swings creaked as they moved in the night breeze. She shivered. She should have brought a sweater. But there wasn't time. Lisa had stolen out of the apartment and waited downstairs to see if Rogan would leave. When she saw him carry down his suitcase, she knew Buddy must be safe. Rogan staggered into the street, where a car nearly hit him. He unleashed a string of obscenities at the driver, which shocked and terrified Lisa as much as anything he'd said that night. She waited until he had turned the corner. Then she went to the playground.

She wandered over to the swingset and sat down. Pressing her face against the cold, rusty cable, she wished her father was home. Then she could ask him what "Uncle Johnny" had meant. And he would tell her it was all a lie. He would laugh and say it was the funniest thing he'd ever heard.

But her father wasn't there. She glanced around the deserted playground. She told herself there might be murderers around, but somehow she didn't care. It would serve her mother right if something happened. Let her worry.

Her mother. Why couldn't it have been the other way around? Why couldn't her real mother have been someone sweet, a stranger who had died in a car crash? No, Lisa thought, it would be even nicer if that stranger were still alive somewhere. She would have survived the car crash and wandered away with a case of insomnia—ambrosia—whatever. She'd have lost her memory. And everyone would have thought she was dead, but one day she'd come back, cured. Then her father would divorce Dee and remarry her real mother, who would look like Ingrid Bergman.

Lisa reached in her pocket. She touched the broken necklace. She'd have to search her bedroom for the St. Christopher medal.

Suddenly, she heard something. She whirled around.

A man was standing by the monkeybars. He wore a long, black overcoat with the collar turned up. Under the coat, she could see a frayed sweater and baggy pants. His face was swallowed up in the shadows. He began to walk toward her.

Lisa was too frightened to move. All her bravado about serving Dee right had suddenly vanished. She could see his face now, narrow and pockmarked. But he had nice brown hair and soft, sad eyes. Drawing nearer, he smiled at her, a sweet crooked smile. "You're out kinda late. Your folks know where you are?"

Lisa said nothing. She tucked the chain back into her pocket.

The man sat down on the next swing. "You live far from here? You shouldn't be here alone. Why don't you let me walk you home?" he asked.

She stared straight ahead. "It's not so late."

"I guess you have a point," he said. "What's your name?"

"Naomi," Lisa said.

"Hmm. How old are you, Naomi? Do you mind my asking?"

"I'm thirteen. How old are you?"

"Twenty-five. Do you think that's old?"

"I don't know. I guess so."

"So why aren't I in the Army, you want to know? Well, I'll tell you, Naomi. The old case of fallen arches. Didn't even know I had them until the draft board told me." He laughed feebly. Lisa was silent.

"Sometimes I talk too much." He paused. "So tell me, are you running away? Not that I mean to pry."

She idly traced a circle in the dirt with her toe. "I just came here to think," she replied.

"Good," he said. "People never really run away. It doesn't matter how far they go, 'cause their problems usually catch up." He sighed. "Take me. I want to be an artist, but instead I work for my father, making cardboard boxes."

Lisa wrinkled her nose.

The man smiled. "Exactly. You see, I want things easy and safe. I'm scared to take risks. When I'm at the factory, I think about painting a picture at the park—one of an old lady feeding the pigeons. A guy will come up and tell me how terrific it is. Just so happens he'll own a gallery on Michigan Avenue. Yeah, I think about that while the machine grinds out boxes, how the pictures I'll never paint will sell for ridiculous prices at a gallery that doesn't exist. It gets me through the day, or at least till coffee break." He smiled sadly at Lisa. "See, I talk too much. Huh, Naomi?"

"That's okay," she said.

"Listen, why don't I walk you home?"

"I guess so," she said, and hopped off the swing.

As they walked through the park, he noticed her fingering the necklace. "Is that broken?" he said. "Maybe I can fix it." They stopped under a streetlamp, and the man examined the chain. "Hmm, it's broken in an odd place, where those beads snap together. You might have to get a new chain."

Lisa shook her head. "I don't want a new chain."

"No. I'm sure this one's special to you. Wait a minute." He ripped a long thread from the inside of his coat pocket. As they approached Lisa's building, he held the chain up to the light and then fastened it together with the thread. He handed the necklace to her. "There you go, Naomi. That should hold for a while. I hope."

Lisa looked down at it. It was one piece again. She couldn't even see where he'd tied it. Smiling, she put the chain around her neck. "Thank you," she said shyly.

"Looks nice on you," he said. "But I guess you already know how pretty you are."

She turned and looked at the building. "Here's where I live."

"They'll be glad to see you. I bet they were worried."

"Maybe." She walked up the steps and then glanced back at him. "Thanks for walking me home. And fixing my necklace. I hope you sell a picture someday."

"Me too." he smiled. "Goodnight, Naomi."

She waited until he had begun to walk away. Then she went inside.

Lisa never replaced the thread that held her necklace together. She'd found the St. Christopher medal, and kept it pinned to the shade of her bed-lamp.

She only spoke to her mother when necessary, and noticed that Dee was no longer working late. Most of the time, Lisa came home from school and shut herself in her room with schoolwork, movie magazines, or Nancy Drew books. She started several letters to Matt, but didn't finish them.

She had reached the point where she didn't care about anything. V-E Day came and went without her noticing. Buddy kept asking her what was wrong. She'd simply shake her head and reply, "I'm tired, that's all."

Her mother knew what was wrong. One night, she knocked on Lisa's door. Lisa was in bed, reading.

"I think we need to talk," Dee said, sitting down on the bed.

Lisa tossed her Nancy Drew book aside and switched off her lamp. "I've got school in the morning."

But Dee didn't move. "I don't blame you for hating me, Lisa.

144

I can only ask you to try and understand. When I knew John Rogan, I was eighteen, only a few years older than you are. I thought I was in love."

"Mother, I'm tired—"

"Let me finish. Now, I made a mistake, and I'm sorry."

"And I'm the mistake. I'm sure you're sorry I was ever born."

"No, that isn't true. I love you, honey. If it weren't for you, I might not have married your father, the most wonderful man I've ever—"

"But he isn't my father! And I bet he doesn't even know. Does he, Mother?" Lisa gazed through the darkness at her mother's profile. "Did you trick him into marrying you?"

Dee was silent. Then she said, "I don't think he knew I was pregnant when we eloped. We've never talked about it, but I think he's always known the truth. But, darling, it doesn't matter what happened thirteen years ago. What's important is that you *are* his daughter, and you've always been since the day you were born. He loves you."

Lisa turned away. Dee touched her shoulder. "Go away," Lisa mumbled into her pillow.

"But we have to talk," Dee said. "Your father's coming home in three weeks."

Lisa sat up. "What?"

"He's gotten a furlough. I got the letter today. He's coming home, and we should be happy. Please, Lisa, we should be happy."

But when her father's homecoming day arrived, Lisa just felt frozen inside. She watched from the crowded gate as her father's train pulled in. "There he is!" Buddy yelled, pointing. And there he was, looking handsome as he stepped off the train in his khaki uniform, his hat cocked to one side of his head. He hoisted his duffle bag and spotted them. Lugging the bag, he raced to meet them at the gate. To Lisa, he looked older, strong and tall as he moved through the swarm of people.

He got to Dee first, scooping her up in his arms and embracing her. Then Buddy pulled at his father's arm, until Matt grabbed him and kissed him, too. Lisa watched from a distance.

"Lisa!" He reached out. Then she was in his arms, pressing her face into his shoulder. Matt kissed her. Lisa began to cry.

That night, her parents went out for a long walk. When Lisa heard them return, she was reading in bed. She quickly switched off her nightstand lamp and hiked the covers up to her neck. She heard her bedroom door open.

"Lisa," Matt said. "I know you're awake, honey."

Silent, she squeezed her eyes shut.

"Come on, faker," he said gently. "I know you were awake a second ago. I saw the light go out."

Reluctantly, she sat up.

He came over and sat down on her bed. "Mom and I had a long talk."

"Where is she?"

"Getting ready for bed. Lisa, do you want to know what we talked about?"

She didn't answer, but just stared solemnly at him with her large eyes.

"We talked about you. Your ears must have been burning."

"My ears are fine," Lisa said numbly.

"I know that, sweetheart. But I'm not sure about you."

"What do you mean?"

"I think we both know, Lisa. A little while ago, you found out something I've known for a long, long time."

Lisa's eyes filled with concern. "It doesn't matter," she said softly.

"Lisa. Sometimes good things happen by accident. And when they do, it doesn't pay to ask why. You just feel lucky. Other times, you have to work at making things right. Honey, as far as you're concerned, I'm the luckiest father in the world. And with your mother . . . I'm pretty darn lucky there, too. You're so precious to me, honey. If it weren't for you, your mother wouldn't have come to me. You don't know how much I loved her then, and love her now. She's had a tough time, Lisa. I want you to try and understand that." He paused. "Does this make any sense to you?"

Lisa shook her head.

Matt bit his lip. Gently, he kissed her goodnight. He got up and turned toward the door.

"Daddy?" Her head was on the pillow, but her sad eyes were open. "I guess I'm lucky, too."

"Why's that, angel?"

"To have you for a father," she said.

Matt went to the bed and gathered her in his arms. Lisa began to cry, and she held him tightly. She could hear her father saying her name over and over. Her father, she thought, her *real* father.

Lisa stared at the necklace in her hand. She slipped it over her head. She hadn't worn Matt's necklace for a long time, but tonight she needed it.

Picking up John Rogan's letter, Lisa was grateful there was no return address. And the East St. Louis postmark on the envelope made her glad he wasn't in Chicago anymore. *You must be doing all right for yourself and making a lot of money,* it said.

Did that mean he was warming up for a loan? Well, Lisa thought, she wasn't her mother. John Rogan wasn't getting a dime from her.

Before she fell asleep, she thought about Bobby Pierce, asleep in the next room. She didn't have to wonder why she always put walls between men and herself. But as she lay in bed alone, Lisa did wonder if she'd ever have the courage to go past those walls.

SEVEN

"They'll be filming the ad at eight," Amelia told Bobby. "Be there on time. And wear a tie."

"Yes, ma'am." He slouched deeper into his chair.

"Don't call me ma'am, for chrissakes. Name's Amelia." She leaned back and lit a cigarette. "I understand from Lisa Weller that you two are planning to audition for the Actors Studio together."

"That's right."

"Well?"

"We were supposed to rehearse at her place last night. But we didn't get around to it."

She gave him a look.

"No, it wasn't like that. We started talking and it got late."

Amelia nodded. "All right, honey. I'm going to level with you. Clients are one thing, friends are another. I saw Ruth Bartlett at a party on Saturday. She's usually a wallflower at those things, but on Saturday, she was doing the mambo. Raymond couldn't keep up with her. I've never seen such a change in anyone. Do you suppose you had anything to do with it?

"Why didn't you ask Ruth?"

"I didn't have a chance. She was too busy talking about you. Nothing juicy, of course, but enough so that I know she really cares about you, honey. She's a very vulnerable lady, Bobby. And so is Lisa Weller. I'm pretty fond of both of them. And I don't want either one hurt on account of you. Do I make myself clear?"

Silent, Bobby nodded.

She sighed. "Anyway, you don't have to worry. I won't say anything to Ruth—or Lisa. I'm going to do my best to stay out of this mess. And you know why? Because against all my better judgment, I like you. I really do, honey. But don't forget—Ruth's how you got in with this agency, and Ruth could just as easily be the reason I toss you out on your ass."

Two college students sit in the front seat of a Dodge, parked at a drive-in. To her boyfriend's irritation, the Girl pulls away when he starts to kiss her.

BOY: Hey, what gives?

GIRL: I just think we should talk. It's important.

She turns down the speaker, hooked to the car window.

BOY: What the hell's so important that it can't wait?

GIRL: Billy, do you love me? I mean, really love me?

BOY: Sure. You're my girl, aren't you?

GIRL: Do you remember the last time you said you loved
me? It was that night I—let you. Do you
remember now?

BOY: Sure, I guess. I still do, babe.

He starts kissing her again, but she breaks away.

BOY: Now what? I already said I loved you. What else
do I gotta say?

GIRL: I want you to say that you'll marry me.

BOY: Are you nuts? We still got two more years 'til
graduation. We can't get hitched now.

GIRL: Why not? Your father can get you a job with his
company. We could make a nice home for
ourselves—

BOY: Why are you harping on this? What's the rush?
God, you act like you're knocked up or something.

The Girl starts to cry.

GIRL: Billy, I'm pregnant.

*No, she doesn't want him to find her one of those
"doctors." She wants to marry him. He has to! Angry,
he tells her he doesn't have to do anything. He leaves the
girl alone in the car. Slowly she turns up the speaker.
With tear-filled eyes, she gazes ahead at the unseen
movie.*

The scene, they both agreed, was quite corny.

For three weeks, Lisa and Bobby had met almost every day, reading and rewriting. The scene had to be perfect in a month. On free afternoons, they rehearsed in Central Park, basking in the warm spring air, and entertaining other strollers. Late at night, they sat in Lisa's kitchen, reading the tattered script while they munched barbecued potato chips and sipped Cokes.

Sometimes, she'd look up from her script and catch Bobby gazing at her. Lisa would quickly glance away, mutter something about a line of dialogue that needed fixing, and everything would be back to business. Safe. She wasn't going to get involved. He'd been around and she hadn't. What had happened to her mother wasn't going to happen to her. She wanted things safe.

When their rehearsals ran past midnight, she'd make up the couch and Bobby would spend the night, always with the bedroom wall between them.

"That couch is giving me a hunchback," Bobby said one day.

"Then you'll be able to play Quasimodo," Lisa replied. She took out a slice of pizza from the carry-out box and set it on the plate. Bobby took a swallow of Coke.

"You got an extra bed in your room. Why can't I use it?"

She shifted in her chair. "Fine. I'll take the couch."

"You don't trust me?" His face expressed mock horror. "Is that it? Afraid I'll ravage you in the middle of the night?"

150

"Hardly," she replied, biting into her pizza.

"I've got it! You can't trust yourself. The temptation to attack me would be too great. Lisa Weller, Fallen Woman."

Lisa nodded wearily. "You guessed it, ace."

"Thought so. Didn't think I could hear your love-starved moans in the middle of the night."

"Do you mind?" she said. "I'm trying to eat here."

He frowned. "Still, that couch is too damn small."

She put down her pizza. "Listen, ace. You start paying rent here, then maybe I'll take heed. Complain, complain."

He got up abruptly. "I've had it, Lisa."

She stared at him. "For God's sake, I was just kidding. You know I like your company."

"Yeah. But you don't trust me."

"Yes, I do. Honest."

"Well, you shouldn't."

She blinked. "What's that supposed to mean?"

"It means any normal guy would've put a move on you ages ago. I've known you for a month, and zero. Nothing!"

"But you're not average, Bobby. You're special. Better than other guys."

"Oh yeah? If I'm such a prince, how come whenever I come near you, you act like I'm the Creature from the Black Lagoon?"

She bit her lip. "My feelings for you are strictly platonic, Bobby."

"Christ!" He rolled his eyes. "There you go with that *word* again! I never heard it before I met you."

"It means I like you. It means—"

"I know what it means." He glared. "Hands off." He picked up his pizza and dropped it on the plate. "It's ice cold."

She got up. "I'll put it in the oven for you."

"Skip it."

"You're mad at me, aren't you?"

"No," he lied.

"Bobby, is it so terrible of me to just want us to be friends?"

"No," he lied again.

"I practically consider you my best friend. Really, I do."

He looked up at the ceiling and chuckled. "Then why don't I just move in? I could be your roommate. We could take turns doing each other's hair!"

"Very funny."

"Really, Lisa. If we're such good pals, you shouldn't mind sharing the same room with me. We could split the rent and save ourselves some dough."

She paused. "I'm almost tempted," she said.

"Then why not?"

"I can think of a million reasons. Two that come to mind are my mother and my father."

He traced a square in front of her face. "Definitely cubic. Your fossils don't need to know everything."

She stared at him. "You're really serious about this."

"Why not? Hell, I'm practically living here these days anyway."

For the next week, the arguments continued. He cited the money they'd both save, the apartment she wouldn't have to give up, the time needed to rehearse for the audition, and the protection his presence would provide. And she could trust him.

On Friday, he took her to see *Rear Window*. Lisa knew the movie was another one of Bobby's ploys to convince her that she shouldn't live alone. Before the lights went down, she sighed and told him she'd given in, but that she'd made a list of ground rules. She took out the list and began reading off items about paying bills and sharing food. And sleeping arrangements. Then the movie started, and during the last, hair-raising half hour, Lisa's hand clutched Bobby's arm and stayed there. Bobby smiled into the darkness.

Afterwards, they strolled down Forty-fifth Street. "You know," he told her, "I always thought you looked a little bit like Grace Kelly."

She groaned. "Not with this nose!" She touched the slight bump near the bridge. "I'm thinking of getting it fixed. That's all

I seem to hear from casting directors anymore, and I've lost too many jobs on account of it."

"Are you crazy? It's what makes you different from all the rest, more interesting."

"So would three arms, but it wouldn't make me prettier."

"If you fixed your nose, you'd be perfect. Don't you know how boring that is? I like your face the way it is."

"Thanks," she said with a smile. "Anyway, it'll have to stay imperfect a while longer. No money, no nose. No nose, no money." She sighed.

She decided that they should put a curtain between the beds, like the Wall of Jericho in *It Happened One Night*.

Bobby smothered a laugh. "Okay. What else?"

"The phone. I don't want you to answer it, in case my parents call."

He stared at her. "I can't answer the phone?"

"Not before nine-thirty in the morning or after ten at night. Until I can figure something else out. Another thing. No bongo drums late at night. No loud music. The neighbors are very touchy."

"Fine, fine."

"And one more thing, Bobby." She looked very serious. "Don't expect me to take a walk if you want to bring girls here. They can't spend the night. And I won't pretend I'm your sister, either."

"What about when you've got a guy here?"

"That you don't have to worry about. Now—last, smoking's okay, but not in the bedroom. I guess that's it. Do you have any suggestions?"

"Yeah. Don't take all day in the can."

"That's it?"

"That's it."

"All right." She smiled broadly. "You can start moving in your things. D-Day is June first. One week from today." She put away the list and sighed. "I can't help being a little nervous about this, Bobby."

"Why?"

"Because the landlord gave me a funny look when I explained what we're doing. Because my parents will kill me if they find out. And because I'm just nervous, that's all."

"Don't be." He shrugged and smiled.

She smiled back. "Gee, thanks. I feel a whole lot better now."

It had been almost a month since Ruth had last seen Bobby. Maybe he'd found a girlfriend, she thought. Or maybe he'd simply forgotten her.

On Tuesday, three days before Raymond was due to leave on business, Ruth stared at the telephone on the nightstand for almost twenty minutes. She and Bobby had had ten wonderful days together, she told herself. She should simply leave him alone. He wouldn't miss her. So why complicate things?

She picked up the receiver and dialed. Impatiently, she counted the rings: three, four, five—She tallied twelve before hanging up. She decided to try again later.

It was ridiculous. The boy was never home. For two days, she called. It got so she could dial his number, put the receiver down, make a cup of tea, and return to the phone to hear the damn thing still ringing. She began to worry.

On Thursday night, she and Raymond sat in the study. He was asleep in front of the TV, his long legs crossed in front of him, his small belly protruding. She reached over and shook his shoulder. He moved his head, but didn't waken.

"Raymond dear. Time to go to bed."

"In . . . minute."

"Are you all packed for your trip, darling?"

"Hmph. Yeah."

"I forget," she said. "Where are you going this time?"

"Mmmmmmm."

"Raymond?"

"Sangeles," he grunted.

"Christina Slade's in L.A. I imagine you'll see her."

"Uh."

Sighing, she got to her feet. Out of habit and boredom, she dialed the number. Holding the receiver loosely, she glared at the sleeping Raymond. Dead to the world. Out like a—

"Hello?"

Her heart froze. Quickly, she hung up. Raymond hadn't budged. A minute later, she was upstairs in the bedroom, the door closed, dialing Bobby's number.

"Hello?" His voice was annoyed.

"Bobby? You're home! I can't believe it."

There was a pause. "Oh, Ruth. Hi. How are you?"

"Fine," she said quickly. "I . . . hope I didn't wake you."

"No. I was kind of snoozing. Then some jerk called a few minutes ago and woke me up. You know the kind? You answer and they hang up?"

"How annoying." She swallowed. "So how have you been?"

"Who, me? Just great. Hey, it's been awhile. How are things with you and your husband?"

"Well." She laughed nervously. "Actually, he's going out of town tomorrow. He'll be gone for a week."

There was a pause. "Did you want to get together?" he asked.

"Do you . . . Bobby? Are you still there?"

Finally, he said, "See, I'm moving to a new apartment tomorrow. Got a roommate. I don't think we should meet there. I mean, with the roommate and all."

"Certainly. I understand." She tried to sound gracious.

"Um, well, we could meet somewhere," he said. "If you want . . ."

Room 519 of the Excelsior Hotel was decorated in pale blue and bleached wood. Ruth had spent the last twenty minutes gazing up at the pale ivory ceiling. Lying in the unmade bed, she laid her head against Bobby's chest and listened to his heartbeat.

"So tell me about this girl," she said, stroking his thigh.

"What girl?"

"The one you're rehearsing with. The Actors Studio audition." She heard his heartbeat quicken.

"She's okay."

"Is she pretty?"

"More or less . . . she looks a little like you. Blond . . ."

"Only she's younger, of course."

"Twenty-two."

"Twenty-two," she echoed. She drew away from him and sat on the edge of the bed. Bobby reached over and traced a finger down her spine.

"You're not jealous or anything?" he asked.

"A little." She looked over her shoulder at him.

Bobby held up a finger. "You're fishing, Ruth," he chided gently.

She got up and picked her blouse off the chair. "Sorry." She shrugged, buttoning the blouse.

"You *are* jealous." He sat up. "Look, Lisa and I just rehearse together. That's all."

"I'm sorry," she said again.

"Don't keep apologizing, Ruth. It's okay."

"It's not okay." She sank onto the chair. "I just can't help feeling you'd rather be with someone else. Someone your own age. And I can't blame you."

"But I wanted to be with you." He tried to keep his voice light, noncommittal, sincere.

"I just don't want you to feel you're being used. I'd hate that. I'm not Raymond. Every girl he helps has to . . . sleep with him." Ruth averted her eyes. "I couldn't bear it if you were only seeing me out of a sense of obligation."

"Ruth, alright already," Bobby said, a little quickly.

"As long as you understand you don't have to see me unless you want to."

"I understand." He got up and went over and kissed her. "Don't worry about this girl. We're just friends. Platonic friends."

156

"All right," she said faintly. "Do we have time for dinner?" she asked, changing her tone.

Bobby reached for his shirt. "On two conditions. I leave the tip. And two. We don't talk about this girl anymore."

"I promise." Ruth smiled. "You can tell me about your new apartment and your roommate. I'm dying to hear all about it."

The clock on the nightstand said eleven-thirty-five. Lisa sat in bed reading. She glanced at the burlap curtain that divided the room. Bobby wasn't on the other side. She didn't like being alone in half a room. He'd said he might be back tonight, or he might stay over with his uncle's friends again. *Might.* She hated not being certain. It meant going to bed without securing the chain lock, not sleeping out of worry. She'd almost felt safer before, living alone.

Footsteps. She heard the chain rattle. "Bobby?" she called. "Is that you?"

"No, it's an ax-murderer."

"Could you fasten the lock?"

"I already did," he said, "I didn't wake you?"

"No, I was reading," she said.

He stood over her. The nightstand lamp cast shadows through her delicate nightgown, highlighting her breasts. Her hair was down and it, too, caught the light. Bobby wished she'd wear cold cream and a retainer to bed. "Can I get you anything?" he asked, trying not to eye her breasts.

"No thanks." She put the book on the nightstand.

Bobby went over to his side of the room and switched on the light in his closet. He began to undress.

"Those friends of your uncle's must really like you," Lisa remarked. "This is your first night here in—"

"I came back last night."

"Not till quarter to one."

"I didn't realize you were punching a clock for me." He hung up his coat and kicked off his shoes.

"Someone's in a bad mood," she said.

"Sorry. Forget it." Pulling off his shirt, he dropped it on the floor of the closet.

"Anyway, it's nice to have you here. After four nights, I was starting to think you'd changed your mind." She yawned. "We ought to rehearse tomorrow, Bobby. The audition's on Tuesday."

Bobby sat on his bed. He stared at her shadow through the curtain.

"Bobby? About the audition. I said we'd better—"

"Yeah, yeah. I heard you. We'll rehearse." He yanked off his socks and tossed them on the floor.

"Bobby? Are you upset about something?" She paused. "Is it about that TV part you didn't get?"

"No, it isn't the TV thing. It's nothing."

"Maybe you should tell these friends of your uncle that you need a breather. Tell them you have leprosy or something."

He went to the dresser and emptied his pockets. "No, I can't do that. They helped me when I was strapped. I don't want to seem ungrateful."

"Well, you're sure going to great lengths to show your gratitude," Lisa said. She glanced at the curtain. She could see his body silhouetted against the closet light. He was taking off his trousers.

"Listen, Bobby. I'm sorry. Okay?"

"Okay." Then the curtain moved and he strolled past her bed wearing only his shorts.

As he started down the hall to the bathroom, she called to him, "Bobby? I don't mean to sound prudish, but I wish you'd warn me before you parade by wearing practically nothing."

He turned back. "Next time I'll whistle. Give you a chance to shut your eyes." Then he continued down the hall.

Lisa slid a hand under her pillow. She felt torn in half, as divided as the bedroom. One part of her resented his presence here, while the other part was disturbed by his nearness, sensing that she wanted something more, much more.

"You must think I'm a complete idiot." Amelia sighed. "It's taken me five days to figure out that your new number is actually Lisa

158

Weller's. I must say, I'm a little surprised. I thought she'd hold out longer than this."

"She is holding out." Bobby smiled slightly. "The whole thing is purely practical. We have a curtain between our beds. The whole bit."

Amelia glanced at him sharply. "You know, it's crazy, but I actually believe you. Any other girl, and I wouldn't." She set down her glasses, picked up a fresh pack of Camel's, and tapped on one end on her desk. "Does Ruth know about your new arrangement?"

Bobby gave her a cautious, sidelong glance. "You said you were going to keep out of my personal life."

"Honey, stay in this business long enough and you'll learn not to believe everything an agent tells you." Amelia smiled. She fished out a cigarette and lit it. "I talked to Ruth this week. She's not a very good liar, either. I gather she's been seeing you. She know about your new roommate?"

Bobby sank in his chair. "I told her I lived with a guy named Mel."

"Mel?"

"Said he was twenty-five. Manager at a miniature golf course."

Amelia laughed. "Well, you're nothing if not imaginative."

"Look, I don't feel too hot about it," he said angrily.

"Ever think it might be easier to tell the truth?"

"She'd never believe me—"

"Why not? I did. Ruth certainly should—she's one of the all-time believers in the better side of human nature. Ask her husband."

"Yes, but she doesn't know Lisa the way you do. Hell, she got all worked up just because I was rehearsing with a girl."

Amelia studied him. "I imagine it hasn't been too much fun lying to Lisa, either," she said.

He looked at the floor. "It's been hell."

"You're in some kind of bind, honey."

He gazed at her. "You're really eating this up, aren't you?"

"I certainly am. But we have business to discuss." She put on her glasses and picked up a manuscript. "I have a new play here.

They're casting it tomorrow. Auditions by appointment, and I got you one. The play's called *Company Twelve*, about a guy in the Army who has a small following in his barracks—*twelve* followers. The religious symbolism is a tad obvious. But it's not a bad play, and it's headed for Broadway." She tossed him the script. "You'll read for one of the twelve disciples. It's not a big part, but it's juicy. There's a marvelous scene near the end of Act Two, when a sergeant beats the hell out of you."

Bobby brightened. "Sinatra just got an Oscar for a scene like that."

"Slow down, sugar. You haven't even opened out of town yet. Anyway, I figure you have a good chance at the part. Audition's at ten tomorrow. I suggest you tell Ruth you can't make it tonight and stay home and study."

He found the passage on page thirty-nine. His hands were cold. He knew they could see the script trembling in his grasp. "Is this where you want me to start? 'I got a letter from my mom today . . .' Is that it?"

"Right," the director called from the third row. "Just the last speech, please."

Standing alone on the stage, Bobby shifted from one foot to the other. He held the script down so the director could see his face. He cleared his throat and began.

" 'I got a letter from my mom today. She said the same stuff about how she's doing fine and all that, but I'm worried about her. She's the type who never complains, wouldn't let on if she was sick or something.' "

Bobby shrugged. Stupid—his shoulder went up and down too quickly. He was reading too fast, too. *Slow down. Feel it.*

" 'See, she's old . . . sixty. I guess that isn't so old, really. Just seems like she's aged since my father died.' "

That's right, hold back the tearfulness. Just a little crack in the voice.

" 'I worry about her being alone. Funny how most of your life, your folks fret over you, and then one day you find yourself doing the worrying. I think about her all by herself in that house, with nothing to do, no one to cook for. She loves to cook, my mom.' "

His eyes watered on cue. He was there now. He was feeling everything this kid was supposed to feel. " 'I can still see her in that blue apron, her hands covered with flour. A strand of hair would fall in her face sometimes, and she'd push it back and get flour in her hair. It'd be a couple of hours before she'd notice it, and I'd tease her about it. She's beautiful, my mom. At least, I stink though."

Oh Jesus.

I stink though.

He closed his eyes and swallowed. " 'At least, I think so,' " he muttered, his face burning. He folded the script and peered into the darkness.

There was silence. Then the director said, "Good read, Bob. Most impressive. We'll call Amelia in the morning, letcha know. Thanks a lot."

It was the sort of restaurant where the diners studied what other people were wearing at other tables and ignored the food itself. The tables were covered with heavy white linen and decorated with single red roses in silver bud vases. A pianist tinkled out standards on a baby grand piano in the corner. Bobby wore one of his Alfred Weeks specials. Ruth wore an understated cocktail dress. Bobby was telling her about his audition for *Company Twelve.*

"That's marvelous," she said. "Do you really think you'll get the part?"

"Yeah, I just feel it. Broadway! Me in a Broadway play." He shook his head with a smile. "Christ, I shouldn't get so worked up until I get the word."

"I'm glad you and Mel finally got a phone," she said. "What is the number, anyway?"

"Damned if I remember," Bobby said. "I'll call you. Okay?"

"No, I have to meet Raymond for lunch tomorrow. Listen, I'll just get the number from information."

Bobby nodded grimly. Hoping Lisa would be out, he took a swallow of beer.

"Why, Ruth! What on earth are you doing here?"

They both looked up. A tall, fortyish brunette stood at their table, wearing a poodle cut and a gold lamé A-line dress. Her mouth was fixed in a smile, while her eyes darted from Ruth to Bobby.

"Well, Monica," Ruth managed to say. "How have you been?"

"Fine, darling. I can see I don't have to ask how you are."

"Oh, this is—Bob Pierce. Bob, Monica Del Monte."

He stood. "How do you do?"

"Charmed," she said, glancing over him thoroughly. She turned to Ruth with a tiny smirk. "How's Raymond, dear?"

"He's fine, just fine."

"I heard he was in Los Angeles."

"Yes. He's due back tomorrow. In fact, Bobby and I were just talking about that. Bob's an actor."

"Oh, really?"

"Yes, I was just saying Raymond might be able to give Bobby some career advice."

"Hmmm, from where I sat, it looked as though you two were discussing something far more intimate."

Ruth took a sip of her old-fashioned. "Well, why don't you go back and sit down then, Monica? You can let your imagination run wild."

The woman seemed nonplussed. Then she uttered an artificial laugh. "I simply stopped by to say hello, darling."

"Thank you," Ruth said coolly.

"Well, Eric is waiting for me." She lifted her chin. "Tell Raymond I said hello." She gave Bobby a final, haughty glance and then crossed the restaurant to where a slim, blond, young man sat waiting.

"Let's get out of here," Bobby said, as soon as Monica had turned her back.

"No. I want another drink."

Bobby glanced at the corner. "They're watching us."

"Let them."

"Who's that squirrel she's with?"

"Eric Somebody," Ruth said. "Her protégé. A poet or something."

"Looks like a drip," he said. "What's Monica's story?"

"She's one of those people at the parties Raymond drags me to. A professional busybody—always full of news about Raymond's latest girlfriends." Ruth took another sip of her drink and smiled slightly. "I can't believe my nerve. But you know, I feel proud to be seen with you. She's probably so jealous right now. I mean, you have it all over that Eric."

"Anyway, who cares?" Bobby said. "By the time she spreads the word, your old man will be back and I'll cool it for a while. No one will believe her."

"But it's wrong." She frowned. "I shouldn't just toss you aside every time Ray returns from one of his trips. It makes me feel ashamed, like I'm using you or something. I won't do that to you anymore, Bobby."

He was hanging on her every word. Was this the kiss-off? Finally? A perfect time for it, friendly parting, nobody hurt.

"It's really unfair to you," Ruth continued. "I think we should be able to see each other even when Raymond's in town."

He fumbled for a cigarette, drained his beer. "Th-that's real nice," he said. "But you're a married woman, Ruth. I think it's a terrific idea. But we've got to be careful."

"I wasn't going to send a press release to Walter Winchell," she said dryly. "But enough with the skulking around. I want us to be together." She looked at him for a long moment. "As long as I can feel you want that, too."

"Hi, Bobby."

Ruth stood in the lobby of the Metro Building. Funny, how just the sound of his name made her heart lurch. She smiled to herself. There must be a million Bobbys in this city. And the girl in the phone booth was talking to one of them.

She glanced at her wristwatch. Raymond was a half hour late

for their luncheon appointment. But at least he'd called to tell her that. Maybe it was a good sign. Maybe there was still some way they could begin to patch things up.

As she pressed for the elevator, Ruth glanced back at the phone booth nearby. The glass door was open and the tall, willowy blonde was huddled over the receiver.

"No, it's Mamie Eisenhower," the girl was saying. "Of course, it's Lisa. Well, tell me, did they call yet? Did you get the part?"

The elevator doors opened, but Ruth didn't move.

"Look, don't worry. Maybe you should get hold of Amelia. They might have been in touch with her . . . No, I'm at a pay phone in the Metro Building. Got a tip on a new TV play and wangled an appointment with the Programming Director."

The elevator doors closed. Ruth stayed in the lobby. Slowly, she pivoted so she was directly facing the phone booth. Young, blond, pretty, twenty-two . . .

"Well, I shouldn't tie up the line. They might be trying to get through to you. Before I hang up, are you going to be home for dinner? Or do you have to see those awful people again? . . . All right, they're nice people, wonderful, but they won't leave you alone and you've been miserable all week. I just thought we could celebrate if you got the part, all right? Okay, call you later. Bye-bye."

She hung up. Ruth quickly turned toward the elevator. The doors opened and they got in together. Ruth pressed the button for Raymond's floor, then stared up at the lighted panel over the doors. Finally, she turned to the girl and managed a smile. "Are you an actress?" she asked.

"Yes. I've got an interview right now, and I'm scared stiff!" She laughed nervously. "Um, are you an actress, too?"

Amused, Ruth shook her head. Then the doors opened and Ruth moved aside to let her out first. "Good luck on your interview," she said.

Lisa started down the corridor, then turned to smile back at her. She held up two crossed fingers.

* * *

Seven actresses sat in the waiting room. Lisa's name was last on the list. Lisa stood by the wall with two of the other aspirants. She hated these cattle calls; she could smell the heartbreak in the room, and it never failed to depress her. The other girls didn't look at each other. They checked their posture, hair, and the seams of their stockings. They had all been through this before, and there was nothing to talk about.

A girl came out of the closed office. Staring straight ahead, she walked briskly through the reception area. Lisa knew what it was like. The quick retreat to the nearest exit while some dignity was still intact.

"Sandra Dunn," the secretary called out. "You can go in now."

A plump brunette got to her feet, took a deep breath, and walked through the door. One of the other girls took her chair.

A minute later, the plump girl was back out, and a second later she was gone. One by one, the other six entered the office and marched back out. As Lisa waited, her nerves began to tingle and her heart began to sink.

"Lisa Weller? Go on in, please."

She stood, nodded like an idiot, and walked toward the door.

The lion's den was a huge, paneled office with a two-corner view of the Manhattan skyline. The hot seat was a high-backed, green leather chair positioned in front of a large mahogany desk.

The man seated behind it was imposingly handsome, Lisa thought. Probably in his mid-fifties, with a full head of silver hair and a cultivated tan. The blue eyes had squinted in the sun of too many beaches, stayed open on too many late nights in casinos and hotel rooms. There was a hardness to his features, except for the jawline, which had softened slightly with age. He didn't stand, but studied Lisa as she walked across the carpet.

"Sit down, Miss Weller."

She sat on the green leather throne, crossed her legs, and pulled her skirt over her knees.

"Do you know what we're casting?"

"No, I don't."

"This part calls for a very spirited girl. An independent and

165

spirited girl, who is nonetheless shy when it comes to men. Almost a young spinster. I have interviewed twenty-nine girls this morning. You are the first attractive woman to walk in the door all morning, Miss Weller. Apparently someone in the casting office feels that anyone who lacks a sex life must be a dog."

"Thank you," she said politely, with a hint of coolness.

"Have you read *The Eternal Soul?*"

"Yes."

"What did you think of the book? Besides the fact that it sold a million copies."

Lisa had decided, while waiting in the outside room, that she wouldn't kowtow to the man responsible for humiliating all those actresses in one morning. "Well, Mr. Bartlett," she said. "I thought it was corny, melodramatic, and preachy."

His eyes narrowed. "Well, we plan to do a television play based on it. Perhaps you might suggest how our writers could improve on this best-seller, Miss Weller."

Lisa didn't look away. "I'd give the mother more depth. She was too bland and weak in the book. The father was too self-righteous. I'd make him less of a windbag. In fact, the only character I really liked was their daughter Nellie."

Raymond Bartlett's mouth twitched. "And how would you describe her?"

Trying to suppress a smile, Lisa gazed steadily back. "I'd say she was a very independent, spirited girl who was nonetheless shy when it came to men. Something of a young spinster, as a matter of fact."

He chuckled and leaned forward. "Very nice, Miss Weller. Now, we've got Thomas Mitchell interested in the part of the windbag father, and Mary Astor or Helen Hayes for the bland mother. Do you object to third billing?"

She faltered. "Third . . . billing?"

"The part of Nellie Sherwood. It's yours, sweetheart." He opened a drawer in his desk and rummaged through some papers. "We'll contact your agent when we're ready to start rehearsals. Probably the middle of next week. Right now, I have a luncheon engagement."

"Oh, thank you, Mr. Bartlett." She forced herself not to gush and stood up.

He was holding out his hand, and Lisa reached forward to shake it eagerly. When she stepped away, she realized he had handed her something. She looked down and saw it was a key.

"What's this?" she asked.

He'd put his hands in his pockets and was jingling his change. She stared at the key again and saw that it was a room key from one of the big Park Avenue hotels.

"I should be finished with lunch by one-thirty. I'll be there around two at the latest."

Lisa drew in a quick breath. "Well, unless you want me to clean the room for you, I don't quite understand."

"I think you do." His voice had sharpened. "You want the part, don't you?"

"Just the one on television, Mr. Bartlett," Lisa said coldly, "and I don't even want that one that badly." She tossed the key back on his desk. "Before I go, I would like to explain that those thirty women you shot down this morning were actresses, not 'dogs.' Professionals looking for work, not exhibiting themselves for your personal amusement. Mr. Bartlett, I wouldn't wait in your hotel room if you wanted me for the lead in *Joan of Arc.* So I suggest you take that key to Room Eight-twelve at the Astor and screw yourself."

She'd assumed the exit line would take her through the door, but before she reached the knob, she could hear him laughing. She turned and saw him still standing beside his desk, his large, manicured hands applauding ironically.

"Bravo, Miss Weller. Very good."

She stared at him.

"Sit down for a minute," he said.

"No, thank you."

"Come on, Miss Weller. Cut the crap and sit down. I want to say something."

She stood stonily, waiting.

"You know what you've got? You've got spunk." Then his grin faded. "And you know what else? I detest spunk."

She stared at him, dumbfounded.

"That's why I can't stand that Nellie Sherwood, why it's taken me so long to cast her. She's lousy with spunk. But you're two of a kind, Miss Weller. Spirited and spunky, and about as sexually frustrated as a woman can get. The part's still yours, Miss Weller." She started to speak, but he cut her off. "I wasn't exactly thrilled by your little speech just now. And if you're anything less than splendid in rehearsal, Miss Weller, you won't know what hit you. You don't do me any favors, don't expect any. That's all, Miss Weller."

She pulled herself up, trying to remember a haughty line from a Joan Crawford movie to exit on. "Good day, Mr.—"

"Don't push your luck, honey," he said. "Out. Now."

Lisa nodded feebly and left. When she got out to the reception area, she saw the woman from the elevator chatting with the secretary. Lisa managed a polite smile.

"How did your interview go?" the woman asked.

"Well, I got the job," she said uncertainly.

"Congratulations."

"Thanks," Lisa said. Even though she had gotten the part, she walked quickly toward the exit. She wanted to be sure whatever dignity she had left was still intact.

Ruth stared after her. The phone rang, and while the secretary was distracted, she slipped off one of her earrings, deposited the other in her purse, and waited. When the secretary was off the phone, Ruth held up the earring.

"Jane, I think the girl who just left lost this. I found it by the door."

"My, and it looks expensive, too."

"I have nothing planned after lunch," Ruth went on. "Listen, give me her address and I'll drop it off on my way home." She watched as Jane handed her an envelope for the earring and then scribbled out the Greenwich Village address for one Lisa Weller.

At Sardi's, Raymond spotted a couple of business acquaintances and invited them to join him and Ruth. Still Ruth welcomed the chance to sit back and smile vacuously, while she thought about Bobby and that girl.

In the cab back to the office, she was very understanding. "It doesn't matter," she told Raymond, who had actually apologized. "I'll have you all to myself at dinner." She paused. "Won't I?"

"Of course, dear." He gave her money for the fare and, with a perfunctory kiss, got out of the cab at the Metro Building.

As the taxi pulled away, Ruth took out the piece of paper and gave the driver the Greenwich Village address.

Standing in front of the brownstone, all the speeches she'd rehearsed were forgotten. The visit seemed as pointless as all those phone calls. Only this time, she prayed he wouldn't be there. Maybe it was all a mistake, she thought—another pretty blonde phoning another actor named Bobby.

But she knew it was him. The girl had mentioned Amelia, the part in a play, and those "awful people" who wouldn't leave him alone. So why was she bothering him now? She bit her lip and glanced up at the building. She knew the answer. Still she had to see him one more time.

She climbed the steps to the front door. Any vestige of optimism faded when she stared at the names by the third bell: WELLER/PIERCE—Apt. C. Taking a deep breath, she pressed the buzzer. Waiting, she studied her reflection in the front door glass. When she'd left to meet Raymond, she had felt rather pretty, but now the prettiness was gone, and she just felt old.

And then Bobby's face merged with hers through the glass. He seemed happy to see her, but then his features darkened. Pausing, he seemed to arrange a smile on his face, then flung open the door with enthusiasm. "Ruth! God, what a surprise!"

Her eyes were downcast. "Hello, Bobby."

"You want to go get some coffee or something? Were you just passing by or—"

"No," she said. "I only stopped to . . ." She reached in her purse, touched the earring, and then caught herself. "Your friend lost—Oh, God. What am I doing? Could I please come in? I think

I'm going to make a scene and I don't want to do it on your doorstep."

He stared at her.

"Bobby, your roommate isn't in, is she?" Ruth asked quietly.

He held the door open. "Come on in. It's downstairs."

The only sounds in the stairwell were the echoes of their footsteps. When they reached the apartment, she saw the door half open. She looked inside at all the quaint feminine touches. "It's very nice," she murmured, stepping into the main room.

"Listen, Ruth. Before you say anything, I want you to see this." He touched her arm. She didn't shake it off, so he gingerly led her down the hall to the bedroom.

"It's very nice," she repeated.

"The curtain," he said. "See? I sleep on the other side. We don't—"

"That's a pretty pattern. Did she pick it out?" Ruth stared at him for a moment, then broke from his grip and retreated back to the main room.

"Ruth, please, understand—"

"I understand, Bobby. You've been *miserable* all week, having to see those *awful people* who won't leave you alone." She looked at him with quiet disappointment, her eyes red. "I heard your roommate on the phone this morning—at the Metro Building. I kept hoping it was another *Bobby* she was talking to, but I heard that and I knew. I only wish I'd known earlier just how miserable I've made you. I'm sorry."

"Please, Ruth. That's not true. I can explain—"

"Don't. I've been forcing you to lie to me all this time. I don't want to make you lie to me now. I'm sorry."

Her head down, she hurried for the door, then stopped. She wanted to scream, do something to release the pent-up anger and humiliation. "*Goddamn it!*" In one strangely satisfying motion, she swung her purse against the wall. The strap broke and the contents flew around the room. Her lipstick, compact, and housekeys tumbled across the carpet.

She turned to him. "Damn you! Why should I feel guilty for all this? You're the liar! How many times have I said you didn't have to see me if you didn't want to? How many? And how many times did you lie?"

"Ruth, you've got it all wrong about Lisa."

"That's not the point! God, don't you realize? Except for my husband, you're the only other one, Bobby. And what kept it from being wrong was thinking you liked me, that you actually wanted to be with me, that you cared."

"I do like you, Ruth."

She got down on her knees and collected the contents of her purse. "Oh, don't lie to me anymore," she hissed. "I'm sick of it. Between you and my husband, that's all I hear. I've been lying to myself all this time, too, thinking you'd want me. Isn't that a laugh, Bobby? What the hell would you want with me?"

"I'm sorry, Ruth. Please . . ."

Then the front door opened and Lisa walked in carrying a grocery bag, her view of the room obscured by a bottle of wine. "Bobby, give me a hand. I told you we were going to celebrate toni—"

Then she saw them and fell silent. Bobby and—was it the lady from the elevator, the nice woman she'd seen in Bartlett's office this morning? She knelt on the floor and shoved things into her purse. She looked as though she'd been crying, and Bobby seemed as if he was just about to. The strangest part of all was that they acted as if she were the one who didn't belong there. "Hi," Lisa said weakly. "Congratulations on the part."

Ruth got to her feet and looked over at Bobby. "So you got it," she said. "I hope it was worth all the heartache I put you through." Then she hurried toward the door. "Excuse me," she muttered to Lisa. "I'm sorry."

"Ruth, wait!" Bobby cried. He started after her, but stopped in the doorway. He and Lisa stood there, listening to Ruth's retreating steps, the sound of the door upstairs slamming shut. Bobby took a deep breath and counted—out loud—to ten.

"What are you doing?" Lisa asked, hesitant.

". . . Nine, ten." He turned and closed the door. "I was counting. It's supposed to make you calm."

"Can I ask what happened?"

With an unreadable look, he took the bag out of her arms and carried it into the kitchen. She followed him, almost on tiptoe. He was putting the wine in the refrigerator as she paused at the door. His back was to her. "Bobby, what happened?"

"What happened?" He swiveled around, his face red. "What happened? Your roommate is a fuck-up, a royal shit-heel, that's what happened!"

He sank down at the table. She leaned toward him and touched his hand. "Oh, no, Bobby. Don't tell me . . . they changed their minds. They gave the part to someone else."

He looked at her and sighed. "No, I got the goddamn part. She probably could have it taken away from me, but she'd never do that. She's too nice."

"Who? The lady who was just here?"

He nodded grimly. "She was the only one who ever really tried to help me. And I hurt her."

She squeezed his hand. "Hurt her? How?"

He drew his hand away and glanced down at the table.

"Bobby, who is she? What was she doing here? Why was she at Metro this morning?"

"She was meeting her husband," he said finally. "He's Raymond Bartlett, the Programming Director."

"Bartlett? Why . . . he interviewed me this morning. He gave me the part in the play they're doing. But what was his wife doing here?"

Bobby's eyes narrowed. "Did he make a pass at you?"

She looked astonished "How did you know?"

"What did you do?"

"I told him to go screw himself."

"And you still got the part?"

"Yes, Bobby, I did. Now will you please tell me what's going on?"

172

Rubbing his forehead, he sighed. "You know those people I've been seeing? Those friends of my uncle?"

She nodded.

"I was seeing Mrs. Bartlett."

She blinked. "What for?"

"Bartlett's been out of town all week. He only came back this morning."

"I still don't understand—" Then Lisa's face suddenly filled with concern. "Oh, Bobby, I'm so sorry! She heard me talking to you on the phone today. It's all my fault! She was helping you, and I ruined it—"

"No!" He drew away from her. "You don't understand! I was sleeping with her."

There was a shocked silence. Lisa gazed at him and a tiny laugh escaped her. "You're joking."

He drew in a sharp breath and closed his eyes. "Ruth helped me out," he said. "She got Amelia to sign me. So I slept with her."

"But she must be at least forty!"

He gave Lisa a sad smile. "Ruth would be pleased to hear that. She turned fifty last month."

"Well, from what I saw of her, she didn't seem like the type that would fool around."

"What about me?" he asked. "Aren't you disappointed?"

"Why?" She laughed. "You—I always knew you were the type. The minute I set eyes on you, I knew you'd been around. I just didn't realize how much. Fifty-year-old ladies, huh?"

"It was different with Ruth. I owed her."

"*Owed* her? For what? For calling Amelia? What did she do, break her arm picking up the telephone?"

"You don't understand."

"I'm not as dumb as you think," Lisa said pointedly. "I know all about the casting couch game. You don't have to play to know the rules. I'm just surprised you'd play for such tiny stakes."

Bewildered, he stared at her. Why wasn't she disappointed in him? Didn't she like him enough to be hurt or mad or just a little disillusioned? The way she acted, it was as if she didn't care.

Lisa smiled wistfully. "Well, I'd like to say I'm sorry you feel so bad about all this, but actually I'm relieved. Maybe you have a conscience after all."

"Hey, if you think I *liked* putting out for all my so-called benefactors, you're nuts. Ruth was . . . different."

But Lisa ignored his defense of Ruth. She was staring at him with amazement. "*All* your so-called benefactors? What on earth . . . You mean, there have been a lot of women?"

"Not just women," he whispered.

The look he'd almost wanted to see was now on her face. It was the punishment, he thought, for what he'd done to Ruth, what he'd been doing ever since that day, years before, when he'd been Mrs. Swift's "slave."

He heaved a sigh and began to tell Lisa everything. All the bodies, the lies, the whoring. Her eyes never left his face. She was expressionless and frozen as he talked about Mrs. Swift and Alfred Weeks and cruising the strip in Los Angeles. As he spoke, Bobby's face relaxed under the pain and his voice grew softer.

"I stayed with this one woman for a week while her husband was gone. Her name was Andria, something like that. Said she knew a guy who could get me on Milton Berle. God, she was terrible, but I managed to believe her. Somehow, I always do. She used to—"

"Shut up."

"I'm sorry," he said, his face twisted. "The reason I'm telling you this is because I hated lying to you all this time. The same way I hated lying to Ruth, only worse, because I didn't *love her.*"

"Shut up!" She pulled away from the table. "God, Bobby, what do you want me to say? What in hell do you expect me to do?" Her eyes brimmed with tears. She stood in the middle of the kitchen staring at him.

"Look, I'll split. Find a hotel tonight and get my stuff in the morning. You—"

She shook her head and fled. Bobby started after her, but the front door had slammed by the time he reached the kitchen door. Head bowed, he stood for a long while. Then, slowly, he leaned over and picked something off the floor—a small, shiny object. He turned it over in his hand. It was an earring.

Dear Lisa,

All I can say is I'm sorry. I shouldn't have told you so much without any warning. I don't blame you for being disgusted. I've been pretty disgusted with myself for a long time. I just couldn't deceive you anymore. Lisa, I love you. I don't expect . . .

"Shit," he growled. He threw down the pencil and tore up the letter. It landed in the garbage with his four previous attempts. Gripping the pencil, he tried again.

Dear Lisa,

I've decided you deserve a break from yours truly for a while. So I'm splitting. I'll call you about the Actors Studio thing. Thanks for listening. I know you were pretty shocked, and I'm sorry.

He hesitated for a moment, then scribbled *Love, Bobby*.

Leaving the note on the table, he went in the bedroom to pack his things. He paused at the foot of her bed and stared at the flower pattern of her bedspread. A pang of longing and regret filled him as he looked around the room at her belongings.

When the phone rang, he stood still, letting it ring a few times before returning to the kitchen to answer it. "Hello?"

"It's me," Lisa said.

"Where are you?"

"In a phone booth in that park near the Fifty-ninth Street Bridge."

"What are you doing way out there?"

"I've just been walking. I got here and suddenly I had this feeling I'd come home to find you gone, with some note saying I shouldn't try to find you."

Still holding the receiver to his ear, he edged over to the table and crumpled the letter. "No, I was just sitting here," he said. "Are you . . . coming home?"

"Yes." She uttered a nervous laugh. "Listen, you want to meet me here instead? The water's so pretty. We could go get something to eat . . ."

"I'll be there," he said anxiously. "Fifteen minutes, okay?"

Lisa waited on a park bench. She stared out at the bridge, a lonely steel-and-mortar titan looming over the indigo water. Slivers of light danced across its rippled surface. She looked up at the sky. The stars were so bright, they seemed fake, like some Hollywood backdrop.

Actually, she felt like a character out of the movies herself, playing a sad, romantic scene on a deserted soundstage. She remembered the night so long ago, when she'd found out who John Rogan really was. She'd run away then, too. And she'd met that sad, ugly man in the playground. She remembered something he'd said, about people never being able to run away from their problems. He was right, she thought. All her walking and thinking hadn't solved a thing.

There was something else he'd said, about being scared to take risks, wanting things "safe." Lisa had thought herself very courageous, going off alone to New York, pursuing a pie-in-the-sky dream. But for all her nerve, she was no better off than that sweet, pathetic man in the park. She always played it "safe" with men. No involvement, no risks, no love.

But it was happening anyway. She loved Bobby.

The realization left her scared and miserable. She'd always been afraid that she'd give herself to a man who would only use her and desert her—as John Rogan had done to her mother. She didn't want that hurt and humiliation.

Bobby wasn't just her friend. If a mere friend had told her what Bobby had just revealed about himself, she wouldn't be so torn up inside, so miserable. She wouldn't feel the huge disappointment she felt now. Bobby was her John Rogan.

176

No, she thought resolutely, he wasn't like that. Bobby was nice. He wouldn't have told her all those horrible things about his past if he hadn't had a conscience, if he wasn't honest, good-hearted. And he'd said—she'd heard him say it right before she'd run out of the apartment—he'd said he *loved* her.

"Oh, what am I going to do?" she asked out loud. She slumped lower on the park bench. "I can't ask him to move. I don't want him to move. I want to be near him. I just won't tell him how I feel. We've got the curtain in the bedroom and he'll be going out of town with the play in a few weeks. You can hold out till then. Out of sight, out of mind. Oh, Lisa Weller, you chicken! Scared little twirp, always running away from love. When are you ever going to—"

Oh, God, no. There was a man in the park. He had probably heard her talking to herself. He was giving her a funny look. He wore a gray suit and carried a briefcase. He strolled down the walk, along the railing that overlooked the river. He was tall, slightly overweight, and his sandy hair was waved high on his forehead. He looked friendly enough, but he was still eyeing her. Lisa gave him a curt smile as he approached the bench.

"Excuse me," he said, with a slight grin. "I know you from somewhere, don't I? Did we go to school together?"

"Not unless you went to Northwestern in Evanston, Illinois."

He chuckled. "Oh, this isn't a pass, if that's what you think. I know you from somewhere." Then he snapped his fingers. "I know! 'Philco Playhouse', right? A couple of weeks ago, you were on TV. Sure. You're an actress, right?"

Lisa smiled. "It was a pretty small part. I can't believe you remember."

"Sure, I do. You were the girl in the bar. My wife and I were watching, and I said to her, 'Look, honey. That gal's got a nose like yours and she's on TV.' See, my wife thinks her nose is ugly—"

Lisa's smile tightened.

The man noticed. "Hey, listen, I didn't mean . . . Well, we thought you did a terrific job on the show. We even looked for you in the end credits. Mona Weller, right?"

"You're very close." She smiled. "It's *Lisa* Weller."

"Right," the man said. "Hey, mind if I get your autograph?" He set down his briefcase and pulled out a pad and pen. Lisa signed it for him. This was the first time someone had wanted her own autograph and not Brenda Dare's.

"Can I have yours, too?" she asked. "You're my very first fan."

He laughed. "Name's Scott Prewett."

"Pleased to—"

She heard someone clear his throat. She looked up and saw Bobby standing behind her. He gave the man an annoyed look.

"Oh, hi," she said. "Bobby, this is Mr. Prewett. He spotted me from that 'Philco Playhouse' bit."

"Are you anybody?" the man asked, hesitating before putting away the notepad.

"What?" Bobby's jaw tightened.

"He was a juvenile delinquent on 'The U. S. Steel Hour' last week," Lisa said quickly. "And he's done dozens of commercials. This is Robert Pierce. He's due for a part on Broadway soon."

"Hey, great." Prewett handed Bobby the pad and pen.

"What's this?"

Lisa coughed. "Bobby, he wants your autograph."

He blinked at the man. "Oh, yeah. Sure." He scribbled his name and returned the pad to Prewett.

The man glanced at the paper with satisfaction. "Well, thanks a lot. Good luck in your careers." With a wave, he strutted off.

Bobby sat down beside Lisa. "Well, whaddaya know," he murmured, pleased. Lisa smiled back, but the happiness in her eyes waned in the silence and she looked out at the bridge.

Bobby swallowed. "You haven't said anything about what I told you tonight."

"What do you want me to say?"

He shrugged. "I don't know."

"I still like you, Bobby," she said quietly. "After everything you told me, I still think you're a nice guy. Sometimes I don't think you know that. You're a good actor, too. I think the things

178

you—told me about just prove you don't believe in yourself
. . . the way I believe in you."

"You're sore at me, aren't you?" he whispered. "For being such a disappointment."

She smiled. "No, I'm not mad at you."

He started to lean toward her, a hesitant look on his face. Lisa got up and moved over to the railing. Bobby followed her. "It's so pretty," she said, gazing at the river. "Can't see how dirty it is at night. And look at all those stars."

He brushed her arm. "Think we'll ever be famous?"

"Oh, sure." She laughed weakly. "The brightest stars in the galaxy."

He looked at the pinpoints of light in the dark, cloudless sky. "Some of those stars up there don't even exist anymore. I read that somewhere. We can still see them, because it takes so long for the light to reach earth. The light keeps shining even after they're gone. Do you believe that's true, Lisa?"

"Yes, I do."

"Stars and movie stars." He smiled. "I guess being a famous actor or actress is the same way. Part of you stays alive even after you're gone. The light keeps shining. God, I hope we both make it, Lisa. More than anything."

EIGHT

Bobby coughed. The pain in his abdomen subsided, and he looked down at the toilet bowl. He grabbed for the handle before he could think too hard and start heaving again. The sound of flushing struck him as warped applause. He wiped his mouth and staggered out of the cubicle.

Lisa pounded on the men's room door. "Bobby? Everything okay in there? They'll be ready for us soon."

"Terrific," he called, trying to sound hearty. At the sink, he splashed cold water on his face and scooped some water from the faucet into his mouth. He checked his reflection: his face was chalk white. During the short trip to the bathroom, his tan had somehow faded.

Stop being so nervous, he told his reflection sternly. After all, they'd passed the preliminary audition two weeks before. They were good. The judges were impressed, all five of them. But he'd never heard of any of them.

He'd heard the final audition could be reviewed by Cheryl Crawford, Lee Strasberg, and Elia Kazan—the Holy Trinity of the Actors Studio. In ten minutes, they'd decide if Robert Pierce and Lisa Weller were the next Marlon Brando and Eva Marie Saint.

This was it, after two months of rehearsing, hoping, and making silly bets with himself: *If you make it across the street before the Don't Walk sign comes on, Lisa and you will get accepted . . .*

He held his breath for a moment. Everything would be all right. Even if they failed the audition, things were going okay. He was rehearsing for *Company Twelve*, and Lisa's play was scheduled to air in three weeks. If they got passed over for the Studio, it wouldn't be all that devastating. There was always next year. But he wasn't sure how he'd be able to face Lisa if he blew it for her. More than just his career was riding on this audition.

"Bobby?" she called again. "Come on! We're on in five minutes. Pull yourself together."

He let out his breath and went out to the corridor. Lisa was leaning against the wall. She was wearing a modest summer dress for her part as the pregnant college girl. She straightened when she saw him. "Bobby, you look terrible."

"Thanks." He slouched next to her. "You look good."

"I've got Kleenex under my armpits, I'm sweating so badly."

"You look cool as a cuke."

"We should think of this as just another audition. We'll do fine. Brando and Clift were probably just as nervous when they auditioned here."

"Yeah?" He felt a little better, but still queasy. "Yeah, maybe they puked in the same toilet I did."

"Where's the prop?" she asked suddenly. "Your popcorn?" It was their only prop; he'd saved the box from the Bijou. She'd filled it with a batch of popcorn for them to nibble on during the scene.

"Oh, shit!" He ducked back in the men's room and, a moment later, returned with the box.

Lisa eyed it warily. Bobby laughed. "Don't worry. It was on the sink."

Suddenly, the stage door across the hall opened. Two people came out. Bobby and Lisa gaped at their competitors. The woman, a heavily made-up brunette, was wearing only the bottom half of a bikini; the man, just a jockstrap. Mumbling to each other, the couple walked casually down the corridor to where their robes hung from a rack.

"Can you believe that?" Bobby whispered. Lisa simply shook her head.

"Lisa Weller? Robert Pierce?" A middle-aged woman with a clipboard that seemed attached to her arm, called their names from the stage door.

They started and then walked over to her.

"You're next," she said. "All you need is two folding chairs, is that right?"

"Yes," Lisa said in a small voice. She squeezed Bobby's arm. Just then the previous couple walked past, this time clothed. Lisa stared after them. The woman chuckled.

"We get a few like that every year. They try to show how free and uninhibited they are. It rarely works." She held the stage door open with her hip. "Well, good luck, you two."

They went up a short flight of steps to the stage. "It's *bad luck* to say that," Bobby whispered, out of the woman's earshot.

"Shut up!" Lisa hissed.

The prop man was setting up two folding chairs on the empty stage. The stage itself was dusty and black. It looked like the perfect site for an execution.

Lisa turned and quickly kissed Bobby on the corner of the mouth. "We'll be fine," she whispered. "We'll be just fine."

The following Friday, Bobby returned from rehearsal to find Lisa sitting in the middle of the living-room sofa. She sat perfectly still, back straight, with hands folded between her knees. An envelope lay on the coffee table in front of her. She slowly turned to look at Bobby. "It came."

He shut the door and went over to the sofa. "What did they say?"

"I haven't opened it yet. I'm too scared. I was waiting for you."

Bobby picked up the envelope. He stared at the return address. The Actors Studio. "Listen," he said, "whatever they say, we'll still—"

"Oh, for God's sakes, open it," she said.

He sat down next to her and ripped open the envelope. Lisa clutched his knee. Then they read the letter together in silence.

*After careful consideration of your application to the Actors
Studio, the judges express their regret that your audition
failed to elicit their full enthusiasm.*

*While capably performed, the material seemed overly
complex for the treatment it received. The pantomime
conveying the restriction of the car was a distraction. The
actress appeared too intelligent, out-of-keeping with the
character of the pregnant girl; the actor's delivery was too
sensitive for the part of the heartless boyfriend. Motivation
here may have been misconceived.*

*You are encouraged to audition again next year. A simpler
scene, more in tune with your own personalities, was one of
the suggestions from our judges.*

Thank you for considering the Actors Studio . . .

"Well," Lisa said after a moment. "Now we know."

"It's my fault." Bobby tossed the letter back on the table. "That
business with the popcorn. Picking it out of my teeth while you
were talking. I blew it for both of us."

"No, they loved it. It was right for your character. It's *my* fault
—I was too ambitious, trying to write my own scene." Her lip
quivered. "Damn! I wanted so much for us to make it."

Slowly, Bobby put his arms around her. She pressed her face
against his shoulder. He felt her tears dampen his shirtcollar. "I'm
sorry, Bobby," he heard her say in a muffled voice. "I'm so sorry."

"It's no one's fault," he said. He was barely able to get the
words past the ache in his throat. His only solace came in holding
her, comforting her. They cried in each others' arms. Gently, he
kissed the top of her head. Cupping a hand under her chin, he
lifted her face and kissed her eyes. His mouth slid down the path
of Lisa's tears, and his lips parted against hers.

She desperately tightened her hold, pulling him with her as she
sank across the length of the couch. Their bodies entwined. He
pressed his face against hers, feeling the wetness of her tears.
Shuddering, he kissed the side of her neck, and Lisa's arms cradled him. His hand found her breast. Lisa drew in a breath.
Awkwardly, she lifted his hand.

"Please, Bobby," she said.

He sat up and rubbed his eyes. "I'm sorry."

"Forget it." She sat up, too. "I'm sorry to be such a tease. It's just . . ." Her voice trailed off. She turned away and unsteadily got to her feet.

"I love you," he whispered. But she was already walking into the bedroom.

Lying on the bed, she fought the urge to run back and lie on the couch next to him, to feel his arms around her and have him remove her sorrow with his touch. She *wanted* him to touch her breasts and to feel his beautiful mouth on hers, feel him inside her. She buried her face in the pillow.

Then she heard him come in the room and sit down on the bed. His hand lingered on her back for a moment. "Can I stay here for a few more weeks? The show's going out of town soon, and you'll have the place to yourself, but I'll still pay."

She numbly looked at him. "Why should you move?"

He glanced down at the floor. "I figured, after the audition, and not making it and everything, you'd—"

"I don't blame you, Bobby." She sighed. "It was the scene that was a mistake, not you. You were wonderful."

"What I mean is, you won't need me around here for rehearsals anymore."

Lisa's eyes widened. "Oh no, Bobby. Don't think so little of yourself," she said softly. "Or of me. I *want* you to stay. I—love you."

He stared at her. With a trembling hand, he brushed a wisp of the blond hair away from her face. Closing her eyes, she took his hand in hers and kissed his palm.

"Lisa, I—"

Looking into his questioning blue eyes, she nodded.

Moving uncertainly, he began to unbutton his shirt. Then he kicked off his shoes. His pants came off quickly, without any slow, teasing charade. This wasn't a performance. It was just what it was—his desire to give himself to her.

Silent, not daring to look at him, Lisa climbed off the bed. She

184

pulled the sweater over her head and stepped out of her skirt. Then she knelt down and took off each of his socks as he sat on the bed. Her hands slid up the backs of his legs, and she rested her head against his thigh.

His fingers descended onto her soft hair. He gazed down at her, his dream becoming reality. Lisa's blond hair spilled over the white of his undershorts, her hand lovingly caressed him behind the knee, and her tears wet his skin.

For a moment, she drew away to remove her slip. As she raised her arms, he buried his face between the warm softness of her small breasts. His fingers traced the lines of her ribs, and she shivered. She unhooked her bra, shyly lowering the straps and letting it fall to the floor. Hungrily, he began to kiss the small white breasts, the rose tips hardening as his tongue flicked over one nipple, then the other.

Lisa was kissing the top of his head. Her tears fell into his dark hair. She closed her eyes and held him, feeling the fear subside. Her body was obedient as he pulled her onto the bed and finished undressing her. Basking in her nakedness, he kissed her stomach, his fingers gliding down the ivory silk of her hip to the soft tangle of hair. She drew in a breath and arched her back as his fingertip found the moist slit.

Then he rose from the bed and pulled off his shorts. Lisa averted her eyes at the sight of his erection. "It'll be all right," he whispered, with a sheepish smile. Gently, he lay down beside her. Her trembling arms slid around his neck, and they kissed.

She wanted to pause and think, So this is it, but there seemed to be no time or need to think. It was enough to feel the contour of his taut, smooth body against hers, the warmth and movement covering her. Lisa's hands grasped his heavy shoulders, as he lifted himself over her and eased open her legs with his knee.

And then he was guiding himself into her. Lisa let out a gasp of pain. Immediately, he pulled back.

"I'm sorry. Am I hurting you?"

"No, Bobby. It's all right," she said, with a pale smile. She pushed against him with her pelvis. He kissed her, stroking the blond hair that spilled against the pillow. Again, more slowly, he moved into her. Lisa's hands roamed down his spine's curve to his tight buttocks. Her legs twined automatically around his.

It still hurt, she thought, but the pain was muted by a growing awareness of their bodies being joined, of hers being filled by him. He began to move within her, slowly at first, and then more rapidly. She felt herself growing more wet inside, the pain easing. They tumbled against each other mutely, almost savagely. Now that it was happening, she wanted it to go on forever, to feel him over her, inside her, pressing his face against hers, his warm breath swirling in her ear.

And then something was happening. She gripped his shoulders and let out a soft, grateful cry. His hands came down and lifted her as he drove himself deeper into her. He threw his head back, and she felt something melt inside her. His aching desire was released in shuddering spasms. Then he fell against her, panting.

They lay exhausted, still locked together in a sweet inertia, listening to their own breathing. She nestled her face against his neck. She felt as if she'd been washed ashore by a warm, sensuous current. Slowly, her awareness returned. She could feel the heaviness of him, but she didn't want to move. She only wanted to luxuriate in the tenderness she felt inside.

With regret, she finally shifted under his weight. He pushed up on his arms and rolled over beside her. "I'm sorry. I'm crushing you."

She just smiled. They touched and kissed each other, lips and fingers caressing warm, moist skin. They admired each other's nakedness. "You've got a beautiful body, Bobby. I guess I can tell you that now. I've always admired it. You've got an ideal body, like one of those Greek statues."

He chuckled shyly. "C'mon, give me a break." He curled up beside her in a near-fetal position. His head rested by her shoulder. He could smell her hair. He stared at her white body, the small round breasts, as if he were trying to memorize them. He began to trace circles around the bud of her nipple. He watched the slope of her rib cage and the firm stomach rising and falling as her breathing steadied itself. "Did I hurt you?" he asked.

She could feel the throbbing cavity he'd left. It burned. "Not too much." She smiled faintly. "Anything that good has to require a little pain." Lisa smoothed back a lock of hair that fell over his forehead. "Don't worry, Bobby."

He kissed the soft, delicate flesh where her arm met her shoulder. "The reason I ask is because I heard that it hurts a woman the first time. I've never been with anyone their first time. In fact, I've never been with anyone I loved, not until you."

Lisa was surprised at her own calmness. Bobby seemed worried about having "corrupted" her, but she assured him that she didn't hate herself or him. There was no guilt, no regret, no shame.

It sank in around midnight. They had taken no precautions. They had risked everything for pleasure. Surely, Lisa thought, remembering her mother, the chances of getting away with it were slim. She sat curled up on the sofa, gazing stonily at her script for "The Eternal Soul." But her heart felt clenched like a fist inside her, tight with fear. How could she have been so careless?

Then Bobby came into the room, his face washed, his shirt unbuttoned. Lisa kept her eyes on the script. He came over to the couch and bent down to kiss the top of her head. "You coming to bed?"

She forced a smile. "Soon."

Bobby sat down. "Which bed do you want me to sleep in?"

Lisa set her script aside. She looked up at the striped shadows where the streetlight fell through the barred windows.

"Mine, I guess," he said, sounding disappointed.

Lisa took his hand. "Bobby," she said carefully, "I love you. What happened today was—wonderful. But I can't afford another chance. Believe me, I want to sleep with you, every night, for that matter, but . . ." Her voice trailed off. "I guess I got lost in the moment. I never wanted to fall in love with you. I guess that's why. I wasn't thinking."

His eyes had frosted over. "So you don't want it to happen again. Is that it?"

Lisa closed her eyes. "Bobby, I'm going to tell you something I haven't told anyone." She opened her eyes and studied him. "Do you remember that fan letter I got so upset about? That first time you were here?"

"The crank who said you were his daughter? I remember."

"Bobby, that letter *was* from my father—my biological father. The wonderful man married to my mother . . . he married her when she was pregnant by this—other man. Bobby, I won't let that happen to me. I might not be as lucky as my mother was."

Then she began to tell him about the time "Uncle Johnny" had come to stay. "I still find it hard to forgive my mother for that," she said. "And I don't want a child of mine feeling bitter about some 'lost moment' I once had. Even if it was beautiful, with someone I loved."

That night, Bobby slept on his own side of the curtain. He lay still, staring at the expanse of burlap. He hadn't told her, but he too was afraid. Love and dependence—those were things he'd learned early not to trust. They were dangerous because they were so easily taken away.

But in the ten days before *Company Twelve* went out of town, they tried to make compromises. Sometimes they slept together, trying to use condoms, but Lisa claimed they hurt. Bobby didn't like them, either. So they tried abstinence, but that was even worse. In their own ways, they were both looking forward to the impending separation.

Two nights before the Philadelphia opening of *Company Twelve,* dress rehearsal wrapped up early. Bobby returned to his hotel in time to catch Lisa's appearance in "The Eternal Soul."

For the first ten minutes, he sat hunched on the edge of his bed. Lisa looked beautiful, but he watched in fear that she'd muff a line or miss a cue during the live telecast.

She'd said her role was important, but Bobby hadn't realized that the whole play revolved around it. Two big-name stars were

188

playing the roles of her parents, but Lisa was the star. And she was good—so good that he stopped worrying after the first commercial. By the second break, he'd forgotten he was watching his roommate. She had become a farm girl named Nellie Sherwood. Lisa Weller had vanished.

When the play was over, he switched off the television and stared at the lingering pinpoint of light in the dark picture tube. He felt envy, pride, and a sense of loss. The moment Lisa had become Nellie Sherwood, he realized she would become a star.

Bobby read her reviews as anxiously as he scouted his own, three days later. He was only mentioned in one of the Philadelphia newspapers.

> . . . The performers try to rise above the banal storyline, but are barely able to stay afloat in the sea of clichés and melodrama. A's for effort, however, must go to Rodger Cromwell, Ben Singer, Michael Leonard, Robert Pierce, Dennis Kinsella, and Tom O'Ryan . . .

"Well, the *Inquirer* liked you." Lisa stood in the kitchen, cradling the telephone receiver against her shoulder. The breakfast table was covered with Philadelphia newspapers that she'd dashed down and gotten from the Times Square kiosk. "Bobby? Are you still there?"

"Yes."

"Don't be depressed. Listen, *Streetcar* got panned in its out-of-town preview." She had no idea if this was true, but she figured Bobby needed to hear it.

"Really?"

"So—you say they're making some changes in the play?" she asked.

"Yeah. That speech about my mother? They're cutting it," he replied. "All I get to say is, 'I got a letter from my mom today. She said the same stuff about how she's doing fine, but I still worry about her.' That's it. The rest went down the toilet."

"Oh, Bobby. I'm so sorry."

"I still get beat up in the third act. They decided to keep that in."

"Good," Lisa said. "Listen, they can do wonders in two weeks. By the time it opens here, you could be a hit. It's happened before." There was silence at the other end.

Then he said, "Speaking of hits—you were great the other night. Every paper in Philly loved you."

"Well, the *Daily News* made a crack about my nose. Let's see, there was 'uniquely beautiful,' 'wanly pretty,' 'offbeat beauty'— all qualified to the hilt, of course."

"The *Times* said . . . wait a minute, I got it here . . . 'Miss Weller has unique beauty and talent. She projects a warmth and candor uncommon in today's crop of young television actresses. She has quite a future in store.' "

Lisa would have been touched that Bobby collected her reviews if he hadn't sounded almost accusing.

"The offers must be rolling in, huh?"

"Oh, a few," she lied. Amelia's current tally was twenty-six. She'd decided to go with Continental Pictures' bid to test her for the lead in *Plea of Innocence*, a courtroom drama based on a blockbuster novel. Her co-star would be Nick Hunter.

"Anything good?" he asked casually.

"Mostly trash," she lied again. "But I'm flying out to Hollywood tomorrow to do a screen test. Not that I have much of a chance. I'll probably go over like a pregnant polevaulter. I should be back in time for your Broadway debut."

Silence.

"Bobby?"

"God," he murmured. "A screen test. That sounds great, Lisa. I'll bet you get the part. What is it?"

"Oh, I don't know. But when Amelia says go, you go." She paused a moment, then added, "It's no big deal."

"You'll knock 'em dead. Let me know what movie stars you see when you're out there. And call me when you find out how you do, okay?"

She could hear the forced warmth in his voice. "Sure thing,

Bobby. I'll be back before you know it, beating the pavements for a part. I miss you."

"Miss you, too. Well, I'd better let you go." He paused.

"I love you, Bobby."

"Love you, too. Bye."

Lisa was not the studio's first choice to play Rosanne, the heroine of *Plea of Innocence*. MGM had refused to loan Kelly. Novak was booked through 1956. Taylor, Saint, and Jones were in various stages of pregnancy. And Hepburn was opening on Broadway in *Ondine*.

So the producers had to back an unknown. Not quite unknown —she'd received critical attention in a highly rated television drama. The producers knew how to hedge their bets.

Until this part, Nick Hunter had been considered a lightweight actor. His swashbuckling adventure films were big grossers, but he wanted a serious role. And Lisa Weller projected the kind of class and New York integrity that Nick Hunter was looking for.

Lisa was disappointed when she learned Nick was shooting a film in Italy and wouldn't take part in her screen test. But it was just as well, she decided later.

The producers decided she needed to be a "real blonde." So her honey-gold hair was lightened to platinum. A padded bra was deemed in order. Then they realized they'd probably have to fix her nose.

But Lisa was as surprised as anyone when she told them, "Sorry, gentlemen. I draw the line when it comes to plastic surgery. My nose stays the way it is." Bobby, she thought, would have been proud of her.

The night before the test, she crawled into her bed at the Beverly Hilton at ten o'clock. There would be a five-thirty call to report to makeup, they'd told her. Some time after four, she finally fell asleep.

Two hours in makeup and six cups of coffee worked a miracle —her face was exquisite, and she'd developed a galloping case of diarrhea.

Between each take of a love scene with a handsome B-actor, she bolted to the bathroom, assuring the crew that her 750-dollar dress needed further adjustments. By the time the test was over, she felt exhausted and anxious. But the money men viewing the test agreed she projected an odd, smoldering sexuality. She was right for the part of Rosanne.

The associate producer called her with the good news. "You were very sexy. They liked that. One said you seemed like a volcano ready to erupt."

"It was the coffee," Lisa said.

"All that's left now is your build-up."

"My what?" she asked, envisioning another padded bra.

"The publicity. We have to get to work on an image for you."

"What's wrong with the way I am?" she asked, two days later. She sat at a long mahogany table with five deeply tanned PR men and two secretaries. The boardroom was filled with smoke and the rustling of papers. All eyes were trained on the profile sheet she'd filled out.

No one answered her question. "So yellow's the favorite color, huh?" one man said.

Lisa shrugged.

"Great. She'll wear yellow in her first scene in the picture."

Another man nodded. "And in all the publicity stills."

"Will it clash with the hair?"

"Will it clash, doll?"

"I don't know," Lisa said. "It didn't when my hair was my real."

"Let's make it cream 'steada yellow. Yeah, a cream-colored dress in the first scene, and in all the—"

"That'll match the hair. Everything should match the hair! Like Harlow."

"Kim's got lavender. You'll be cream. The Cream Girl. Could even get a dairy tie-in."

"That sounds faintly obscene," Lisa murmured.

"The kid's right. How about polka dots? How do you feel about that, honey?"

After four hours, it was decided she would carry a cream-colored rose to all her public functions. The first scene in the film was shot in the rain, so a trenchcoat would become her trademark. Though on the profile she had written, *I've got a boyfriend, and my love life is none of your business*, it was agreed she would have "a crush" on Nick Hunter, her co-star.

But she put her foot down when it came to her entry into show business. They had decided she'd be a librarian in New York, where a talent scout had discovered her in the stacks, reciting Shakespeare.

"Okay. So you'll just be 'working at a bookstore.' "

The press release carried the story. Lisa underwent three days of photo sessions, dressed as everything from a hillbilly to a princess, each shot featuring the cream-colored rose.

A press conference was scheduled, to be held in New York in five weeks, when Nick Hunter would return from Italy. At the conference, Lisa would meet her co-star and be presented to the public as Continental Pictures' newest discovery.

She left the Burbank Airport with her hair a shade lighter and a trenchcoat thrown over her shoulders. A few photographers were there to witness the latest star's departure. They didn't catch a shot of Lisa stuffing her rose in a terminal trashcan.

Bobby's play opened at the Court Theater. Lisa and Bobby held vigil at Sardi's, waiting for the early reviews. She was nervous; it was his turn for the spotlight, and she wanted him to be able to bask in it. She glanced across the table at him. He was in high spirits.

"A toast!" He held up his glass. "No more bit parts for either one of us!"

"Hear, hear!"

They drank and laughed, each proud of the other's success. He liked her new hair color; she loved his new suit. He congratulated her for keeping her nose; she praised his performance in the play.

"Aren't we both just so wonderful and talented?"

"Hey, you forgot beautiful, for chrissakes!"

They were on their third round of drinks when the latest in

a steady stream of well-wishers stopped at their table. Bobby looked up. It was Ruth.

"I just wanted to tell you how marvelous you were tonight, Bobby." She looked composed and elegant, but there was something apologetic about her manner. "I always knew you could do it."

Looking at the two women on either side of him, Bobby wanted to slink under the table, but he forced himself to stand. "Um, Ruth Bartlett, this is Lisa Weller." He cleared his throat.

"We've met," they said in unison. Then they laughed nervously.

Lisa got to her feet. "Excuse me. I have to use the powder room. It was nice to see you again, Mrs. Bartlett."

Ruth nodded. "By the way, Raymond and I loved your performance in "The Eternal Soul'."

"Thank you." Lisa smiled and left the table.

Ruth timidly gazed at Bobby. "I—just wanted to come by and say how happy I am for you."

He pulled out a chair for her. Ruth perched on the edge. "I came with Amelia. We both loved you in the play."

"Thanks, Ruth," he said, returning to his chair. "Um, did you get the earring?"

She blushed and glanced down at the tabletop. "You were very sweet to send it. I still feel the need to apologize for the scene that day, Bobby. I acted terribly."

"No need to apologize. You had every right to say what you did."

She just smiled faintly.

"I'll always be grateful to you, Ruth," he said. "If it weren't for you, I wouldn't have been in that play tonight."

"You wouldn't have met Lisa, either," she said softly.

"So—how are things at home?"

"Improved. Somewhat. He's still not perfect, but more—attentive. We're actually going to travel *together* next month. Paris."

"Sounds great."

Ruth tilted her head and regarded him warmly. "You two look

nice together, Bobby. She's a lovely girl. I'm very glad for you. I really am."

Amelia was seated at the vanity table applying fresh lipstick. Lisa smiled at her in the mirror.

"I love what they did to your hair," Amelia said, without turning. "I want a full rundown on tinseltown tomorrow, at the office. Two o'clock okay?"

"Fine," Lisa said listlessly.

"What's wrong, honey?"

She sighed. "Nothing. I just left Bobby with Mrs. Bartlett. I can't help feeling sorry for her."

"Oh, she'll get over him. Menopause crush. Don't worry about Ruthie."

Lisa sat down next to Amelia. "What did you think of the play tonight?" she asked soberly. "What did you *really* think?"

Amelia put away her lipstick. "Bob did a good job in the part. That's why I wanted him to do it—I knew he'd do well, that it would be exposure, at least. I just hope that bomb runs long enough for someone to see him."

NINE

Nick Hunter was the kind of cad a girl could bring home to meet her parents. Lean, mustached, and darkly handsome, he had been born in Baton Rouge and supposedly lost his virginity at eleven, when a parlor maid seduced him. "I often wondah what happened to that li'l gal," Nick would muse for interviewers. In his three years as a box-office draw, he'd had as many paternity suits brought against him and eventually dismissed. But the love-struck testimony made for great copy.

Amelia had warned Lisa about her co-star. The studios had set up a momentous "first date," a New York premiere of Nick's latest film, *Scoundrel of the Sea*. Lisa was given an evening gown, mink stole, diamond choker (all to be returned to the studio), and a cream-colored rose.

Nick's limousine was due at any moment. Lisa sat in front of the mirror in the Greenwich Village apartment, wondering what she could say to bring Bobby out of his mood.

His play had closed after eight performances. Amelia had tried to bank on the exposure with television parts, but they weren't star material. Lisa, on the other hand, had starred in another TV drama, to rave reviews. And as his roommate's press notices and fan mail grew, so had Bobby's resentment.

Their lovemaking didn't help matters; it was abbreviated, bringing him to the point of excitement and then leaving him feeling cheated.

"Do I look okay?" she asked, turning from the mirror.

He was heading for the bathroom. "Yeah, terrific. Don't forget the goddamn rose—it's in the refrigerator."

Lisa slammed down her hairbrush. "Would it kill you to be civil, just for tonight? I happen to be rather nervous."

"How would you feel if I had a date with Marilyn Monroe?"

She sighed. "It's just a publicity deal. Why do you insist on taking everything personally?"

"The guy's a phony, Lisa. A goddamn wolf! I mean, his cock isn't attached to him—he's attached to it!"

She snorted. "I'm not jumping into bed with him, if that's what you're worried about."

Bobby gave her a long look. "Well, then Nick Hunter's in for a big surprise," he said and brushed past her.

She stood staring after him. She could hear the water running in the bathroom. Then the door opened.

"Okay," he said. "You look terrific. I wish I was Nick Hunter."

She ran over and kissed him. "Sorry to be such a jerk," he murmured and put his arms around her.

"I'm sorry too, Bobby."

The doorbell sounded.

"He's here! Oh God, where's my purse?" She broke away and flew into the bedroom to snatch up the mink. "Listen," she called, "wait up for me, okay?"

The bathroom door slammed. Lisa grimaced.

Outside, a chauffeur waited at the front step. "Are you with Mr. Hunter?" she asked the driver tentatively.

"No, sugah pop, *you're* with me," a voice said, and Nick Hunter appeared from around the side of the car.

The movie pirate looked even more handsome in a tuxedo. He wasn't a storybook prince—his neck wasn't thick, and three small birthmarks marred his right cheekbone. Yet Lisa felt instantly drawn to him.

Inside the limousine, on their way to the Astor Theater, she gave Nick a wary smile. "Considering your reputation, I'm not sure I'm completely safe back here with you."

"What do y'all hear about my reputation, sugah?"

She stared at the driver through the window divider. "Oh, a lot of things I've read. You know, in those magazines . . . *Confidential*. I read them, but I don't buy them. I'm not sure I buy everything they say about you, either."

"Such as?" He smiled.

"Well, let me think. You sleep in the nude. You're not really from the South. You're secretly married. You have seven illegitimate children. Your mustache is fake. You're really a homosexual. You like little girls. Your . . . genitalia is twelve inches long. You only have one testicle. You hate acting. You're an alcoholic. You smoke reefers. You never touch the stuff. Even though you've made four pirate films, you're deathly afraid of water. You can't swim." She turned to him. "Stop me when you've heard enough."

"It's all true." He smiled.

"Even the mustache?"

"Pull it and see."

She stared at his amused expression.

"Most people," he said, "believe what they wish about me."

Lisa nodded. "I'm learning about images myself. They're trying to create one for me. I'm finding it an uncomfortable experience. Must be a challenge for you. There's little *you* could do to shock people, I imagine."

"Oh, I could get married, retire, move to Gary, Indiana."

"I can't picture that," she said.

"You think I'd be unfaithful to my wife?"

She shrugged. "I think it's hard to break a habit you've had since age—what?—eleven?"

He smiled at that. "She was a colored gal, about forty. I used to peek through the keyhole in her bedroom. She never laid a hand on me. I didn't lose my cherry till I was twenty-two, sweetheart. A late bloomer. If I'd been goin' at it like this since age eleven, I'd be six feet undah by now."

Lisa regarded him. "Funny about that accent of yours," she said. "How it seems to come and go."

Nick Hunter laughed. "You don't miss a trick, do you, sugah?" He looked amused. "I was born in the South, but we moved to California when I was six. Well, *Southern* California. I went to New Orleans when I was twenty-five. Sometimes my voice can't make up its mind where—or who—the hell I am."

"And how long has it been since you were in New Orleans?"

"I'm thirty-three, honey, but I like to keep 'em guessing. Just like you, honey." He touched her hand and smiled, but his eyes were serious and penetrating. "Just like you."

Hair done up in pincurls, Lisa sat on the floor going over the script for *Plea of Innocence*. They would start principal photography in New York in four weeks, then shoot interiors in Hollywood. It was her first look at the script, and she had to admit she was impressed.

Bobby sat on the sofa above her, leafing through the *Daily News*. Lisa cuddled near his legs for warmth. The heat in the apartment wasn't turned on, and she had her feet bundled into a pair of Bobby's argyles, her hair dryer trained on her icy toes.

Glancing over the paper, Bobby wondered what Hunter would think of his future co-star if he saw her right now. Bobby was the only one who saw this Lisa. When Hunter looked at the carefully coiffed, expensively dressed starlet, what did he know of the real person underneath? Nothing, Bobby hoped. Though she'd now attended a dozen premieres and parties with Hunter, all she ever said to Bobby was that it was "tiresome" or "a bore."

"You and Mr. Sincerity decided what you're going to be for this Halloween blast?" he asked.

She didn't take her eyes off the script. "He said something about going as Oscars. You know, gold tights, gold paint, swords."

"I may throw up."

"I knew you'd like it."

He flipped over the newspaper. "Don't y'all pay me no nevah mind. I'm jess jealous, sugah pop."

"Well, you have no grounds to be. He hasn't so much as kissed me—in private, anyway."

Bobby tossed the paper aside. "You sound disappointed, for chrissakes!"

"Well, it's not as if I don't like the guy. He's charming and handsome and very pleasant. Not like his public image at all. You should know about that, Bobby. Look at me!"

The doorbell rang.

Lisa glanced up. "It's past ten," she said, frowning.

"Probably Nick and his dick. I'll show them right in."

Lisa gave him a look. "Can you control yourself for one—?"

But he was already on his way to the door. In the lobby, he didn't recognize the middle-aged man waiting out on the steps. But there was an eerie sense of familiarity about him, all the same. Bobby stared at the man's shabby coat, the drooping stance, the oily hair, the crooked nose. "Can I help you?"

The man chuckled. "Yeah. I wanna come in. That okay with you?"

"You rang my apartment," Bobby said coldly.

"So okay. Sorry, hotshot. So I rang the wrong bell."

"Which apartment do you want?"

"Apartment C. Weller. Ya mind?"

Bobby didn't move. "Why do you want to see her?"

"I'm a friend. Of Lisa's.

"Well," Bobby said, "she doesn't want to see you now. Or ever. So why don't you just take a hike, okay?"

A soundless laugh escaped from the man's throat. "I happen to be her old man. Who the fuck are you?"

"Someone who's going to make sure you never come here again," Bobby said evenly. "Now, why don't you do us both a big favor and get lost?"

Rogan's face darkened. "Look, jerk-off, she's my daughter, got that? My daughter! I have a right to see her."

Bobby drew a deep breath and stared at the pathetic figure. Pity tugged at his heart. "Look, Mr. Rogan. I'm sorry, but she really is tied up right now. I think you'd better just—"

200

"Outta my way, creep!" Rogan tried to push past him, but Bobby grabbed him by the collar and shoved him back out on the step. Rogan stumbled and fell against the railing. Recovering, he crouched in a defensive stance and glared at Bobby.

"Look," Bobby said. "I don't want to repeat this. You come here ever again, and you're one dead scumbag. Is that clear enough for you?"

Rogan dusted off his cheap suit and retreated down the steps to the street. From the sidewalk, he looked up at Bobby. His face was mottled, and he stabbed a finger at the younger man. "You'll be sorry for this, jerk-off. I'll make you pay."

Bobby remained in the door and watched the shabby man make his way down the street, kicking trash out of his path savagely.

When he went back into the apartment, Lisa looked up. "I went in and made us some tea," she said. "It's just freezing here! God, to be in Hollywood and sunshine! So, who was it at the door?"

"Some poor old wino. Took a while to convince him this wasn't the Salvation Army."

Lisa smiled. "Good thing I didn't go to the door," she said. "I always end up giving those poor old drunks a few dollars. My protector," she said to Bobby. "Saving me from myself."

Lisa stood in the middle of the Brooklyn Bridge, her hands in the pockets of her trenchcoat. The revolver in her right pocket was moist from the sweat on her palm.

Bobby stalked up behind her. Sensing him, she turned. The chilly wind from the river made her eyes water. "Well, it's been a long time, doll," he said, flipping up his jacket collar. "You've been neglecting your old pals, Rosanne. Ever since you took up with that society bum."

"Phillip isn't a bum."

He smiled. "How would old Phil and his rich crowd feel if they knew about us? Don't think you'd get invited to their tea parties after that—"

"Just what do you want from me, Luke?"

"Ten grand. Your boyfriend will never miss it."

"Forget it!" she retorted.

"You're gonna miss all those tea parties, dollface," he sneered.

"You wouldn't—"

"Sure, I'd tell them."

She drew out the revolver and, trembling, aimed it at his chest. Bobby took a step back. "Christ! What are you—"

"*Cut!*" the director bellowed. He threw his cigar stub into the water below. "What did you just say?"

Lisa looked nervously at Bobby. "You can't say 'Christ' in films, Bobby. That wasn't in the script."

The director was marching into the pool of artificial light that flooded the bridge walkway. His pudgy face was pink with rage.

"Didn't you study your script, kid?"

"Of course! But that line was all wrong. I just thought—"

"We don't pay you to think! We don't pay you to rewrite the script!"

"But it was wrong. The line was wrong for the character. He wouldn't say, 'Why, you little fool,' when she pulls out a *gun*, for chrissakes. He'd be a little more shocked than *that.*"

"You think you know the character better than our writers?"

"I think I know good writing better than your writers."

Lisa sighed. "Bobby, you—"

But the director had turned and called for the script girl. "Honey, who's that jerk?"

"Look, sir," Bobby said. "I'm sorry, I just thought—"

"Don't think. Just read what's in the script."

"He will, Mr. Daniels," Lisa broke in. "I promise."

"Good," Daniels said, and stomped back to his chair.

But Bobby cast her a wounded glance. "Why did you take his side? You said last night that the line stank!"

"Yes, but you really shouldn't change it while the cameras are rolling. It's called being uncooperative."

"I happen to care about the motivations of my character!"

"Well, so do I," she said, "but you shouldn't let it interfere with the movie's schedule." She stared at him. The role was so small, he couldn't afford artistic temperament. Not after she and Amelia had pushed him for the part as the murder victim in *Plea of Innocence*. This was his only scene, and evidently he wanted to make the most of it. But he went about it the wrong way and didn't seem to understand that his poor attitude reflected on her, too.

"I fight for what I believe in," he was saying hotly.

"That's wonderful," Lisa said wearily, "but let's just do it as written, okay? Daniels is no Kazan, Bobby. He really won't know the difference. Anyway, it's getting late and they don't like to pay the crew overtime. And I'm freezing."

Seven takes later, the director was screaming at another "improvement" Bobby had made in the script. Though Lisa had liked the alteration, Bobby wasn't handling the discussion well. This time, she stifled her impulse to defend him.

They finally wrapped at one o'clock in the morning, leaving the scene unfinished. Everyone went home tired and out of sorts.

Lisa didn't speak during the cab ride. It wasn't until they were back in the apartment that she finally said, "What the hell was the big idea?"

"I was about to ask you the same thing. You knew damn well those changes I made were right."

"Fine," Lisa said, hunting through the kitchen cabinet for the hot cocoa mix. "When you're a star, you can disrupt the set and dictate changes. Until then—"

"A star? You mean like you, Lisa?"

She slammed down the tin of cocoa. "Okay, Bobby. Let's have it. I've been waiting to hear how much you resent my success. So let's hear it now."

"I've been busting my butt for seven years, trying to get someplace! You're in New York less than a year and you're starring in a major picture. Christ, no one's that lucky!"

"Don't you think I know that?" she shouted. "You think I wanted this to happen so fast? It's not as great as it looks, Bobby. There's no room for mistakes. Ten million people watch to make sure they'll see when I fall. I'm not secure as an actress, but I have to pretend I know everything!"

"My heart bleeds," he said. "Pretty traumatic, Lisa—fifty fan letters a week, write-ups in all the papers. That can really eat away at a person."

"It hasn't made my life any better. I still get depressed. It hasn't changed me." She looked down at the floor. "Just because you're so hungry for fame, don't assume I am."

"You want it just as much."

"I don't think so," she said. "I wouldn't ever do what you've done for fame. I couldn't sell myself like that." She immediately regretted her words, but he'd heard. A wary look crossed his face.

"Then why are you running around with Nick Hunter?" he said slowly. "If that isn't selling yourself, I don't know what is."

She switched off the stove with a sigh. "Good. I knew we'd get to Nick eventually. Bobby, I like him. I think he's a nice person. But I don't love him. I love you. I'm not selling out by doing promotional events with Nick—I'm just trying to cooperate with the studio. Which brings us back to the point." She paused. Bobby didn't know how instrumental she'd been in getting him the part; she didn't want to tell him unless she had to. "I wish you'd try to cooperate with Daniels a little more. I think you'll do fine in the scene as written. Now, how about some cocoa?"

He glanced down at the floor for a moment. "I'm sorry."

She went over and put her arms around him. As they held each other, she had the uncanny feeling they were playing a scene written for two parting lovers.

Midday light filtered into the office and fell on Amelia's drained face. "Didn't get much shut-eye," she told Lisa as she lit a cigarette. "Your director called me at three in the morning. After hearing what he had to say, I couldn't go back to sleep."

Lisa shifted. "What did he say?"

"Honey, I'm sorry. Bob's off the picture."

Lisa shut her eyes. "Does he know?"

Amelia nodded. "He came by earlier. I managed to get him a commercial; he's over there now. It's a good thing, because I wanted to see you alone. There's . . . something else, and I think you should be the one to tell him."

"What?"

"You've got to move out. You can't live with him anymore."

"Why, for God's sake!"

"Because more and more people are interested in you these days, honey. In your life. If it ever got out you were living in sin, it could ruin your career."

"But—"

"You don't remember what happened to Ingrid Bergman?" Amelia's face was cold. "She was a bigger star than you, and after the Rossellini business, they still blackballed her. You're just starting out, Lisa. If your arrangement with Bobby ever hit the papers —and it will—the columnists will paint you as a scarlet woman from coast to coast. Half the studio already knows."

"I don't care."

"What about your parents? You think they want to see their little girl splashed across the *Movietone News?*"

"I'll tell them. I was going to anyway. Amelia, I can't dump Bobby just because some studio head doesn't like my personal life. I can't sell out on him."

"Honey, you don't realize the risks involved. This isn't some little image problem. This is your career we're discussing. You're really willing to give up an entire career for an ego-ridden little hustler like Bobby Pierce? C'mon."

Lisa stared at her steadily. "You once told me that smart decisions were tough to make. Well, you were right. This hurts. But I love Bobby and I'm not going to leave him."

"You honestly think, Lisa, that Bobby would make the same sacrifice—for you?"

Lisa knew the answer. But she evaded it. "He won't have to. Actors don't have to be virgins. This kind of scandal can only help a man's career."

"I'm not talking about that! Bobby is not established, and if this were discovered, both of you would be finished." She lit another cigarette. "When I first offered to represent Bob, a casting director wouldn't use him in a commercial. When I pressed, he said he'd met Bob before, at a party given by a man named Alfred Weeks. He told me Bobby had been living with this Weeks character for over a year.

"I know about that. Bobby told me himself."

"Did he also tell you Weeks was once a card-carrying Communist? A fellow traveler?"

"What!"

"From what I can gather, Bobby didn't know. But enough people in this business do. Weeks moved to Rio two years ago to avoid the investigations. I haven't told Bob. It's not the homosexual angle that worries me—that's been going on for years with actors. But right now, the Red scare is still a concern. Look, Lisa," she continued, "I've told myself Bobby wasn't going to get famous overnight. He could still work. But I didn't count on you giving him a spot in your limelight. These allegations could hurt both of you. And I didn't count on Daniels asking me last night if it was true that 'this Pierce kid was a pinko once.' " Amelia looked grim.

"Is that why they fired him?"

"That, and his difficulty on the set. By the way, tonight you reshoot the bridge scene with another actor."

"That's why I should stick by him," Lisa said defiantly.

"No, honey. If you continue with him, he'll become news. Just as much as you. It's too soon to throw him to the wolves. The Weeks mess is bound to come out; he'll be labeled a subversive. You'll be labeled immoral. It'd ruin you both."

"But if I left—why would that prevent it?"

"In a few years, none of this may matter. As long as he doesn't know how deeply it's affecting him right now, he won't worry. He can still work. He still has a chance to become the big star he wants to be."

Amelia stood up. "But not now. Your relationship is too dangerous, for both of you."

Lisa wanted to scream that it wasn't fair. But she knew Amelia, as usual, was right. If she didn't leave Bobby, their careers could both be ruined. When she looked up, Amelia was smiling sadly.

"That's what I meant, honey. When I asked if Bob would make the same sacrifice for you."

That night, the bridge scene was shot in three takes. The young actor playing Luke recited his lines convincingly. And as Lisa confronted her former lover, her character's heartbreak and anxiety were there in her eyes, and in every word she spoke.

"You're home early." Bobby sat at the kitchen table. It was littered with cut-up newspapers.

"What are you doing?" she asked, taking off her coat.

"Your press clippings." Carefully, he worked the scissors around her review. "I figured you'd want them for a scrapbook."

Lisa winced.

"Sorry. I just wanted to make up for being such a jerk last—"

At that, she ran for the bathroom. Bending over the cold water, she tried to splash away the tears that threatened to come.

"So I screwed up again." Bobby stood in the doorway.

"No, Bobby. I just feel bad, that's all."

"Listen, I deserved to get the ax. You were right. I shouldn't have given him an argument. You don't give anyone trouble, and you're the star."

She wiped her eyes with a towel. "I'm not talking about that," she said, her voice strained. "Bobby—we can't live together anymore. I'm sorry . . ."

He stared. "Why? Is it the studio? Are they pressuring you to move?"

She gazed down at the sink. "Yes." She couldn't look at him. "We start filming in Hollywood next week, and they want me to move out there anyway. Bobby, I wish there was some way we could stay together. I—love you."

"There is a way, you know," he said. "We could, well, get married."

"No, we couldn't!" she cried. "God, I'm sorry, Bobby. I have
. . . I've got my career to think about."

"I wouldn't ask you to give up your career!"

She wanted to say she *would* give it up for him. But would he
abandon his dream for her? Could he bear not finding work
because he was 'suspect?'

"We can't get married," she said, finally. "And we can't stay
together. Please, believe me, it's for the best. For the both of us."

He glared at her with stony contempt. "I figured this would
happen," he said. "So that's the way you want it?"

She felt the tears start again, the ache in her throat. "No, it's
not," she cried. "Please, Bobby, don't hate me. It's just the way
it has to be."

"I don't hate you, Lisa." His voice was quiet. He managed a
smile. "You tried to help. It was you who got me that part in your
picture, wasn't it? Nobody said anything, but I knew. And I'm
grateful. I'll always be grateful. So like you say, it's just the way
it has to be."

It was the best performance Bobby ever gave.

TEN

Dear Bobby,

This is the seventh time I've started this letter. I couldn't decide on the tone. Cheery? Apologetic? It makes me realize I've never written to you before. Anyway, I decided on the "honest" approach, which will probably see me through a couple of paragraphs before I rip this up. I'd phone, but it's 11:30, which means it's 2:30 your time. And every time I call, you're not home.

I guess this letter must be about as welcome as Uncle Johnny's was for me. I wish our last days together had not been spent avoiding each other, but I am glad you decided to stay on at the apartment.

The picture is going very well. We should finish on schedule in a couple of weeks. I'm looking for an apartment. Apartment hunting isn't the same without you. Anyway, I miss you and you can write to me at the hotel here (hint, hint).

Nick took me to a party at—are you ready?—Hedda Hopper's. There were almost as many photographers as guests! And every guest there was a movie star. Amid all that glamour, I felt like a schoolgirl. But Susan Hayward actually <u>recognized</u> me, and we managed to have a nice conversation. I worked up enough nerve to ask Gary Cooper to pass the hors d'oeuvres, but I couldn't say a word after he had touched them. John Wayne said, *"Excuse me, little lady"* when he backed into me. Janet Leigh said she liked my dress, and she made Tony Curtis fix me a drink. I was tongue-tied. Then Hedda grabbed me and started telling Jennifer Jones how sweet I was, which was a laugh because compared to Jennifer Jones, I felt about as delicate as Rocky Graziano. But most of the night I stuck with Nicky to avoid making a complete idiot of myself. But it was fun. I kept wishing you could be there with me.

I missed you at Thanksgiving, too. It was my first away from my family, but you were the one I missed. I tried to call, but no answer. I imagine you were having a turkey sandwich at the Automat. Nicky ended up taking me out for roast duck. It was all very grand, and Nicky was his charming self. But I would rather have been at the Automat with you.

I do miss you, Bobby. I miss staying up all hours talking, and then going to bed together. I miss you like crazy.

Please, write.

Love, Lisa

Dec. 14, 1954

Dear Bobby,

I saw you on <u>Mystery Theater,</u> and you were wonderful. You looked very sexy. Even Nicky thought you were awfully good. We were both disappointed you weren't on longer.

Why haven't you written? I sent you my new address.

The film is all wrapped up and a new agent Amelia recommended has sent me some awful scripts. Actually, some aren't bad. But I miss Amelia! You could tell her your troubles. This new guy is all business. I envy you still having her.

I'm running out of room on this card. <u>Please write</u>. Take care. I love you.

Merry Christmas, Lisa

Nick sat behind the wheel of his Porsche convertible, his curly, black hair ruffled by the breeze. He wore a tuxedo that flattered his tan; he was all black and white and brown.

Nick and Lisa were finished with the film and all their publicity dates now. It amazed Lisa that after nine months, she still had a crush on Nick. And he still hadn't tried to do a thing.

On this spring night, they were headed for the Pantages Theatre to see a special sneak preview of *Plea of Innocence.* Maybe they wouldn't get to the theater until the film was over, Lisa thought. Maybe Nick would have an accident and she'd be spared the two-hour death awaiting them on Hollywood Boulevard.

Nick smiled. "You want me to pull ovah so you can throw up?"

"No, thanks. I already did that at home." She fidgeted with the cream rose, and another petal fell off. But she was pleased with the emerald green evening dress; the slit to mid-thigh might draw attention away from her windblown hair.

"Relax, sugah pop. No one's going to boo you. Maybe throw some jujubes, but they won't all boo."

He was right. No one booed as the face of Lisa Weller filled the forty-foot screen, in Technicolor and Cinemascope. Then she spoke and words came out of the ten-foot mouth.

No one hissed. Lisa was amazed. They'd paid money and didn't seem to mind watching her up there. After the first half hour, a hypnotic quiet settled over the audience. Maybe, she thought, they were all asleep.

In the middle of her dramatic monologue, Nick squeezed her knee. Lisa looked over. His fingers inched under the slit in her gown and began to trace a line up and down the inside of her thigh. Lisa stared up at the screen. The bastard had picked this moment to make a pass! She slammed her knees together, trapping his hand. Nick let out a surprised yelp.

"Shh!" "Shut up!" "Quiet!" Censuring murmurs filled the seats around them. The vexed whispers of her audience hung in her ears. *Her audience,* sounding as if something precious had almost been snatched away from them.

The applause began as the final credits rolled. It reached a crescendo when Nick and Lisa were escorted to the lobby. Mobs of people rushed after them, squeezing through the theater doors; hands reached over ushers to touch Lisa and Nick.

She took a step behind Nick, but he grabbed her hand and thrust her forward. The applause and cries of "We love you, Lisa!" overwhelmed her. She wanted to hide behind Nick, but he held up her hand in a sign of triumph. A teenage boy tried to snatch her rose, and Lisa willingly gave it to him. More hands grabbed at her—a sea of hands. She kept smiling and nodding until Nick had to pull her into the limousine.

"This one here says, 'I want more Lisa Wellah and less Nick Huntah'," Nick announced cheerfully. He waved the audience response card for the whole table to see. Producers, studio executives, stars, and reporters were gathered at Chasen's for the post-preview party. The consensus was that they had a hit.

"This one says, 'Great picture. The girl is a dream.' "

" 'I want to see this movie again.' "

" 'Lisa Weller is a knockout!' "

Lisa read one: " 'What's-her-name has a funny nose.' "

Everyone roared, including Lisa, while the reporters made note of her good-natured humor. Nick leaned over and kissed her as the flashbulbs popped.

Excusing herself, Lisa dashed across the alley to the bar, where there were phone booths in the vestibule. She needed privacy for this call.

Bobby just had to be home now. She had counted four rings when she noticed Nick outside the booth. After two more, she hung up and stepped out of the booth.

"He's not home, huh?" Nick said, with a faint smile.

"Who?"

"That boy in New York. Bobby."

She sighed. "No, he's not answering his phone. Would you buy me a drink, Nick? I feel like getting good and drunk tonight."

The bar was dark and uncrowded. Nick and Lisa took a booth near the jukebox where Rosemary Clooney's "Hey There, You With the Stars in Your Eyes" softly teased them.

"You're awful hung up on that boy, aren't you, sugar pop? I think he's crazy, myself. Not answering any of your letters or calls."

"He has his reasons." Lisa frowned over her wineglass.

"You've been carrying that torch for months," Nick said. "When are you gonna put it down and give old Nicky a chance?"

"They're probably wondering where we are," Lisa said. "We should get back."

He shook his head. "You and I conveniently slipping away? They love it. Makes good copy." He put his hand over hers. "I think it's a shame we only got something going on in the papers, Miss Weller. Think how disappointed they would be if they found out the truth. Our big night, and you're slipping off to call your boyfriend."

"I'm sorry, Nick. It's just—when you have really good news, you want to share it with someone you're close to."

"And you couldn't share it with me?"

She managed a smile. "Well, you were part of it."

"And I behaved like a cad," he said. "Sugah, I have a confession to make. You were so goddamn good up there, I wanted to take away from it. Sitting in that theater tonight, I realized you were the star. I guess I didn't want anyone stealing my thunder." He looked at her sheepishly. "You must think old Nicky's a real bastard."

She laughed. "At least old Nicky's an honest one."

"You wouldn't care to keep on seeing this honest bastard, now that we're finished with the picture?"

"You're the only friend I have here," Lisa said, smiling.

"You're my only friend, too, sugah."

"That's not true. You have loads of friends."
"Yes, but none as good as you, Lisa. None like you."

Variety: May 20, 1955

". . . *Plea of Innocence* is a well-acted, well-photographed courtroom soap opera. It is slick, stimulating, and about as intellectually nourishing as a box of popcorn. But in a change-of-pace role as the ambitious lawyer, Nick Hunter shows a talent for serious drama, albeit melodrama. He gives a credible performance, but is eclipsed by his co-star, newcomer Lisa Weller. In her film debut, the twenty-two-year-old fulfills the high expectations of her television work in last year's *Eternal Soul*. She is magic . . . "

June 7, 1955

Dear Bobby,

Well, I guess you know by now that the movie is doing well, and the critics were pretty nice to yours truly. Have you seen it yet? I just signed to do a drama about slum life in New York, called Streets of the City. *I play a social worker. Naturally, it's being shot here in Hollywood, but the script is beautiful and I'm excited about it.*

I get close to two hundred fan letters a week (well, aren't you impressed?), but I don't hear from you. I told my secretary to be on the lookout for anything from "Bobby," but so far she's only come up with false alarms. If you haven't gotten my drift by now, this is the Make Him Feel Guilty approach. It's a new one I'm trying on you. All my other tactics have failed.

I miss you so much. Nicky is sick of me talking about you. He can't understand why I'm so miserable.

I'm sorry about this letter. It's boring and full of self-pity. I just want you to know how much I miss you and love you. I never stopped loving you, Bobby. I wanted to marry you. Please believe me when I tell you that my reasons for moving

away weren't entirely selfish. I was doing it for you, too. I
know that sounds hokey, but it's true.

Well, it's late, and I've got a magazine interview early
tomorrow morning. So I'm (mercifully) wrapping this up. I
miss you.

Love, Lisa

The unopened letter came back two weeks later, marked ADDRES-
SEE MOVED: NO FORWARD: RETURN TO SENDER. It was amid seventy-
eight other letters Lisa had received that day. Fan letters.

The New York Daily News; October 14, 1955

HOLLYWOOD (UPI). NICK HUNTER TO WED
LISA WELLER. Nick Hunter, 35, and Lisa Weller, 22,
today announced their engagement at a party given in their
honor by Sheldon Edwards, head of Continental Pictures.
The couple costar in the hit film, *Plea of Innocence*. A wedding is planned for November, to be held in Miss Weller's
hometown, Chicago . . .

Bobby shoved the newspaper down the counter. He sat in Crom-
well's Drugstore over his third cup of coffee. Amelia didn't have
any jobs for him, and he wasn't exactly dying to go on rounds,
as it was raining like a son of a bitch.

He propped his chin in his hand. How many other slobs in here
were actors? Two years back, he'd shared this counter with guys
like James Dean, Paul Newman, Ben Gazzara, and Tony Franciosa. He'd seen them at casting calls from time to time. Dean, who
had died just two weeks before, was already a legend. Newman
had just starred with Sinatra and Eva Marie Saint in a TV version
of "Our Town" (Christ, another production of *Our Town* that
had passed him by). Gazzara and Franciosa were both starring on
Broadway. How had all of those guys gotten so far so fast? When
was *his* break going to come?

Why couldn't Amelia do for him what she'd done for Lisa?

Lisa had been on the cover of *Look* last week; he'd bought the issue, just as he'd picked up *Life*—the issue with her and that phony, Hunter, on the cover. He'd saved all her reviews, every magazine that had an article on Lisa Weller. His room at the Iroquois was cluttered with her memorabilia: the wicker Chianti bottle and candle; a blue scarf; a used-up lipstick she'd left behind. He had all her letters. But he wasn't going to write back, not until his luck had changed. Not until he was a success.

Sighing, he frowned at the paper. A shadow crossed the page. It belonged to Lyle Garrett, a brown-haired, blue-eyed Romeo with a self-confident smile and a lot of connections. "Hey ya, Berto. How's it hanging?"

Bobby lit a cigarette. "Hell, I'm great, just great. Got a million-dollar picture deal. That's why I'm sitting here like a jerk."

Garrett laughed. "Listen," he said, "I'm gonna do you a favor. Remember Stella Sanders, that pin-up broad a few years back?"

"Like ten?" Bobby snorted. "Yeah. She made a couple pictures, didn't she?"

Garrett nodded. "Listen, she's in town for this awards show and she needs an escort. Not for the show, but for afterwards. Catch my drift?"

"When did you become a pimp, Lyle?"

"Hey, just trying to do a favor, man. I heard you weren't getting too many breaks, Berto, and this Sanders broad just might have the right connection." He nudged Bobby. "She'll pay. And she's not bad-looking, either. I'd take her out myself, only I got a walk-on, Steve Allen, last minute thing."

"Congrats."

"I told her I'd find her somebody good. She'd go for a guy like you. Whaddaya say?"

Bobby stubbed out his cigarette. He glanced out the window. "No thanks, Lyle. Rain's let up. Think I'll go see if there's anything cooking over at NBC."

Garrett shrugged. "Don't say I never did you any favors, buddy."

But Bobby was already heading out the door.

ELEVEN

It was the first time Lisa had ever put on lipstick before going to bed. The white lace gown had cost three hundred and twenty dollars and it seemed to weigh about three ounces. Did she look sexy? She scrutinized herself; she couldn't tell. Why did this feel like another audition?

There was no reason to be nervous. Nicky was, after all, her best friend in the world—her confidant. Maybe she didn't love him the way she loved Bobby, but he was attractive, charming, and above all, he was patient.

Yes, Nick was cooperative. He'd come to dinner at the house in Evanston. Her mother had adored him. But Nick's charm was lost on Matt. Later, Lisa learned Nick's betrothal speech had consisted of, "Well, Mr. Wellah, I rake in close to a million a year aftah taxes, which is—correct me if I'm wrong—more than you-all make. So I can support your daughtah all right. How bout it, Dad?"

Still, Lisa was crazy for him. There was something uncomplicated and fun about Nick. And now they were married. Well, she just had to look beautiful tonight, to keep the fantasy alive. If only she could get over her stage fright. Her hands were cold. Her feet, too. Beneath the delicate lace, her nipples grew hard. Shivering, she rubbed her bare arms: gooseflesh.

The damn hotel bathroom was freezing. Her toes became numb against the cold marble floor. She padded to the door and opened it. A current of Lake Michigan air hit her as she entered the dimly lit bedroom. Nick stood near the bed, his arms folded over his bare chest, his teeth chattering. A pair of blue silk pajama pants hung low around his trim hips. The French doors to the terrace were open, the curtains billowing with the November breeze. "Nicky, what—?"

He pulled her against him in answer. She drew a startled breath before he pressed his mouth to hers, parting her lips with his tongue. She shuddered at the sudden warmth of his kiss. Feverishly, her cold hands rose and caressed his smooth back. Trembling, she squeezed his buttocks and pulled him against her.

Nick drew down the thin strap of her nightgown and brought his hot mouth to her breast. As he sucked the swollen nipple, Lisa let out a tiny, grateful cry. She rubbed against him, lace to silk, and felt him grow hard.

Then he was pulling her toward the bed, where he shucked off his pajama bottoms. They scurried under the gold quilted coverlet and huddled together. Nick tugged the top of her nightgown down past her breasts. "God, you're beautiful," he murmured, kissing each hardened nipple. Abandoning her shyness, she reached for his erection. Holding the warm shaft, she felt his body quiver.

He pushed up her nightgown and his deft hands moved beneath the material, over her thawing flesh. Climbing on top of her, he cradled the small of her back and lifted her hips. The hairy chest she'd admired in so many pirate movies now pressed against her breasts. She touched his face tenderly, and he took her fingers in his mouth. His smooth cock teasingly glided up the soft inside of her thigh. Then he entered her.

As he moved deeper inside her, she felt pain. It reminded her of Bobby. Nick didn't stop to ask if he was hurting her, and she didn't want him to. It wasn't part of this performance: the cold room, the warm bodies. Nick had made the fantasy easy for her in his skilled way. The desire to make love was as urgent as the need to survive the cold.

The tendons in his neck were bulging above her. Lisa closed her eyes. She felt his muscles grow rigid, and then the hot gush.

218

After the release, his body relaxed. Their breath was visible, coming in quick pants in the frigid room. Nick kissed her. "That was fucking fantastic," he gasped. "Or rathah, fantastic fucking, Mrs. Hunter."

She really wished he hadn't said that. But Lisa managed an obligatory chuckle. She kissed him. "Now, Nicky," she said, "do you think we could close those goddamn doors?"

They honeymooned on the French Riviera, but seldom left their suite at the Carlton. Nick was insatiable. He wanted sex to seem spontaneous, even if it meant surprise attacks in the bathtub, during dinner in their room, on the floor, standing up or sitting down. She was grateful there wasn't a chandelier, or he might have wanted to try it swinging from that. Still, he fascinated her.

The novelty of being Mrs. Nick Hunter didn't wear off when they returned to his 800,000-dollar ranch house in Beverly Hills. Every evening, Lisa would sit in bed watching the Evening Ritual. In his silk pajama bottoms (he had several dozen bottoms and no tops), Nicky would brush his teeth and wash at the bathroom sink. And then, just before snapping off the light and coming to join her in bed, he'd pause at the mirror for a moment. He'd pick up his small custom-made comb and groom the famous mustache. Flick, flick, one for each side.

He never knew she was watching him each night, nor how much those two flicks with his comb captivated her.

Six months later, it drove her up the wall.

If he had to comb out his silly mustache, why couldn't he just use the brush, for God's sakes? Always the same comb, and never for anything else but the hair above his lip. Sometimes, when she saw him pause at the mirror after brushing and washing, she knew he'd go for that stupid comb, and she wanted to scream.

When Nick left for the Belgian Congo to do a jungle epic, Lisa was almost glad.

According to *The New York Times*, *Streets of the City* was "one of the best films of the year . . . as the concerned social worker, Lisa Weller delivers a touching and honest performance."

The movie, however, was only a critical success. The public seemed apathetic when it came to realistic drama about slum life in New York. But Lisa's popularity didn't suffer from the modest reception at the box office. Being married to Nick helped. The fan magazines loved them both, giving Nick and Lisa as much attention as they'd once showered on Tony and Janet, and Eddie and Debbie. LISA & NICK AT HOME. THE HUNTERS ON HOLIDAY! LISA WELLER: "I WANT TO BE A MOTHER!"

But she didn't want to be a mother. It was bad enough having Nick. The fantasy was dead, and she didn't want any children aboard a ship that could be sinking. Against her Catholic morals, Lisa got a diaphragm.

She concentrated on her career. She wasn't bound to a studio contract and was able to choose her own scripts. Most of the parts offered were for sweet, vulnerable things; she was in danger of being typecast. She chose a comedy called, *Never Again*. It was set in Rome where Lisa, a divorced American, got pursued by an Italian movie star, as well as her ex-husband. Predictably, the divorced couple reunited.

She was attracted by the character, who was sophisticated and sexy. Besides, she wanted to see Rome and get away from Nick for a while. He had scheduled a television appearance, and so they kissed good-bye.

Three weeks later, a Rome tabloid carried a blurry picture of Nick frolicking on a secluded beach with a topless brunette.

Although Lisa was nominated for an Oscar for *Streets of the City*, she figured she didn't stand a chance. Still, as she lay in bed the night before the ceremony, she tried to rehearse an acceptance speech, just in case. She rolled over and glanced at Nick. Should she thank him in her speech? Hardly, she thought, and shut her eyes.

She and Nick presented the award for Best Cinematography. Their stunning evening clothes and cute ad-libs were enough to dispel rumors that their marriage was already on the rocks.

The fifth name read for the Best Actress nominees was Lisa's.

Nick patted her knee for the press and grinned at her. She smiled back and tried to keep smiling as the camera focused on her. Be a good sport, she told herself. Why was she so nervous? She wasn't going to win.

"May I have the envelope, please?"

Her stomach took a dive. Am I still smiling? she wondered. What if I win? What'll I say? I'll trip going up there—

"And the winner is—"

Not me, Lisa thought, grinning like an idiot. Look poised. Chin up. Everyone was applauding. She'd missed it! Who'd won? Nobody got up. She glanced at Nick. He was leaning forward and whispering. "Hell, sugah pop, you were better than her . . . "

Lisa smiled. She applauded. Shit.

Every weekday morning, Lisa's secretary, Estelle, came to the house to brief her on appointments. Estelle was petite, red-haired, and twenty-three. In addition to her other duties, Estelle was responsible for handling Lisa's correspondence, including her fan mail.

Lisa sat in the study. "Okay," she said over her coffee. "Tell him I'm sorry but I do not have any pictures of the inside of my mouth. But thank him for his interest. Next?"

Estelle held out the next letter. "I thought your father's name was Matthew," she said.

"It is." Lisa stared at the letter, but didn't reach for it.

"Well, this nut signed it, 'Your Dad, Johnny.' He seems to—"

"Throw it away."

Estelle shrugged. "Okeydoke. I just thought you'd get a laugh out of it, that's all." She tore the letter in pieces.

"Anything else?" Lisa asked, rubbing her forehead.

"There's a kid in Santa Barbara. Big fan. Has multiple sclero —one of those diseases. She's laid up in the hospital and her mother wants a letter or a phone call."

"What am I doing tomorrow?" Lisa asked.

Estelle consulted her notes. "Hairdresser at nine. The Bob

Crosby Show from eleven to one. Then lunch with Nick. Dance class from two till four. *Photoscreen*'s shooting the 'At Home' layout at five, and you're addressing the UCLA drama school at eight." Estelle looked up and smiled faintly. "I can pencil you into the bathroom at four-thirty-five."

"Cancel the dance class," Lisa said. She studied the letter. "I'm going to drive to the hospital at Santa Barbara."

"Fine," Estelle said. She scribbled in her book. "Just don't promise you'll hit a home run for her."

"Cute, Estelle. Anything else?"

The secretary glanced at her correspondence pile. "I know you quit asking this about a year ago, but . . . there's one here signed 'Bobby.' "

"Where?" Lisa reached for the note. But when she saw the letter, she was hit with disappointment. It wasn't his handwriting. The return address was Lincoln, Nebraska. A teenage boy asking for her autograph. She tossed the letter on the desk. "Send him an eight-by-ten. The sexy one." Lisa strolled over to the window and listlessly stared at the swimming pool in the backyard.

"Well, that's it," Estelle said. "I'm having my thighs waxed in twenty minutes. I'm out of here." She stood up.

"Before you go, Stell, could you get me Amelia Foster on the phone?"

When Lisa picked up the phone, she heard Amelia's familiar baritone. "Honey, I haven't heard from you in months. How are things?"

"Pretty good."

"Yes, you sound chipper as hell. What's wrong? Trouble in paradise?"

"No more than usual."

"I was just thinking about you," Amelia went on. "A young blonde came in here. Said she wanted to be the next Lisa Weller. I told her there was only one."

"Is my picture still up in the waiting room?" Lisa smiled.

"Oh, I should've taken it down when you went to Hollywood, but I've made you an exception to my rule of newcomers only.

It's still there. So's Bob's. And that's really why you're calling, isn't it, honey."

"Why, how is Bobby?"

"About the same as when you left." Amelia sighed. "I got him a small part in a Broadway show. It flopped. He's back to doing commercials and walk-ons. At least he's making a living."

"You wouldn't drop him, would you, Amelia?"

"Well, let's face it, honey. He hasn't gotten very far in three years with me. And I've busted my ass to keep him in work."

"But if you quit on him, he'll never get anywhere. You're the best agent in town!"

"Now, don't try buttering me up. Or making me feel guilty. I've tried my best with him. In fact, if it weren't for you, I would've given Bob his freedom a long time ago. I've been very patient with him."

"Amelia, please don't give up on him."

"Don't worry. I plan to keep trying, honey. But I do not make promises I can't keep."

"Thanks, Amelia," Lisa said. "Does he ever—ask about me?"

"No. But then he can always get hold of the fan magazines for updates, can't he? I read them once in a while. I get the impression Nicky's back in action." Lisa listened to Amelia's low chuckle. "Don't tell me Nicky's roving eye has anything to do with this sudden concern about your old flame?" Amelia continued. "Because if that's true, you're on the wrong track. You tell your husband that between you and me—and all our friends —we can finish him in that town if he doesn't shape up. You're a bigger star than he is and he needs you now."

"Frankly, I don't know if I want to fight for him that badly."

"Well, at least tell the s.o.b. you're onto him. You don't want to end up looking like a prize fool. Y'know, it's funny. I've got several rules. One is, I try not to butt into other people's business. The second is, if a client doesn't get anywhere with me in three years, I refer him to someone else. And number three is, the day after they're gone, I take down the office picture. So tell me. How come with you I keep breaking the rules?"

Lisa laughed. "I guess I'm just a pain in the ass."

"No, honey. It's because you're different. And that's what makes you a star."

Nick was filming a Civil War picture at Continental. Lisa decided to drive over to the studio. On lot sixteen, Nick, dressed as a Confederate general, was talking with a handful of cavalrymen outside their tent. Lisa stood next to the camera and watched until the take was finished. She endured the autograph seekers and even the director, who was making a fuss over her spontaneous visit. Finally, Nick joined the group and gave her hand a mock-courtly kiss. Lisa turned to the smitten director. "Mind if I steal your star for a few minutes, Bert?"

"Sure. Take an hour. We're setting up the next shot anyway."

They drifted away from the small crowd that had gathered. Nick took off his gray general's hat and wiped his brow. "What's up, sugar pop? We were supposed to have lunch tomorrow, not today."

"That reminds me—I've got to cancel. I'm visiting a girl in the hospital tomorrow. A fan," Lisa replied.

"That's all right."

"You don't seem too upset," she observed.

"You-all got your fans. I won't stand in the way."

They strolled along the lot until they reached a replica of a small-town Main Street. Lisa perched on the front step of a house that said JUSTICE OF THE PEACE. Nick sat down beside her. He straightened the sword that hung from his yellow sash. "Well, I do believe the last folks to set here were Van Johnson and June Allyson. I recall him carving their initials in that tree over yonder."

"You look very handsome in your uniform," she said tightly. "I feel I should be wearing hoop skirts and bows. But I always feel that way when I'm with you, Nick. It's as if Hollywood were your plantation. You brought your Yankee girl here and taught her how to act in front of the native folk. I'm grateful, Nick."

"Sugah, I haven't the slightest idea what you're talking about."

"Nicky, you know, most plantation owners had several mistresses, in addition to their tolerant wives. I'd just like to remind you that those days are over."

"I still don't know what you're driving at."

"All right," she said curtly. "I'll put it in language you can understand. If you-all don't stop screwing around, I'm divorcing you, sugah pop."

"What makes you think—?"

"Oh, please, Nick! Give me credit for a little intelligence, will you? I'd name names, but you're due on the set in an hour!"

He stared at her. "How long have you known?"

"Since Rome."

"Lisa, those gals, they don't mean a thing to me."

"Good. Then it should be easy for you to stop seeing them."

And he did. At least, Lisa thought so. Either that, or he was being very discreet. But the marriage didn't improve. She threw herself into her work. *Never Again* became a hit, though reviews were mixed. Her opinion was that the film bordered on moronic, and she ran for cover, taking a serious role as a nurse in a war epic.

Lisa's character, Nurse Ellen Beats, was torn between devotion to her fiancé, an ambitious lieutenant, and her sudden attraction to a bold young private. Rugged Steve Brock was cast against type as the staid fiancé. A hot newcomer, Hank Robb, portrayed the arrogant, carnal private. Lisa had love scenes with both actors. The romantic embraces with Steve Brock and the mounting sexual tension in her scenes with Hank Robb worked temporary magic on her marriage. The days on the set were like nine hours of foreplay, and she'd rush home to consummate her passion with a very receptive Nick.

Then Nick had to go to Mexico City to work on a film. He'd been gone a week, and all Lisa could think about was sex. At the same time, her love scenes with Hank Robb were being filmed.

Nurse Beats changed the dressing on a shrapnel wound in the private's shoulder. Shirtless, he sat in his hospital bed studying her with a mixture of contempt and desire.

Robb had a few actorish quirks. One was his insistence on

225

being naked under the sheets. The set was cleared of all but the principals and necessary technicians. Lisa was nervous. The steamy atmosphere was only increased by the fact that several times, Hank had come on to her after the cameras had ceased to roll.

"You don't like me very much, do you?" Nurse Beats said after covering the wound with a fresh bandage. Her hand lingered on his chest for a moment. "I think I know why. It's because I know you better than anyone. You try to act tough, but inside you're a scared little boy who wants to be loved."

"You're wrong." He held her with steady blue eyes. "I do like you."

She sank down on the edge of the bed.

"Why don't you ever let your hair down, Nurse Beats?"

She smiled nervously. "Hospital rules. The hair must never touch the back of the neck."

"Take it down," he whispered. "Take it down for me, Mary Ellen."

Slowly, she removed the nurse's cap and unfastened the pins from her hair. Hank moved his fingers through the silky blond strands. The moan that escaped her wasn't in the script. He pulled her head down to his, and their lips met.

"Cut!"

At the end of the day, Hank Robb entered Lisa's trailer. Lisa had already changed into her street clothes. Hank stood in the door wearing a yellow bathrobe. "Damn." He gave her a crooked grin. "I was hoping you'd still be in uniform."

She sat down before her mirror and began to apply lipstick. "You were wonderful today, Hank."

"I'm a dying man, Nurse Beats," he said. With one motion, he untied the sash of his robe.

Lisa got up quickly and began throwing things into an overnight bag. "Look, Hank. I do find you attractive, but right now, I've got to—"

"God, don't tease me. I want you, Lisa. I know the feeling's mutual. And Nick's far away in Mexico City."

"I know." Trembling, she shut the suitcase and picked up her purse. "I'm leaving for the airport and I'm taking the first plane down there. Nick will probably thank you for this, Hank."

As she brushed past him, Lisa glimpsed Hank's naked body beneath the partly opened robe. With all the self-control she could muster, Lisa fled from the dressing room.

She was still thinking about the scene in the trailer when she reached Nick's rented villa. Without bothering to ring the bell, she reached for the handle and discovered the door was open. She hurried through the plush rooms, eager to find Nick.

The bedroom door was also open. Lisa started to enter and then froze when she saw what was on the bed.

It was a nude woman. She seemed to be a contortionist, her head buried between her legs, lovingly exploring herself. Her hands, the fingernails painted a vivid red, stroked the ripe, olive-skinned ass, which obscured her face.

Then Lisa realized it was not one woman, but two. The girl on top straightened as she knelt over her partner. Tawny red hair cascaded to her shoulder blades. Neither of the women had seen her. Lisa felt embarrassed, thinking that she must have entered the wrong villa. She turned to tiptoe away.

Then she heard it. "That's fucking fantastic. Or rather, fantastic fucking."

Both women giggled and turned to smile toward the corner of the room, on the other side of the door. Lisa stepped inside and saw Nick. He was naked, seated in a hardbacked chair. A third girl—dark-skinned, maybe sixteen—rocked in his lap, astride him. They both faced the bed. As Nick squeezed the girl's young breasts, her eyes crossed the room and widened when she saw Lisa. Nick's gaze followed.

The scene froze, its mock carnival atmosphere dissipated. Lisa cleared her throat. "I hope it's true what they say, Nick," she said, "about how easy it is to get a Mexican divorce."

TWELVE

"I don't understand!" Bobby complained, pacing Amelia's cramped office. "Christ, that jerk couldn't even inhale without coughing! I'm the best smoker going. Damn! Eight hundred dollars, they'd said."

Amelia nodded patiently from behind her desk. "Okay, honey. You're a better actor. You're a better smoker. But you didn't get the job. I know it stinks, but—"

"Well, it's not fair! If I'm so hot, how come they picked that Walters clown for the cigarette ad?"

"You really want to know?" she asked warily.

He sank into a chair and stared at the carpet. "Yes, I really would."

"The sponsor didn't like you. Finito. I don't mean to sound heartless, but that's show biz."

He shrugged. Then he laughed faintly. "I guess I shouldn't be surprised."

Amelia lit a cigarette. "Honey, you're twenty-nine years old. Don't you think this young rebel act has run its course by now? You're good, but baby, you are trouble. You're a scene grabber. Other actors don't want to work with you. You argue with directors. You give everybody a headache, Bobby." She took a long drag and sighed. "I'm wasting what's left of my breath."

"I don't make trouble on the set," he answered. "Not anymore. That was years ago."

"Five years," she said soberly. "That's how long I've been your agent, Bob. And you haven't gotten very far. I'm not blaming you, and God knows I'm not blaming myself." She looked at him levelly. "But I think the time has come for you to find someone else to represent you. It just hasn't worked out with me."

Bobby stared at her in disbelief. "What? Just because a sponsor didn't like me? Amelia, you must be—"

She held up her hand. "I can't help you anymore, Bob. I'm sorry."

"I'll—I'll try harder. I'll take anything you give me. I just want to work, I want to act."

"You want fame," she said. "I can't make you famous, baby. I'm not a promoter. You need a showman, someone who'll get your name in the paper, someone who'll exploit you to the hilt. I don't operate like that. You'll have to go somewhere else."

"Where?"

Amelia stubbed out her cigarette. "I don't associate with the type of agent you need. Even if I did, I wouldn't refer you. I like you, Bob. I'd rather see you work at becoming a good actor than a household name. So while you shop around, I'll continue to be your agent. It'll look better." She tried to smile. "I'm sorry I couldn't give you what you wanted, honey."

"Don't bother with the crap, Amelia," he said. He stood. "I'll find someone else. If you're through with me, you're through." He fumbled with the doorknob. Then his hand dropped at his side. "Amelia?" he said in a low, stunned voice.

"Yes?"

"Thanks for trying."

He left the office and crossed the reception room, past the framed photographs on the wall. The secretary was at the typewriter; he could still hear tapping as he walked down the hall.

Sam Sheen was the kind of agent Amelia would never recommend: an exploiter, and a slimy exploiter at that. Mr. Sam Sheen was fat. He wore a cheap toupee and an even cheaper plaid jacket. Perched behind his desk, he brandished a chewed-up cigar and told Bobby, "I don't think I want to handle you, kiddo. Nothing personal."

"I need work. I don't care what it is. I'll do it."

Sheen spilled a few ashes on Bobby's résumé and whisked them away with a hairy hand. "Looks like you've done some pretty tony crap, here. I doubt you would take just anything."

"Yes, as a matter of fact, I would." He'd been living on canned soup and macaroni and cheese for the past two months. The rent was due on his room at the Pioneer Motel, where he'd moved after the Iroquois had proved too expensive.

Sheen sat back and smiled. "Well, if you're really desperate . . . "

Bobby hesitated, then nodded.

"So all right. Think I can do you a favor, kiddo. I gotta friend who makes movies . . . "

And so, after years of trying, Bobby Pierce landed a leading role in a film. The movie was in color, with a running time of fourteen minutes. The title was *Thirsty Lady*.

He was to be paid 350 dollars. He told himself a lot of famous actors had probably paid their dues doing stag films, calendar shots, and the like. Even so, he grew a mustache to do the movie. He loaded his hair with Wildroot and arranged it in curls. He told himself not to worry; no one would be looking at his face anyway.

The movie was shot in one day in a warehouse in Brooklyn, with a crew of three: the director, the cameraman, and a flunky who tended lights, props, and makeup. Bobby's co-star was a buxom, twenty-seven-year-old bottle-blonde who called herself Kandy Sweet. Her real name, she told him under her breath, was Susan Zimmerman. With her Monroe hairdo and Botticelli figure, she was not unattractive, but she was unmistakably a bimbo.

Bobby stood in his undershorts and watched Kandy emote. She sat on a bed, her sturdy legs apart. The gold kimono she wore was spread open to expose large, pendulous breasts. The brown nipples and shock of black pubic hair negated the Monroe effect. She was drinking beer from a long-necked amber bottle.

The cameraman moved in for a close-up as Kandy licked the rim of the bottle and poked her tongue into it. Tilting her head back, she plunged the entire neck into her mouth. Beer spilled over her lips and throat.

Bobby felt disgusted.

"Great, Kandy!" the director cried. "In-fucking-credible!"

Then Kandy gagged and beer started running into her nose. She yanked the bottle out of her mouth and coughed harshly. "Shit, I'm choking to death—"

"Cut!"

Bobby chuckled. Kandy looked annoyed. "What's so fucking funny?" She wiped her face.

He suddenly pitied her. Probably a poor little girl from the Bronx who'd started out to be the next Lana Turner. Just like the rest of the dreamers. "Nothing," he said. "Forgive me."

"I'd like to see *you* take something this size in your mouth, creep."

"I'm sure he has," the director said archly.

"I said I was sorry." He wanted to tell them to go to hell. But his days of being difficult were over, he told himself. It was, in fact, just what had driven him to this. Besides, he needed the three hundred and fifty. He tried to swallow his anger as the director placated Kandy.

They resumed filming, and she continued to play with the beer bottle. "You about ready, Tom?"

"Bob."

"Yeah, right. Well, let's go. We don't want to waste time waiting for you to get a hard-on."

Kandy was pouring beer over her breasts. The sight of it cascading over her nipples aroused him, and he vigorously rubbed himself. He tried to pretend he was alone. He was tempted to fantasize about Lisa, but that only made him feel ashamed.

He made his naked entrance. Taking Kandy by the hair, he

brought her face down to his groin. She wrapped her mouth around his erect penis and mechanically began to slide it in and out. He was able to hold back for the series of maneuvers and positions called for. He tried to look as if he were enjoying himself: working his tongue over her like a mad man, flexing his buttocks, twitching his hips.

"Great," the director called. "Un-fucking-believable! This guy is un-fucking-believable!"

Bobby smiled to himself. Praise at last.

After they filmed the obligatory "come shot," the prop man handed Bobby a towel. "You finished with me?" he asked.

"Yeah, for this one. But I'd like to use you again. What did you say your name was? Tom—Peters, was it?"

Bobby hesitated. Then he nodded. "Yeah. Tom Peters."

"Well, you were in-fucking-credible, Tom. You can shower up over there. Then we'll give you your money."

"Thanks." His head down, he wandered toward the shower room. He heard the director instructing poor Kandy.

"Okay, baby. Smear that over your tits, then lick your fingers. Real sexy—that's right, baby."

In the grimy stall, he braced himself against the wall. He was exhausted, shaking violently. Under the lukewarm trickle of rusty water, Bobby scrubbed himself for ten minutes, but when he emerged, he still didn't feel clean.

While Doris and Rock were box-office champs in 1962, Tom Peters became a big name in skinflicks, top-billed in such mini-epics as *Milkman's Due, Naughty Nymphettes,* and *Velvet Trap.*

Bobby found it easier to think of Tom as a different person; that way, he didn't hate himself so much. When Tom wasn't shooting a stag film or posing for porno mags, Bob Pierce made the rounds and answered open casting calls. He managed to land a few bit parts, but Tom Peters was an underground star, having signed an exclusive contract with Good Time Productions. He had a reputation for being capable of anything. In *Deep Double Trouble,* he serviced two blondes at once. *Mixed Doubles* had him involved

232

with two women and another man. *Bad Girl Connie* included bondage. And *Lonely Sailors* featured Tom teamed with another man and an Oriental girl.

The title of his nineteenth film was *Puppy Love.* He didn't have the guts to ask about his co-star for that one. There was no use raising a stink until he knew for certain what he'd be required to do.

Riding the bus to the Brooklyn warehouse, Bobby told himself he needed the work, the money. If he refused this film, they could fire him. Maybe it would just be a Great Dane licking him or something.

He hadn't even taken off his jacket when the director threw an arm around his shoulders and led him over to the set. Bobby looked down at his co-star and winced. "Christ," he said.

"Cute, ain't she? You're gonna feed it to her in the mouth. It's gonna be our best yet, Tom. *Puppy Love.*"

As the man turned to smirk, Bobby suddenly slammed him in the jaw. The man toppled back and collided with a spotlight. He landed on the floor with a cry. The tall, heavy light smashed down, barely missing him. Wiping the blood from his mouth, he stared at Bobby with rage. "You fucking scumbag! You—"

"I quit! Find yourself some other pervert!" Bobby shouted.

"You're finished in this business, Peters. I'll see you *never*—"

"Thanks. Just what I was hoping to hear." Bobby turned and walked toward the door. Then he stopped and looked back at the set. His face twisted with pain.

The blonde was sitting on the bed, clad in nothing but a pair of pink panties. She stared back at him with a look of childish fear and confusion. She couldn't have been more than ten years old.

Baldrini's Deli was the first place he saw with a beer sign in the window. He was going to get very drunk, if only on beer. The place was good and dark; it smelled of corned beef and ground coffee. Christmas songs played on the jukebox as he entered the store.

Christ, it was Christmas. He sat down at the lunch counter and ordered a beer. One quickly became four. Christmas, a swell time to be out of work. Well, he'd given himself an early Christmas present today. After a year, he'd gotten a little self-respect back. It felt good. He wondered what he could do about the kid back there. Call the cops? Have her scumbag parents arrested? You're a ward of the state now, kid. Merry Christmas. Ho ho ho.

Drink up. Drink to the death of Tom Peters, king of the sleazeballs. Toast the demise of a dream. He'd been chasing it for twelve years now. A guy got tired of running after something for that long. Time to hang it up. He had once told himself if he'd gotten nowhere by thirty, he would quit. He should have thrown in the towel a year ago.

The last of the lunch crowd shuffled out, and the Italian behind the counter switched places with the girl at the meat case. She wore a black waitress uniform. She looked Italian too, and skinny. Late twenties, probably. A kind face. No makeup. Her brown eyes appeared perpetually tired and amused. Her stiff Jackie Kennedy hairdo was the only thing about her that didn't seem soft.

He watched her clean the empty tables. There was something sweet about the way she stretched her little body, totally unconscious of his eyes. After the last table was bussed, she went over to the jukebox and put on a Chubby Checker tune. She turned and smiled at Bobby. "Hope you don't mind," she said, in a charmingly laconic voice, a two-o'clock-in-the-morning voice. "I love that Christmas stuff, but you need a break from it once in a while. How you doin'?"

He nodded and held up his half-full glass.

"I meant, are you drunk yet? That's your fifth beer. I been keeping score. Why you drinkin', huh? Girl or a job?"

"Yeah."

She laughed and came over to lean on the counter. "Both?"

"I don't have either anymore," he shrugged.

"Aw, you must have a sweetheart. Good-lookin' guy like you."

"I did once, six, seven years ago."

"And you're still broken up about her? She must've been real special, huh?"

Bobby smiled sadly. Lisa Weller was still special. Tucked away in her Beverly Hills mansion, she kept to herself and left the gossip to Tinseltown. She'd gained a reputation as a serious, cooperative actress, very selective in choosing her roles. Even her divorce from Nick Hunter had escaped bad publicity. And she frustrated the gossip-mongers by never dating one man for too long. It frustrated Bobby, too, because she wasn't written up in the fan magazines, and he couldn't read about her unless one of her new movies was released. She seemed, like all great stars, untouchable.

"You're thinkin' about her now, aren't you?" The girl smiled.

He looked at her. She was attractive in a clumsy way, the type of girl who might bump into a wall and say "Excuse me."

"You know, you're beautiful," he heard himself say.

She laughed. "Huh, now I know you're plastered. I'll get you some coffee."

As she poured him a cup, Bobby smiled at her. "What's your name?"

She set the cup in front of him. "Sylvia Baldrini. A mouthful, ain't it?"

"What are you doing working in a dump like this?"

Sylvia rolled her eyes. "Well, my father owns the place. That was my brother, Dom, helping you get blotto."

"Oops . . ."

"That's okay." She shrugged. "I know it's a dump. In fact, business stinks, except at lunchtime. But I get to keep my tips. I'm saving for a trip to Europe. I ought to be able to get there by 1975. You want some food? Can I get you a sandwich? We got good corned beef here."

"No, thanks." Mentally, he rearranged her stiff hairdo and put lipstick on her wide mouth. Then he realized he liked her fine just the way she was. Real.

"You sure? Eat something, you'll feel better."

"No, I'm okay. Thanks."

"So give him the check already!" Dom passed behind the counter. Sylvia muttered something in rapid Italian, and Dom looked at her sharply. "Five drafts and a coffee, Syl. Make out the check."

She smiled sheepishly at Bobby and scribbled on her pad. Nodding, he reached for his wallet. Inside was his last paycheck for posing in a naked muscleman magazine. No cash. "Jeeze," he muttered, groping in his pocket for change.

"He don't got the money." Dom folded his arms. "Dollar forty-six, pal. Don't you got it?"

"I'm sorry. All I have is fifty-three cents and a check they're probably going to stop payment on."

"He could give us an IOU," Sylvia suggested.

"IOU, shmew." Dom glared at him. "Okay, lemme see this check. 'Two hundred dollars.' Uh, you Tom Peters?"

"Well, yes and no. It's not my real name."

"What? You a criminal or something?"

"No, I'm an actor."

"What's this Good Time Productions?"

"The company I worked for. Look, the check's no good. I quit the job and the check won't go through." He dropped the fifty-three cents into Dom's outstretched hand. "Sorry, you'll just have to trust me for the rest."

"What you break, you pay for," Dom had told Bobby. Then he'd left the kitchen and gone upstairs to watch the Giants game on TV.

Sylvia set the plates and silverware to dry after Bobby had washed them. "Forgive Dominic," she said. "He's very—suspicious."

"He must scare away a lot of boyfriends."

"Huh. No boyfriends."

He handed her a plate. "Aw, you must have a sweetheart. Good-lookin' girl like you."

Smiling, she set the plate on the drying rack. "Well, I meet a lot of jerks in this place."

"Like me?"

"Oh, no, Tom. I think you're real nice."

"Bob. That's my real name. Bob Pierce."

She considered it for a moment. "Roberto? I like it. How come you changed it?"

"For this job I had. It was—like a disguise."

"What'd you do?"

Idly, he scrubbed a plate. "I did stag films."

Her eyes widened. "You mean like the dirty movies they showed at Dom's bachelor party? Naked girls and—?"

"Naked men, too. I was one of them."

Flustered, she moved away to get another towel. Her large, brown eyes avoided his. "But you quit, huh?"

"Yeah. I quit. I guess you think I'm some kind of creep, huh?"

"No, Roberto." She looked up at him and smiled. "As a matter of fact, I think you're kind of cute."

Bobby didn't have to work Christmas Day, but he went to the deli that afternoon. It was the Baldrini family dinner, and as official dishwasher, he was their newest member. Dressed to the teeth, the clan was gathered in the restaurant. A Christmas tree glowed in the corner. Cardboard pictures of Santa Claus and greeting cards were stuck up on the walls, festooned with tinsel. Carols played on the jukebox. The tables were pushed together to form a banquet setting. Before dinner, Dom's four children had already broken six ornaments and snapped the head off a Wise Men from the Nativity set. Sylvia's teenage twin sisters were home from parochial boarding school, and they both developed instant crushes on Bobby. The twenty-year-old brother, Angelo, was on furlough from the Army, and he chewed off Bobby's ear about "that ratfink Castro." Dom's wife was friendly and quiet, and Dom still eyed him suspiciously. Sylvia, shy in a black dress and pearls, stayed at Bobby's side all through the meal.

Dominic Sr. carved the turkey and led the family in prayer: " . . . And God bless Roberto for his good work in the kitchen, and his company at our table." After dinner, the wine flowed and the family sprawled around the table, singing carols, arguing, and laughing. Sylvia held Bobby's hand under the table. As everyone was singing "Oh, Little Town of Bethlehem," Bobby whispered to her that he was going outside for a moment.

"You want me to come?" she asked softly.

"That's okay. I just want some air."

He slipped outside into the snowy evening and stood by the deli window, framed with blinking, colored lights. He looked at the family gathered around the table. They were singing "The First Nöel" now. One of the kids was off-key. Bobby watched them with wonder, and warm tears stung his eyes.

After a moment, he saw Sylvia get up and go into the kitchen. She emerged wearing a coat. Then the door to the restaurant opened and she stepped outside.

"Bobby, it's freezing out here. You okay?" She touched his arm. "You're crying."

He nodded at the frosted glass. "Look at them," he whispered. "I didn't know families could really be like that."

"Huh, pretty obnoxious sometimes."

"God, you're lucky." He took a deep breath. "I wish I had that."

"You do," she said. "C'mon inside. We need a baritone."

He started to kiss her, but she twisted away. "Dom's watching."

Bobby pulled her away from the window, and they kissed. He felt her arms go around him and he tasted the wine on her lips. She giggled. "Your mustache—it tickles."

"I'll shave it off."

"No, I like it. Makes you look like Nick Hunter."

He gave her a sour smile. "Then I'll definitely shave it off."

"No! I *like* Nick Hunter. He's so cute. I think that Lisa Weller was a fool to let him go."

Gently he pulled away, then shoved his hands in his pockets. "What's wrong?" she asked.

Bobby glanced up at the snowflakes glistening against a streetlight. For a moment, he listened to the muted singing from inside.

"You know how I told you about when I was an actor, a legitimate actor?"

"You still are," she said with encouragement.

He gave her a strained smile. "Anyway, remember that girl I lived with for a while?"

"The one who left you for her career? Yes, but do we have to talk about her now?"

"I think I should tell you. The girl was Lisa Weller."

Sylvia stared at him. A skeptical laugh escaped her, but she read the seriousness in his face. After a moment, she took his hand and smiled. "Well, then," she whispered. "Lisa Weller really is a fool —for letting *you* go, Roberto."

THIRTEEN

As Lisa Weller stepped out of the church, shutters clicked and the few assembled reporters scribbled notes. Nick hadn't been able to take time from his new detective series, but he sent a beautiful wreath of white roses. Other celebrities had sent telegrams, which were read during the service. But the most famous person at the chapel was Lisa Weller and, unwillingly, she became the focus of attention at Amelia's funeral. As far as the reporters were concerned, the others in attendance were pretty slim pickings.

Lisa had hoped to find Bobby there, and felt even more isolated by his absence. It had been thirteen years since they'd seen each other. For a while, he'd popped up on TV occasionally, but after 1960, he'd seemed to vanish. Maybe he'd felt both she and Amelia had let him down.

But he should have come, she thought, as she left the services. The chilly autumn wind seemed to cut right through her. Even if Bobby was disappointed in her, he should have come for Amelia's sake. Maybe he hadn't heard. News services always devoted more space to the stars' obits than those of their agents, the people who had helped make them.

"Amelia Foster, sixty-three, New York talent agent, died today from a cancerous tumor of the brain. Miss Foster was well known for nurturing young talent and advancing the careers of such notable performers as Veronica Haze, Nick Hunter, Lisa Weller, and Hank Robb, among others."

It was just a small item in the back of the *Times*. Bobby could have missed it.

Now that Amelia was gone, Lisa missed Bobby even more. Together, they had kept alive a chunk of her life—the best parts. Those lean times in New York: auditions, bit roles, the dreams, studying, and struggling.

There was, however, one familiar face among the mourners. Three pews ahead of Lisa had sat Ruth Bartlett. Despite the silver in her blond hair, Ruth appeared a good decade younger than her sixtyish years. But she seemed different from the woman Lisa had met so long ago, no longer sweet and vulnerable as Bobby had described her. She watched Ruth walk down the church steps leaning on the arm of an attractive man in his thirties. Lisa felt reluctantly curious about the man. Word had it that Raymond Bartlett was gravely ill. Turning from her limousine, Lisa smiled at the couple as they approached.

"Miss Weller? I guess you don't remember me."

"Certainly," Lisa replied coolly. "How are you, Mrs. Bartlett?"

"Fine." She touched Lisa's arm for a moment. "You know, when Amelia was so ill, I knew she didn't have much in the way of coverage. I spoke to the head physician about contributing toward her medical expenses, and he told me you'd already taken care of it. That was a lovely thing you did."

Lisa nodded. Her eyes slid over to Ruth's companion.

"Oh, I'm sorry. This is Brendon."

"How do you do?"

"I admire your work a great deal, Miss Weller," he said. Lisa studied him. There was something familiar in the way he spoke her name.

Then Ruth squeezed his arm. "Darling, could you bring the car around?"

He nodded and smiled again at Lisa. "Nice meeting you, Miss Weller."

She watched him start for the parking lot, then turned to Ruth. "Congratulations," she said icily. "He's very good-looking."

"Well, thank you," Ruth said, a nervous edge to her own voice. She paused and glanced at the sidewalk. "Miss Weller . . . Lisa . . . I realize this is awkward, but I was wondering if you had kept in touch with Bob Pierce, what he's doing now?"

"I'm sorry. I've lost touch with him, too. I'm sorry I can't help you. Perhaps . . . Brendon can."

"Brendon?" Ruth looked puzzled. "My son never knew Bobby."

"Your son?"

"Yes. Didn't you know that?"

Lisa laughed suddenly. "No! No—I thought he was your—"

"My—oh for God's sake." Ruth smiled. "I think our friend Amelia would have had a very good laugh at us if she were here."

Lisa nodded. She could imagine the wry baritone voice mocking her. She blushed. The words "Miss Weller" that had jarred her had been spoken by a younger version of Raymond Bartlett. She shook her head. "I'm so sorry, Mrs. Bartlett."

"Ruth." She smiled. "You know, we don't know each other very well, but in some respects I feel we're very much alike. You see," she went on, "outside of my marriage, there was never anyone but Bobby."

Still dressed in black, Lisa stood in the kitchen of her Beverly Hills home eight hours later, pouring herself a glass of wine. Glass in hand, she strolled toward the study, where a Beatles song was playing on the stereo. It was her favorite room in the house, cheaply furnished and private, the one part of the austere mansion where she could feel comfortable about putting her feet up on the furniture.

She could smell the pungent aroma of marijuana as she entered the room. Nick Hunter was stretched out on the sofa. At age forty-eight, Nick's hair was grayer and longer, and he managed to get away with dressing in blue jeans and a rumpled shirt without looking ridiculous. He put down his pipe and smiled as

Lisa marched over to the stereo and turned down the volume.

"I never should've given you a key," she sighed. "I see more of you now than I did when we were married."

He moved his feet as she sank down on the couch. "Did you water my plants," she asked, "or just smoke them?"

"All watered. What's the matter, sugah? Why the rotten mood?"

"Jet lag and a funeral." She fanned the air. "I wish you wouldn't smoke that stuff in here."

"Oh, you're no fun, sugah pop. Wake up and smell 1967. Join the revolution. You don't sleep around, you don't do drugs, you don't drink."

She brandished her wineglass.

He shook his head. "You're just a product of the Establishment, sugah. Next thing I know, you'll be selling me Girl Scout cookies."

She kicked off her shoes and propped her feet in his lap. "I guess you're right, Nicky. I'm a square. Today I realized I've gone to bed with only three men. I'm thirty-five years old and I've 'known' only *three men!*"

"Who's the third?"

"Hank Robb. It was after the divorce. On again, off again. Lasted a couple of years."

"Almost as long as we did," Nick said. "Was man number one there today?"

"Bobby? No, he didn't show up."

"Whatevah happened to him?"

Lisa sighed. "I don't know."

"You never saw him again?"

"I wanted to," she said. "Every time I went to New York. Thanks to Amelia, I always knew where he was. But I didn't see him, because I was married to you at the time. Unlike some people I know, I had this ridiculous notion about fidelity."

Nick smiled wryly. "What about after you dumped that cad you were married to? Didn't you try to see him then?"

"It was too late," she frowned. "By then, Amelia had let Bobby

243

go. She didn't have a clue as to where he was." Lisa drained the rest of her wineglass. "Anyway, I never saw or heard from Bobby again. Fade out. The end. Another broken heart production."

She pulled her feet off Nick's lap and set her empty glass on the coffee table. "On that depressing note, I'm calling it a night. Hope you're not too stoned to drive yourself home."

"Wait a minute," he said. Glancing at his wristwatch, Nick jumped up from the sofa. "There's this show we've just *got* to watch!" He switched on the television set.

Over the tube came a shot of the Leaning Tower of Pisa and the title credits. A chorus brightly chirped the theme song:

> . . . Never Again! That's what she said,
> No, Never Again! She'd rather be dead!
> Never again! Never Again!

"Oh, shit," she muttered, watching herself in the ten-year-old movie.

"Hey, that's a catchy tune," Nick said mockingly. "You all look pretty good there, sugah. Damn good. Were we married when you made this?"

"Yes. I was in Rome and you were humping some beach bunny in Santa Monica." Lisa watched her character step out of a taxi and take a picture of the Fountain of Trevi.

She found herself admiring that girl on the TV screen. The young actress in that film had two Oscar nominations and a respectable career ahead of her. The woman watching her hadn't made a movie in two years. She was a victim of the current emphasis on male "buddy" films. The few good roles for actresses were offered to the under-thirty stars like Faye Dunaway and Julie Christie. Lisa Weller was at that difficult age: too old to play nubile heroines and too beautiful and young to take on mature character parts.

On the television screen, the young Lisa Weller was just meeting her Italian co-star when they broke for a commercial. "We'll be right back," said the announcer, "with *Never Again*, starring Paulo Padrioni and William Long."

"What about Lisa Weller?" Nick yelled indignantly.

Lisa felt the same ire. She'd had top billing in the film, but her supporting players were more popular now. It was the way of the business, she told herself. She shouldn't let it bother her. Besides, she'd be mentioned when they returned from the break.

"We now return to *Never Again*, starring Paulo Padrioni . . . "

Yes, and . . . ?

"William Long . . . "

And?

"And Tilly Goldtree."

"Tilly Goldtree?" Nick howled. "What the hell? She's just a character actress! This was your movie!"

Grabbing the *TV Times*, he threatened to phone the station and complain. But she snatched the magazine out of his hands. "Oh, for God's sakes, Nicky." She laughed. "It's no big deal."

But after he left, Lisa looked up the movie in the *TV Times*. It was given a half-page endorsement featuring a shirtless Paulo Padrioni: "11:30 Tonight—Rome Romance with Paulo Padrioni in *Never Again*. Also starring Tilly Goldman and William Long."

Lisa put down the magazine and decided it was time to reconsider the few scripts that were being sent to her. Two years was a long time away from the public eye. She knew she had better get another part, and soon, before she was totally forgotten.

What the hell had possessed her to do a musical? Lisa knew she was starring in a turkey when she viewed the rushes. Maybe Shirley MacLaine, Julie Andrews, or Petula Clark could have pulled this one off, but not Lisa. After two months of coaching, her singing and dancing were passable, yet she still felt uncomfortable in the drippy modernization of *Cinderella* from a Broadway musical called *Carefree Cindy*. As if the title wasn't enough to turn her stomach, the wardrobe and makeup were even more embarrassing. She knew she looked good in a miniskirt, but not these shapeless, rainbow-colored jobs, with clashing colored tights, go-go boots, and fat plastic earrings. She knew she looked pathetic: a thirty-six-year-old woman dressed as a teeny-bopper. They'd cut her hair to imitate Twiggy and bleached it white. Lisa confided to one of her costars, "I look like a goddamn martian."

Every day on the set was a grueling ordeal. Her body took a beating going through the dance numbers, and her morale flagged with the knowledge that the picture was a piece of crap. At least she'd be able to make a final payment on that monstrosity of a house. But it was faint comfort.

Carefree Cindy vaulted over its already astronomical budget. Numbers were shot, scrapped, restaged, reshot. Delays extended the schedule from three to five months. Looking for a scapegoat, the accountants settled on "temperamental star." Lisa was livid. But there wasn't much she could do except try to put on a good face. It was horrible, lying through her smile during interviews to promote the film.

"I think it's such a cute title." *It makes me want to vomit.*

"Oh, Frank George, the director, is marvelous. And the dancers all worked so hard." *This wasn't my idea; don't blame me.*

"No, I haven't seen it yet, but I'm dying to." *I'm dying.*

The truth was that she hated the film and her performance in it. She felt grotesque.

The critics and public agreed. *Carefree Cindy* was a twenty-million-dollar disaster. Its star became box-office poison.

"Okay. What you do is make another picture right away," said her agent, Morris Cooper. Lisa sat in his elegantly appointed office at the Cooper-Ritz-Gibbs Agency. She and Morris passed back and forth a dog-eared script that was prophetically titled *Desperate Measures*. "You should do it, Lisa. You've got to bounce back before they have a chance to bury the body and say the final prayers."

"Oh, I'll bounce back with this, all right. Like a bad check. This makes *Carefree Cindy* read like *Waiting for Godot*. No, Morrie, I can't make two dogs in a row. Then I'll really be buried."

"It's the best I can offer you right now, sweetheart." He shrugged.

"Then I'll wait until you can offer something better."

He took off his glasses and looked at her. "Honey, I won't lie to you. That may be a while."

Lisa threw down the script. "You know, Morrie, five years ago, you wouldn't have bothered showing me something this bad. Am I really that washed up that you think I'd even consider this trash?"

He put his glasses back on, but turned away. "Let me just say you can't afford a long break from working right now. It's not only bad for your image, it's murder on the pocketbook, too, honey. I was talking to your business manager this morning, and he tells me—"

"I know. Don't bother." She had less money now than when she'd been doing bit parts in New York, except now she was deeply in debt. She owed a staggering amount to her business and publicity firms, and she was still working on Amelia's medical bills. "Well, the house is mine to sell. I can pay everyone off with that."

"Sell the house?" Morris stared at her. "Right after a bomb like *Cindy*? Do you know how bad that will look? Why not take a billboard on Sunset that says, 'Lisa Weller Is Broke and Desperate', for cryin' out loud!"

"Well, she is!" Lisa cried. "I don't care how it looks, damn it. It's true. I'm going to sell the house and move into a nice apartment. I hate that drafty old place anyway."

"But if you don't do another film—"

"Okay." She sighed. "If you want me to keep working so the American public will know I haven't died of shame, I'll do TV. Nick's been bugging me to make a guest spot on his show. I'll do that."

Nick's detective show was a hit, and for good reason. Each week, Detective Lance Stone investigated the murder or kidnapping of a model or chorus girl, centerfold or hooker, exotic dancer or stewardess. In Lisa's episode, she played a movie star whose life was being threatened by her maid. The episode drew high ratings, mostly due to the curious reunion of Hollywood's former happy couple.

Lisa spent little time in her new duplex, opting instead to tour with road show productions of *Cat on a Hot Tin Roof, Summer and Smoke,* and *Desire Under the Elms.* She took time to do a TV movie that garnered her an Emmy nomination, but not the award itself.

Movie deals, however, were no longer being offered, and the television projects were mediocre. She got another agent and settled for second billing in a TV movie about a policewoman posing as a nun to trap "The Convent Killer." Guest starring roles on "Marcus Welby, M.D.," "Medical Center," "Columbo," and "Then Came Bronson" kept her visible on the small screen for a couple of years.

In 1972, she joined a dozen assorted stars in a disaster film called *Tornado! Variety* wasn't kind:

> . . . after a four-year absence from the big screen, Lisa Weller returns to try and lend some class to the silly proceedings. Despite her still-ravishing looks, she is hardly more than set decoration. It's a shame an actress of Weller's caliber is saddled with such idiotic lines as "I didn't realize how much I loved my family until the tornado destroyed our home . . ."

Nick set the copy of *Variety* on the kitchen table. Lisa stood at the stove, watching the spaghetti cook. "You know, sugah, they're right about one thing. You still look like a goddess."

"Thanks, Nicky." She stirred the pasta. "I just wish some producers read that review."

"Hell, how many parts do you think there are for a sexy, beautiful, forty-year-old?"

"It's not fair," she sighed. "Actors your age always get teamed up with nymphets. And actresses my age are lucky to get—" She turned from the stove and shook her fork as she spoke. "Do you know what I'm stooping to next week? I'm doing a pilot for a new sitcom about a widow trying to raise four fun-loving children. They're calling it—are you ready for this?—'Kids Will Be Kids.' Talk about nauseating. Four scene-stealing little brats and me. If they decide to make a series of it, I'm turning in my SAG card and becoming a hooker. There's less shame." She went back to stirring the spaghetti.

Nick got up to freshen his drink. Lisa glanced at him sharply. "Take it easy on that stuff, Nicky. Dinner's almost ready."

Smiling, he poured a half-glass of bourbon and gave her waist a squeeze. "None of my other ex-wives nag me like you do, sugah."

"None of them feed you, either."

He brushed the blond hair behind her ear, and she felt the cool glass graze her neck. He kissed her earlobe. "Is it true what they say about a gal reaching her sexual peak at forty?"

"Nicky darling, you pull this every time you come over."

He kissed the nape of her neck. "Hmm. Maybe sometime I'll catch you in the right mood."

"I've got news for you, cutie," she said. "You're better as a friend to me than you ever were as a husband."

He abruptly pulled away. Gulping down his drink, he set his glass down on the counter. "Did it ever occur to you, sweetheart, that you-all weren't the world's greatest wife?"

Dumbfounded, she turned to regard him. "I just meant I wanted things to stay the way they are with us, Nick."

"I know what you meant. So I stepped out on you a lot. Ever wonder why? How do you think it felt being married to a gal who never stopped loving another man? Goddamn it, Lisa. How do you think it felt?"

His anger took her by surprise. "I was never unfaithful to you," she said quietly.

"Yes, you were. Every time you thought about him. Bobby Pierce was nothing but a hustler, a no-talent con-man bit-player who never got anywhere except into your pants. A nobody."

"That's enough, Nick."

"You still love him. After eighteen goddamn years, you still love him."

"Just get your coat and leave. Okay?"

"I'll get my coat all right, sugar."

Angry, she followed him out to the hall. Yanking the coat from the closet, Nick drew something out of the pocket. "Maybe you'd like to see what the old boyfriend's been up to, hmmm?"

It was a paper bag. Inside the bag was a magazine. Nick shoved it into Lisa's hands. She looked at the cover and began to tremble. Under the banner GOOD TIME PRODUCTIONS PRESENTS TOM PETERS IN *More Than a Mouthful* there was the black-and-white photo of a naked, mustached man clutching a woman's blond hair, her face poised above his crotch.

"What the hell is this?" she asked in a low voice.

"You don't recognize Mr. Wonderful? You don't recognize the love of your life, sugar pop? Well, there are more pictures inside, but not too many show his face."

She forced her eyes to take in the photo again. Past the closed-eyed ecstasy and the mustache, she saw Bobby. And beneath her shock and disgust, her heart broke for him. She didn't have to look at the awful pictures inside; she already knew it was Bobby. The boy who would do anything in pursuit of his dream.

"Where did you get this?" She glared at Nick, tears of hate in her eyes.

"Private investigator. Hired to find whatever happened to Bobby Pierce, from Amelia Foster's Class of 1960. That magazine's ten years old. Your boyfriend made plenty of them, by the way. Starred in stag films, too. Oh, you were right about him, sugar. Old Bobby was one hell of an actor. I saw one of his movies. He was very convincing. No wonder you fell for him—"

"*Stop it!*" She struck him across the face with the magazine. He tore it out of her hand and threw it to the floor. Lisa beat at him with her fists, but Nick made no attempt to halt the blows. Finally her tears slowed, and he held her.

"I'm sorry," he whispered finally. "I couldn't let you throw your life away on someone like that, Lisa. You mean too much. I couldn't stand it." He stroked her hair as she pressed her face into his shoulder. "He's married now, honey. That's what the man told me. Works in a restaurant in Brooklyn. Married a waitress. He's got two kids, Lisa. Please, honey," he crooned, stroking her hair. "Don't look back. It only hurts more. Sshh. Don't look back, sugar."

FOURTEEN

It was definitely too hot to cook. Bobby had brought home barbecued chicken and potato salad from work. The family sat at the kitchen table in shorts and T-shirts, their thighs sticking to the plastic dinette chairs. A game show blared over the TV propped on the radiator panel.

Sylvia wasn't watching the show. Her new Farrah Fawcett hairdo had gone limp in the heat. Still, she looked pretty with her deep tan and the Pabst Blue Ribbon T-shirt showing off every curve of her still-fetching figure. She put down her iced tea. "Just once, I'd like to eat dinner without that stupid TV going."

Bobby glanced over at his ten-year-old son. He could clearly see himself in the boy: thin, black-haired, the large blue eyes and the guileless expression that sometimes even fooled his father. "You heard Mom," he told the boy. "Turn off the TV, George."

"Oh, never mind, honey," Sylvia muttered. "Let him watch if he wants. Shannon, eat!"

The reedlike, chestnut-haired, five-year-old frowned at her plate. "I can't. It's chicken."

"I thought you liked chicken, honey," Bobby said softly.

"Not anymore. It's gross. This was once a cute little chicken. I can't eat it. It's too gross!"

"You know how they kill chickens?" George volunteered. "They cut off their heads and—"

"Hey!" Bobby said in a sharp voice. "Wanna live to be eleven?

Put a lid on it, kiddo." His demeanor changed swiftly as he turned back to his daughter. "Honey, I know for a fact that this chicken we're eating was never cute. This was the ugliest, creepiest chicken that ever clucked. But very tasty. Now, just try a few bites."

George turned up the volume on the TV.

"*. . . Pete Peters, we still love you in reruns of 'Those Crazy Conways.' Here's the question. True or false? A dog's mouth is cleaner than a human's.*"

"Hey, old buddy," Bobby said patiently. "Does that have to be so loud?"

"But I can't hear, Poppy."

"*Well, I've kissed some dogs in my day . . .*"

Bobby tried again with his daughter. "Just a little bit, honey."

"Please, Daddy, don't make me," she whined. "Can't I have Cap'n Crunch instead?"

"Can you believe it?" Sylvia sighed. "This from a girl who ate a caterpillar when she was four."

"*Lisa Weller, we're all looking forward to your new movie. What's it called?*"

Bobby put down his fork. He stared at the TV. She looked lovely, but out of place sharing a panel with eight washed-up performers.

"*Well, Skip, it's a thriller . . .*"

"I'll eat her dumb old chicken, Poppy," George said.

"Quiet a sec," Bobby hissed. He knew Sylvia was scowling at him, and he felt guilty. After all these years, she was well aware of why his eyes were riveted to the flickering screen. But he continued to stare at the television.

"*. . . 'Scream in the Night', and it's opening around the country in time for Halloween.*"

With a clatter of silverware, Sylvia got up from the table. Bobby glanced at her retreating back as she flounced into the bedroom. Lisa was still on-camera.

"*Well then, Lisa, our next question for you should be simple. Alfred Hitchcock made three films starring Grace Kelly. Name them . . .*"

Bobby heard the bedroom door slam. He handed his fork to George. "Here, buddy, coax your sister to eat a little." He ruffled the boy's dark hair and headed toward the bedroom.

She'd turned on the air-conditioning unit full-blast. Bobby shivered as he stepped into the room. Sylvia sat on the edge of the bed, her thin back to the door. She turned her head away as he sat down beside her.

"Why aren't you in there watching her?" she asked.

He didn't reply, because he was asking himself the same question. "I'm sorry, Syl."

"Huh."

"Syl, please, look at me."

"No." She gave her head a shake. "I'm a mess. I look at her and I watch you watching her. Now, how am I supposed to compete with *that?*"

He stroked her back. "Honey, I think you're the most beautiful girl in the world."

She cast him a suspicious glance over her shoulder.

"You are, Syl," he said. "When you come to the deli sometimes, I see the way guys look at you. You're still a knockout."

"Huh, but compared to Lisa Weller . . . "

"Syl, she's a movie star! Do I get upset every time you moon over Paul Newman?"

She swiveled around. "I never slept with Paul Newman! And I don't carry a picture of Paul Newman in my wallet."

"I don't have any pictures of Lisa in my—"

"Don't lie. I've seen it. It's hidden between the snapshot of George and your Social Security card."

"It came with the wallet, for chrissakes! I just never threw it out."

She frowned. "Well, maybe you should."

"All right, I will," he said gently. "What else do you want me to do?"

"Tell me how beautiful I am again. It sounded nice."

Sighing, he put his arm around her and pulled her down onto the bed. With a shaky breath, she slid her hands up his back, under the sweaty T-shirt. Their bare legs interlocked, and he kissed her mouth, then her neck.

"You lock the bedroom door?" she asked.

"Hmm-mmm."

"Do you still love me, Roberto?"

"Mmmm . . . "

"Good. Because I have something to tell you."

"Mmm?"

"I'm pregnant again."

Bobby lay awake, unable to sleep or move. George was curled up beside him, his arm sprawled across Bobby's stomach. Shannon, sleeping on the other side of George, left her mother alone. The heat wave had driven the kids into the only air-conditioned room in the apartment. At first Bobby didn't mind; he liked the feeling of closeness with his children, a feeling he'd never had with his own father. Had the old man ever worried about him the way he did about George and Shannon? Had Cameron—in his sane moments—suffered the same premonitions about his boy being kidnapped, murdered, or run over by a car? George had been in school for five years now, and still Bobby worried that one afternoon, his little boy wouldn't come back. He didn't even want to think about Shannon starting kindergarten in the fall. Did all parents live with this perpetual sense of dread about their children?

At least having the kids in bed with him allowed Bobby the luxury of unimpaired parental protectiveness. He could watch them sleep, instantly comfort them from a nightmare, listen to them breathe.

However, after six nights of George's skinny, sweaty body pressed against his, and lovemaking with Sylvia reduced to a "quickie" in the bathroom, Bobby was ready to risk placing the kids back in their own beds. Maybe he could dip into the budget and buy a fan for the kids' room. The image of Shannon poking her finger past the screen into the blades—blood spraying everywhere—suddenly flashed through his mind. Well, they couldn't afford the stupid fan anyway, he thought.

They couldn't afford this baby, either. Besides, he was getting too damned old. He was in pretty good shape for a guy of forty-six: he only had a few gray hairs, no pot belly, and still rated some interested stares from female customers. But when this latest child hit fourteen, sixty-year-old Dad wouldn't exactly be playing tackle football with him.

And at forty-one, Syl wouldn't have an easy time, either.

He wanted to roll over, but George moved and he didn't want to wake him. He'd given a hell of a performance earlier that night, when Syl had told him. "Boy, honey, that's great! Oh, well, so the deli's going under. I'll get another job. . . . Don't worry about the money right now. No, forget that. I'm not going to dip into your savings. That money is paying for our second honeymoon —Europe, just like you'd planned when you started saving it. Hell, one more room won't be that much expense. Don't worry about it, Syl. I'm so happy, I could bust."

Busted. Broke. Lose a job, gain a child. It was time to look for work.

He had forgotten, in eleven years, what it was like. All that time, he'd managed the Baldrinis' deli. Everything was relative, he thought, when factory work and custodial jobs suddenly seemed like shots at stardom. When he heard about an opening at a downtown gas station, he felt as if he'd been offered the lead in a major motion picture.

The job was offered through a friend of the owner, a regular customer at the deli. The meeting with Osborne, the owner, was held at Osborne's office, a messy, dumpy, little place behind a Brooklyn warehouse. Osborne was also messy and dumpy, a middle-aged, seemingly dull-witted man—but he owned the warehouse, as well as four gas stations and a parking lot in Manhattan. He surveyed Bobby for several minutes of requisite chitchat. "Well, you seem like an okay guy," he said finally. "What do you know about cars?"

"I worked as a parking attendant a few years back." Say about twenty, Bobby thought. "Used to work on a few once in a—"

"In other words, you don't know a tire from a windshield wiper."

"Ah, that's right."

"Well, don't worry, you'll learn quick. I think ya got what it takes, kid. I like ya. Gonna work ya overtime the first couple of weeks. Now, I got two openings. One's here in Brooklyn, pays six-fifty an hour, good hours. Other's in the city, Broadway theater district. Only six an hour, but you could make manager in a few months if you play your cards right."

Bobby hesitated for precisely thirty seconds. The Brooklyn job had convenient hours and was closer to home. He looked at Osborne. "Well, I'm pretty interested in the Broadway location," he said. "And th-the possible management position."

When he told Sylvia about the new job, she was thrilled. The first weeks were murder. During the long hours, he learned about distributors and carburetors, while a block away, actors auditioned, curtains were raised, and dreams were born. Every night Bobby came home ready to break something. Sylvia's patience and sympathy amazed him. "I wish you could have gotten something in Brooklyn," she said wistfully from time to time, and it only made him feel worse. He never told her about the Brooklyn opening. That was the first lie concerning his new job.

The next lie came on Halloween night. They took the kids trick-or-treating and then came home to count the loot. George and Shannon were in their room, climbing out of their costumes. He and Sylvia sat at the kitchen table sorting through the candy for anything unwrapped or suspicious looking.

"I have to work late tomorrow," he said with studied casualness.

"Jesus, who gave out Fig Newtons? Talk about cheap." She shoved the cookie aside, unwrapped a Milky Way, and took a bite. "I thought you finished that overtime stuff a week ago."

"Yeah, but Tony wanted to show me how to replace shocks. Anyway, I should be home by nine."

"I hate lies."

He laughed nervously. "What do you mean, Syl?"

She licked her fingers. "I'm going to have to tell George his Milky Way looked funny, so I threw it out. I hate lying."

Bobby sat in the semidarkness, staring at the dingy floor. It was seven o'clock. An hour earlier he'd left the station. Syl would probably call and find out he wasn't there. She didn't usually, but with his luck, tonight would be the exception. Then she'd notice he smelled of popcorn instead of gasoline. She'd find out.

The reviews for *Scream in the Night* had been good. A low-budget homage to Hitchcock. A tour-de-force performance from veteran actress Lisa Weller. He glanced around the theater. Packed. Good, her movie was making money. Maybe she'd get some good parts after this. The lights went down, and he shifted in his seat.

The movie was a spine-tingler. Lisa had the audience on the edge of their seats as the unsuspecting victim of a psychotic killer. It was *her* movie—for three-quarters of an hour, anyway. Then came the scene where her car broke down on a dark, lonely highway, and she walked to a deserted gas station, where she stepped into a phone booth to call for help. Lisa Weller's phone booth was comparable to Janet Leigh's bathtub in *Psycho*. After fifty horrifying seconds of knife-wielding and bloodletting, Lisa was dead. The scene grabbed Bobby by the throat. He'd never seen her die on-camera before. For the rest of the movie, he sat lost in reverie.

When it was over, he listened to the comments around him. "God, was that scary!"

"I couldn't stop thinking about Lisa Weller, even after she was dead and all."

"I always liked Lisa Weller's old films."

"She's aged so well."

"Sloppy Joes okay?" Sylvia asked when he came in the door.

"Sure, fine, honey." He sat down at the table and kicked off his shoes.

"It'll be a couple of minutes," she said, taking the Tupperware container out of the refrigerator. "Want a beer?"

"I'll get it."

"I'm right here, hon." She set the can in front of him.

"You don't have to fix dinner for me," he said. "You should be resting."

"It's no trouble. Besides, you've been working hard all night. No wonder Mr. Osborne considers you his golden boy. So—you learn about those brakes or whatever?"

I'll make it up to you, he thought. Lying to you. I went to Lisa's movie, honey, and she was great. It made me feel better in some funny way. She'll be back in the limelight now. I can stop worrying about her career. It'll take the heat off me somehow. I'll make it up to you. I still love you, swollen belly and all. . . .

"It wasn't brakes," he mumbled. "Shocks. Replacing shocks."

"I almost called you."

"Oh?" He looked up warily.

"Yeah. Your old girlfriend was on the Merv show, plugging her new movie."

And he'd missed it! He managed a twisted smile. "So, did she talk about me?"

"You know, I hate to say it, but she seems like a real nice person. Damn her." She dropped some bread into the toaster and took a sip of his beer. "Ever think about getting in touch with her?"

He smiled. "I'm sure she's forgotten all about me by now. That was twenty years ago."

"I'll bet you anything she hasn't. You should write her, tell her about your lovely wife and wonderful children." She gave him a wry look, then got up to stir the Sloppy Joe mix.

A year of working overtime was starting to pay-off. Osborne had not only made Bobby manager of the Shell station, he'd also asked his "golden boy" if he wanted to buy the place. Osborne was retiring and moving to Las Vegas, and the deal he'd offered Bobby had been too good to refuse. With the nestegg from Sylvia's waitressing days plus their savings, Bobby had managed to offer him a meager down payment. While it was slightly premature, Osborne insisted that Bobby post his name across the station's plate glass window: ROBERT PIERCE, OWNER. At last, his name—in large, silver letters—for all the Broadway theater-goers to see.

Of course, Robert Pierce, owner, was nearly broke from the monthly installments, hospital bills, and higher rent payments. But he knew it was only temporary. The new apartment was close to their old place. George and Shannon each got their own room, and Sylvia was thrilled to finally have a dining room. That was where Bobby sat early one morning, burping the new baby, Edward, and idly glancing at the entertainment page of the newspaper.

He went over an article about new movies and plays coming to town that summer: *Interiors, Foul Play, Grease, National Lampoon's Animal House, Heaven Can Wait*. No new movies with Lisa. Maybe *Scream in the Night* was just a fluke. Couldn't be. She had been nominated for an Oscar for Best Supporting Actress. She didn't get the award, but the film had raked in a fortune at the box office. Maybe she was holding out until another good part came along.

He felt wet slime on his shoulder, and he juggled Eddie and took the diaper off his knee to wipe the baby's chin. By now, Bobby was used to smelling like baby puke. "Thanks a lot," he told the infant. "I drag my ass out of bed to feed you, and this is the thanks I get."

He picked up the bottle and the baby reached for it. "Oh, time for another round?" He put the nipple in the baby's mouth. "Okay, take your time for a change, handsome."

He turned back to the paper, and then struck gold.

> . . . And *Star Child*, Gregor Goethals' long-awaited drama about a film actress coping with her son's suicide, is slated for December release. Advance word is that Lisa Weller, as the distraught mother, gives the performance of her career. Ms. Weller has been announced for the lead in John Met-

calf's new comedy play about voyeurism, *The Birdwatcher*, scheduled to open here at the Helen Hayes Theatre in September . . .

The Helen Hayes Theatre was just three blocks from his Shell station.

FIFTEEN

New York City—October 1978

Five curtain calls. Not bad, Lisa thought, as she sat back in the limousine on her way to the hotel. *The Birdwatcher* was eight weeks into its run, and a hit. But there was now a film offer, and it was tempting to give someone else a chance in the play. Besides, she'd discovered she missed L.A. New York depressed her. Too many memories.

She stared out at the nighttime neon of Broadway, occasionally catching her own somber reflection in the glass.

"Miss Weller?" The driver glanced at her in the mirror. "Mind if I stop for gas? We're running on empty. Just now noticed it."

Smiling wearily, she pulled her stole around her shoulders. "Well, Buzz, that sure puts a crimp in my whole evening, but go ahead."

"Thanks, Miss Weller."

He pulled the limo into the station at the corner. Lisa watched an attendant amble out of the office, his hands in his pockets. He looked like someone out of a Western, ready to draw his gun.

Buzz got out of the car. He ducked his head back inside.

"Sorry, ma'am. This will only take a few minutes. Should have filled her up before I left the barn."

"Don't worry, Buzz. I'm in no hurry." She glanced out the window. The attendant stood in front of the light, his face lost in shadows. She sensed him peering in at her. She managed a smile.

Buzz called out, "Fill her up with unleaded, okay, buddy?"

"Okeydoke."

Trying not to yawn, she rolled down her window for some night air. The man passed the car, and she gave him another smile.

"Recognize her?" the driver asked him. "I'm carrying precious cargo tonight. That's Lisa Weller, the actress."

"For God's sakes, Buzz," she groaned.

But the attendant had approached her window, and she took a secret delight in his excitement. "Well, I'll be! Whaddaya know. It *is* Lisa Weller!"

"See? You made his night, Miss Weller," Buzz said.

"Oh, Buzz," she said, "I bet you didn't do this to Barbra Streisand when you drove her around last month!"

"I seen all yer movies," the attendant piped up. "I seen that one, *Fate Is My Destiny*, five times."

Lisa looked at him, startled. "You sat through that turkey five times?"

"Yeah. I thought you was great in it."

She thanked him and then retreated further into the car. He was quite good-looking; the attention of good-looking men embarrassed her these days. And he reminded her of Bobby. For one breathless moment, she had that same old feeling. It had happened a few times before. But the name on his shirt said "Art" and his accent was Brooklyn/Italian.

"I'm your biggest fan," he was telling her.

"Thank you." She smiled past the ache of memories and then turned away. Stop gawking, she told herself. Stop torturing yourself. Wherever Bobby was, he was married now.

Buzz was telling the man that she would give him an autograph. She was no longer in the mood to play gracious movie star. "Buzz, please," she sighed. "Just pay the man. I'm sure he gets a lot of show business people in here."

The attendant probably thought she was snubbing him. She sighed. "Now, Buzz, give him a good tip. He's been very patient with us."

It was a bad idea to disillusion fans. And the resemblance to Bobby was indeed eerie. The same blue eyes. As he stepped toward her window, his face—Bobby's face—seemed to plead with her, to say, "Don't you know me?"

She became suddenly aware of everything going on around her: Buzz climbing back behind the wheel; the car shifting under his weight; the smell of gasoline; the October air stinging her eyes; and Bobby, standing in front of her.

Her throat closed around his name. Why would he want her to recognize him, she suddenly thought. He was on the outside, and she was on the inside. She wanted to tell him it didn't matter, that being a great actor, a great gas station attendant, didn't matter.

"You know"—he smiled and glanced down at the pavement— "I really would like your autograph, Miss Weller. I mean, if it's no trouble . . . "

The charade saddened her. *All right, Bobby. I'll play this scene any way you want it. I won't take away any of your foolish pride.*

She drew an envelope from her purse, then dug out a pen. Pausing over her signature, she looked up, giving him one more chance to drop the façade. "Your name?" The pen wobbled as she looked steadily at him.

"Art. Make it out to Art."

"Art," she echoed. "Buzz," she called, "be a dear and reach in that glove compartment. There're some passes in there—give a couple to Art here."

Bobby stepped away from the window. He could hear Buzz praising her to the skies. "Yes, I'm a saint," she called, as she added something on the inside of the envelope flap.

He returned to the window. She spoke to him cordially, invited him to see the show, bring his wife. She secretly hoped he wouldn't. Handing him the envelope, she smiled. "There you go. It was nice meeting you . . . Art."

"Thanks a lot, Miss Weller."

Her smiled waned and she rolled up the window. "Okay,

Buzz." Closing her eyes, she sat back while Buzz started the engine.

As the car pulled out of the station, she didn't allow herself to look at Bobby. It hurt too much to look back. She wondered suddenly if he'd ever find that hidden message. But it didn't matter. She'd seen him again. That was the only thing that counted.

Bobby felt as if he were auditioning for a show instead of watching one. Lisa's superb performance couldn't soothe his nerves. Anticipation, guilt, and desire formed a potent cocktail in his stomach, and he squirmed through the witty play in misery.

He'd told Sylvia he was working the graveyard shift. He'd told Tony that Sylvia was sick, that he was taking the day off. He'd made six o'clock reservations at a fancy restaurant to wine and dine Syl, hoping it would ease the guilt. And it gave him the excuse to wear a coat and tie as he rushed off to "work."

He'd given himself the whole night. And when he returned home in the morning, Syl would fix him breakfast and keep the kids quiet while he slept. He felt like a dog.

He didn't have to go backstage, he told himself. Lisa didn't know he was here. He could leave now if he wanted, go home, tell Syl the godawful truth, endure her wrath, and hate himself for passing up an opportunity to see Lisa again. Either way, he'd end up hating himself.

Glancing down at his trembling hands, he wondered if he should take off his wedding ring. He hadn't removed it in fourteen years. But he hadn't seen Lisa in twenty-four. Did he even have a chance with her? In a way, he hoped she'd reject him. No choice, no guilt. He'd been rejected by her before, and it had hurt. But he'd gotten over it. Learned to live with it, anyway.

When the final curtain descended, Bobby had no memory of what the play had been about. The applause swelled and clamored like his heartbeat. After four curtain calls, the cheers subsided and the theater began to empty.

He waited until the aisles cleared, then grabbed his coat, got to his feet, and moved toward the stage. He felt as if his breath were being pumped out of him. He made his way to the side door, then backstage and down the narrow hallway.

When he found the dressing room, he couldn't make himself knock. Inside were voices, a woman jabbering, a man responding, "C'mon, Leslie, we'll never get a table if we don't leave."

Bobby backed away as the door opened and the middle-aged couple in evening attire started down the hall. For a moment, he was unaware that the door had remained open. Then, turning, he saw Lisa. The blond hair was piled on top her head, and her still-youthful face looked freshly scrubbed. She wore a floor-length satin robe, its cream color a shade lighter than her skin. She didn't move. Her gray eyes regarded him with a trace of hesitation.

"Hello, Lisa," he said. For a moment, he doubted that she'd heard him.

Uncertainly, they stood in the doorway, gazing at each other like strangers on a first date. For a moment, neither spoke. Then Lisa uttered a skittish laugh. "Would—would you like to come in?"

Sheepishly, he stepped into the room. The walls were white-painted brick. Bouquets of flowers filled every corner. The vanity table was cluttered with makeup jars, tissues, and scripts. Telegrams and clipped reviews framed the brightly lit mirror.

Lisa closed the door and then busied herself at a side table. "I was just about to have some coffee. Can I pour you a cup?"

"Thanks. I take it black."

She smiled faintly. "I know."

"So, did you like the play?" she asked, handing him the cup.

"Yes, I—it was wonderful. You were wonderful in it, really wonderful." His mouth wasn't working right, too dry. He sipped the coffee.

"Glad you liked it," she said. "Is the coffee all right?"

"Yes, it's—it's—"

"Wonderful?"

He managed a smile. "Yes."

There was a moment of silence. Lisa retreated to her makeup table. Setting down her cup, she picked up one of the scripts. "I just signed to do a movie," she said. "It's really a good part. We start filming next month. I hate to leave the play, but it's one of those things. I—" She tossed the script back on the table. "God, I've missed you, Bobby," she whispered. "You don't know how many times I've pictured this—seeing you again."

She turned and wrapped her arms around him. He could feel her warmth through the smooth satin robe, the fragrance of her hair.

"I was so worried that you wouldn't come," she said.

He kissed her, afraid to hold her too close, afraid that she'd melt into some daydream. He kissed her again.

After a moment, she pulled away. Gently lifting his left hand, she studied his wedding ring. A bittersweet smile crossed her face.

"Do you love her?"

"Yes."

"She doesn't know you came here tonight, does she?"

"No. But she knows about us. Everything. I told her a long time ago. She knows I haven't quite gotten over you. I never have, Lisa."

"But she doesn't know you came here tonight," she repeated, softly touching his face.

"I told her I was working the graveyard shift."

"Then we've got until morning." She bit her lip. "Bobby, I don't know her. I don't know your wife at all, not even her name. You say you love her. But tonight you came here. So what are we going to do? I'm leaving it for you to decide."

His throat went dry again. He held her hands in his. He felt torn by a sweet pain he didn't know how to assuage. "I don't want to hurt anyone, Lisa."

"I know," she said. "But Bobby, twenty-four years is a long time to ache." Slowly, she kissed him again.

* * *

They hadn't realized it was raining until they stepped out the stage door. The theater, like a giant cocoon, had sealed off the rumble of thunder. They ran two blocks in the downpour. She shielded her head with his copy of the *Playbill* until they reached the bar.

The oak-paneled tavern was almost empty, with a few theatergoers straggling in for a nightcap. Lisa and Bobby chose a secluded booth away from the lights and chatter. A small hurricane lamp glowed in the center of the table. They peeled off their damp coats and ordered brandies. The waiter recognized Lisa. He asked for an autograph, and she graciously obliged. Bobby wordlessly stared at them, trying not to frown.

After the waiter left, Lisa caught her breath and dabbed her moist face with a cocktail napkin. "All right," she sighed, giving Bobby a wry smile. "I guess I can take it. What's her name?"

"Who?"

"Your wife. Tell me about her."

"Well, her name's Sylvia. It was Sylvia Baldrini before we got married. That was in 'sixty-four."

"Baldrini? Sure she didn't marry you just to get rid of that?"

He managed an uncomfortable laugh.

Lisa crumpled up the soggy napkin and tossed it in the ashtray. "I'm sorry," she murmured. "I'm acting catty. I'm jealous." She tried to smile. "Really, tell me about her. Is she nice?" Lisa quickly shook her head. "No, you're married to an ax-murderess. Dumb question."

"She's very pretty—not as pretty as you," Bobby said coolly. Then he smiled. "She's a better cook, though."

Lisa laughed. "I'll have you know I've graduated from macaroni and cheese."

The waiter returned with their brandies. They drank in silence, their smiles waning. Finally, Lisa put down her snifter and glanced around the bar. "Have you ever been in here before?"

It was an opening line for strangers, and the awkwardness of her question didn't escape him. "A few times. I work a couple of blocks from here."

"Why didn't you want to talk to me that night?" she asked quietly. "In the gas station, I mean."

He shrugged. "I don't know. I guess I was embarrassed, ashamed."

"Why?"

"Hell, I'm a gas pump jockey, Lisa. Remember me? I was going to be a famous actor. A big, important man. Well, now I'm a nobody."

"Don't you think you're important to your wife and children?"

"Let me tell you something. George—he's my oldest—he'd rather have Starsky or Hutch for a dad." He took a sip of brandy and frowned. "I can't really blame him, either. I'd give anything to be one of those actors, just to be somebody important."

She took his hand and squeezed it. "You'll always be important to me, Bobby."

He looked at Lisa and noticed the fine lines that had accumulated around her eyes and neck, the traces of silver in her blond hair, untamed by the rain. Yet her beauty transcended her age. She still made him feel vulnerable and weak.

Delicately, he stole his hand from beneath hers. "I wish I could really believe that, Lisa. But it's kind of tough. I've always wondered why you left me."

"I didn't want to. I would have given anything to stay with you."

"Then why didn't you?"

She took a deep breath. "I couldn't ask you to give up your career for me."

"What do you mean?"

"It was Amelia who told me I had to stop seeing you," Lisa answered quietly. "She thought you'd panic if you found out. Your friend—God, I've never been able to forget his name—Alfred Weeks, he was once a Communist."

Bobby laughed, startled. "That? He told me about that. I knew. Hell, it was before I ever met him. They could never pin anything like that on me."

"In 1954 they could have." She gazed at him sadly. "And they did."

"I don't believe it. Weeks would have cleared me."

"No, he couldn't have. He left the country after you moved out —to avoid the witch hunt. Apparently, though, some of his friends remembered you. And back then, you were still fresh in their memories. You couldn't afford to be in the spotlight, Amelia felt. And living with me, marrying me, Bobby, would have put you there.

"Anyway, that's why I moved out, why I couldn't marry you. They were starting to print all those stories about me, prying into my personal life, the whole 'star' build-up. The limelight shows a lot of blemishes you'd just as soon keep covered. I've always been afraid they'd dig up something about my real father. And back when you and I were living together, I was afraid that my publicity would include you. It was just too soon after Alfred Weeks for that to happen."

Bobby imagined the scandalous stories, and he smiled tightly. "I guess I would have taken off too, under the same circumstances. That might have been a lot of bad publicity for you."

She looked at him in pain. "I left for you, Bobby. I didn't want to. It was your career I was thinking about. That bad publicity would have ruined your chances of ever being employed as an actor! But with me gone, you still had a chance to keep acting, ride out the witchhunt, and maybe even in time grasp that dream of fame. I left because I was thinking about *your* career, not mine."

"But why didn't you tell me?" All those wasted years, he thought. The wasted, bitter years.

"You mean, give you that choice? Your dream or me? How could you expect me to ask you that? Maybe—maybe I couldn't face finding out. So I left."

Slowly, he shook his head. "But all this time I thought you really didn't love me. I thought you left for your own career."

"No, I did it for you." With a sad smile, she reached over and smoothed the unruly lock of hair that still fell over his forehead.

270

"You see, I loved you, Bobby. I still do. You've always been important to me."

The bar closed at three o'clock. The rain had settled to a dull, cold drizzle. Lisa and Bobby were a little drunk when they hailed a cab. On their way to the Plaza, they sat in the back of the warm taxi and reminisced about their time together in the basement apartment in Greenwich Village. They laughed about the strange neighbors, the battles over the bathroom, the ruined dinners.

Lisa noticed the driver glancing back at them with a smile. "I bet you'll be happy to get rid of us," she remarked as they neared the hotel.

"Yeah," Bobby said. "Are we obnoxious enough for you?"

"You kiddin'?" he said. "You folks been my best fare all night. It's good to hear a couple back there laughing and all. Most married folks I get sit back there and don't even talk to each other."

Bobby glanced at Lisa, and she turned to look out the window. But he felt her squeeze his hand.

They sat in the lobby of the Plaza for nearly an hour, talking of Amelia and Nick and Ruth feverishly, as if a simple lapse would be an excuse to call it a night. Finally, Lisa yawned and lifted Bobby's hand to glance at his watch. "My God, it's almost five."

"We're running true to our old form." He smiled. "I don't have to be back until six-thirty."

"Well, I have a matinee at two. I should catch some sleep." She focused her eyes on his face. "I think we've avoided the obvious long enough, Bobby. Do you want to come upstairs with me? It's still your decision."

He took her hand, but couldn't look at her. "I don't know, Lisa. There are so many risks involved."

"You're thinking about Sylvia and your children." She smiled wearily. "I guess maybe you've grown up. At the start of this evening, I was hoping you hadn't. But now I'm glad." She got to her feet.

"Well, can I walk you to your room?"

"On one condition. No long good-bye at the door. I don't want to undermine our resolve."

"I promise, no long good-bye. Besides, you'll be in town . . ."

"Only through next week," she said. The elevator doors opened. Lisa wrapped her arm through his, and they stepped inside. "I'm leaving the show to do a movie. Next Saturday's my last performance."

"Well, can't we see each other before you leave?"

"I don't think so. See, Nick's flying in tomorrow night. He wants to stay, then go back with me."

"Oh." Bobby fell silent. He glanced up at the lighted numbers above the door.

She sighed. "It's hard to explain about Nick and me. We aren't really living together. But we have a sort of a commitment." She gave Bobby a wry smile. "He's very jealous of you, and not without good reason."

The elevator doors opened and they stepped into the corridor. "Anyway," Lisa said, "I'm not just thinking about Nick and what he'd think. There's Sylvia, too. Here I am."

At her door, he paused. "Then I guess we won't be seeing each other for a while."

Lisa took out her key. There were tears in her eyes as she tried to laugh. "I sense that long good-bye coming on."

Bobby managed a smile. "Well, then, I'll see you in your next movie. *Star Child*, right?"

She nodded. "See you in the movies, Bobby."

"Listen," he said. "Let me give you my address at the gas station in case you want to write or something. Though you don't have to if you don't—"

"No. I'd like that." She pulled out a gold pencil and scribbled on a pad as he gave the address. She seemed to have difficulty writing it, Lisa Weller, the scribbler of a million autographs.

"I promise I'll write back this time," he said.

Lisa put the pencil and pad back in her purse, then unlocked the door and opened it. Turning, she smiled at him, the tears still captured in her eyes. "Take care, Bobby," she whispered.

When they embraced, his lips brushed her cheek. His heart ached with that old, familiar feeling, having her in his arms.

Finally, Lisa pulled away. Head down, she turned, went into her room, and gently closed the door.

There was still an hour-and-a-half to kill before heading home. Bobby found an all-night greasy spoon and ordered some breakfast. He was feeling the effects of four hours of Lisa and alcohol, and he hoped the food and coffee would sober him up for the trip home.

He thought of Lisa and felt a pang in his gut. But he'd made it—he hadn't shed a tear, hadn't taken her to bed. Yes, he'd grown up. And she thought more of him for his show of character, his noble refusal.

As he finished his coffee, he decided he wasn't that drunk after all. His thoughts were now clear, painfully clear. And he realized he'd never answered the question Lisa had held onto all these years. They'd managed to avoid it, maybe because as she said, she'd already guessed the answer.

Of course, his dream of fame would have come first. Bobby stared at himself in the coffee shop window, the first streaks of dawn already showing outside. Even now he'd still sell himself for it. Given the chance, he'd still sacrifice everything—abandon Lisa, forsake Sylvia, even the kids.

He was sober now. But suddenly, Bobby desperately wanted to go out and get very, very drunk.

SIXTEEN

Everyone connected with *Star Child* knew it was a good film. But they hadn't really expected it to be a hit. After all, the story of a movie actress and the son who commits suicide was hardly the kind of plot that made people line up around the block. But they did. And the film proved to be one of the top moneymakers of the year.

Star Child reaped seven Oscar nominations, among them Lisa Weller for Best Actress. She was a favorite of the Vegas odds makers, and a favorite of the press as well. The newsstands were choked with cover stories on the actress who made over-forty look good, as the slogans said. She was the media darling, the "Hollywood survivor" who had captured the public's imagination. Even her starlet days of twenty-five years before were nothing compared to the uproar over her latest triumph.

The acclaim was not ignored by the producers of the Oscar Awards show, who gave Lisa the coveted assignment of presenting an honorary Oscar to veteran director Sir Cedric Gardner. On the morning of the ceremony, Lisa, dressed in jeans and a sweatshirt, stood on the stage of the Los Angeles Music Center and rehearsed her slot in the show. It took an hour to set up the lights and film clips, while Lisa stood patiently at the podium and rehearsed her speech praising Sir Cedric's career.

As she left the Center, it occurred to her that she'd given little thought to her own speech, in case she received the Oscar that night. She laughed a little. Why did she always wait until the last moment to think about these things?

Crossing the entertainment complex, her mind was full of modest rejoinders, and she barely noticed the elderly man who held the door open for her, though she smiled and thanked him. A gray-haired man in a shoddy brown suit with no tie, grinning with the adoration of a devoted fan.

She crossed the street and began listing the people she should thank. As she neared the parking lot, she heard a car horn blare. Turning, she saw the old gray-haired man standing in front of the car, delivering obscenities with such rage that she felt more alarmed than amused. Then his voice became strong and familiar. The ravaged face with its dark, angry eyes and slightly crooked nose suddenly became recognizable.

She thought back to the last time she'd seen Uncle Johnny, on that chilly Chicago night outside the apartment building, his lean figure stomping down Newguard Avenue while she cowered in an alleyway. Now, in the palm-lined street under the bright California sun, he seemed so feeble and pathetic.

John Rogan caught her stare. Waving the car aside, he moved back to the curb and came toward her. His smile reflected a father's pride at his daughter's graduation day. "Lisa, honey," he whispered entreatingly.

You're not my father, she wanted to say. My father's with my mother in Florida, and they're very happy, so just leave us alone, just go away somewhere and die. What was it about him that suddenly made her feel like a frightened, angry child? She stared at him coldly and pressed her lips together.

"Lisa, honey, doncha know me?" He reached out to touch her, and she took a step back.

"What do you want?"

He laughed with a rough cackle. "Just wanted to take a look at ya, Lisa, that's all. Just wanted to see ya again, babe."

"Well, you can see me on TV tonight. I don't want to see you." She felt a pang of guilt as she watched her words knock the silly smile off his face.

"That any way to talk to your old man? After all these years?"

"Yes, thirty-five years. Why all of a sudden do you want to see me now?"

"Didn't you get any of my letters, honey?"

She took her sunglasses out of her bag and put them on. "Yes. I threw them away."

"I didn't think it was in ya to be this cruel."

"Maybe it's an inherited trait."

His voice was barely a whisper now. "Lisa, why do you hate me so much?"

The question left her mute. For the first time, the mist cleared and she was able to see the loathsome Uncle Johnny as he might have been fifty years before: a scared high-school boy, unable to deal with the responsibility of a pregnant girlfriend.

"I've seen all your movies," he was saying.

She worked up a smile, and he looked so grateful, her heart nearly broke for him.

"How's Dee?" he asked. "How's your mother?"

"She's fine." Lisa wondered why he looked so much older than Matt and Dee. It was as if every crime and hard knock had left a scar on that once crudely handsome face. Had he always been down on his luck, this pathetic man? Was she his only possible source of money? Or perhaps his only source of pride.

"Y'know, I used to tell people I was your father," he said. "I —I cut it out though. Figured you maybe wouldn't like it. Y' know, it wouldn't look good if that ever got out. Might really hurt you, and your mother. Anyway, I stopped."

"Thank you. That was very considerate of you."

He shrugged and shifted in front of her. "Yeah, well, I figure the newspapers would have a field day with a story like that. Especially now, you so well off and me not knowing where my next dime's coming from. That wouldn't be good publicity for you now, if it ever got out."

She stared at the shabby suit. "You know, if you need money, I wish you'd just come out and ask for it. You almost sound like you're trying to blackmail me."

He laughed coyly. "Oh, I wouldn't call it that."

"I've played this scene in a couple of my movies. I'm waiting for you to say, 'Blackmail is such an ugly word.' That should be your next line."

He looked at her narrowly. "Y'know, maybe you aren't taking me seriously. I'm doing you a big favor keeping my mouth shut all this time. Especially now, with your big movie and everything. Some people might pay me a lot of money for information about you."

"You know, it's really amazing," Lisa said. "For a minute there, I was stupid enough to think I meant something to you."

"You do," he said. "You mean a lot to me, honey."

"Oh, really? Just how much? A thousand dollars? Five thousand? Just how much is a lot?"

His eyes blazed with contempt. He drew a sharp breath and then said, "Ten thousand, to be exact. That's how much you mean to me, you superior bitch."

"You won't get ten cents from me."

"Then the whole world's gonna find out that Lisa Weller's a bastard."

"I think they'll realize just who the bastard is, Uncle Johnny." With a curt smile, she turned away and headed for her car.

Rogan began to thread his way through the maze of Cadillacs, Mercedeses, and BMW's. "You'll be sorry you didn't treat me with respect! I only wanted to see you because you meant something to me. That's a laugh! I wouldn't treat a dog the way you've treated me. You'll fucking well pay."

She paused at her car. "What I can't figure out is why you waited until *now* to pull this. I mean, I'm not surprised that you're trying in your pathetic way to blackmail me. But I've been in show business for twenty-five years."

"I tried to see you, goddamn it! I wrote to you. Christ knows why the hell I would want to associate with a prize bitch like you. I even tried to see you in New York—at that apartment of yours. Some *punk* tossed me out. I told him I was your father, and the prick threatened to kill me if I ever came back. He kicked me out!

This punk boyfriend of yours. Whaddaya smiling for? I'll make you sorry, you snotty bitch."

He was still raving as Lisa climbed inside her car and started the engine. She wasn't listening to him. She was still smiling and thinking of Bobby, of those nights so long ago when he'd get out of bed to investigate a noise for her, when he'd answer the door to chase away a peddler or a drunk leaning against the buzzer.

So Bobby had protected her from John Rogan, to the point of never telling her about it.

Rogan banged on the car as she began to pull away. "I'll make you pay!" he screamed, as she drove off. "I'll fucking destroy you."

Sylvia gave a tired laugh as she switched channels on the TV. "Are you a masochist or what? Every year we have to watch this nonsense, and every year you end up getting depressed." She found the channel and then came back to sit beside Bobby on the couch.

He didn't say anything, because she was right. He never missed an Oscar telecast, and the show always left him frustrated, because he wasn't part of it. He wasn't up there at the podium making the acceptance speech he'd had in his head since high school. He wasn't among the stars filing into the pavillion amid a throng of fans and flashbulbs.

"There's Roger Moore—a presenter tonight—and his lovely wife," said the announcer. "And beautiful Lisa Weller, nominated in the Best Actress category."

"She makes me sick," Sylvia said. "Nobody her age has a right to look that good."

Lisa seemed luminous, her white chiffon dress slit to reveal her remarkable legs, her blond hair pulled back to show off a pair of sparkling diamond earrings so large, they had to be paste.

She'd never written him. In a funny way, Bobby didn't care. It was enough that she was still a part of his life. And more than anything, he wanted her to win tonight.

"They're right though," Sylvia said. "She *is* beautiful. Says something for your taste. You're going to think I'm nuts, but sometimes it's hard not bragging to Tina or Alice that you had a thing with her. I mean, my husband slept with Lisa Weller. How many wives can say that?"

He laughed. "You *are* nuts."

"Not so nuts that I'd actually tell them." She patted his knee. "Besides, they're already impressed just knowing my husband now owns his own gas station. Thank God, no more night shifts. I'm so proud of you, honey."

Bobby smiled for a moment. He put his arm around Sylvia and watched the TV.

As the show progressed, he sipped beer after beer and puffed his way through a pack of cigarettes. They were finally getting to the major awards. The show was starting to seem like a long wait in a doctor's office. The only bright moment had been Lisa's poised presentation of a special award to some senile director. Elegant and radiant, she was a breath of fresh air.

When they announced the Best Actress category, Bobby sat forward on the couch.

"Can we turn to something else?" Sylvia teased.

Bobby managed a nervous chuckle, but he didn't tear his eyes away from the screen. The presenter seemed to read off the nominees' names with deliberate slowness. Lisa's name was last. As the camera focused on her, Bobby felt a pang when he noticed that Nick Hunter sat next to her, squeezing her hand.

The envelope was about to be opened. The five nominated actresses were shown simultaneously. Lisa's face was a serene mask. Bobby wondered how she could look so calm when he was ready to crawl out of his skin. He almost didn't want to watch, in case she lost.

"And the winner is . . . " The presenter paused and smiled, half to himself. "Lisa Weller for *Star Child!*"

Bobby leaped to his feet and broke into applause.

"You're blocking the TV, sweetheart," Sylvia sighed. She

reached up and pulled him back to the couch. Then she wrapped her arm around his, and they watched as Lisa ascended the steps to the stage. The ovation for her swelled.

She received the statuette and stood nodding gratefully, waiting for the applause to die down. "Thank you," she said finally. "I'm so honored merely to have been nominated, to be included in the company of four great actresses. Oh, this is such a thrill."

She tried to compose herself and blushed charmingly. "I want to thank everyone connected with *Star Child*. So many wonderful, talented people. They made me look good. Mom and Dad . . . hello, Nicky . . . " She waved slightly. "Thanks for being there when it counted." Smiling past emotion-charged tears, she held up the gleaming Oscar. "And I—I want to also share this with someone very special. Bobby, if you're watching, I love you and this is yours, too."

Then she turned to the audience. "I thank you with all my heart." As she stepped away from the microphone, the auditorium rocked with applause.

Bobby stared at the screen, his eyes filled with tears. He hoped that Sylvia wouldn't spoil the moment with an understandable show of jealousy, a sarcastic remark. But she only kissed him. "Well, honey." She smiled. "After all these years, you're finally a part of the Oscar Awards."

He smiled back and he could almost feel the heavy gold statuette under his fingertips.

The telecast was over, but celebrities still jammed the brightly lit stage. TV cameras continued to roll as the winners were interviewed and photographed. Lisa posed with the other winners, then with the Best Actor Award recipient. Finally, she faced the press all alone as it formed a circle around her.

"How does it feel, Miss Weller?" someone shouted.

"I'm waiting for someone from Price-Waterhouse to tell me they made a mistake." She laughed, clinging the Oscar statuette to her chest. "I'm totally bowled over. It's wonderful!"

"Who's Bobby?" another reporter piped up.

She smiled protectively. "A friend of mine."

"Aren't you going to say?"

"No." She grinned. "So you can stop asking."

"Did you think you were going to win?"

She opened her mouth, about to answer, when a startled cry rang out of the crowd. Hesitating, she stared as a sudden break appeared in the circle of reporters. Then a newswoman was pushed to the floor near Lisa's feet. An elderly man in a shabby brown suit shoved past the cameraman. He was holding something in his hand.

The news broadcasts would show the tape again and again. The shots sounded oddly muted, like two small firecrackers popping. Lisa dropped the gold statuette as the red stain bloomed on the sleeve of her white gown. At the second shot, her head suddenly snapped backward. Then her legs sank from under her and she fell to the floor.

The movements of the camera were rickety and blurred. The soundtape was filled with noises of confusion, startled screams. Somehow, the camera had pointed away and never caught the gaping red-black hole where Lisa's left eye had once been.

A third shot rang out. The camera wove over the panicking crowd. No one had seen the old man in time to restrain him. Before John Rogan could be grabbed, he had stuck the barrel of the revolver into his mouth and pulled the trigger.

The newsclipping would be endlessly dissected and analyzed before a horrified nation. Crucial frames would be blown up and featured in newspaper and magazine stories. Eventually, people would become almost indifferent to the repetitious, slow-motion ballet of death: Lisa Weller, a beautiful marionette, her strings abruptly severed; the soft pops of gunfire; the warbled cries of confusion and shock.

That night, Bobby had waited up to watch the late news, hoping to see more coverage of the Oscar presentations. Sylvia had teased him, "Oh, you just want to hear your name again."

"Don't you want to hear it, too?" He smiled.

She was about to speak, but turned quiet as a photo of Lisa came on the screen in a black-framed box behind the newscaster's shoulder. In the picture, Lisa smiled and clutched her trophy. But the newsman's face was grim and distraught.

"Tragedy tonight, following the Oscar ceremonies in Los Angeles. A short time after the Academy Awards broadcast, Lisa Weller, winner of the Best Actress award, was shot down by an unidentified gunman. We switch you now to Brian Mattson in Los Angeles."

"What?" Sylvia cried.

Bobby sat in shock. He told himself he hadn't heard right. The young reporter stood in front of a crowd of bewildered celebrities and journalists.

"I'm told the assailant is dead. Miss Weller's condition is still unknown. She was struck by at least one bullet and she did—um —she did fall. Four shots are believed to have been fired. Miss Weller has been rushed to the hospital."

"Oh, my God," Sylvia whispered. Blindly, she reached over to grab Bobby's hand. It was cold and damp, almost lifeless.

His vacant eyes gazed at the TV screen. He said nothing.

For several hours they sat watching as the vague, contradictory reports began to crystallize into fact. But finally it was announced: Lisa Weller, winner of the Best Actress award earlier that evening, was dead.

Within twenty-four hours, the story on John Rogan was out. He was identified as the actress's real father. He had been in and out of jails all his life. Among his few belongings, discovered in a downtown motel, were old news clippings about his famous daughter. No one could explain why he'd killed her or himself. The press seemed satisfied to point up his disreputable past and let the rest settle into horror and mystery.

But Bobby couldn't stop thinking about that night Rogan had come to their door, how he'd pitied the strange old man. They'd both lost her. For a while, she had been the only decent thing in their miserable lives. But Bobby had found Sylvia. Rogan had only the memory of Lisa, and she'd wanted no part of him. Bobby understood why John Rogan had killed himself just seconds after destroying the only thing he'd ever really loved.

Sylvia's compassion only made him feel worse. She comforted Bobby through his crying fits, and jumped up to change channels on the TV whenever the horrible newsclip was rerun. He knew why she was being so nice. How could she compete with a ghost? Still, he felt awful. His uncontrollable sorrow was a series of stabs at her ego. She begged him to take the rest of the week off, but in a strange way, he looked forward to work.

When he returned to the station three days later, he gave Rusty the night off. He welcomed being alone, but every time he sat at the desk, his mind drifted toward the unthinkable, and so he busied himself straightening up spare parts and rummaging through the trash on his desk, throwing out old flyers and unused manuals, reading the junk mail.

Then his hand paused and he noticed an envelope addressed to him. He picked it up and something rattled inside. When he tore it open, a tarnished necklace spilled into his hand. Numbly, he stared at the familiar handwriting, at the date of three days previous.

March 27

Dear Bobby—

I'd promised myself I wouldn't pester you, but here I am, doing just that. Call it therapy. In three-and-a-half hours I'm supposed to be at the Oscar Awards, and this nominee is a bundle of nerves.

For more reason than one. This morning, I ran into an old acquaintance—the infamous Uncle Johnny. He wanted money, of course, and I pretty much told him to go to hell. He also referred to a night in New York when he'd come to visit. You never told me about that, Bobby—my dear, sweet, Bobby. Well, my thanks comes twenty-five years too late, but there it is.

283

Whether I win tonight or not, I want you to have something, too. My father—the one who counts, that is—sent this to me when I was twelve, when he was in the Army. I wore it for months thinking it would protect him and me, too. Now I want you to have it, because you protected me and asked for nothing. I don't expect you to wear it. I doubt Sylvia would like that, and I don't blame her. But you might make a key-chain out of it or keep it at work. Anyway, this chain means a lot to me, Bobby, and I want you to have it.

Take care.

Love,
Lisa

Bobby caressed the chain's tiny metal beads. Even though his throat ached and his eyes burned with tears, he glanced at himself in the darkened plate-glass window. He still couldn't break that actor's habit of checking his own expressions. He held Lisa's necklace in his hand and watched himself cry.

Past his reflection, he saw a car pull into the station. It was a limousine. Automatically, he jumped up from his chair and rushed out of the stationhouse. Then he caught himself in the doorway. Letting the door close on his back, he tucked Lisa's necklace into his pocket.

Bobby counted to ten. Then, wiping his eyes, he went to fill the customer's gas tank.

EPILOGUE

In the weeks after her death, Lisa Weller was hardly out of the public eye. She graced the covers of eleven national magazines. A ninety-minute special, full of film clips and interviews, was hastily prepared and aired during prime time. The networks battled to acquire film rights to her life story; six publishers announced forthcoming biographies. The tabloids had a field day speculating on her death and her relationship with her father. There were stories of a death wish, visits from the grave, secret love affairs with all her leading men.

Matthew and Dee Weller, residents of Clearwater, Florida, since 1974, closed their doors to the press and had their phone number changed. Matthew "Buddy" Weller, a surgeon in Alexandria, Virginia, gave in and hired a police guard to protect his wife and three children from harassment. And shortly after the funeral, Nick Hunter left for Europe to do a film. The press was barred from the set at the actor's request.

The wall of silence that sprang up only whetted the curiosity of the press and the public. Just when people most wanted to know who the real Lisa Weller was, there seemed to be no one willing to tell them. And no one to answer the question that plagued every reporter—who was the man Lisa had mentioned on Oscar night, the mysterious "Bobby" for whom she had professed love only moments before her death?

It was a question that occurred to the chief story editor who sat in the conference room of *Candid* magazine. *Candid* was a glossy gossip weekly, published by a reputable newspaper chain. Three men and two women sat around the table in a fog of cigarette smoke. They were discussing their strategy for a special issue devoted entirely to Lisa Weller.

"All right," one editor said. "We've ruled out Robert Redford, Robert DeNiro, Robert Wagner, Robert Duvall, Robert Mitchum, and Robert Vaughn."

Another editor nodded. "And Robert Preston's out. So are Robby Benson, Robert Stack, and Robert Blake. So who's left?"

"Rob Petrie?"

Everyone laughed.

"Maybe she had an affair with Robert Kennedy," one woman suggested. "No one said you had to be alive to play in this game."

"No one said Bobby had to be a man, either," a reporter named Leonard Furlong remarked. "Maybe it's short for Roberta. Who's to say she wasn't a lesbian? After all, she never remarried."

The first editor glared at him. "If Lisa Weller was gay, Walter Cronkite's a Hari Krishna."

"Maybe it was her dog."

"Maybe it was her sled." The chief story editor grinned. "This whole thing is turning into a farce." He puffed on his cigarette. "I think we're all barking up a red herring. This Bobby was the most important person in Lisa Weller's life. But he's most likely someone we've never heard of. He could be anyone from a high school crush to a man she sat next to on the red-eye shuttle once."

"Terrific," an editor groaned. "All we have to do is sort through everyone she ever met in her whole life for someone named Bobby."

"So what if this guy turns out to be a nobody?" Leonard Furlong asked. "What then?"

"He won't be a nobody after we get through with him." The chief editor smiled. "We'll make him as famous as Lisa Weller herself."

* * *

It was Open House night at George's school. Bobby and Sylvia looked at the school projects, talked with the teachers, and then hurried home. Bobby had given himself the graveyard shift to break in a new employee. He had about an hour to lecture George, change his clothes, eat dinner, and get to work.

While Sylvia reheated some stew, he put on his workpants and transferred change and keys to his pockets. Sylvia hadn't noticed he had a new, though slightly tarnished, key-chain. Buttoning his shirt, he came out of the bedroom and bumped into his thirteen-year-old son.

"You gonna yell at me now or later, Poppy?" George asked.

"Let it wait till tomorrow," Sylvia called. "Dinner's almost ready. You've got to get to work, hon."

Bobby suddenly felt bone-weary. The last thing he wanted was to spend the night at that miserable gas station—even if it was his. The doorbell shrilled, and he headed for the intercom, ready to cuss out whoever was interrupting his dinner.

"Is Robert Pierce home?" a male voice asked through the static.

"Speaking. Whozzat?"

"I'm with *Candid* magazine, Mr. Pierce. May I come up and talk with you for a moment?"

"We got all the magazines we need, pal. Thanks anyway."

"No, you don't understand," the man said quickly. "I'm a reporter for the magazine. I'd like to talk to you . . ."

Bobby glanced at Sylvia. She turned from the stove and shrugged.

"Okay, I'll meet you in the hall." He pressed the buzzer for the downstairs door. "I'll see what this guy wants," he told Sylvia.

"Well, show him in."

"The place is too much of a mess."

Sylvia started to protest, then merely rolled her eyes and went back to fixing the meal.

"I'll just be in the hall," Bobby said. "Be back in a minute." Sylvia didn't answer. Great, Bobby thought, shutting the door on little Eddie's squalling.

The reporter was in his early thirties, a trim, athletic-looking man with a notebook tucked under his arm. He gave Bobby a pleasant, insincere smile. "Robert Pierce?" he asked, extending his hand.

Bobby shook it warily. "Yeah?"

"Well, thank God. At least you're the right age and color," the man said enigmatically. He laughed. "You don't know how many guys I've seen today. Let me get this straight. You were once an actor?"

Bobby looked at him narrowly. "Who are you?"

The man laughed again and pulled out a business card. "Len Furlong. My magazine's doing a feature piece on the secret love of Lisa Weller. The man she mentioned in her acceptance speech. Did you watch that night?"

"Yes."

"Then you heard her mention a man named Bobby. Well, I've been talking with the people who knew Lisa Weller, the people who worked for her. Found a gal by the name of Estelle Landis. She was Lisa's personal secretary from 'fifty-five to 'sixty-three. Said Lisa had given her instructions to set aside any mail that was signed 'Bobby.' And the director of her first film remembered she'd had a boyfriend when she was living in New York, guy named Robert Pierce. An actor. So I've been talking to every Robert Pierce in the Greater New York area, and believe me, it's no picnic."

"Well, you've found me," Bobby said flatly. "What do you want to know?"

The reporter uttered a skeptical laugh. "Now how do you expect me to believe you're the right Robert Pierce? The thing is, my magazine's prepared to pay ten thousand dollars for the rights to this Pierce guy's story. His picture—along with Lisa's —will make the cover of the issue. And probably the covers of a lot of other magazines, too." He smiled to himself. "But not until we've scooped them. In addition, I've made a deal with a publisher to ghost-write an authorized account of the affair between Lisa Weller and this Robert Pierce. Not to mention promotion tours, talk shows, the works."

"That's all just for knowing her?"

Leonard Furlong's smile widened. "Well, Bob, there's knowing and there's *knowing*. And we're banking on just how well you —or this Robert Pierce—knew her. We've already had all that saccharin garbage from the others she worked with. We want to know what Lisa Weller was like in bed. What she drank. If she used drugs, slept around. What were her hangups about the old guy, her father. That sort of thing."

Bobby's jaw stiffened. Furlong continued.

"Anyway, if you're really the right Robert Pierce, you've just walked into a gold mine, baby. We're not only talking a good deal of money here, but you're going to wind up being a celebrity yourself, Bob. Maybe even as big as Lisa Weller."

Behind Bobby, the door opened and the shrill sound of Eddie's crying echoed into the hallway. Sylvia poked her head out.

"Honey, dinner's ready. You'll be late for work if you don't come and eat."

He turned. "Yeah, in a minute, Syl."

He looked back at the reporter and saw the sly look of interest spread across the man's face as the situation before him seemed to fall into neat little pieces. He watched the man take in his clothes, the script on his workshirt pocket. "Are you—ah, a custodian or something?"

"I work at a filling station. I own the place."

"I see. Well, of course, you realize that before we can start giving you all this money and getting the publicity machine rolling, we have to verify that you are in fact the right Robert Pierce." Furlong gave him a brisk smile. "For openers, maybe you might tell me the name of the man who directed Lisa Weller's first film."

He'd never forget Mario Daniels. How Daniels had treated him like scum. Bobby looked at Furlong and shoved his hands in his pockets. He studied Furlong's patronizing smirk. He only had to say "Mario Daniels" and the smug reporter would become a docile pet. Two words were his passport to fame, the realization of every dream he'd ever had.

Idly, he pulled the keys out of his pocket. Gazing down at the tarnished metal chain, he realized why Lisa had sent him the old necklace: *I wore it for months thinking it would protect him and me, too. Now I want you to have it, because you protected me and asked for nothing . . .*

"Well, do you know the director's name?"

"Ahh—it kind of escapes me right now," Bobby said slowly.

The reporter shrugged. "How about her agent at the time? You should remember that. According to this director, Bob Pierce had the same agent."

Bobby gripped the key-chain. He could suddenly see Amelia Foster's office before him. And the slender blonde in the corner typing. He was aware of Furlong beside him, hanging on his answer. Who would have thought that simply having known Lisa would make him an important man? But maybe, just maybe, he was already important.

He held the key-chain in his hand a moment longer. And a triumphant smile slowly came to his face. Bobby looked up. "I guess you got me on that one, too," he said. Turning, he opened the door, then glanced back at the man.

"I'm just a gas station attendant, bub. You're talking to the wrong guy. I never knew Lisa Weller. I never knew her."